ELEANOR DARK

(1901-1985) was born in Sydney, Australia. The daughter of the writer and Labor politician Dowell O'Reilly, who introduced the first bill for Women's Suffrage into the New South Wales Legislative Assembly, she grew up in an intellectual and political household. She began writing early, publishing her first story at the age of nineteen.

In 1922 she married Dr Eric Dark, going to live with him in Katoomba, in the Blue Mountains outside Sydney. Here she combined her career as a writer with that of a doctor's wife and the mother of two sons. Her first novel, *Slow Dawning*, was published in 1932, followed by *Prelude to Christopher* (1934) and *Return to Coolami* (1936), both novels winning the Australian Literature Society's Gold Medal. Throughout the 1930s Eleanor Dark took an overtly political position in opposition to the growth of fascism abroad. In 1935 she joined the Fellowship of Australian Writers with, amongst others, Marjorie Barnard, Flora Eldershaw, Dymphna Cusack and Kylie Tennant. Eleanor Dark's political preoccupations became increasingly evident in her fiction of the 30s and 40s. *Sun Across the Sky* was published in 1937, and *Waterway* in 1938. In 1941 she published the first volume of an historical trilogy, *The Timeless Land*. Acclaimed in Britain, the United States and Australia, it has also been dramatised on television. The trilogy was interrupted with the publication of *The Little Company* in 1945, but resumed with *Storm of Time* (1948) and *No Barrier* (1953).

One of Australia's most distinguished writers, Eleanor Dark lived for some years on a farm in Queensland, the setting of her last novel *Lantana Lane* (1959), before returning to the Blue Mountains where she died in 1985.

ELEANOR DARK

LANTANA LANE

WITH A NEW INTRODUCTION BY
HELEN GARNER

PENGUIN BOOKS – VIRAGO PRESS

PENGUIN BOOKS
Viking Penguin Inc., 40 West 23rd Street,
New York, New York 10010, U.S.A.
Penguin Books Ltd, Harmondsworth,
Middlesex, England
Penguin Books Australia Ltd, Ringwood,
Victoria, Australia
Penguin Books Canada Limited, 2801 John Street,
Markham, Ontario, Canada L3R 1B4
Penguin Books (N.Z.) Ltd, 182–190 Wairau Road,
Auckland 10, New Zealand

First published in Great Britain by William Collins Sons and Co. Ltd. 1959
First published in the United States of America by Penguin Books 1986

Printed in Finland by
Werner Söderström, a member of Finnprint

TO ANN
WITH LOVE

CONTENTS

INTRODUCTION

Eleanor Dark was born in Sydney in 1901, to a bookish and political family. Her father was the poet and man of letters Dowell O'Reilly, who worked as a schoolmaster and in the Commonwealth Public Service and who was briefly a Labor MP. About her mother I have no information. The young Eleanor, according to information provided by A. K. Thomson in *Understanding the Novel: The Timeless Land*, one of those mysterious and useful little cribs one unearths in public libraries, flourished intellectually from the start: she read at three, and by seven was writing verse and stories. She was educated at a private school and went to business college to become a stenographer. She appears to have taken it for granted that she would become a writer; she published her first verses at nineteen, and at twenty married Dr Eric Dark, a man who seems always to have supported her strongly in her work and her ambitions.

Dark is described, in Thomson's little book, as "an intensely practical and hard-working woman", a keen gardener, a hiker and bushwalker, who designed the family's house at Katoomba in the Blue Mountains west of Sydney, and who with her husband made a second summer home in a cave: "A rock in the floor was blasted away," writes Thomson, "and the floor made of white ants' nests. Fireplaces were made and rough furniture, and the table was a slab of rock."

Dark's love for the land and her knowledge of it came from a great deal of serious hiking and mapping of the area, activities which provided the solid research basis of *The Timeless Land* and also the wonder and respect for the ancientness of the country seen, for example, in *Return to Coolami:*

... in the gullies, through a dim green light and on soft earth that gave out a damp, rich smell, you might walk under tree ferns whose ancestors had been tree ferns before you grew legs and came to live on dry land.

The few photographs of Eleanor Dark that I have seen, all head-and-shoulders portraits, show her as broad-faced, with thick dark wavy hair cut shortish, a wide but rather thin mouth in a most determined set, and very striking, very large dark eyes which are always turned away from the camera. Her expression is serious and private.

Lantana Lane is Eleanor Dark's last novel. It appeared in 1959. Until I was asked to write this introduction I had never heard of it. To most Australians who were at high school in the 1950s, Dark was known as the author of the fattish historical novel *The Timeless Land* (1941; part of a trilogy) which we studied in fifth or sixth form. The strongest memory I had of this book is an early scene in which an Aborigine stands on the cliffs of Sydney Harbour (which bore for him, of course, a different name) and watches the approach of the sailing ships carrying the first European settlers to his land. It is a scene that the subsequent near-destruction of the Aboriginal race makes into an image of piercing irony.

Eleanor Dark's name returned briefly to public notice several years ago when a television series was made of *The Timeless Land.* Writers are accustomed to being passed over in the hooha that launches TV events, and Dark was no exception; but it is hard to imagine this old woman, living in the Blue Mountains, being much interested more than forty years after its publication in yet another interpretation of her most popular novel as little more than a colonial costume drama.

The TV series, using alcohol as the metaphor for racial destruction, touched lightly on the fatal impact of white settlement on the Aborigines, but paid little or no attention to the damage which, as Dark points out in her novel, greed and plunder did to the ancient land with which the Aborigines had lived in harmony. She uses the image of rape—but rape, it seems to me, within an already established relationship—when she says of her character based on Governor Phillip:

He heard them crying out to her insatiably, "Give! Give!" and was aware of her silent inviolability which would never give until they had ceased to rob.

If this strikes us as modern, we may be equally struck by this account, also from *The Timeless Land*, of Carangarang, elder sister of the main Aboriginal character Bennilong and a maker of songs: she sings,

... but the words faded as swiftly as they had been born; smitten with fear of her own temerity, she glanced round apprehensively upon a ring of startled, hostile faces. They said nothing, but she understood their condemnation.

Her younger sister, too, made songs that "were not such as men might make ... To the men she was like a faintly pricking thorn in the foot which they could not discover."

The women novelists of Australia between the 1920s and the end of the Second World War were no "faintly pricking thorns". They dominated the country's fiction output: Dark, Katharine Susannah Prichard, Barnard and Eldershaw, Dymphna Cusack, Kylie Tennant, and the two most brilliant, Christina Stead and Henry Handel Richardson, both of whom fled the place and worked abroad for virtually their entire careers. It is the mark of the ability of Australians to distort our own cultural history that a novelist like Eleanor Dark, a critical and popular success for twenty years and twice a winner of the Australian Literary Society's Gold Medal, should now be someone whose name produces blank looks, whose books have almost all been out of print for years, and who is omitted from the Oxford Anthology of Australian Literature (published 1985 and by any standards a conservative selection).

Drusilla Modjeska's important book *Exiles at Home* (Angus and Robertson, 1981) has brought fresh attention to the women writers, solidly on the left and subsequently all but forgotten, who dominated the Australian novel of their time. Dark is one of these writers, but even in Modjeska's book she remains a shadowy figure.

In her early novels *(Prelude to Christopher,* 1934; *Return to Coolami,* 1936; *Sun Across the Sky,* 1937; *Waterway,* 1938) Dark was stylistically some way in advance of her resident female contemporaries. In my fossicking among the rare personal reports about Dark, I have picked up an impression that her early technical adventurousness (time compression, flashback, etc.) and in particular her interest in psychology did not endear her to certain influential supporters of social realism who were devoted to the establishment and consolidation of a nationalistic Australian literary culture.

She may not have found congenial the heavy stress laid on social realism by Nettie and Vance Palmer and their network of commentators and writers, but her novels make it abundantly clear that her political sympathies lay with the left. In *The Little Company* (1945), the most explicitly political of her novels, written during the Second World War and reissued now by Virago with a rich and knowledgeable introduction by Drusilla Modjeska, Dark tackled crucial questions about the meaning of war and the role of the radical and the writer in a world whose social and political fabric was being torn apart. She was never an activist, however, and rarely went to literary or political functions; it was her husband's name that appeared on the Council for Civil Liberties masthead.

A Melbourne historian who interviewed Eleanor Dark ten years ago in his research for a biography of one of her contemporaries on the left remarked to me that she was "reflective, and not opinionated, unlike most of the people I interviewed from the old left whose responses tended to the automatic. She was easily the most impressive person I interviewed. She was a person who was still thinking, and who was prepared, if she had no grounds for opinion, to say nothing at all." He described her, in her middle seventies at that time, as "well preserved, fine-boned, without make-up, very attractive, sitting up there in her beautiful house on the edge of the escarpment, chain-smoking and looking out the window and thinking before she spoke."

But Dark and her husband were branded fellow travellers in a period when any criticism of Australian society could bring accusations of communism. They were so harassed for their politics in the fifties that Dr Dark's medical practice suffered, and they were obliged to leave Katoomba where they had long lived and worked, and move for a time to a small farming community in Queensland.

Then, for most of that decade, Dark's silence.

Then, in 1959, *Lantana Lane*, a novel so strikingly different from her other works as to "make one gasp and stretch one's eyes".

It is probably impertinent to make ignorant guesses about an artist's state of mind, but *Lantana Lane* strikes me as a novel written by a happy woman. Its tone is light, lively and benevolent. Its humour is benign. Its observations of human behaviour, while razor sharp, are affectionately knowing, and informed with an attractive, amused tolerance. Its wit is without malice, blackness or strain. Its feminism is no more vitriolic than a firm but gentle chiacking of men in their self-importance and laconicism. It is not a novel of conflict, of character development, of strain and resolution. It is a contemplation of a particular microcosmic isolated little farming community "round the corner from the world". It is a book written with pleasure by a mature artist in calm command of her craft.

The Timeless Land, Dark has said, "necessitated a fearful lot of study and research and, not being a scholar, I was very tired of that." *Lantana Lane*, on the other hand, clearly springs from personal experience. The only evidence of scholarliness here, apart from Dark's superb handling of syntax, is the easy familiarity the unnamed narrator (who employs a god-like and gender-hiding "we") demonstrates with certain Great Works of our culture: The Old and New Testaments, the Arthurian legends, Dr Johnson, Tennyson, Freud and the works of Richard Wagner. These learned references are bandied about with a breath-takingly light-handed cool, and give rise to some of the book's most hilarious sequences.

It's a "slow read", as they say, a wonderfully leisurely piece of writing, as if the easeful sub-tropical climate in which the farming community lives had affected the prose and structure of the book itself. Into her language of syntactic formality and wide vocabulary Dark slings sudden colloquialisms which blast the seriousness sky-high. The loveliest example of this is the chapter called *SOME REMARKS UPON THE NATURE OF CONTRAST with Special Reference to the Habits and Characteristics of Ananas comosus and Lantana camara and an Examination of their Economic and Psychological Effect upon Homo Sapiens.* This marvellous dissertation on the uncontrollable tropical weed, the bushy and massive lantana, in which the scientist's calm detachment keeps giving way to outbursts of cursing by the tormented farmer, is perhaps the showpiece of the book, not only for its sparkling language ("the feckless and slovenly lantana"; "the stiff, tough, soldierly pineapples" — this woman is a mistress of anthropomorphism) but because it is also a dissertation on the epic struggle of humankind against nature, and because of the tremendous possibilities of lantana as an image for the human unconscious.

This last I find specially satisfying and entertaining because of Dark's early difficulties with the Australian social realist school who turned their backs on what it no doubt saw as the side alley of Freudianism.

The beauty of this symbol did not strike me until a friend remarked to me, while I was reading the book, that her husband had dismissed his own unconscious by describing it as "a deep dark hole where I throw things I don't want to think about, and I never see them again". Dark's phrase "Throw it Down in the Lantana" sprang to my mind. The lantana, this pestiferous spreading plant, Australia's version of Brer Rabbit's briar patch, is the hiding place for many an unwanted object:

What would *you* do with tins and dead marines? What would *you* do with the old iron bedstead, the rust-consumed tank, the roll of useless wire netting, the ancient pram, the buckled bicycle wheel, the kettles, saucepans, egg-beaters and frying pans which have earned an honourable discharge? What would *you* do with the broken vases, medicine bottles, crockery and looking-glasses; the half-used bag of cement, now set like a rock; the worn-out gumboots, and the mouldering remains of your late grandmother's buggy? True, an incredible amount of junk will go under the house, but there comes a time when space there is exhausted—and then how thankfully we turn to the lantana! With a soft crash, and a sound of splitting twigs, discarded objects of all kinds, shapes and sizes fall through the green leaves, and discreetly vanish into the twilit world below.

And what is revealed when the mass of lantana is thinned or bulldozed or poisoned or destroyed will be, we imagine with a shiver, as momentous as the discoveries in store on the day when the sea shall give up its dead. It delights me to think of Eleanor Dark slyly slipping this image under the social realist rabbit-proof fence.

Dark's attitudes to the relationships between women and men are, in *Lantana Lane*, at their most benevolent. In earlier works she showed women frustrated and even driven mad by the contradictions forced on them, but the little community of Lantana Lane is so tightly knit and its people so interdependent that their situation is almost tribal: women's work is highly valued. Dark writes about the habits and roles of men and women in a pre-women's liberation movement way: without a political message, she presents the matter as a fact of nature, but oddly this enables her to point out with apparent innocence of motive things which any woman writer today could barely draw attention to without being accused of rampant man-hating.

The sequence in which "a youth named Barry James" carves a new road with a bulldozer, besides being a piece of writing of the most inspired brilliance, delicacy and strength, handles with controlled humour the fact that "the types of construction which most excite (men's) enthusiasm are those which demand, as a preliminary, excavation or demolition on a massive scale".

Bulldozed, with its paean to the machine and its sceptical respect for and witty sallies on manly skills and concerns, is beautifully counter-balanced by an earlier chapter called *Gwinny on Meat-day*. This sequence is a *tour de force* of another order. Here Dark gives us what is perhaps the book's greatest creation, the character of Gwinny Bell.

And when you see her working down in the pines, or pegging out her vast quantity of vast garments on the line, or striding along the Lane to visit one of the neighbours, you seem to hear Wagnerian music, and lo!—the scene dissolves. Fade out the serviceable working clothes, or the best frock of gay, floral rayon; fade out the felt slippers, or the patent leather shoes; fade out the battered, weekday hat, or the Sunday straw with its purple flowers, and its little pink veil. Fade in accomplished draperies which reveal the limbs they should be covering, and shining breastplates which proclaim the curves they guard; fade in gold sandals laced about the ankles; fade in a horned helmet over blond, wind-driven hair. Fade out the timber cottage sitting on high stumps, crowned with corrugated iron, and surrounded by pineapples; fade in an abode of gods, resting on legend, crowned by clouds, and surrounded by enchanted air. Fade out, Lantana Lane . . . and fade in, Asgard!

Although I long to quote further from this wonderful chapter, I refrain out of reluctance to pre-empt others' pleasure. Suffice it to say that Gwinny Bell and the feats of her "fabulous memory" brought tears of laughter, admiration and envy to my eyes. It is dazzling writing, and the purest tribute to the working lives, the teeming brains and the splendid competence of ordinary women everywhere.

Helen Garner, Melbourne, Australia, 1985

The Lane

LANTANA LANE leaves the highway so unobtrusively that, although it is the only side road between Tooloola and Dillillibill, strangers sometimes miss it. There are many car tracks leading off to half-hidden farm gates, and the Lane, at its junction with the bitumen, looks much the same as these. There is no signpost; if there were, it would bear the name Black Creek Road, for only by the inhabitants of the district is this mile-long strip of red earth called, in half derisive affection, Lantana Lane.

It follows a winding, hilly course along the crest of a ridge from which (where the lantana permits) one may look down across sloping farmlands to Black Creek on the one hand, and Late Tucker Creek on the other; both are tributaries of the Annabella River, whose estuary is visible from a point where the Lane, coming to an abrupt end at the top of a steeply plunging hillside, overlooks a stupendous view. Miles of farmlands lie below, lightly linked by ribbons of red road to the clustered roofs of little towns, and beyond them blue ocean and white beaches proclaim a stretch of the long, Queensland coastline, fading north and south into a haze of distance. Until this point is reached, however, one sees very little except the high walls of lantana, between which there is just room for two cars to pass, unless their owners are faddy about paintwork; but this we dwellers in the Lane have long since ceased to be. We are more concerned for our springs, axles and universal joints.

And with reason. The surface of the Lane is composed, for

9

the most part, of football-sized boulders thinly overlaid with the native earth—or, at the bottoms of the hills, where this has washed down upon them, deeply buried. In such places vehicles proceed with comparative smoothness except in rainy weather when, as likely as not, they are unable to proceed at all; for our soil combines with water to produce a mud of such slipperiness that even our dogs cannot walk on it without skidding. Then there is The Bump between Kennedys' and Dawsons'; among so many bumps, it claims the distinction of capital letters, for it is bedrock, a section of the earth's crust here nakedly exposed, and pity help you if you hit it unwarily. There is The Dip, too, just opposite the Griffiths', where it is nearly always greasy because of an underground seepage. And of course there is The Tree blocking half the road at the foot of Hawkins' hill; but we shall have more to say about this later.

And yet, despite all these hazards, we are fond of the Lane. A dead-end road must obviously develop a character quite different from that of a thoroughfare. Heaven only knows who the travellers along the Tooloola-Dillillibill road may be; the flash of sun on their paint and chromium is all we ever see of them. But if a car turns off into the Lane, it is making for one of the farms behind the lantana; it is one of us; or one of our friends; or Wally Dunk, delivering the groceries; or Doug Egan on his big truck, collecting our fruit for market; or Sam Ellis approaching, honk, honk, honk, to leap from his van at our gates, thrust the bread into the boxes nailed to their posts, and be off again, honk, honk, honking the news of his arrival all the way down to Ken Mulliner's. We do not need to look up from our chores, for we know them all by the sound. Thus there is a cosy, family atmosphere in the Lane, and those who live in it will stoutly assure you that it is by far the best part of Dillillibill.

Jack Hawkins' grandfather once owned all the southern side of the ridge, and most of the northern slope as well. There was no Lane in those days, no Dillillibill, and only a bridle track to the railway town of Rothwell. But since then the land has been subdivided and re-subdivided until there are now ten farms fronting the Lane. The largest of them is only thirty-five acres, the smallest is eight, and the rest are all between twelve and twenty. Those rural Moguls who measure their properties in square miles would doubtless be amused by our presumption in claiming to be on the land at all ; and indeed, we have only a toe-hold.

But we hold on tight. In the cause of survival many forms of life develop many strange faculties and physical characteristics—and small farmers have developed powerfully prehensile toes. This has been made necessary by the Curse which has relentlessly pursued them down the generations for six thousand years.

The first of their kind, as we may recall, took over a going concern, and his status was that of a caretaker rather than a proprietor. His instructions were to dress and keep the garden—nothing whatever being said about re-planting, grafting, cross-pollination, original research of any kind, or even developmental work. But the garden (containing, as it did, samples of every form of vegetation), was more than one pair of hands could dress and keep, so Eve was rung in to help—as she still is, on all one-man holdings.

Now when men pry into mysteries they are called scientists, but when women do the same thing they are called inquisitive, and if we are to reprobate the inquisitiveness which began the search for knowledge, we cannot but view with some reserve the scientific genius which has so stubbornly pursued it, even into the dreadful fastnesses of the Atom. Eve's husband was clearly a bloke with a sluggish intellect and no ambition ; we have her, and her alone, to thank for the fact that we now know enough to blow ourselves into small pieces. But in common justice we must bear in mind the disadvantage under which she laboured. She was not really at all inquisitive about atoms ; her curiosity was directed towards quite different matters. And being entirely innocent of knowledge, she could not possibly be expected to know that all knowledge interlocks, and that fiddling with one bit disturbs the whole cohesive structure. Of course the Creator of the garden knew this very well, having just spent a solid week designing and manufacturing parts for assembly into a working model ; and to see one's unique achievement endangered by a pair of ignorant meddlers (particularly when they have been created, merely as an afterthought, to preserve the status quo) is enough to make anyone curse.

So Eve and her offsider were for it. The great anathema was uttered. Cursed was the ground for their sake ; in sorrow should they eat of its fruits ; thorns and thistles should it bring forth, and with the sweat of their faces should it be for ever bedewed. So exactly has this maleficent prophecy been fulfilled throughout the centuries, that we cannot fail to marvel at the persistent way in which each generation produces a fresh crop of mugs not only willing but eager to dare its bane for the sake of possessing a bit of earth of their own.

To the stern and awful voice of the Lord has now been added the somewhat peevishly didactic voice of the Economist. Even the most junior apprentice to this craft knows, and will tell you with assurance, that the small farmer is doomed. He is done. He cannot compete. He cannot afford to be mechanised, and if he is not mechanised he is not in the race. Nor can he live-through-the-bad-years-on-the-fat-of-the-good-years, because the good years no longer produce much surplus fat, and in any case (whether owing to Acts of God or acts of nuclear research), seem to be getting worse, and farther between. He has become—to put it quite plainly and brutally—an Anachronism. Whenever he is warned by the economists of all this, he listens a trifle absent-mindedly, and does not answer back. There is one reply which he might make, but never does—and this is a pity, for it is based upon figures, which are things economists respect very highly. Those who have consulted certain tables compiled by insurance companies will have noted that farmers live longer than any other description of people except clergymen. We cannot account for the longevity of the clergy (indeed, it would appear to conflict with Professor Freud's theory of wish-fulfilment, since they may be supposed to hunger for the hereafter), but it is clear that farmers live long precisely because they indulge in such anachronistic habits as rising early, working hard all day in the open air, retiring early, and sleeping like the dead. They are therefore in a position to look those who warn them in the eye, and retort : " Better a live farmer than a dead economist."

The ten Anachronisms in the Lane are all alike in that they fulfil the prophecy of the Book of Genesis by sorrowing, sweating and contending with noxious weeds. And they are all alike in that an economist would need to do no more than cast an eye over their account books to say : " I told you so." But these are the similarities of their condition as practising farmers ; their dissimilarities of personality and background are so marked that the observer is driven to enquire what common factor it can be which has brought them all together in Lantana Lane. He will discover, if he examines the matter, that on only four out of the ten farms are to be found people who were born, so to speak, with brush-hooks in their hands—namely, the Hawkins, the Bells, Herbie Bassett and Joe Hardy. Now some are born farmers, some achieve farming, and some have farming thrust upon them. The Hawkins, the Bells and Joe Hardy were born farmers ; Herbie Bassett had farming thrust upon him ; but the rest have achieved farming, and they have found their way to it by paths so strangely various that we shall pause for a moment to glance at them.

Aub Dawson had a newsagency in a Melbourne suburb fifteen years ago, and his wife, Myra, was a cashier in a large store before she married him. He is a solid, active, rubbery little man who, in those days, used to gamble on the horses—which, as he often remarks now, are drearily predictable compared with the things farmers gamble on. Myra tells us they made quite a lot of money out of the newsagency, but quickly lost it again on the race-tracks, so at last Aub woke her up in the middle of one night, and said he had been thinking. When he says this she always knows that she is going to hear something very cynical beginning with " Listen, love," and what she heard was this :

" Listen, love—remember that little farm we used to talk about when we were engaged ? Right. Well, I thought I'd play safe, and make some money instead. So now I get up in the dark, and work like hell all day seeing that everyone gets their crosswords, and comics and cheesecake, and I make some money. Right. What happens to it ? We both like a flutter, so we put it on the wrong horse, and lose it. Now suppose we put it into a little farm instead—what happens then ? We still get up in the dark and work all day seeing that everyone gets their vitamins, and we're still gambling, and we still lose our money. Right. Which way would we rather lose it ? "

Put like that, it was really quite simple, and within six months Aub and Myra were settled in the Lane. Aub bets on this or that market, instead of on this or that horse, and usually bets wrong. He gets a hunch that Melbourne is rising, and sends his fruit there —and Melbourne falls ; next week he backs Sydney, and Melbourne pays top price. But he says it's all good, clean fun, and Myra swears that she would find the life quite perfect if only she weren't so allergic to ticks.

Henry Griffith is an Englishman, and was once a lawyer. His wife, Sue, also English, was the daughter of an archæologist and a French pianist of no mean repute. She is one of those women who would look elegant in a cornsack girdled with a bit of string, but she is usually to be seen around the farm in shirt, shorts and gumboots. To these she frequently adds headgear in the shape of a tea-cosy—gorgeously striped in rich shades of green, yellow and vermilion—whose purpose is to remind her that she has left the iron switched on, or a cake in the oven; but its effect, in combination with the rest of her toilette, is to make her look rakish and enticing, like a musical comedy she-pirate. As for Henry, it is difficult to imagine what can have prompted him to choose the law as a profession, for he likes to get things done fast. He also has a lively sense of humour, and a massive bump of irreverence ; had it not been for the fact that he is an extremely stubborn cuss, persistent in pursuing a course that he has set, these qualities would surely have bumped him out of the legal profession before he was fairly into it. As it was, he hung on grimly until his thirty-sixth birthday, when he took the day off, and had time to reflect.

He reflected that the effort of spinning out for months matters which could have been settled in hours was already producing in him symptoms of acute nervous irritation, and might well end by giving him stomach ulcers; that he seemed constitutionally unable to experience that sharp thrill of horror which shook his colleagues when they encountered a departure from precedent; that a time might come when he would not even want to laugh at the multitudinous absurdities which surrounded him; and that his partner was a pompous ass upon whom some day, he would surely inflict actual bodily harm. He put all this to Sue, and it terrified her; so when he suggested that they try farming in the Antipodes, she immediately rushed out and bought their steamship tickets. Thus they arrived in the Lane where, as they agree, impecuniosity is chronic, and absurdity by no means unknown—but pomposity is blessedly absent.

Ken Mulliner is not much over thirty, but he has been many things—soldier, carpenter, taxi-driver, bus-driver, garage mechanic; he met his wife when he was driving the bus, and she was its conductress. We know of her only from hearsay, however, for as soon as she saw the prospect of farming ahead, she found herself a tram-guard, and told Ken he could go and grow pineapples by himself. Ken does not appear to have been at all cast down at finding himself duly and legally released from the bonds of marriage; in fact his elder sister (who often brings her two boys to stay with him), has expressed the opinion that he was never so pleased about anything in his life. Certainly— if one may judge by his cheerful, ugly face, his brightly roving eyes and his sardonic grin—the unfortunate affair has caused no damage to his psyche.

He farms in a slap-happy sort of way, working furiously for a few months, and then disappearing for a week or two. He doesn't keep a cow, or fowls, because he says he likes to be able to walk out any time, and just shut the door behind him. (This, by the way, is a mere figure of speech. We do not shut doors when we go out—far less lock them; probably the only key in the Lane is the one old Mrs. Hawkins keeps hanging on a nail in case someone's nose begins to bleed.) But this desire to be untrammelled in his comings and goings seems to have been always noticeable in Ken, for his sister tells us he once got down from a bus he was driving, left it standing there bulging with passengers, and was seen no more for six months. She also assures us that he held the record for the whole Army in the matter of being A.W.O.L.

Bruce Kennedy and his wife were both teachers. He is a tall, thin man who speaks slowly, and she is a short, dumpy woman who speaks fast. He works to a relentless timetable, and reaches his deadline triumphantly, like a sprinter breasting the tape; but there are times when he becomes possessed by a desire to do something which will serve no purpose other than exercising his muscles or his grey cells—both of which, his wife thinks, are too active anyhow. He is much given to mental arithmetic, and does many useful sums, but also many others whose usefulness is not so apparent; for he will suddenly produce discouraging statistics about how many hours per year they spend washing-up, or how many times Marge will have to loop the wool round her needle before she finishes knitting her new scarf. He has even been known to tackle the problem of how long it would take to fill a ten-foot square room entirely with paint, if you painted it once a year—assuming, of course, that you had somewhere to stand during the later stages of this chore, though why anyone should assume such a thing, we do not know; at all events, Bruce derived some mysterious satisfaction from discovering the answer to be fifteen thousand years. His degrees were in science, and even before he turned farmer he was always reading books about agricultural theory and experiment. He belongs to the compost and organic manure school of thought, views chemical fertilisers with reserve, and will talk for hours about methods of controlling erosion, the need for preserving soil-bacteria, and the evils of monoculture. He is enthusiastic about worm-casts, and frequently invites Marge to admire them; indeed, one is tempted to wish that the common earthworm were a more sensitive and responsive creature than it appears to be, for on Bruce's farm not even Royalty could be more warmly and respectfully welcomed.

Marge gained her academic qualifications in the faculty of Arts, and her whole approach is less erudite. She has an eccentric theory that farms should be pretty as well as productive, and consequently she is always galloping through her farm jobs, or leaving her domestic ones undone, so that she can find time to plant a flowering tree, or sneak some of Bruce's compost to put round her gerberas. They have a son and a daughter—both married and living down south—who think they are crazy.

Tim Acheson was a bank clerk until about five years ago, and his wife, Biddy, was a typist. Tim is a good-looking young chap with a ready laugh, but when he is not laughing he wears a rather harassed expression. Possibly, in his former capacity he saw too many farmers' bank statements; at all events, he works as if a mortgage did close behind him tread, and Biddy swears that he once talked in his sleep about overdrafts. No matter how early we get up in the morning, there is always a light burning in the Achesons' kitchen, and no matter how late we stay out working, we can always see Tim, still plugging away until the darkness swallows him. Biddy says they occasionally talk of the time when they both worked eight hours a day, and they agree that sunrise to sunset doesn't seem as long as that did. Not while you're doing it, she adds pensively, but you ache more after you're in bed.

As for Dick Arnold (and you may believe this or not, when you see him in his mudstained jeans, and note the state of his hands), he once managed a beauty salon in a fashionable city hotel. Even now, when he goes to Church, we catch a glimpse of him as he must have been then—large, suave, well-barbered and well-tailored, with a trick—doubtless perfected as part of his professional stock-in-trade—of bending over the weaker sex in a protective and confidential manner. Despite this—or perhaps because of it—the womenfolk in the Lane were at first apt to vanish in confusion when they saw him coming, for they all felt that he must be noting with contempt their un-permed, unmanicured, un-groomed and generally un-glamorous appearance. But when they learned that his wife, Heather, who had worked in the hotel office, first attracted his favourable attention because she was the only one of several girls so employed who never patronised his establishment, they were reassured; and since Henry Griffith reported him as saying it was a treat to see women who looked like women, and not like bloody film stars, they have quite recovered their self-respect.

Observe that the occupations in which all these people were formerly engaged are highly reputable ones. No curse has ever been called down upon them, nor has any been the subject of solemn warnings, either human or divine—though it is true that Shakespeare made Hamlet say some pretty bloodcurdling things about beauty-culture. They are all respectable avocations, and you can even make money at them. Why, then, have they been so rashly abandoned for the sweat and sorrow, the thorns and thistles of a pursuit blighted by an age-old malediction? Why have the Dawsons, the Griffiths, the Kennedys, the Arnolds and Ken Mulliner all deliberately chosen to become Anachronisms?

It is a simple question of heredity. We can only regret that Genesis tells us nothing about how Eve brought up her sons, but presents them to us fully grown—the elder farming, and the younger keeping sheep. But we may confidently assume that during Cain's formative years his mother must still have been feeling a bit browned off about that Curse; a bit defiant; a bit inclined to toss her head, and say to her firstborn that in her opinion there was really nothing so marvellous about that garden. You just took seeds from things, and put them in the ground, and up came plants. Anyone could do it. She could do it. Cain could do it if he wanted to, and she'd like to see any son of hers scared off by a lot of bogey-talk about sweat and thistles. The idea!

So Cain, nurtured on subversive propaganda, grew up a rebel, and meddled with creation, while Abel (who was more the caretaker type, like his father), took care of sheep. And in Cain's posterity the urge for farming has persisted to this day—though there have been those who strayed into other paths. We have explicit Biblical information, for instance, about some who went in for cattle, some who dealt in musical instruments, and some who worked in the metal trade; and, as we have just noted, there are many in Lantana Lane who at first ignored the summons of their blood, and addressed themselves to callings not their own. But in the end, given half a chance, they will all find their way back, rejoicing, from ease to adversity; they will return, singing hosannas, from liberty to bondage; they ask nothing better than to till the ground, come sweat or cyclone, come drought or depression, come curse or creditors; and if the voice that thundered o'er Eden has not taught them sense in six thousand years, the voice that now analyses their economic predicament, and coldly foretells their ultimate extinction, might just as well pipe down. Cursed they may be—but they are cussed too.

Turning from the Old to the New Testament, we may recollect an occasion when a certain seafaring type told Paul that the freedom he enjoyed as a member of the master-race had cost him a packet; and Paul replied, rather loftily: " But I was born free." In a like manner, perhaps, do Joe Hardy, the Bells and the Hawkins regard their neighbours who have come late to farming.

Joe is nowadays not often visible at close quarters. We see him working among his pineapples, and he lifts a hand in answer to our waves, but he is of a solitary disposition, and rarely leaves his property unless some crisis in the affairs of a Lane-dweller calls for an extra pair of hands. Then he willingly appears—although, in fact, he has only one really effective hand to contribute, the other having been injured in a cyclone. He lives alone except for his Uncle Cuth, and his blue kelpie, Butch.

Alf Bell hardly ever leaves his pines, either. He is a large, dark lump moving slowly up one row and down the next, all day and every day. No matter how brilliant the sunshine, it never seems able to arrange its shadows in such a way as to lend Alf clear definition; he is just a shapeless object which we know to be a man because it moves. At first one thinks him surly, for he seldom speaks, and when he does his voice is an inarticulate rumble, like a roll of drums. His wife, Gwinny, does his talking for him, and interprets him to us. " Alf says ..." she tells us ; "Alf thinks ..." And thus we have learned that Alf is a person worthy of much respect ; a person with immovable convictions and uncompromising standards of behaviour ; a person with an almost agonisingly sensitive and accurate perception of what ain't right.

Jack Hawkins is a lean man of middle size and middle age, with a deeply lined face, a very quiet voice, and a remarkable gift for looking cleaner and sprucer than anyone in the Lane. He is our Oracle. As the ancients took their problems along to Delphi, so we take ours along to Jack—though the analogy is perhaps defective, for it seems that a good deal of skulduggery went on at Delphi, and you had to pay through the nose for advice, whereas what you get from Jack is free, and dinkum.

Now that we come to Herbie Bassett, we are stumped. We don't know what to make of him. He behaves like a descendant of Cain in that he tills his minute patch of ground, but we suspect a bend sinister somewhere. We think Abel was his true progenitor, for if ever there was a bloke who liked to leave nature alone, that bloke is Herbie Bassett. No ; when it comes to Herbie, we give up. He belongs to no group in the civilised world, though he might have found himself at home, perhaps, in some primitive tribe before progress sneaked up on it ; or in Eden, before Eve.

Here they are, then—a bunch of unrepentant anachronisms assembled in Lantana Lane. They are all—except Herbie— farming because they like it. True—true—they will declare, if questioned, that farming means drudgery, misery, penury, monotony, anxiety, bankruptcy and calamity ; that it is a mug's game, perpetually bedevilled by floods, droughts, tempests, soaring costs, sinking markets, debts, gluts, weeds, mud, viruses, nematodes, fruit-fly, bean-fly, top-rot, base-rot, black-heart, water-blister, white scale, gall wasp, bunchy-top, tip-wilt, melanosis, backache, heartache and holes in the tanks ; that anyone who chooses such a dog's life is a beetle-headed, fool-hardy, fatuous, gullible, impractical and deluded numbskull, and for two pins they would walk off the flaming place to-morrow. Nevertheless, they like farming.

" By golly ! " they will snort bitterly. " Just take a look at us, and then take a look at the graziers ! They have it all taped out —half the work, and a hundred times the profit ! They're the Government's little white-headed boys, all right ! " (And is not this the very voice of Cain, contrasting the genial commendation of his brother's offering with the cool reception accorded to his own ?) But growl and grumble as they will, the fact remains that they are farming because they want to, and they will continue to farm until they die—or (like Cain) are driven out. For let us make no mistake, driven out many of them have been, and will be. We need not here usurp the function of the Economist by enquiring into the nature of the power that drives them ; it is enough that the bone is pointing straight at their hearts.

But so long as the seasons are still permitted to follow each other in their appointed order, and behave more or less as they have always done ; so long as the sun, moon and stars are not crowded out of the sky by satellites, and the rain is not too radio-active ; just so long as this will the posterity of Cain mulishly defy every power on earth or in heaven for the undisputed possession of one small plot of earth. For although any farmer will, at the drop of a hat, denounce farming in the terms we have quoted, he will also say, now and then : " It's a good life."

And both times he is right.

The Narrow Escape of
Herbie Bassett

THE LANE's oldest inhabitant is Jack Hawkins' mother, who was born where she still lives—aged eighty-six—with her son and his family, on its south-western corner. The next oldest is Herbie Bassett, who has also lived in the Lane all his life—but he is only fifty-three.

Herbie's mother died when he was about sixteen, and he and his father worked the place for the next ten years or so, until his father died too. It had been about fifty acres once, but by then it had dwindled to twenty, and after his father's death Herbie sold another twelve, keeping only a narrow strip which runs south-ward from the Lane, fairly level at first, and then—growing steeper and steeper—plunges down to Late Tucker Creek.

Herbie got married a few years later, but his wife was delicate, and they had no children. Her health kept on going from bad to worse, and for a long time before she died she spent most of her time in bed, so Herbie had to do nearly all the domestic chores as well as his own work. But he was—and still is—a brisk, neat, methodical little man, and everything was always in apple-pie order. In those days he used to have a few sidelines to supplement his earnings from the farm. He made picking-baskets —enormously strong, with a metal band passing right round the bottom, and woven into the handle, to support the weight of the pineapples—and he made smaller and lighter ones, too, which he sold to the women for shopping baskets. He also made *objets d'art* out of seashells and fragments of coloured glass or china which he embedded in plaster of paris plaques, and often arranged so that they spelt out some legend, such as HOME SWEET HOME, or COUNT YOUR BLESSINGS. But this was mainly a labour of love, and he gave most of them away as Christmas presents. He was a good cobbler, too, and mended boots and shoes for everyone in the Lane. Though he was as fine-drawn as a fiddle string, and often looked haggard, no one ever heard him complain; and considering how small his place was, he seemed to do well enough. We all thought it rather hard on him that his wife—who came from the city—was not a bit interested in farming—but only after she died did we discover that Herbie wasn't either.

What Mrs. Herbie was interested in was interior decoration. She was always surrounded by very shiny and colourful magazines describing, illustrating and extolling a state known as Gracious Living. This state was to be attained, they said, by acquiring picture windows, free-standing fireplaces, piazzas, cocktail bars, barbecues, and a great deal of glittering gadgetry for the kitchen. It was also a help if you made one wall of your living-room lime green, and the others shocking pink; and it was of vital importance that you should remember to call the room where you slept with your husband the Master Bedroom. Herbie really couldn't do anything about picture windows and free-standing fireplaces, but he felt he could at least co-operate in this last matter. By that time he was sleeping in the other room, though, and rarely entered the Master Bedroom except to take trays to his wife, so he suggested that the Mistress Bedroom would really be a more accurate phrase; of course the words were no sooner out of his mouth than he realised they didn't sound right at all, and Mrs. Herbie's expression showed clearly that they weren't. Poor Herbie often put his foot in it when he tried to show an intelligent interest in Gracious Living. Perhaps his worst blunder was over the board. The magazines, although indulgent enough about the naming of houses, made it clear that The Trend was towards

numbers—which, however, must not be displayed in figures, but
as words. So Mrs. Herbie asked her neat-fingered husband to
paint the word THREE on a board for her, which he was very
glad to do ; but he argued that their place was the second in the
Lane, and should therefore be TWO. When she explained that
odd numbers went on one side, and even numbers on the other,
he wanted to know how she knew they were not FOUR, seeing
that none of the other places had numbers you could go by. To
this she replied rather tartly that they were going to be THREE
because it looked nicer than FOUR, on account of being longer,
and if any of the other places wanted to put up numbers they
could just fit in with hers, so would Herbie please get on with
it, and do it with that black shadow effect which made the letters
stand out. It so happened that she had a bad turn just afterwards,
and Herbie, desirous of having a really nice surprise ready for
her when she was better, bethought himself that SEVENTEEN
was even longer than THREE, and he worked late into the night
producing a board which would have done credit to the most
accomplished professional signwriter. His wife wept when she
saw it, and said it was done lovely, but it wasn't any use. When
Herbie, in great distress and bewilderment, asked why, she wept
harder and said there weren't seventeen places in the whole of
the Lane, at which Herbie scratched his head and pointed out
that there weren't any numbers either, so why couldn't she have
any one she liked, and she'd said the longer the better ? . . . But
she was adamant and inconsolable, so he threw the board down
under the house and got to work hurriedly preparing another
shorter one for THREE ; this was duly put up, and much
admired, and it lasted until white ants got into the gate many
years later. But the most imperative rule for Gracious Living
was undoubtedly an operation known as Bringing the Outdoors
Inside. Mrs. Herbie was never able to interest the rest of us in
this very much, though, because it is a thing which occurs quite
naturally in our part of the world where we are always finding
mud, leeches, ticks, Noogoora burrs, bulldog ants, Cobblers'
Pegs and even snakes littering our floors.

However, it was acknowledged that Mrs. Herbie studied all these mysteries very closely, and she was the recognised authority on them. Of course it was her dream to pass from study to achievement, and to this end she bought a ticket in the Casket every month—or rather (for she herself rarely went out), arranged that Amy Hawkins, her next-door neighbour, should buy one for her. She knew perfectly well that her chance of acquiring the requisites for Gracious Living by this means was about a hundred thousand to one—don't we all ? But since her chance of acquiring them by any other means was precisely nil, she very sensibly persevered, and passed many happy hours making lists from her magazines of the things she would buy when she received a cheque for six thousand pounds.

Now of all the narks known to psychological science, there is none worse than the man who seeks to set himself above his fellows by loftily declaring that he despises money, doesn't want money, and wouldn't know what to do with it if someone left it to him in a will. Everyone wants money. Nevertheless, " money " is a very elastic word, and due allowance must be made for the fact that Mr. Rockefeller's notion of wealth would be substantially different from that of, say, Herbie Bassett. Herbie often thought it would be pleasant to have plenty of money, but he thought it only when he had to cut down his tobacco to pay a bill, and then his idea of plenty of money was just enough to pay all his bills without ever having to cut down his tobacco.

He was worried at first by his wife's monthly bid for riches, because the thought of Gracious Living terrified him, and he was afraid her ticket might win. Moreover, he was a man who liked life to proceed placidly, and he found the recurring cycle of anticipation mounting to a climax of excitement, and then plummeting into an abyss of despair, very trying. But he endured it with patience (having been lavishly endowed at birth with this quality), and, as the years went by, and Fortune continued utterly to ignore the numbers on her tickets, was gradually reassured ; he even had a feeling, sometimes, that he was buying her all the satisfactions of Gracious Living very cheaply, and with little inconvenience to himself. The whole business seemed simpler and more harmless than ever when Amy Hawkins—having decided to give up growing vegetables, and buy them from Herbie instead—took to deducting the ticket money from what she owed him, so that he was not troubled about it at all.

After his wife died he allowed this custom to continue because —like many other people, including such wise and illustrious folk as statesmen—he had found that it was easier to let customs alone than to alter them. Amy now not only bought his ticket, but kept it, paid herself for it, and looked up the results, so there was no need for him to give it a thought, and he didn't. True, she said to him every month : " No luck, Herbie ! " and he replied : " Can you beat it ? " But this exchange was no more than a polite formula, like saying : " Lovely day ? . . ." or " Nice drop of rain ? . . ." And he came to regard it, in his increasing preoccupation, as merely a form of polite greeting peculiar to his intercourse with Mrs. Hawkins.

For he now had much more important things to think about. He had discovered that he, too, had ideas about Gracious Living, and that these, unlike his late wife's, could be translated into reality without any expenditure whatever.

As far back as he could remember, Herbie had always liked to look at things, and as far back as he could remember he had always been hauled away in the middle of looking at something to milk a cow, or make cases, or run a message, or plant beans, or pick pineapples, or wash his hands, or brush lantana. Now, for the first time in his life, he seemed to see opening before him the miraculous possibility of an existence in which he could look as long and as hard as he liked.

He was not choosy. He would look at anything from a sunrise to a separator, but he had to take his time over it. He was quite willing to study machines—or, for that matter, human beings— if only they would keep still long enough, but they rarely did, so he was driven more and more to nature, whose activities and metamorphoses proceeded at a pace which allowed leisurely contemplation. He was no mute, inglorious Burbank, and his interest was not scientific. If a flower had red petals, that was all right with him, and it did not occur to him to wonder if he could turn them blue. He liked to observe the golden pollen on its stamens, but was content to believe that the wind and the bees knew their business, and felt no desire to do officious and impertinent things to it with a camel-hair brush. He found weeds just as rewarding to look at as the more useful or decorative forms of vegetable life, but could have named only those which are a bane to farmers, and must therefore have a name to be cursed. However, looking at things with the attention he felt they deserved obviously required a great deal of leisure, and he had always patiently assumed that leisure was, for him, an unattainable luxury.

Now he was not so sure. He was beginning to believe that it might be within his grasp, and he soon realised that if he were to grasp it he must first make some changes in his way of life. He began by getting rid of everything in the house except necessities, which left him with a bed, a table, a broom, a bucket, three blankets, two towels, a stove, a cupboard, a spoon, and a few oddments of crockery. Having sold his surplus household goods, and disposed of such unsaleable trifles as remained by throwing them in the lantana, he looked round his bare dwelling with as much pleasure as his wife could have felt in contemplating the most graciously equipped house that ever was lived in.

Do not fall into the error of imagining that Herbie now began to lead a feckless, sordid, grubby sort of life. Not at all. He regularly scrubbed his house out from end to end, and there were so few things in it to be out of place that nothing ever was. He hung his washing on the line punctually every Monday morning —a pair of shorts, a shirt and a towel. A bath towel—for he had perceived that tea towels are necessary only if you wash up, and washing up is necessary only if you cook, so he lived with sumptuous simplicity on bread and butter, cheese, raw eggs and vegetables, milk and fruit. He kept his knife in a sheath hanging from his belt, and cleaned it by pushing it into the ground, rinsing it at the tank tap, and drying it on his shorts. He brewed tea some six or seven times a day in a billy out of doors, and his stove remained cold except when he wanted to dry his boots.

Herbie is far from lazy. He has never minded doing a little work, and he continued to keep two acres under cultivation, milk his cow, feed his fowls and tend his vegetables. The rest of his land he left to be slowly swallowed up by lantana, and when he recalled how much of his life had been spent in brushing the stuff, he felt very peaceful and luxurious as he watched it creeping like a slow, green tide over his paddock, and knew he needn't do a thing about it. Sometimes his contentment was disturbed by a few guilty qualms, for there was a good deal of groundsel getting in too, and he had been brought up to hate groundsel like the devil. But he meant to get it out some day when he wasn't so busy. His training had never gone far below the surface of his mind, and underneath there were depths of conviction which told him the main business of life was to be happy.

He now began to be very happy indeed. It was noted that he lost his taut look, put on a bit of weight, and grew quite rosy. He was, if anything, more brisk, neat and methodical than ever as he went about his irreducible minimum of chores, for now there lay beyond them glorious, uninterrupted hours of looking.

If he specialised in anything, it was sunrises. He was unable to milk as early as his neighbours did, because sunrises cannot be taken in at a glance, or even in a series of glances ; they emerge from darkness, and are not over until full daylight, and Herbie had to sit them out on his east verandah from beginning to end. Throughout the day clouds occupied a good deal of his time, and since staring upward causes a crick in the neck, he pursued this particular study lying flat on his back. Some people—Aub Dawson was one—took a long while to get over the idea that there must be some purpose in Herbie's odd behaviour. " What's he do it *for* ? " Aub would demand. " What's he trying to get *out* of it ? " But when such people asked Herbie what he got out of it, he only baffled them further with the simple word : " Dunno." This is his favourite word. It saves him endless trouble and discussion. Aub, who really could not bear to think of all that good, concentrated gazing going to waste, developed the theory that if a man spent most of the day staring at the sky, he must at least become a good weather-prophet. So he used to ask hopefully : " Change coming, Herbie ? . . ." " Rain blowing up ? . . ." " Might get a thunderstorm, eh ? . . ." But Herbie always answered, with his slow, amiable smile : " Dunno." And at last Aub fell back upon cynicism, and remarked that this, after all, proved him as good a weather-prophet as most. Similarly, when Herbie had been keeping his eyes fixed un-winkingly on a pineapple plant for a couple of hours, he had nothing to say about it afterwards. He just liked to stare, and his pleasure in staring was incommunicable.

He was on excellent terms with everyone, but he had only one real friend, and this was Tommy Hawkins, who was five years old. Tommy had a brother, Dave, a couple of years older than himself, and another, Keithie, who was three, so his mother sometimes thought it strange that he should so often abandon his games with them, and run off across the paddock to spend a few hours with Herbie. The truth was that he had recently acquired a farm of his own, and he found Herbie particularly acceptable as a companion simply because he appeared to be the only person who fully understood that the reality of imaginary things is not the same as the reality of real things. Even Dave and Keithie were a little shaky on this point. Dave was apt to do his pretending in a slightly shamefaced manner which quite spoiled Tommy's concentration, while Keithie became utterly confused, and reduced the whole art of make-believe to an absurdity. As for grown-ups, they were hopeless ; all but Herbie.

Tommy knew perfectly well that his farm was not *real* real, and he sometimes became weary of the fiction—kindly upheld by all the neighbours—that it was. However, Amy Hawkins has taken great pains to teach her children manners, so when some

well-meaning adult paused to pat him on the head, and enquire
how things were going on his place, he always replied that they
were going good, thank you. He knew the language of farmers,
and had lately added to it the word " damn," which rather
disturbed his mother, ". . . though really," she would sigh, " the
way he says it, so sort of natural, it doesn't sound like a swear-
word at all."

" Put any beans in down at your place, Tommy ? " some great
goat would ask, and Tommy would reply, humouring him :

" I put 'em in long ago."

" They doing all right ? "

" They was getting the damn bean-fly, but I sprayed 'em."

" Tanks getting low, I suppose ? "

" No, they're full up . . . or they might be just two rungs
down."

" Half your luck ! Mine are pretty near empty."

" Mine were too, but the damn rain last night filled 'em up
again."

" Go on ! We didn't get any rain here."

" Down on *my* place," Tommy would reply firmly, " there was
twelve . . . no, twenty inches, and me damn tanks are full, and
me damn dam's full too."

And he would smile a little sideways smile, indulging this
great goat who knew nothing at all about imaginary reality. Did
he not betray it by his questions ? For what would be the use
of such a farm as Tommy's if things went wrong on it ? It
would be no better than a *real* real one. He had taken suitable
steps to guard against this. He had an assistant known as Me
Man on to whose shoulders he could push such jobs as he did
not care to be bothered with himself ; those which he did attend
to were never waiting to be done, but always already accomplished, with complete success ; and he made good use of " to-
morrow." He had also taken the precaution of supplying himself
with a road of such surpassing badness that no wheeled vehicle
save his own could negotiate it, thus checkmating the embarrassing suggestions of his acquaintances that they might come

along and have a look at this place of his one day. Herbie, of course, was never guilty of such a solecism.

A farm of this kind was no trouble at all. Tommy could possess and enjoy it without feeling—as he knew all the other farmers, except Herbie, did—that the cultivation of the soil was a tyranny from which there was no respite. He needed, like Herbie, a tremendous amount of leisure for enjoyment—every waking moment, in fact—and he refused to tarnish the pleasures of farm ownership with anxious cares. So when he wandered over to Herbie's place, he felt at home. Herbie's farm was, of course, a *real* real one, but that did not seem to worry Herbie much. And when they spoke of Tommy's, it was clear that Herbie not only understood the advantages of imaginary reality, but wished his own farm might share them.

" You not putting in any more suckers, Herbie ? "

" I reckon I got enough in now. How much've you put in ? "

" Two acres. No, three." Tommy pondered, and felt that it was perhaps a pity he had not made it five while he was about it. " But I put in another acre of bananas, too," he added expansively, " and a hundred damn paw-paws."

" You got a man to help you, though," Herbie pointed out.

Tommy smiled his wise and secret smile. Herbie's farm was better than most real real ones, but it would clearly be better still if it were like his own.

" You picking to-day, Herbie ? "

" No, I been around, but there ain't enough to make up a case."

" Me man's picking down at my place—he'll get fifty, I reckon."

" Got your cases made ? "

" I got enough for to-day. I'll be making more to-morrow."

" Ah," said Herbie with a perfectly genuine sigh, " that's the best day for making cases—to-morrow."

Tommy's father—who well knew that a prosperous farm must be mechanised—had given him a tractor for Christmas, and when

Herbie needed any hauling done Tommy pedalled it down to the fence, and Herbie lifted it over, and Tommy did the job for him. Herbie (who was mechanised only to the extent of a home-made wheelbarrow) found this a great convenience, for Tommy's tractor was well known to be of almost unlimited horse-power, and had recently dragged a log weighing one hundred tons up the hill from Late Tucker Creek in less than five minutes. All its machinery was clearly painted on its side, and a trifling adjustment with a spanner—or a stick, if no spanner were handy—converted it instantly to a bulldozer. One morning when it had been so converted Tommy announced vaingloriously :

" I could shift that damn lantanna of yours in one day, Herbie, I bet."

" Reckon we better let it be, Tommy. I got all the land I can manage."

" Well, there's that damn patch of groundsel—I could shift that."

" No hurry—it ain't going to seed yet awhile."

But Tommy was being properly brought up by a good farmer, and he said severely : " Me dad says it don't do to let groundsel get a hold."

True. Herbie eyed it uneasily. It did not occur to him (and this, no doubt, was why Tommy so valued his company), to say with amused and indulgent heartiness that Tommy had better go and get it out, then ; for he had committed himself to the reality of imagination, and though the imaginary situation must be treated as real, he must not insult Tommy by seeming to suggest that Tommy actually believed it to be so. He must not subject Tommy to the embarrassment of finding himself and his tractor pitted, in very truth, against a forest of groundsel. Tommy trusted him to stall ; and he stalled.

" Maybe I'll get on to grubbin' it out," he conceded, and added hastily : " To-morrow."

But Tommy would not allow this. He knew all about to-morrow. Herbie must not suppose that because he kept the demands of his farm within reasonable bounds, he could ignore its real reality, and play about with to-morrows in this shameless manner. " There's too much to grub out," he objected. " It'd take you months and years. You want a damn bulldozer."

" Well," countered Herbie, " I might buy a bulldozer one day."

" When ? " demanded Tommy ruthlessly ; and Herbie, hard-pressed, replied : " When I win the Casket."

Herbie was very busy all the next morning. First there was a finer sunrise than usual, prolonged by a bank of low-lying cloud which filled the air like a luminous red dust. Then, when he had just finished his milking, and was going down to his pines to do some chipping, he almost trod on a very newly-shed snake skin, so he had to squat on his heels and study that for a long time. After he had been chipping for an hour or so, he noticed that someone had begun burning off on the far hillside across Late Tucker Creek, and the spectacle of blue smoke melting into the blue sky was one which could not be passed over in a hurry. So what with one thing and another, he was only just returning to the house when he saw the Kennedys' Land Rover stop at the Hawkins' with their meat and mail. He didn't eat meat himself, or read newspapers, and no one ever wrote to him except to send bills, so he was neither surprised nor disappointed when the Rover went past his own gate without stopping. He lit the fire for his billy, cut himself a hunk of bread and a hunk of cheese, made his tea, and sat on the steps very contentedly, eating and drinking and gazing with great interest at a dead lizard. He had just peeled a bird-pecked pineapple, and was holding it by its green top, and eating steadily round and round it, when Tommy arrived, and demanded at once :

" You going in to buy your bulldozer 's'afternoon, Herbie ? "

Herbie shook his head.

" Got to save up a bit more yet."

" Why ? " enquired Tommy. " You got tons of money now you won the Casket."

" Eh ? I never won no Casket."

" Me mummy says you did. I heard her telling Mrs. Bell over the 'phone. She said it was in the damn paper."

Herbie sat with the pineapple half-way to his mouth, staring at Tommy, but for once he saw nothing at all. He didn't believe it, but he was vaguely frightened. It seemed to come over him all of a sudden that such a thing *could* happen, and he felt that he had been terribly and stupidly careless.

" Go on," he said slowly, " you must've got it wrong."

" I never ! " cried Tommy with indignation.

" She must've meant something else," Herbie insisted doggedly.

" She never ! " Tommy was getting annoyed. " You come and ask her, then," he challenged. " Come on ! "

" I haven't finished me dinner," Herbie protested weakly, and took a small bite of the pineapple to prove it. He had an overwhelming instinct to sit still and keep very quiet.

" You can eat a damn pine while you're walking, can't you ? " demanded Tommy, hopping with impatience. " Come on—don't you want to know if you can get your damn bulldozer ? "

Herbie did not. He felt like an insect being prodded with a stick. He only wanted to be left alone.

" You go," he suggested. " I got a bit of a pain in me leg. You go."

Tommy went, streaking across the paddock to the boundary fence, ducking under the wire, and racing up towards his own house, yelling : " Mum ! Mum ! "

Herbie sat there on the step feeling very confused. For many years the sum of six thousand pounds had been associated in his mind with Gracious Living, and Gracious Living had been associated in his mind with his wife ; therefore, when his wife died, Gracious Living had died with her, and it had seemed that there could be no further connection possible between himself and six thousand pounds. He was now tormented by a suspicion that this might have been faulty reasoning—but it was still powerful enough to comfort him a little. Herbie Bassett simply DID NOT acquire vast sums of money. More comforting still, however, was the sudden realisation that it would be damn silly if he did; for his contemplation of natural phenomena had imbued him with one conviction, namely that strange things often happened, but not damn silly ones, and, since he never read the newspapers, he erroneously supposed this rule to apply, also, to the arrangements of mankind. Most comforting of all was the thought that if it had been true Amy would have been over herself to tell him—and Jack too, and all the family, and most likely the neighbours would have got wind of it. . . .

So he began to feel a good deal better. There was no need to worry, he told himself, and forthwith ceased to do so, because right above his head he noticed a long path of rippling white cloud trailing across the otherwise empty sky like the wake of a ship on a blue ocean. He had his lunch things to put in order—there was the billy to be emptied, and the pannikin to be stood upside down, and the knife to be cleaned—but he knew how slyly clouds could sneak off or melt away while you weren't watching, so he left his chores undone, and was just about to settle down on his back when Dick Arnold drove past, caught sight of him, waved a hand and shouted:

" Congratulations, Herbie ! "

Herbie sat down suddenly on the steps because his legs began to wobble. It *was* true, then. . . . It was *true*. . . . There opened up before him like the pit of Hell an intolerable, dark, endless and indescribably menacing vista of things he would have to do, beginning with buying drinks for everybody, which he would have done very gladly if he could have done it without being present himself, for he was not a drinking man. And he would have to go to banks, which were places he disliked intensely because there was nothing to look at except bits of paper, and these, he had found, usually meant trouble of one kind or another. He would have to be talked at; make decisions; answer questions; fill in forms; be interviewed, perhaps and have his picture in the paper; buy a suit, even; buy all sorts of things. He might have to develop his farm . . . plant up the rest of his land . . . get some machinery, and a ute . . . learn to drive them.

. . . He was rich, and rich people were never left alone. He would never have time to look at things again. . . .

This prospect of change and turmoil distressed him so much that the eyes he lifted as Amy Hawkins scrambled through the fence and came running towards him, were quite wild, and grew wilder when he noticed that she was jubilantly waving a slip of paper over her head. There! Hadn't he known it? Bits of paper always meant trouble. . . .

She called out breathlessly:

" Well, Herbie—at last! You've waited long enough!"

Speechless and stricken, he could only stare at her, and she gasped out chidingly as she came up to him:

" Why, what's the matter with you? Tommy told you, didn't he? You look like you'd lost five pounds instead of winning it!"

Five pounds? . . . He blinked. He breathed deeply. He smiled. He took the ticket and looked at it almost with affection. Five pounds needn't cause much disturbance. A man could take five pounds in his stride; that was what he called a real nice little amount of money. His smile broadened to a beam, but faded as he glanced up and saw that the cloud had already disintegrated into a few wisps. There's what money does, he thought bitterly; takes your mind off things for a while, and then they're gone, and you know you'll never get another chance to see them just that way again. . . . But he mustn't grouse. It had been a narrow shave. After all, the five pounds would just cover the rates nicely. But he wouldn't buy no more Casket tickets; it was too risky.

Tommy, who had scuttled down at his mother's heels, now proclaimed triumphantly: " See, Herbie, I never did get it wrong, did I? Mum, Herbie's going to buy a bulldozer! He's going to buy a bulldozer, and shift his groundsel!"

" Ah-ha!" cried Tommy's mother. " That'll be the day!"

The Deviation (1)

THE ERUDITION of Dr. Johnson was such that we hesitate to contradict him, but our experience in the Lane seems to disprove his theory that none are happy but by anticipation of change. We must concede, perhaps, that a little change for the better in our financial affairs would make us even happier than we are, but on the whole we are pretty care-free, and the only thing which periodically afflicts us with uneasiness and despondency is precisely the anticipation of a certain change which threatens to overtake us at some future time. We do not exactly brood upon it, but every now and then something happens to recall it to our minds, and then we speak of it as The Deviation.

A few years ago it began to be rumoured that the Department of Main Roads was casting a critical eye upon our district, and particularly upon that part of the highway which lies between the Lane and the township of Tooloola. No one was at all surprised to hear it. The official definition of a perfect road is well known to be the same as Euclid's definition of a straight line, and this stretch of bitumen is so far from being the shortest distance between two points that it must cause acute shame and anguish in the Department. What more likely, we reflected, than that some road-planner, seated at a desk with a map in front of him, should suddenly have noted that if he laid one end of a ruler upon Dillillibill, and the other upon Tooloola, it would lie roughly along the Lantana Lane ridge? What more certain than that he should observe, further, another ridge running out from Tooloola

37

upon approximately the same line ? And after that, what more inevitable than that he should thump his desk, and cry loudly : " Eureka ! " ?

Looking more closely, he might of course regard it as unfortunate that there should be the gorge of Late Tucker Creek between the toes of these two ridges, and that half a mile upstream Hawkins' Falls should drop it perpendicularly about a hundred feet ; but what, he would surely ask himself, is a little matter of a steep mile or so, with a few hairpin bends, and a bridge at the bottom ? True, it would slightly mar the beautiful straight line, but would it not be far less damaging to the Department's prestige than the ridiculous, wide loop which, following the crest of the main ridge, at present links Tooloola with the Lane ?

All this seemed so plausible that we never really doubted the truth of the rumour, even before Horrie Bates (who is on the Shire Council, and may be supposed to have inside information) assured us that a major reconstruction of the Tooloola-Dillillibill road was undoubtedly being considered. He added rather sourly that in his opinion it would go on being considered for the next thirty years ; but we were inclined to dismiss this as wishful thinking. For if our road-planner had, indeed, drawn The Deviation with his ruler, he must have gone further and, with a fine abandon, scribbled out The Loop—thus relegating Horrie and others to what would then become a local road, dependent for its maintenance upon the Shire Council. And Horrie, as a Councillor, knows what that would mean.

But what would it mean to the Lane ? . . . We weigh the pros and cons. We remember the squeaks, rattles and sagging springs of our long-suffering vehicles, and think of bitumen. We sigh over the scratches on their paint, and remind ourselves that on a main road we could meet the oncoming traffic without getting off into the lantana. On the other hand, we wonder whether they really know what Late Tucker Creek is like in a cyclone ; and whether, even in the most halcyon conditions, The Deviation would serve us better than The Loop. One school of thought holds that it would save time, while the other argues that the steep grades and hairpin bends would cancel out the shorter distance—but this point is never debated with much heat, for, as Ken Mulliner so often says, what's the hurry ? And in any case, we are well aware that when all this considering is going on, our convenience will not be a very weighty factor.

On a far warmer note of interest, we discuss resumption—for this pill is always followed by the sugar-plum of compensation. Everyone agrees that (at all events as far as Aub Dawson's place), there would be no real need to resume anything, for the poor visibility on our corners is due not to their sharpness, but to the encroaching lantana. We are not so naïve, however, as to imagine that a bend of any description would be tolerated if it could possibly be straightened, and the only way to straighten the Lane would be to shave bits off our properties. Not very big bits. Regarded as proportions of our acreage, they would hardly be missed. But the point which we are prepared to argue with force and eloquence is that they would be our best bits, our most level bits, our most accessible and easily worked bits—and therefore bits for which we may justly urge our claim to handsome compensation.

But towards its eastern end, the Lane veers slightly northward before fading out into a track, and the ridge descends through Aub Dawson's farm, and Dick Arnold's, to the creek. If our guesses are right, The Deviation will here call for resumption on a scale which implies most seductive compensation ; Aub names a sum which makes our mouths water, and pugnaciously declares that if he doesn't get it they will have to build their ruddy road over his dead body ; and Dick is hardly less truculent. You would think, to hear them, that they are panting for the action to begin. They even boast, with a great show of hardihood, that they will go down in history as the only blokes in the neighbourhood who ever made a nice little packet out of their farms.

This does not deceive anyone. They, like the rest of us, are grievously torn. Whatever Dr. Johnson may have said, anticipation of this change brings no gladness to any of our hearts. For the Tooloola-Dillillibill road is more than a link between two little towns ; it is also one section of a north-south route which gathers in, at various points, the traffic from vast inland areas— and The Deviation would make us part of it. Do we really want to be part of anything so busy and important ? Do we really want to find ourselves on all the maps ? Should we really like being on the way from anywhere to anywhere else ? Ah ! These questions—which we never discuss at all—are the ones which give us pause ; we know that if the Lane ever becomes a through road, it will be the Lane no longer—and somehow we like it as it is.

Till You Come to a Green Ute

IF YOU should ask the way to Lantana Lane, you will be told, most likely, to drive along the Tooloola-Dillillibill road, and turn off when you come to a green ute. This form of direction is, admittedly, a little less than foolproof, for occasionally the ute is not there. But it nearly always is. Joe Hardy only uses it once a week on the farm, and hardly ever drives it on the roads, so the residents—quite reasonably taking the view that a green ute is more easily spotted than an inconspicuous, lantana-shrouded turning—customarily proffer it as a landmark.

Joe is a gangling, taciturn, middle-aged bachelor; rather a villainous looking person, if the truth must be told, for he has a broken nose, and a long scar running down the left side of his face from the corner of his eye to the corner of his mouth; this distorts his features, and gives him an evil leer which is gravely misleading. His left shoulder is higher than his right, and his left arm—not much use to him now—ends in a hand from which three fingers are missing; he also limps badly. When Heather Arnold's sister came to the Lane once for a fortnight's visit, she was frankly terrified of him, and could only with great difficulty be convinced that his favourite relaxation is neither murder, arson, blackmail, rape, nor even drink—but draughts. He is a notable draughts player, but since no one in the Lane was, until a few years ago, proficient enough to sit at the same board with him, he used to have a standing appointment with an old lady in Dillillibill on Sunday afternoons. He lives with his Uncle Cuth

and his black kelpie, Butch, in a corrugated iron shack on the
corner; he had a house once, but it was blown down in a
cyclone, as we shall relate, and he has never got around to re-
building it.

In these parts most houses stand up on stumps high enough
to provide room beneath the floorboards for innumerable things,
including, of course, the family's motor vehicle—be it car, truck,
ute, tractor, jeep or jalopy. Joe's house, however, had been
erected, for some inscrutable reason, upon stumps a bare four
feet high. The construction of a shed, and access thereto would
have been not only costly in time and money, but a waste of good
pineapple land, so Joe merely brushed a bay in the lantana outside
his fence, and parked the ute there. In those days—what with
driving in to the store a couple of times a week, and taking a day
off now and then to go fishing, and attending the pictures on
Saturday nights, and keeping his draughts appointment in Dillillibill every Sunday—Joe had the ute out pretty frequently, and it
had not yet begun to serve as a substitute for a signpost. This
came later, and was due to his Uncle Cuth.

Uncle Cuth, who first made his appearance in the Lane a few
months before the particular cyclone which we have mentioned,
is a wiry, bow-legged little man with a shock of grey hair and a
drooping grey moustache. He is to be seen in all seasons wearing
an earth-coloured flannel shirt, patched khaki trousers precariously
supported by a length of string, sandshoes which were once
white, and a sailor's cap. (Since he has never been to sea, and has,
in fact, spent the greater part of his life well west of the Dividing
Range, no one is able to account for the cap; but there it is.) His
main preoccupation is food, and his favourite comestible eggs—
because, as he says, they go down easy, and don't give you no
trouble when they're there. He has so passionate an aversion to
water that he cannot bear it to touch either his person or his
garments, and will not stir out of doors in even the lightest shower
of rain. He is enveloped, consequently, in a strong, goat-like
odour, reinforced by the fumes from a noisome pipe which juts
aggressively from his mouth throughout his waking hours.

His arrival in the Lane provoked much comment (for Joe had always lived by himself, and was known to prefer solitude), but by now he is as familiar, and as permanent a feature of the landscape as the lantana. He simply turned up one morning and announced that fifty years of matrimony was as much as any man could be expected to stomach, particularly now that eggs were sixpence each down in Sydney, and his old woman rationed him to one a day. Having inspected Joe's fowlyard, and counted his Australorps, he declared his intention of living henceforward as a bachelor with his bachelor nephew; so long as the tucker was good, he observed tolerantly, he would not complain.

Joe's house had three rooms not counting the kitchen, and a verandah as well, so he said he reckoned that would be all right. They needn't get in each other's way, and Uncle Cuth could look after the fowls, and take a turn at cooking the meals, and lend a hand in the pines now and then. At this Uncle Cuth became extremely angry, asserting that he did not propose to exchange one slavery for another, and Joe heard for the first time a phrase with which everyone in the Lane has since become familiar. "Exploitin' an old man!" cried Uncle Cuth indignantly. "Y'orter be ashamed!" With these words he took to his bed— or, more accurately, to Joe's bed—and stayed there.

Joe scratched his head, shrugged, and went about his business. A few days later he thought he would have a word with Jack Hawkins, so he strolled across the Lane and found Jack mixing spray in his shed. Joe, as courtesy demanded, conversed for some minutes about the weather, and then came to the point.

"Got me old Uncle Cuth over there," he began. Now of course Jack—and everyone else, for that matter—knew perfectly well that there was an old bloke staying with Joe Hardy True, Uncle Cuth had retired to bed within a few hours of his arrival, and remained invisible ever since, but his presence was no secret all the same. There are no secrets in the Lane. There are conventions, however, one of which is that you do not appear to know your neighbours' business, but civilly wait until they see fit to inform you of it, and Jack therefore responded, on a delicate note of surprise :

" That so ? "

" Come to stop, he says."

" Go on ! "

" Lives down near Sydney, but he's shot through."

" What's the idea ? "

" Couldn't stick his wife no longer."

Jack fell silent. He is a good husband, and a contented one, but the married man does not exist who could hear such words without a faint thrill of sympathy, or contemplate without a guilty twinge of admiration a fellow-husband who has shot through. Joe, as a bachelor, strongly disapproved in principle ; but he knew his uncle's wife.

" Wouldn't say I blame the old sod," he conceded. " Wouldn't mind havin' him around the place if he'd do a bit here and there to earn his tucker. But he stays in bed."

" What's wrong with him ? " asked Jack staring. Joe looked baffled.

" Nothin' I can see. He et five eggs for breakfast. When I tells him if he can sink 'em at that rate he orter feed the chooks at least, he goes crook and says I'm exploitin' an old man. ' Me exploitin'?' I says to him. ' Break it down ! ' I says." Joe's face assumed an expression of injured bewilderment. " What's he think I am," he demanded, " a bloody capitalist ? "

" How old is he ? " inquired Jack. Joe ruminated for a moment and then replied : " Depends."

" What d'you mean—depends ? He must be *some* age."

" Well, when he gets to skitin' how his wife was jealous on account of him jokin' over the fence with the lady next door, he reckons he's sixty-seven, but when I says anythin' about work, he says he's seventy-nine or eighty-two. All I know, he eats like he was seventeen, and he gets through more terbacca than I do meself. Boosts me store bill, I can tell y'."

" Doesn't he get an old age pension ? "

" Too right, he does. But he reckons he's got to put by for a rainy day. I asks him what about *my* rainy day, but all he says is young fellers like me don't have no sympathy with the problems of old age." Joe looked anxious. " D'you reckon that's right, Jack ? "

Jack shook his head in a troubled way. His own old mother more than pulls her weight in the family, and can milk a cow or pack a case of citrus with the best of us ; but she was probably in his mind as he said slowly :

" I wouldn't like to say, Joe . . . they do have their problems, the old ones. Seems a bit hard to turn him out. . . ."

" I never meant to turn him *out*," Joe protested. " I was just thinkin' he orter . . . well . . . lend a hand, like. S'pose he might, after he's settled down a bit ? . . ."

" He might, too," agreed Jack, relieved. Joe sighed.

" Thought I'd ask if I can take that old stretcher you threw down in the lantanna last year ? . . ."

" Stone the crows, Joe, it's got one leg broken, and the wire mattress was all holes when I threw it out—it'll be rusted clean away by now."

" I can prop it up on a crate, and nail a few planks across—or a sack or two, p'r'aps."

Jack looked rather shocked.

" You're welcome, of course, Joe," he said with slight reserve, " but it's not going to be much of a bed for the old chap."

" It ain't for him," Joe said, surprised. " It's for me."

When the cyclone hit the Lane the roof of Joe's fowlhouse began to flap up and down, and Joe went out to fix it. That sentence, with a different name substituted for Joe's might be included in any account of any cyclone ; someone's fowlhouse roof always begins to flap, someone always goes out to fix it, and the result is very frequently disastrous. It is well known that during such climatic disturbances the air is apt to be full of solid bodies flying with great velocity in different directions, and that a wise man, consequently, remains indoors. Nevertheless, when his fowlhouse roof begins to flap, wisdom forsakes him, and out he goes.

In this case, however, it appears that Joe acted not entirely upon his own initiative. Certainly Uncle Cuth urged him forth, excitedly declaring that if the roof went, the fowls would surely succumb to the fury of the wind and rain, and the egg supply would be indefinitely interrupted. Joe, who knew the age, condition and holding-power of every nail on his property, assured his uncle that if the roof went, the sides would go too, and the fowls, thus released, would find shelter under the house. Uncle Cuth derided this theory, pointing out that fowls were the stupidest of all created things, not even excluding sheep, and this Joe was compelled to admit, though he continued to insist that they had at least enough sense to come in out of the rain.

" Heartless, that's what y'are ! " shrieked Uncle Cuth above the increasing roar of the gale. " Never a blinkin' thought fer the weak and helpless, whether it's fowls or old men ! You get out there and nail that roof down, quick and lively ! I ain't one to stand by and see dumb creatures suffer, I tell y' straight ! "

It appeared to Joe, after he had pondered this for a moment, that standing by was precisely the programme which Uncle Cuth envisaged for himself in this crisis, and he therefore retorted with some asperity :

" Why don't y' get out and nail it down y'self, then ? "

This threw Uncle Cuth into an alarming paroxysm of rage.

" Tryin' to murder me now, eh ? Tryin' to get rid of me ! Not enough to go exploitin' an old man that never did y' no harm, y' want to be the death of him too ! That's what a bloke gets from his own fleshanblood when he's old and wore out, and don't ask no more'n a quiet corner to die peaceful in ! Yeller, that's what y'are ! Call this a cyclone—why, blast me buttons, I been out sailin' on Sydney Harbour in worse blows than this 'ere ! No guts, the young ones haven't got nowadays—yeller, the whole flamin' lot of 'em ! Yeller ! "

Joe reached for his old oilskin. " Aw, shut y' trap ! " he said surlily, and opened the door. The blast made him stagger, and

flung Uncle Cuth backward on to a sack of potatoes. " What the
hell y' think y' doin' ? " he screeched furiously. " Give me me
death, lettin' in the rain like that ! . . ." But Joe was gone, having
—with great difficulty—dragged the door shut behind him.

A spinning sheet of corrugated iron, borne along about five
feet above the ground by an eighty-mile-an-hour gale is a fairly
lethal object, and Joe—as everyone agreed later—was extremely
lucky not to be decapitated. He was knocked out cold, though,
and the damage he sustained accounts for the peculiarities of his
present appearance which we have already described. Uncle
Cuth, who was watching from the window, became more
enraged than ever, for Joe's prophecy concerning the fowlhouse
was fulfilled, and the hens, suddenly exposed to the full fury of
the elements, were scattering in all directions. Even as he
watched—shaking his fist at the prone figure of his nephew, and
shouting imprecations the while—two of them became airborne
and passed overhead at a great altitude, taking with them an
incalculable number of his potential breakfasts. And there, to his
gibbering indignation, Joe continued to lie, quite disregarding,
with characteristic selfishness, the threat to his aged relative's
nourishment.

But Uncle Cuth's attention was now abruptly deflected, for at
this moment the roof blew off the house too, and he was hardly
able to get himself across the Lane to the Hawkins', where he
arrived, half-drowned and chattering with wrath, to inform Jack
and Amy that it fair beat him what the world was coming to when
an old man rising ninety was left to fend for himself in a bloody
cyclone. Jack and his eighteen-year-old nephew, Bill, went out
and brought Joe in ; they reported that there was not much left
of the house, but the fowls had established themselves beneath
what there was. They expressed the fear, as they laid Joe on a
bed, that there was not much left of him, either.

The telephone lines were down, of course, so they could not
ring for the doctor, who lived twelve miles away. He could not
have reached them in any case, because half an acre of Jim

Greenfield's bananas had slipped down the hill, and were now obstructing the main road. So they patched Joe up as best they could, and Uncle Cuth retired, after a hearty meal, to Bill's bed, where Bill later joined him—but only for a few minutes; he finished the night on a sofa in the living-room because, he said, the air was better there.

The cyclone passed in due course, the telephone lines were repaired, the bananas were heaved off the road into the scrub on the downward side (where, by the way, they are still growing and flourishing) and the doctor arrived. He was plastered with mud, and swearing wickedly, having been bogged three times on the way; but he tidied Joe up, rang the ambulance, rang Bruce Kennedy and told him to go and meet it in his Land Rover and pull it out when it got bogged too, and thus finally got Joe away to hospital. Before leaving he informed Jack and Amy that Joe should not survive, but probably would, because damn fools always did. Uncle Cuth truculently enquired what was to become of an old man of ninety-two now that his only relation had deserted him, and young Bill, looking him in the eye, replied that he didn't know, and couldn't care less.

That was all very well, but in the Lane we have an unwritten law which ordains that when anyone suffers misfortune or disaster caused by an act of God, the neighbours rally round. Bill's aunt and uncle therefore bade him shush, and convened a meeting in their house to which everyone came except Herbie Bassett (who was also in hospital, having succumbed to appendicitis on the very eve of the cyclone), and Sue Griffith's Aunt Isabelle (who was left baby-sitting for the Achesons.)

After due discussion Jack Hawkins and Tim Acheson were entrusted with the task of taking up a house-to-house collection for Joe in Dillillibill and its district; it was also resolved that approaches be made to the Football Club, the Cricket Club, the Tennis Club, the Bowling Club, the Ladies' Aid Society, the Parents and Citizens, the C.W.A., the Rotarians, the Junior Farmers, the various Church organisations, the School of Arts and the Orchid Society, with a request that they bestir themselves to arrange functions to swell the fund. The men agreed that between them they could keep Joe's pines pretty clean if they worked out a roster for a couple of afternoons each week ; Ken Mulliner volunteered to rebuild his fowlhouse ; Amy Hawkins made herself responsible for his fowls ; and Bill announced that he would look after Butch. Then there was a pregnant pause. An unuttered question hung in the air.

Who would look after Uncle Cuth ?

No one spoke.

We are not affluent people in the Lane. As primary producers we are, of course, frequently described by our legislators as The Backbone of the Nation, but we do not feel that this title, honourable as it is, really helps us much. We get by, but with nothing to spare—and we never know from one week to the next what is going to happen to The Market. Moreover, it must be understood that Dillillibill is not a large community, despite an impression to the contrary which may have been gained from the imposing number of social, sporting and cultural bodies just listed. Most of us belong to several of them, and in some families their members belong, between them, to all. There are only five members of the Orchid Society, for instance, and every one of them belongs to at least four other things, and their wives to two or three more. So the handing over of a contribution to the house-to-house collection would by no means be the end of any family's duty in the matter ; indeed, so far as the ladies were concerned, it would be but a bagatelle. They, as members of the Tennis Club, would make cakes for a Social, and then, as members of the C.W.A., make more for a Euchre Party, and again, as members of the Ladies' Aid, still more for a Concert; next, as the mothers of Junior Farmers, they would provide supper for a dance, and as the wives of Rotarians do the catering for a Monster Fair on the sports ground ; after this they would apply themselves to the making of jam, tea-cosys, aprons, coconut-ice, felt rabbits and other useful articles to furnish stalls at fêtes under the auspices of the various Churches. Finally they would attend all these functions, surrender an entrance fee at the door, take tickets in a number of raffles, pay sixpence to guess how many beans there were in a bottle, and, as the proceedings drew to a close, buy up such flotsam and jetsam as might still remain on the tables, including, very probably, a coat hanger they had spent last evening covering, or half a chocolate cake baked that very morning in their own kitchen.

All this they were more than willing to do for Joe who—despite his taciturnity and his somewhat unsociable habits—had always been where he should be when any of his neighbours found themselves in a predicament.

But Uncle Cuth—— ?

The women kept their eyes on their knitting. Tim Acheson lit the wrong end of a cigarette. Bill Hawkins stared moodily at the floor. Jack rose, and with great care moved the clock on the shelf two inches to the left. Ken Mulliner cleared his throat, and said :

" Seems the police have been making a few enquiries about Joe's relations. . . ."

Ken has a brother-in-law who is a policeman at Rothwell, so he spoke with authority, and his neighbours hung upon his words. After all, they had been saying in their hearts, old Grizzleguts *has* got a wife somewhere, hasn't he? . . . And a home ? . . . And a pension ? . . . Why should *we* . . . ? Now hope revived.

" It was when they thought Joe might conk out, see ? " Ken explained. " Got to know who to notify—next-of-kin, and all that. . . ." A murmur, faint but fervent, acknowledged the correctness of this. " But they couldn't find none," continued Ken, " only Uncle and his wife, and it seems she's sold up her house and gone to live with a friend in New Zealand." He added morosely : " So that's no good." And though not a word about the disposal of Uncle Cuth had yet been spoken, his hearers understood him perfectly.

They went on knitting or smoking, and avoided each other's eyes. They were not resisting the inevitable, but merely backing away from it. However, it continued to bear down upon them as the inevitable will, and at last Alf Bell, the Lane's uncompromising authority upon ethical behaviour, made some deep, rumbling noises in his throat, and everyone turned to his wife for a translation. Gwinny put her knitting down on her capacious lap, and interpreted :

" Alf reckons it wouldn't be right to leave the old chap stranded, like. What with eight of us in the house we're a bit crowded, but Tristy's going off on his National Service next week, so we'll have a spare bed then. I s'pose we could take Uncle. . . ." She met Amy's eye, which was signalling a warning, and added rather hastily : " Mind you, I wouldn't say we'd keep him on indefinite, seeing the doctor says it might be months before Joe's out of hospital—and even then it isn't as if he's got a house to come back to. . . ."

There was another painful pause. Jack and Amy were exchanging glances, and at last Amy succumbed.

" Well, as he's here he might as well stay on a bit. . . . Say a fortnight, Gwinny, and then he could go on to you." They looked at each other for a moment, and then applied themselves with intense concentration to their knitting ; neither of them even glanced at the others who, nevertheless, wretchedly realised that an example had been set. Marge Kennedy sighed briefly, and reached across the table for her husband's cigarettes—an action which everyone recognised as symbolic of the general desperation, for she had given up smoking three months ago.

" If someone'll lend me a stretcher," she said, " we could fix up that glassed-in corner of the verandah for him. For a fortnight." She lit her cigarette, and inhaled recklessly.

Biddy Acheson spoke up in some agitation :

" Look . . . I don't know, I'd like to help, but with a baby in the house . . . it's not only the work I mean, it's . . . well, hygiene, and all that, because you know he's *really* . . ."

Again there was a pause. No doubt Biddy's words had sharpened certain misgivings, and everyone was thinking, in agonised agreement, that Uncle Cuth *was* really. . . . But all communities are blessed with at least one invaluable person who calls spades spades, and stinks stinks; who voices the thoughts which others are too scared, too bashful or too wary to express, and who with bracing ruthlessness, illumines the fogs of reticence with glaring truths. Such a person is Myra Dawson.

" Oh, well," she declared heatedly, " it seems we're the mugs. He's got us all flumdoodled. I'll take the old bludger for a fortnight. . . . But . . ."—the eyes turned upon her widened expectantly—" if he comes to me he's darned well got to wash sometimes; *I'm* not living with that pong around me all the time! And he's got to work sometimes. I've got my hands full as it is—haven't we all ? " Heads nodded. " And we've all got our own families and our own bills to think of." They nodded harder. " So what I say, girls and boys, is I'll take him on for a fortnight, but I don't see why he shouldn't earn, say, about a quarter of his keep. Do you, Gwinny ? "

Gwinny is not without her flights of fancy, but in everyday matters she is an invincible realist; she spread her knitting out, looked down at it over her majestic bosom, and replied with deliberation : " I don't see why he shouldn't, but I don't know if he would."

Rebellion is catching, however, and now others were aflame.

" Nothing heavy, of course," said Amy, " because after all, he *is* an old man. But there are plenty of little jobs. . . ."

Everyone began to speak at once. " Branding cases . . ." " Weeding the vegs . . ." " Feeding the fowls . . ." " Sewing up bags . . ." " Packin' a crate or two . . ." " Clipping the hedge . . ." " Burning the rubbish . . ." Dick Arnold, whose idea of Heaven is to lie late in bed, dreamily suggested : " He could milk one morning a week. . . ." Sue Griffith cried hopefully : " He could chop some kindling for my copper. . . ." Biddy said : " He could collect the eggs. . . ." To this last, Aub Dawson rejoined promptly : " Not *my* eggs, he couldn't."

" And what's more," announced Myra with vehemence, " I'll find a change of clothes for him, and we'll all see that the ones he isn't wearing go in the copper ! And at least twice a week he'll have a bath, if I have to put him into it myself ! "

This was greeted with squeals of appreciative endorsement, and there were even a few male guffaws, though the men now had a slightly guilty air, as if they were basely handing over one of their sex for torture at the hands of the eternal enemy. Those among the enemy who had so far refrained from committing themselves, now did so, not only with alacrity, but even with a certain relish ; and when Amy had dispensed cups of tea, everyone went home, satisfied that Joe's disordered affairs were under control, and leaving the Hawkins' to acquaint Uncle Cuth with the arrangements which had been made for his comfort.

As it turned out, he sampled all his hosts in turn, but remained with none for the full fortnight. Amy Hawkins, in some agitation, rang Gwinny Bell.

" Gwinny, I've just got to warn you—he's on his way down to your place . . . yes, I know, but it's no good, he won't stay. I've done my best—three eggs and five slices of toast for his breakfast, hot dinner with pudding and all, meat or eggs for his tea—and talk about smokos . . . ! Six scones and four slices of cake's nothing to him ! Why, when it comes to eating, he makes even Bill look like a pecker ! What's that ? . . . No, love, I *can't* stop him—I tell you he's on his way. I've been arguing with him this last hour, and all I get is he's not going to stay where he's being exploited. . . . What ? . . . Well, two mornings he took the chook-bucket down to the fowl-run, and when he brings it back he says he's that worn out he's got to have a lay down, and that's the last we see of him till dinner-time. And once Jack asked him to knock up a couple of cases, but he only got the ends done, and then he says he's sprained his wrist. Without the word of a lie, Gwinny, he hasn't done another hand's turn, and what set him off this morning was I asked him to get me some kindling—not chop it, mind you, just bring it up from the stack—and then he starts to create, and give me this exploiting stuff. . . . Well, I'm real sorry, Gwin, I'd have kept him if I could, but short of tying him down . . . What ? . . . Bath ? . . . Look, love, don't be funny. You try, that's all I say ! *You* try—and good luck to you ! "

She replaced the receiver, returned to the kitchen, filled a bucket with hot water, laced it liberally with disinfectant, and reached for her scrubbing brush.

Thenceforward Uncle Cuth's career as a guest followed a pattern which varied only in minor details. He began by expressing to each new host and hostess in turn his opinion of those from whose home he had just been brutally driven out by starvation, persecution, harsh treatment and shameless exploitation. He declared that he might be a friendless and helpless old man, but he had sperrit, and he wasn't going to be exploited by nobody ; he had therefore transferred himself to the hospitality of his hearers in the hope that he would, under their roof, be treated with ǝɥ̟ respect and consideration due to one who was practically a centenarian. So if Mrs. Bell—or Mrs. Kennedy—or Mrs. Acheson —was just making a pottertea he wouldn't mind a cup, and if there was a bitterterbacca lying around he'd just fill his pipe, and then he wouldn't be no more trouble to nobody because he was fair wore out with workin' for them other slave-drivers, and only wanted to have a good lay down, and a bit of a nap before dinner.

Things would go well enough for the first few days. His plate was generously heaped, the packet of tobacco was passed to him when he desired it, and only the most tentative hints were dropped about small tasks waiting to be done. But by degrees the hints became requests, and the requests more peremptory in tone, so that at last he was compelled to point out that he could not clip the hedge since privet always gave him hay fever, and had since he was a boy ; that owing to rheumatics in his right shoulder, he was unable to make cases, chop wood, or even lift anything heavier than a tea-cup ; and that a pain in his legs which had, for twenty years, baffled the entire medical profession, was apt to catch him suddenly with such violence that he could not walk, nor even stand. He also suffered from a complaint called carbuscles ; the Lane spent much time in speculating whether these were, like corpuscles, situated internally or, like carbuncles, worn outside, but nothing was ever discovered about them except that they utterly precluded any activity whatever. It was usually at the stage when he began to speak of his carbuscles that a note of acrimony developed in his intercourse with his host and hostess; but not until he discerned in them a disposition to lay hands upon his clothes—and even upon his person—for the purpose of immersing them in water, did he make up his mind to move on. He might have stayed the course at Ken Mulliner's if Ken's sister had not turned up for a few days. As a policeman's wife, she is strongly prejudiced against people who do not conform to the accepted pattern for respectable house-holders, but she is also firmly convinced that anyone can be made respectable by continued exhortation. Uncle Cuth stood her for two days, and then arrived at the Dawsons', gasping out: " Clacketty-clack ! Clacketty-clack ! Strike me handsome, I never thought I'd fall so low as feelin' sorry for a copper, but I dunno 'ow 'er 'usband can take it ! "

Meanwhile, Joe's dilapidated green ute stood, day in and day out, at the corner of the Lane, and Nature, seeing that it was abandoned by man, adopted it. The bay of lantana in which it stood became a bower arching above it, and a rambler rose entwined itself quite charmingly over the bonnet and around the headlamps. Dead leaves drifted down on to the tray, and rotted. Rain washed them, mixed with the accumulating deposit of dust, into cracks and corners where blown seeds took root, and grew. Beside one of the rear wheels a pumpkin plant established itself, and became a luxuriant vine which clambered ever higher. Kookaburras made a regular perching place of the hood, and a family of mice which nested in the stuffing of the seat became a source of great annoyance to Butch, whose custom it had once been to take a nap there every day ; but Jack Hawkins had seen that the cab was securely closed against the weather, so there was nothing Butch could do about it except stand on his hind legs on the running-board, and bark furiously at them through the glass. Bill Hawkins used to start the engine up occasionally, but he never had time to brush the lantana, or disentangle the rambler rose, or pull the weeds out of the tray; in any case, they were doing no harm. As for the pumpkin vine, it might just as well be left alone, Amy pointed out, to produce pumpkins.

And we all began to say: " Just keep on going till you come to a green ute. . . ."

At this stage we might almost have added : ". . . with a little bloke looking at it," for Herbie Bassett had, of course, returned from hospital by now, and he spent much of his time sitting, or squatting, or prowling about near it. His main pleasure in life has always been gazing at things—so long as they keep still, or move (like a snail, a cloud, or the growing tip of a plant) at a pace which allows him to take his time about it. He had never studied motor vehicles, for even when they were stationary he found himself unable to forget that they were essentially mobile objects which might, at any tick of the clock, begin to move at forty miles an hour; this made him nervous, and destroyed his concentration.

But now there was one available which conveyed no such disquieting impression, since it had all the appearance of being permanently anchored to the ground by rose and pumpkin vines, and incorporated into the lantana as inextricably as a fence. He therefore gave himself up to almost continuous contemplation of this rare spectacle, and to an exhaustive study of the natural processes which were submerging it, leaf by leaf, in rampant vegetation.

It was about the time when Herbie first noticed the pumpkin forming that Uncle Cuth presented himself at the Arnolds', and as they were last on the list of those who were to entertain him, everyone was beginning to wonder rather wildly what would happen next; for the latest medical bulletin held out no hope of Joe's return for some time.

Uncle Cuth had been no more than five days with the Arnolds, however, when he created a sensation by declaring that he had made his own arrangements for the future. He was going to stay with Herbie Bassett. He reckoned he weren't going to be exploited no more by a lot of skinflints that was only trying to

get free labour out of him, so he was going to Herbie, because
Herbie was the only bloke in the Lane not plumb-crazy about
work, and there wouldn't be no flamin' women around to push
soap and towels at him, and try to sneak the clothes off of his back.

On this note of defiance, he walked out the Arnolds' gate, and
up the Lane towards the green ute. Immediately all the telephones
began to ring in all the houses, and by the time Uncle Cuth
reached the corner, Herbie was the only person in the Lane who
did not know what was in store for him.

Squatting on his heels, he was studying the pumpkin when
Uncle Cuth walked up. It was about the size of a marble, and
it was growing in midair from a stem which had reached out
from one of the back wheels, and attached itself to an overhanging
branch of lantana. Herbie was quite excited about it, foreseeing
days—nay, weeks—of absorbing occupation and, in due course,
a climax which might well prove to be dramatic ; for clearly, as
it grew bigger it would also grow heavier, and something would
happen. What ? Would the stem break ? Would it develop a
kink which impeded its circulation, and condemned the infant
pumpkin to premature extinction ? or would it subside, gently
lowering its burden to the ground ? . . .

Uncle Cuth, standing beside him, said :

" Huh."

Herbie, without lifting his eyes, replied politely, but absent-
mindedly :

" Huh."

Uncle Cuth, bending down, examined the pumpkin, and
expressed the opinion that it would never come to nothing.
Herbie remained silent, for he had no preconceived ideas on this
or any other subject ; he merely wished to observe, and whatever
happened was all right with him. But he did not want to be
disturbed just now, nor to have his attention deflected, because
he really had two things to watch at once. Near the pumpkin
there was a corkscrew-like tendril stretching out towards a tall,
dead stalk of Stinking Roger, and it had only a centimetre to go.

Now Herbie had watched tendrils at work in many varieties of scandent plants—those of peas (which he held to be assiduous, but incompetent), beans (which he considered enterprising and efficient), passion-fruit (which, in his opinion, were not only marvels of tenacity, but had also provided inspiration for the coiled steel spring), and others too numerous to mention—but watch as he would, he had never yet managed to see a tendril at the precise moment of its first contact with a support. So when Uncle Cuth announced that he was bound for Herbie's house to take up his abode there, and expressed the hope that Herbie's hens were laying, because he'd been pretty near starved lately, Herbie only said "Huh" again, and continued to watch the tendril with passionate attention. Uncle Cuth therefore went on his way, found a packet of tobacco on Herbie's table, filled his pipe, and lay down on Herbie's bed where he smoked peacefully and congratulated himself upon his escape until he fell asleep.

Meanwhile the Lane was buzzing with excitement. Everyone had said over the 'phone to everyone else that really, you know, it *might* work, and why hadn't they thought of it before? Anyhow, they must now do their best to make it work, and to help poor Herbie. Marge said she would send a dozen eggs, and Gwinny thought she could rustle up a dozen too, and Amy declared she would get Bill to take a stretcher and a couple of blankets over, and Biddy had just baked a cake that would do nicely, and Sue contributed an apple-pie and a pound of butter, and Myra Dawson and Heather Arnold each had a loaf to spare, and Ken Mulliner sacrificed a whole, unopened packet of tobacco. So by the time Herbie got home there was a generous stack of food on his table. Uncle Cuth did full justice to it, and then retired again to Herbie's bed. Herbie adopted the stretcher, which he set up on the verandah ; this enabled him to watch the stars—a study so enthralling that he could not imagine why he had neglected it before—and he resolved never to sleep indoors again. But it kept him awake for a great part of the night, so he formed the habit of taking a siesta during the day. Being thus so fully occupied with his chores, his forty winks and his daily engagement with the pumpkin vine, he had no time to spare for his guest; but since Uncle Cuth had nothing to do but eat and sleep, and could do as much of both as he pleased, this suited him very well. The Lane, having held its breath while awaiting the outcome of the new experiment, released it in a long sigh of relief, and continued ardently to pile Herbie's table with eggs, tobacco and other delicacies.

In this way matters proceeded very smoothly and pleasantly until, at last, Joe came home.

The Joe who came home was, of course, markedly different from the pre-cyclone Joe—and not only in appearance. His capacity for manual labour was greatly impaired, and a significant change in his attitude to Uncle Cuth was also discernible. With the aid of the neighbours he built himself the shack which he still occupies, using such materials as he could salvage from the wreck of his house; this dwelling consists of a sizeable room which combines the functions of kitchen, living-room, and Joe's bedroom, and a second very small apartment which belongs to Uncle Cuth.

He occupied it, at first, under protest; indeed, under physical duress. He had been very comfortable at Herbie's, and protested that nothing would make him return to be the exploited prop and mainstay of a nephew who had callously deserted him in his hour of peril. Besides, he added, his dear old friend, Herbie, needed him.

This was overstating the case, but it was a fact that during the last week or two of his stay, his company—or, more correctly, his presence—had afforded his host some pleasurable hours. For it had occurred to Herbie quite suddenly that he was wasting a unique opportunity. He had always mournfully accepted the fact that human beings were no good at all for his purposes, being even more restless than motor vehicles; and besides, although it is not rude to stare fixedly at a car or a pantechnicon, it is very rude indeed to stare fixedly at a human being. The discovery that neither of these disadvantages applied to his guest had been a momentous one. Uncle Cuth was content to remain perfectly motionless on a bed for hours at a time, and far from betraying any discomposure when Herbie sat down nearby and subjected him to a close, and prolonged scrutiny, seemed to find it a natural tribute to his interesting personality. All the same, Herbie had not yet exhausted the wonders of the ute, and the pumpkin problem was growing every day more engrossing, and each night the stars demanded longer study, so he found Uncle Cuth almost an *embarrass de richesse*, and was beginning to lose weight, and get dark circles under his eyes. So when Joe came along and fetched Uncle Cuth home by the scruff of his neck, Herbie saw them go with composure, if not without a lingering regret. And Joe, having marched his violently protesting relative across the threshold of their new abode, delivered himself of one grim sentence : " If y' gotta be a bludger, y'ain't gonna bludge on nobody but me."

Well, that was that, and they settled down together. Joe couldn't do as much work now as he had done before, so not many cases of pines went out from his farm, and the cheques which came back must have been small ; but the fund tided them over, and Joe made Uncle Cuth throw in his pension—cutting short his attempted remonstrances with the dour remark that if there was one thing he had better not mention in Joe's hearing, unless he wanted to get thrown out on his ear, that thing was a rainy day. It was also remarked in the Lane, with wonder and satisfaction, that Uncle Cuth (carbuscles or no carbuscles), was sometimes to be seen chipping in the pines, and frequently to be heard hammering in the shed. He raised his voice loudly, of course, against this cruel exploitation, but Joe merely retorted that the trouble with him was that he'd never been exploited enough, but, by golly, he was going to be now.

Joe didn't feel equal to going fishing any more, and his injuries made him awkward in driving the ute, so he rarely went in to the store, and never to the pictures. He thought of selling the ute, but he wouldn't have got much for it, and it saved him a lot of heavy lugging on the farm, so he kept it. The neighbours arranged to fetch his meat, and mail and groceries for him, so that was all right, but, bereft of his weekly movie, his thoughts began to turn longingly to his draughts. He accordingly sent a message to the old lady in Dillillibill enquiring whether their weekly contest might be resumed, and received a reply to the effect that she would be eagerly awaiting him, and thirsting for battle, on the next Sunday, and every Sunday thereafter.

He was greatly cheered by this prospect—particularly when Gwinny (who has a sister in Dillillibill, and visits her every Sunday), volunteered to transport him there and back. When all was satisfactorily arranged, the Lane dared to hope that his disorganised life was once more settling down to a peaceful and regular routine.

With what consternation was it learned, therefore, on the Saturday morning, that Gwinny's sister had just rung Gwinny to tell her that the old lady had died suddenly of a stroke, in the very act of getting her draughts-board out from the cupboard where it had lain unused for so long. Joe was terribly upset by this, and confided to Amy Hawkins that he felt real bad about it, because he couldn't help being afraid it was the excitement that did her in. He went along the Lane collecting white flowers from everyone, and Biddy Acheson made them up into a very fine wreath, and Jack Hawkins drove him in to attend the funeral.

It was difficult, now, for Joe to look sad—or, indeed, anything but sinister. But we all knew that he *was* sad, and felt very sorry for him, and very useless, because although we could help him in some ways, we could not help him about draughts. We knew our limitations. We realised that there was now no one within, perhaps, a radius of a hundred miles, who was qualified to compete with Joe at this venerable game of skill.

But Bruce Kennedy (who is the least contemptible player in the Lane) did, at last, pluck up courage to go and offer himself, in all humility, as a poor substitute for the old lady. He returned, goggle-eyed, with news which swiftly flashed along the Lane. Joe, in the greatness of his need, had begun teaching Uncle Cuth to play draughts—and already Uncle Cuth had twice wiped the floor with him.

After that we knew that Joe's problems were at an end. He still swears at Uncle Cuth, and Uncle Cuth still screeches at him, but they need each other. Nothing will ever part them now except death, and we are not worrying about that yet; Joe is clearly indestructible, and Uncle Cuth—whatever his age, and despite his numerous infirmities—looks good for another twenty years.

The ute stands, week in and week out, at the corner, and although the vegetation is not now quite so thick about it, and Butch once more takes his midday nap on what the mice have left of the seat, it still has an air of being rooted. So when we have occasion to direct our friends to the Lane, we feel safe enough in saying:

" You can't miss it; just keep going till you come to a green ute."

Quite Abnormal

OUR CLIMATE, as anyone in the neighbourhood will tell you, is ideal. There is the wet, of course, which makes life rather sodden for a while, and admittedly we get a cyclone now and then, but no one seriously disputes our claim that the weather is—normally —just about perfect.

We are perched high enough to escape extreme heat, even in midsummer, and as for our winters, they are widely and justly celebrated. By day an ardent sun pours down its ultra-violet rays upon us, and even when darkness falls, the air is not cold, but only pleasantly nippy. You never saw such stars as we have burning over us in the cloudless night sky, nor such swarms of moths as flit about desiring them. Our dews are lavish; they drench the grass, spangle the cobwebs, trickle down the pineapple leaves, and conspire with the early sunshine to set the whole landscape glittering like a jeweller's window. As for moonlight, we would not wish to lay ourselves open to a charge of being ignorant and unscientific, but it is a fact that there seems to be much more of it here than elsewhere, and it has a dazzling, refulgent, lustrous, radiant and brilliantly luminiferous whiteness which we venture to say is unique.

Of course there was the ten-months drought a few years ago ; but that was quite abnormal. Our average annual rainfall is eighty inches, and we simply do not have droughts. Nor do we have bushfires. The scrub just won't burn, and anyone who has tried to get rid of lantana by putting a match to it, has learned

63

the meaning of frustration—so it was entirely owing to the abnormal conditions that we spent most of that December racing from one farm to another, brushing breaks, and burning back as the flames came romping up the gullies towards our pineapples.

As for frosts, it is only very rarely that we see a light, silvery powder on the ground in some low-lying spot, and the time when four farms lost about twelve acres of pines between them must be regarded as the exception that proves the rule. We do cop the winds a bit, particularly the westerlies, and the north-westerlies, and the easterlies come in from the sea pretty fiercely, and the southerlies are sometimes bad, too. But it is well known —having been established as part of the district's folk-lore since old Mrs. Hawkins was a girl—that no wind lasts more than three days; even when one does go on for three weeks, you will notice that there is nearly always a sort of lull after the third day. Cyclones just have to be accepted; at least we never get them in the winter, though there was that July a few years ago when we had three—but that was quite abnormal, too.

Naturally one expects the wet to be wet, but when we have got it over, the rest of our eighty inches comes down as needed, at well-spaced intervals. So we were rather shocked one year when, instead of taking itself off at the appointed time, the wet settled down with us. Aunt Isabelle—blandly ignoring the reassuring noises made by politicians—always referred to it as *la pluie atomique*; but be that as it may, there was hardly a break in the rain from February to September. This was a grievous blow not only to our pockets but to our local patriotism, for we are proud of our climate. Hordes of shivering fugitives from the south are only too glad to flee to it every winter, and we, for our part, are very willing to share it with the poor things. But we cannot say that they showed a proper spirit during that trying time. It hurt our feelings to hear them making satirical remarks about The Sunshine State, for anyone should know that you cannot judge a climate by a spell of crazy weather.

So we repeat that—making due allowance for the kindly rains

which fill our tanks and reanimate our crops—we live perpetually under a benignant sky. Each day, unfolding from its dew-sparkling sunrise, proceeds through a golden morning to a mellow afternoon, and a crisp, star-spangled night ; any meteorological aberrations which, from time to time, disturb this felicitous routine are, we assure you, quite abnormal.

Gwinny on Meat-day

AT SCHOOL, when learning the art of literary composition, we were bidden first to introduce our subject, then to develop it, and finally to produce a conclusion; this formula we shall now adopt. First we shall introduce Gwinny; then we shall introduce meat-day; then we shall examine the two in combination, and by that time, we trust, a conclusion will have occurred to us.

Gwinny Bell was born in this district, but she was twenty when she came to live in the Lane. She had then been married to Alf for two years, and their eldest child had already won a Blue Ribbon at a Baby Show. The brothers and sisters who followed him have since won others—so many that Gwinny has made them into a cushion cover. But this is by no means the only family trophy. Nowadays Gwinny contents herself with awards for her jams and bottled fruits, but before her marriage she won many laurels at swimming, tennis and basketball. Alf, in his younger days, was a champion weight-lifter and shot-putter, and he still tosses crates of pineapples around as if they were match-boxes. The two elder boys bid fair to follow in his footsteps, and the elder girl has collected two Certificates of Merit for physical culture. As for the twins (who are known, naturally, as Ding and Dong) they have had the three-legged race at the school sports all sewn up for several years now, and their younger sister only recently carried off several prizes in the girls' under-ten events.

All this athletic prowess seems quite a matter of course when you consider Alf and Gwinny. Alf stands six feet two in his bare feet, and weighs seventeen stone; we doubt, however whether he would have qualified, even in his youth, as Mr. Universe, for his physique, though powerful, is less reminiscent of the Greek god than of the gorilla. In strength and size Gwinny is a fit mate for him, but her Amazonian proportions are beyond criticism. She has abundant, fair hair, not yet touched by grey, and worn in thick plaits around her head, bright blue eyes in a fresh and comely face, and she carries herself like an Empress. In a way she looks too young to be the mother of two grown-up sons and, a nineteen-year-old daughter, to say nothing of solid, twin school-boys, and a bouncing schoolgirl. But when you see them all together—as you do every Sunday morning, when they assemble, brushed and scrubbed, for Church—it is clear that only Gwinny could have mothered such a family.

And when you see her working down in the pines, or pegging out her vast quantity of vast garments on the line, or striding along the Lane to visit one of the neighbours, you seem to hear Wagnerian music, and lo!—the scene dissolves. Fade out the serviceable working clothes, or the best frock of gay, floral rayon; fade out the felt slippers, or the patent leather shoes; fade out the battered, week-day hat, or the Sunday straw with its purple flowers, and its little pink veil. Fade in accomplished draperies which reveal the limbs they should be covering, and shining breastplates which proclaim the curves they guard; fade in gold sandals laced about the ankles; fade in a horned helmet over blond, wind-driven hair. Fade out the timber cottage sitting on high stumps, crowned with corrugated iron, and surrounded by pineapples; fade in an abode of gods, resting on legend, crowned by clouds, and surrounded by enchanted air. Fade out, Lantana Lane . . . and fade in, Asgard!

Or, to put it more briefly, fade out Gwinny, and fade in Brunny.

Gwinny was, of course, called after the erring and somewhat shrewish consort of King Arthur, whom she in no way resembles. You might think that, having carried this name through life, she

would have had enough of Malory (or, more probably, Tennyson), but on the contrary, each successive christening in her
family has demonstrated afresh her addiction to the Arthurian
romance. For this, however, neither Malory nor Tennyson may
be held directly accountable. The story, as we have it from
Gwinny's own lips, is as follows :

Her parents were devout folk who sent their children to Sunday
School, where the eldest girl was so impeccably regular in her
attendance that she was rewarded with a handsome and lavishly
illustrated book entitled *Tales of the Round Table*. Introduced into
the house just before Gwinny (the youngest) was born, this work
had a profound effect upon her mother, who determined to name
her new child Guinevere if it were a girl, and Arthur if it were a
boy. It turned out to be Gwinny, and Gwinny was reared upon
jousts, chivalry, Excalibur and the Holy Grail ; the grosser
aspects of life at the Court of Camelot appear to have been, very
properly, omitted from a Sunday School prize.

Gwinny's mother so frequently lamented the fact that she had
discovered the entrancing land of Lyonesse too late to bestow the
names of its knights and ladies upon all her children, that Gwinny,
when the time came, resolved to console and delight her with
grandchildren who should enjoy this advantage—and has faithfully carried out her plan. The eldest boy is Tristy, the second is
Gally, and the elder girl is EElaine. Then come the twins.
Gwinny says she did think of Balin and Balan, of course, but she
felt they were a bit *too* unusual, so she decided upon Gareth and
Lancelot—names which, as she pointed out, would have shortened
nicely to Garry and Lance, only someone started this Ding and
Dong business. (Someone also started calling Alf King Kong,
but since this might have hurt his feelings if it came to his ears,
it was dropped.) There is general agreement that the youngest
child got off easily with Lynette.

We know what you are thinking ; Gwinny appears to have
missed something. What, you ask, no Arthur ? . . .

No ; no Arthur. On this point Gwinny is dumb—but Rumour
is not. And what Rumour says is that when Alf was courting

Gwinny, he had a very active and pertinacious rival—a massive young footballer, whose name was Arthur Bilpin—and one evening, at a Church social, these two fell out. Students of the classics will find the incident reminiscent of that great encounter between Hector and Achilles, for it seems that young Bilpin's nerve temporarily failed, and Alf pursued him three times round the parish hall before they came to grips. Then he turned at bay ; for a few sensational moments it was Rafferty's rules, and no holds barred, but at last a haymaker from Alf stretched his antagonist on the grass. What Gwinny thought about this scandalous affair we cannot say, but she married Alf. Alf himself was overcome by shame and remorse, for he knew it was not right to indulge in mayhem at a Church function. The fact remains that in his family there is, conspicuously, no Arthur.

But it is not difficult to guess what Gwinny has called their farm. Hereabouts the farms are rarely named, though some people feel that this is a pity, and always mean to set an example with a board on the gate ; but somehow they never do, and the farms continued to be known as Smiths', Browns', Joneses, and Robinsons'. Often they do have what we might call private names, but these are strictly unofficial, and the Postmaster-General's Department never hears of them. Ken Mulliner's house, for example, is surrounded by nut trees, so he calls it Nuttery Hut, and Jeff Jenkins, who has a poultry farm the other side of Dillillibill, naturally capped this with Chookery Nook. Dick Arnold, with stately simplicity, calls his place The Pines, and the Griffiths, whose house is in a pretty advanced state of disintegration, always refer to theirs as Tobacco Road. But although Gwinny went to a lot of trouble painting CAMELOT on her gate in red letters, beautifully edged with gold, the name was never generally adopted. This may have been due to some slightly embarrassed feeling of delicacy on the part of the neighbours, because the Bells' is a picket gate, and when Gwinny painted the name, she had to put the letters on separate pickets, which was quite all right until the last two fell off, and then it looked rather silly. However, by that time the whole gate was pretty decrepit, and a year or so later Alf built a new one ; so far Gwinny has not put the name on it, and we all just call the place Bells'.

Gwinny is really something of a prodigy. Besides all her other skills and attributes, she can attend to an almost unlimited number of things simultaneously, and she has a memory which would put any elephant to shame.

Let us join her for a few moments at tennis—not when she is playing (though she does play, of course, and is no mean performer), but when she is sitting out. Sue, Marge, Myra and Biddy are having a ladies' doubles, and Gwinny is seated (very upright) on the bench outside the wire, conversing with Amy about the forthcoming Church Fair, watching all that goes on, and knitting a jumper with an extremely complicated pattern for EElaine. We cannot presume to say, guess, or even tentatively imagine just how her remarkable brain works, but if we were able to make a recording not only of her speech, but of her concurrent thoughts, it would probably run something like this :

" Yes, I said I'd go to the cake stall with Aunt Isabelle (purl 5, knit 2) but we really need a third (I must get home in time to press Gally's trousers for to-night), and Alice can't help this year of course (knit 2, slip 1, pass the slipped stitch over), so I asked Edith, Tony, you'd better call the dogs away from the tea things (repeat this row three times), and she said she could come in the morning, it's thirty-love, Marge, that ball just got the line, but she has a dentist's appointment in the afternoon, look, love, Keithie's playing with a cow-pat (that's two rows), Myra, the jeep just went down the Lane, so Aub should be here soon, pick up that cardigan, Lynette, it's getting trodden on, so I'll try to find someone else (three rows). Hi, Sue, it's to the other side, your ad. Ken, how about lighting the fire for tea, no, the games are five-four, Biddy, you served first (decrease once at the end of the next and every alternate row fifteen times), but it's a bit hard, because everyone's doing something else (that cow in the Lane looks like Griffiths' Blessing), you'll find the tea in the biscuit tin, Henry (purl 5, knit 2 together, make 1, wool forward knit 1, slip 1, purl 5, knit 2 together, turn), that was a let, Marge,

I heard it touch, children, come away from the tank, but I expect we'll manage if we have to, yes, I brought some milk, Dick, it's on the bench in the shed, Myra, you're serving from the wrong side, yes you are, it's thirty all (knit 2, slip 1, wool round needle knit 1, purl 3, knit 1, repeat three times), it just means I can't leave the stall, see, because Aunt Isabelle gets the change mixed, Ken, don't let the children go near the fire. (I hope Tristy remembers to pump some water for the washing. . . .) "

Gwinny can keep this sort of thing up indefinitely, and think nothing of it. She is never confused, she never forgets anything, and nothing escapes her notice. She is the only person in the Lane who is really equal to meat-day.

Except for Herbie Bassett and Joe Hardy, we all have calendars, with certain days marked, hanging beside our telephones. Gwinny rarely refers to hers, but the rest of us are always rushing to them in a panic, thinking : " *Is* it our day ? . . ." And relaxing with gasps of relief. No, thank goodness, it isn't !

But even our calendars sometimes fail us. Myra Dawson once turned over two leaves by mistake, and marked July instead of June, and Heather Arnold had a dreadful time for a while, because Dick insisted on regarding calendars as spills for lighting his pipe. When this kind of contretemps occurs, someone's 'phone rings, and a voice says apologetically : " Look, I'm awfully sorry to bother you, but *could* you tell me if it's our meat-day ? "

Now and then, too, things are thrown into fearful confusion because somebody has to go down to the city on his meat-day, or is invited to a wedding, or succumbs to 'flu, or is in some other way unavoidably prevented from fulfilling his duty. But Gwinny can always rattle off an accurate account of even the most complicated adjustments.

" No, it *was* Dawsons' day on Tuesday, but they changed with Kennedy's and then Kennedys found they couldn't go either, so they rang Arnolds, and Dick went, so that makes this Friday Dawsons' day, and next Tuesday will be Kennedys', and the

Friday after that should by rights be ours, but we have to go and see Alf's sister in hospital, so we've changed with Ken Mulliner, and we'll take the next Tuesday, and then we'll be back at the Griffiths, and we can go on by the calendar unless Sue and Henry have visitors for lunch that day, and if they do they'll have to swop with Hawkins, and do the following Friday instead, and that'll get us back to the Achesons."

Time was when the butcher brought our meat to our doors twice a week. But nothing can stay the onward march of progress —which, indeed, gathers impetus so rapidly that it begins to remind us of an incident which once occurred in Gadara. It is difficult to work and stampede simultaneously; consequently the three sections of the community which always keep on working whatever happens (namely, farmers, artists and housewives), are liable to get trampled on. So now the meat is brought from Rothwell, dumped on the verandah of the store at Dillillibill, and after that it's up to us. We try to be philosophical about this little alteration in our domestic arrangements, and hope that it means someone is better off somewhere.

Behold Gwinny, then, on her meat-day, glancing hurriedly at the clock as she puts the dinner in the oven, and calculating that if she is not kept waiting too long for the mail, she will just about get home in time to take it out. She has put on her floral rayon and her white sandals, but goes hatless and stockingless, for this is not a visit. She makes no list, because of her fabulous memory, but she checks over in her mind that she needs salt, soap, matches, a new dish-mop and a dozen twopenny duty stamps for herself; that she has to get a reel of number forty white cotton for Myra, two dozen fourpenny stamps and four letter-cards for Bruce Kennedy, and three air-letters for Aunt Isabelle; that she has to leave some eggs at the store for Sue Griffith, and pick up a rotary-hoe blade which someone is leaving there for Ken Mulliner, and get him a packet of ready rubbed, and post letters for the Achesons, and collect Joe Hardy's groceries.

She hurries down the steps, waving to Alf and the boys, who

are picking in the farther patch, and drives the ute out from under
the house. EElaine, who is packing in the shed, puts her head
out to call : " Timber-chalk ! " and Gwinny waving again reassuringly, adds timber-chalk to her mental list as she turns out
the gate, and sets forth along the Lane. She drives fast, but of
course (being Gwinny) efficiently. It is no thanks to the owner
of a placidly ambling cow, but entirely thanks to her unshakeable
presence of mind, that there is not a skittled Jersey at the bend
before Achesons'; and had it been anyone else's meat-day, Amy
Hawkins would not have been observed racing breathlessly,
waving her arms, from her house to the back gate. But Gwinny
observes her—we can only suppose out of her left ear, because
Doug Egan's truck, with a load of wood-wool and fertiliser, has
just come round the corner, taking up two-thirds of the Lane—
though not, admittedly, more than it needs. Gwinny adroitly
steers her offside wheels on to the last available inch of roadway,
gets by with a centimetre to spare, and stops neatly at the
Hawkins' gate.

" Ooooo-ff ! " gasps Amy. " Oh, dear, am I puffed ! I heard
you coming, but I thought I was going to miss you." She
produces papers and money from her apron pocket. " Listen,
Gwinny, would you mind getting some things for me at the
store ? Here's the list. And you might just ask if they've got
laying-mash in yet ? And this is a pattern I promised Helen Miller
—I said I'd get someone to leave it at the store for her. And this
is for Mrs. Hughes, eight and tenpence (yes, I know there's
thirteen and four here, but I'll tell you about the other four and
six presently). This belongs to the raffle money, but I got mixed
because the kids were playing up, and gave her eight and tenpence
short. And the four and six is for stamps—a dozen fourpennies
and half a dozen pennies. And if you wouldn't mind just posting
these letters, only this one has to go by air mail, so it'll want
extra postage, and you can put it on out of the stamps you
get. . . ."

Gwinny undertakes all these commissions imperturbably, and
continues on her way. She herself would never get mixed, and

give someone eight and tenpence short, even if all her kids were playing up at once, but she feels no scorn for Amy. She bowls briskly along the main road, and should anyone ask her to-night —or six months hence, for that matter—what she encountered on this two-mile stretch, she would reply without hesitation : "A Land Rover, young chap in glasses, some fowls in the back— Australorps. Jim Bray driving his cow along to the Mullinses bull. Pale blue Cadillac with a Victorian number-plate, man and a woman with a lot of luggage and some golf clubs. Mal Rayner from Rothwell, in his Ford—going to see his girl at Tooloola ; had his right hand bandaged up. Tom Andrews with a load of pigs for the saleyards. Old Blatt's dog, limping on its left hind leg." It would be no matter for surprise if she could recite the numbers of all these vehicles, too.

Without appearing to take her eyes off the road, she also possesses herself of much interesting local information. From certain garments hanging on the line, she knows that Maud Ashwell's sister is staying with them again ; from branded cases outside the Wylie's shed, she learns that they are now sending their fruit to Adelaide ; from a glimpse of Judy Blake walking across to the Grahams with a billy in her hand, she understands that the Blakes' cow has been dried off ; and from the sight of Des Wilkie unloading a bag of cement from the boot of his car, she correctly deduces that he is going to mend his leaky tank at last. All these matters automatically file themselves in her mind, to be produced when required as material for conversation.

Arrived at the store, she parks her ute, and is immediately accosted by Bill Weedon from The Other Road. (There are only two roads—not counting the main highway—in Dillillibill ; our Lane, and the one which we call, condescendingly, The Other Road). Bill has a sugar-bag full of potatoes, and he would be obliged if Gwinny would just drop it at Ken Mulliner's . . . and how's Alf keeping ? . . . And what's the chance of a drop of rain ? . . . And Cheerioh.

Gwinny descends from her ute, and looks about her as she straightens her skirt. The store stands a little back from the road,

know better, and ought to be ashamed of himself.
also two English newspapers for the Griffiths, a
…per for Ken Mulliner, and a scientific journal for Bruce
These form the foundations for neat piles arranged on
… along the seat beside her, and she adds to them thus:
…ns, Arnold, Hawkins (only a circular), Acheson, Master
…awkins (that's for his birthday), Dawson, Dawson (from
…nd, that must be Myra's mother), Griffith, Tommy
…Dufour (French air-mail—funny writing !), Griffith
… fruit cheque), Kennedy, Acheson (that's Biddy's sister,
… say her baby's arrived), Hon. Sec. Bowling Club (that
…Hawkins') Bell (receipt for the insurance), Mulliner,
…Bell (about time Olive wrote !), Kennedy (that's his
…e), Arnold (that's *his* fruit cheque, but I bet he didn't
… for his last lot), Hon. Sec. Tennis Club (goes with
…cheson, Dawson (that's his fruit cheque—he *would* be
… Newcastle just now !), Bell (that's our fruit cheque),
… Kennedy (wonder what the V. stands for ?), Tommy
…Bell (that'll be my pattern), Mr. T. Bell (now who's
…g to Tristy? . . .) parcel for Tommy Hawkins (bless
…doing all right. . . .).

…verything is sorted, and each bundle secured by an
…d, she starts up her engine and—thinking again of her
…eps on the gas. About a mile short of the Lane she
…Herbie, who has been keeping an appointment with a
… which is sending up a new, perpendicular trunk from
…e in a manner which calls for constant observation. She
…ick him up, but tells him to ride in the back so that he
…e meat out of the sacks, thus saving her a few minutes.
…lunteers to take the Hawkins' parcel in while she is
… Joe's, so when she stops at the corner, he jumps out
… for the gate.

…" says Gwinny, stopping him in his tracks, and
… him back with a jerk of her head. "Papers—mail—
…groceries—tell Amy they've got laying-mash in, and
… on Tuesday fortnight."

with a camphor-laurel tree and a couple of petrol bowsers in
front of it, and about these assorted motor vehicles are negligently
parked. The Post Office opens off one end of the store verandah,
which is crowded with Dillillibillians waiting for their mail ; at
the other end, Bill Hawkins, as Secretary of the Cricket Club, is
pinning on the wall a notice which says that the D.C.C. will play
the M.C.C. (away), on Saturday the 18th—but this does not
mean what you think it does ; the Dillillibill boys will go no
farther than Malandaba. Just at Bill's feet the sacks containing
the meat are piled, and towards these Gwinny makes her way,
pausing to separate and admonish two little girls who have
come to blows over a bright green ice-block. She mounts the
steps on to the verandah, and begins to pull the sacks about,
reading the labels affixed, and setting aside those destined for the
Lane.

While she is thus engaged, Jenny Robertson from The Other
Road comes along to greet her, and ask her to tell all the womenfolk
in the Lane that the next meeting of the C.W.A. will take place on
Thursday week. Gwinny immediately objects that this won't do,
because Thursday week is the Bowling Club's monthly Ladies'
Day ; Jenny claps her hand to her head, and says, oh cripes, she
had forgotten—how about Friday week, then ? A dog sidles up
and begins to show more interest than he should in the sacks,
so Gwinny routs him with a smack he will remember, and points
out to Jenny that most of the ladies will be very busy on Friday
week, preparing for the Junior Farmers' ball on Saturday. But
there's nothing on for Tuesday fortnight, so she can tell the
Lane to keep that day, if Jenny will attend to The Other Road.

She then grasps the sacks, takes them over to her ute, and
returns with Sue's box of eggs—this time entering the store, where
she is at once involved in several conversations while waiting to
be served. But she manages some small items of business at the
same time. All the Dunks—father, mother, son and daughter—
are busy attending to their customers, but Gwinny catches Mrs.
Dunk's eye, sets the box on the counter, and calls out : " Eggs—
Griffith." Mrs. Dunk nods, jerks her head towards the floor near

the entrance, and responds : " Rotary-hoe blade—for Ken."
Holly Dunk, sorting newspapers, looks up to say that Joe
Hardy's groceries are in that carton over there, and Gwinny, as
she nods acknowledgment, perceives Mrs. Hughes coming in,
immediately collars her, and gives her, together with eight-and-
tenpence, a lucid explanation of how this sum came to be
erroneously abstracted from the raffle money. She then hoists
Joe's box of groceries on to her hip, picks up the rotary-hoe
blade, and makes another journey to the ute.

Returning once more, she posts all the letters (except, of course,
the airmail one), re-enters the store, places the pattern for Mrs.
Miller conspicuously propped up against a pyramid of tins containing baked beans, and, observing Mrs. Dunk momentarily at
liberty, proceeds with her own purchases, and those of Amy
Hawkins, not forgetting to ascertain that laying-mash is now
available, and to buy the reel of cotton for Myra Dawson. By
now Holly has the newspapers sorted, so there is a bulky bundle
ready for the Lane, and presently Gwinny once more emerges,
laden, into the sunshine, and crosses the road to deposit her
burdens.

Now for the mail. She finds the Post Office counter lined four
deep. Mr. Davis, the postmaster, whom nothing can hurry,
astonish or disturb, is waiting with monumental patience while
Jenny Robertson (a bit of a muddler, Jenny), scrabbles in her bag,
strews the counter with sixpences, threepences and coppers, and
finally admits in despair that she is fourpence ha'penny short.
Mr. Davis briefly instructs her to drop it in some day, and waves
her aside. Things go ahead pretty briskly then, until Old Blatt
has to collect a registered package, and sign for it ; this threatens
to create another bottleneck, so Mr. Davis moves him up to the
far end of the counter, where he can take his time over it, and
turns to Gwinny.

Gwinny says rapidly :

" Three dozen fourpennies, half a dozen pennies, four letter-
cards, three air-letters, one dozen twopenny duties, and mail for
the Lane."

While he is assembling her ne
at her elbow again with anoth
scrawled bit of paper.

" Gwinny, I've got to arrange
they're playing the Tooloola juni
they want everyone to play ever
get it worked out. . . ."

Gwinny is watching the clock
She glances with astonishment at
interrupts hurriedly, but kindly :

" It's quite easy, Jen. You war
or numbers for one team and le
One and two play a and b, three
on for the first round, and then
three and four play e and f, and
in the third round one and two p
play a and b. . . ."

" Have a heart ! " cries Jenny

Gwinny snatches a telegraph fe
writes the whole thing down for J
and goes off, chewing her handker
Mr. Davis is ready with Gwinn
seconds Gwinny is ready with the
There is still air-mail postage to l
when she has done this, and drop
returns to the ute to sort the mai

This she does sitting in the dri
it without pause while several oth
to her for a few minutes, and ther
paper for every house in the Lane,
copy of the *Farmers' Weekly* for e
women's magazine with a lovely p
cover, and one copy of a men's n
cover which is the kind of picture
hopes Tristy and Gally do not see
people !) Joe Hardy's Uncle Cuth

---

enough to
There are
sporting p
Kennedy.
her lap, an

" Hawk
Tommy H
New Zeal
Hawkins,
(that's thei
probably t
goes with
Dawson,
fruit cheq
get much
Ken's), A
sending to
Mrs. B. V
Hawkins,
that writi
him, he's

When
elastic bar
dinner—s
overtakes
fallen tree
the old on
stops to p
can get th
Herbie vo
delivering
and make

" Hoy
beckoning
stamps—
C.W.A.'s

Thus briefed and laden, Herbie sets out again, and Gwinny, having gathered up Joe's belongings, ducks under the wire near the green ute, and takes a short cut through the Cobblers' Pegs to the door of his shack, which stands open ; she can see Joe and Uncle Cuth far away down in the pines. The table is swarming with ants (and no wonder, she thinks, with all those crumbs left lying around) so she sets the box of groceries on one chair, with the meat on top, lays Uncle Cuth's disgraceful magazine on another, and buries it beneath the newspaper and the *Farmers' Weekly*, which has nothing more suggestive on its cover than a picture of a self-priming, non-corrosive, high-pressure centrifugal spray pump. Next she seizes a broom, and with a few swift strokes sweeps the ants and crumbs from the table and out the door, after which she replaces the broom and bustles back to her ute, where Herbie is awaiting her.

Down the Lane she goes, and stops at the Achesons'. Herbie's gate is almost opposite, so he again offers to do the delivering, and swears that he will not fail to tell Biddy about the C.W.A. meeting. This enables Gwinny to go straight on to the Griffiths'; here Aunt Isabelle comes running out to collect everything, and astounds Gwinny by fervently pressing her French air-mail letter to her lips. Gwinny decides to ring Sue this evening about C.W.A., because Aunt Isabelle does not seem to be in a state to remember messages ; she waves farewell, and drives on to the Kennedys', where she finds Marge grubbing about in her garden, so everything is quickly disposed of, though Bruce comes hurrying up at the last moment with a pile of sacks which he would like her to dump at Ken Mulliner's if she wouldn't mind.

Gwinny wouldn't mind at all, and continues along the Lane, waving to EElaine as she passes their own packing shed. The Dawsons have gone down to Rothwell for the day, so she enters their house by the kitchen door, rearranges the things in the fridge to make room for the meat, puts the mail on the table with the reel of cotton on top of it, finds Myra's grocery list, and scribbles : " C.W.A. Tues. fortnight " on the bottom of it. She then proceeds upon her way, feeling that luck is really with her when she finds Dick Arnold waiting for her at his gate ; she has got through it all in quite good time, and there is no one left now except Ken. He is nowhere to be seen, which is a pity, because she doesn't think she can manage his meat, his mail, his papers, his rotary-hoe blade, his bag of potatoes and his pile of sacks in one journey to the verandah. However, she manages them in two, starts up the ute again, turns in the narrow road with one dazzling sweep, and makes for home.

Gaining her own kitchen at last, she deposits her burdens on the table, and hastens to open the oven door. Had she been late, EElaine, of course, would have rescued the joint, but this has been unnecessary, and all is well. Thanks to Herbie, and her other bits of luck, she has reached home with a good ten minutes to spare before she need call the family in. So she ties an apron over her frock, and begins to set the table. She thinks she might even get a few rows of knitting done before it is time to dish up.

Faith is rewarded, for no less than three conclusions punctually present themselves.

The first is that human beings reveal their more amiable aspects, retain their good humour, and keep their affairs coasting along not too badly when engaged with others in a loose, flexible, slapdash and not particularly efficient system of their own devising ; but immediately begin to betray extreme prickliness, asperity, mistrust and jealously of their rights—to say nothing of a really distressing solemnity—upon finding themselves strait-jacketed in a tight, unyielding Organisation. Should some well-meaning, but grievously misguided Authority ever set up a Lantana Lane Meat Transport Committee, with a Constitution embodying Rules contained in Clauses and sub-Clauses, and providing penalties for Neglect or Evasion of The Same, we shudder to think of the arguments, the stallings and the recriminations which would ensue.

The second is that Gwinny is wasted in the Lane. For in the outer world Organisation is firmly entrenched, and we must make the best of it. There are literally millions who, given a pencil and a bit of paper, could (and do) whip up blueprints of quite infallible Systems capable of dealing with every conceivable problem in human affairs, except humans. Consider the multifarious enterprises which, with the passing years, grow bigger and bigger, better and better, more and more perfectly organised until no one can cope with them any more. How they need a Gwinny! Consider that we are moving steadily from the many mickles to the muckle which they proverbially form—the little businesses being swallowed by the big businesses, the suburbs being swallowed by the cities, the little nations crouching beneath the wings of the big nations from whose benevolent shelter they never will emerge; consider all this, and then reflect that some day one solitary human being will be called upon to administer the ultimate Muckle. . . . Heaven shield us if it should be anyone but Gwinny!

Therefore, the proposition that she should prepare herself for this high destiny by seeking, somewhere outside the Lane, a sphere where her remarkable gifts might be more fully exercised, is the essence of our second conclusion.

And our third is that we hope she won't.

Our New Australian

THE SMALL, elderly lady whom you may often see hastening along the Lane—usually accompanied by a large, gambolling Boxer—is Aunt Isabelle. We should perhaps introduce her more formally as Mme. Dufour, but she made it clear from the beginning that she was not only Sue Griffith's aunt, but the aunt of the whole Lane, so we all address her accordingly.

The dog is Jake, who also lives at the Griffiths'. This seems the most diplomatic way of putting it, for the question of who actually owns him is in constant dispute. Sue and Henry emphatically declare that he belongs to Aunt Isabelle; Aunt Isabelle vehemently insists that she gave him to Tony; and Tony (who is a generous little boy, and means it quite kindly) refers to him as "ours." No doubt Jake finds this confusing, but it cannot altogether explain his permanently puzzled expression, for wrinkles of bewilderment were already deeply graven on his puppy brow when he first arrived with Aunt Isabelle. (Of this arrival we hope to speak later, for it created no small sensation.)

Our communal aunt is an active, vivacious and extremely voluble lady of sixty-eight. Unlike Jake, she is neat in her movements, and, far from being puzzled by life, is prepared to explain to anyone at a moment's notice anything from politics to pig raising, or from religion to relativity. Nor does she stop at explanation. She is always ready to act—sometimes with results which, however disastrous, are dazedly conceded to be interesting and original, and sometimes with embarrassing success.

82

Her theory that the mixing of timber for crates and cases would produce a pleasing variety of shapes and sizes proved, in practice, entirely correct, particularly when she ingeniously worked in a few bits of old three-ply which were lying around ; and in the ensuing altercation with Henry, he certainly came off second-best —for how may dreary standardisation and shocking waste be logically defended ?

For a time it was her custom, when packing pines, to enclose chatty little notes drawing attention to the fact that the fruit grown by my-nephew-Mr.-Griffith was of unparalleled excellence ; or pointing out that the trifling bruise on the pineapple in the middle of the top row was caused when the dog of my-nephew-Mr.-Griffith knocked it off the bench, and was of no consequence at all ; or sternly protesting that the cheque received by my-nephew-Mr.-Griffith for his last consignment was entirely inadequate, and she would expect more liberal ones in future. The only result of this, however, was a chilly reply, scribbled on the foot of the agent's statement, that correspondence could not be entered into.

But Aunt Isabelle is a firm believer in correspondence, and enters into a great deal of it, so she was soon writing, instead, to the Prime Minister, describing the trials of those engaged in agriculture, and bidding him instantly reduce by half the cost of tanks, fertilisers, fence-posts, case timber, nails, wire netting, wood-wool and all farm machinery ; this was felt by everyone to be a gallant gesture, though it produced no result at all.

She has explained to us her reasons for deciding to emigrate, and it seems that they were these :

Firstly : Tony is a little cabbage, from whom she could not bear to be permanently separated.

Secondly : If she had been present at her sister's deathbed which unfortunately was impossible, since her husband had chosen to die at the same time, and *les convenances* had demanded her attendance at his side, though to say that she mourned his demise would be to tamper with the truth, for he was not only unfaithful (". . . which one must expect, is it not ? ") but also dull, which is unendurable and inexcusable, her sister would certainly have exacted from her a promise to watch over Sue ; for Henri, though a man of energy and intellect, is, like all Englishmen, a little mad, and lacking in that realism which is the predominant characteristic of the French.

Thirdly : Although her family had for several generations been accustomed to city life—and in Paris, too, where culture and sophistication are admitted to have reached a peak unattained elsewhere—she did not forget that her remoter forebears had been peasants such as those depicted by the immortal Millet, and therefore it was clearly her duty to join Henri and Suzanne in their new life, so that they might have the advantage of drawing upon the knowledge of agricultural matters which she had doubtless inherited.

Fourthly : She likes pineapples very much.

Fifthly : She possesses the spirit adventurous, and is not yet so old as to be incapable of sustaining the little hardships of life in *les backblocks*, nor so far into her dotage that she may not hope to contribute something to a young country which could with benefit add to its native vitality a measure of the serene and mature wisdom of the older civilisations.

These are powerful arguments, and we received them with respect, though the conclusion of her fifthly raised a few eyebrows, and Aub Dawson was moved to remark that he hadn't noticed Europe being so serene during the last forty years.

But whatever her reasons for throwing in her lot with us, we are delighted to have Aunt Isabelle, and she does add an exotic note to our scene. We could wish that she appreciated our climate a little more, but the fact is that she does not approve of air at all, unless it is strictly controlled within four walls. Not that she hesitates to spend much time out of doors, for, as she constantly declares, she came here prepared to share all discomforts, and brave all perils. But it grieves us to see her step out into one of our glowing mornings attired in long, woollen trousers, two sweaters, a cardigan and a balaclava.

On the whole, however, she has undergone the ordeal of assimilation with remarkable ease and rapidity. She plays her part in all our community affairs, being on no less than five committees, whose proceedings she greatly enlivens. She is to be found presiding over a stall at every fête, for she is without peer as a saleswoman. (However, it is always unobtrusively arranged that Gwinny shall share this duty with her, to prevent financial chaos.) She volunteered, upon one occasion, to address the Junior Farmers on the subject of Successful Pineapple Growing, and although—as Bill Hawkins remarked—the recommendations of the Ag. and Stock (for thus do we always refer to the Department of Agriculture and Stock) are sometimes difficult to remember, no one will ever forget the rules laid down by Aunt Isabelle. She is also in great demand as a baby-sitter, and when Jeremy Acheson lisped a few words of a French song with which she had regaled him and his little sister, everyone was entranced except Sue and Henry, who exchanged rather uneasy glances.

She confesses that she was never a keen follower of *le sport* in France, but she now regards it as her duty to share the enthusiasms of her adopted country, and never fails, during a Test Match, to enquire how many goals have been scored on either side. She authoritatively analyses the techniques by which Hoad and Rosewall have so successfully defended the Melbourne Cup ; and since Aub Dawson is known to be keen on racing, she has a long standing argument with him about whether Don Bradman was, or was not, the greatest jockey of all time.

At our week-end tennis she is one of the most regular and interested spectators. This close and constant association with the game has made her a connoisseur of its finer points, and no one can tread on a line anywhere, even during the fastest rally, without being sharply reprimanded for foot-faulting. Nor will she condone Henry's practice of executing subtle little drop-shots from half-volleys, for she says this is not hitting the ball, but merely allowing it to bounce from the racquet, which is not sporting at all.

Occasionally she declares her intention of taking her turn as an umpire, and, assisted by everyone, ascends the high stand. Upon such occasions the four players realise that some little time will elapse before the game gets under way, so they assemble at the net for a gossip while they wait. Aunt Isabelle, meanwhile, despatches someone to fetch her a cushion from one of the cars, drapes several cardigans over her knees, and calls Tony to bring her dark glasses, which may be in her bag, or perhaps on the seat of the ute, or possibly on the table in the shed, though it is conceivable that she left them at home. She next demands paper and a pencil (". . . for the accuracy in scoring is essential "), and, when all is arranged to her satisfaction, looks with astonished displeasure upon the group at the net, and cries severely : " Tcht ! tcht ! Have we all day to waste ? *Commençons!* " She then becomes so busy applauding successful shots, lamenting unsuccessful ones, scolding the men for hitting hard at the women, and encouraging the women to hit hard at the men, that she forgets all about scoring for a while, and, when she remembers it again, says reassuringly : " No matter ! We shall call it the deuce, for that is just to everyone."

Indeed, there is no aspect of our life in which she does not share, and some of our habits she has not merely adopted, but ardently embraced. For instance, few of us can now match, and none can surpass, her addiction to tea. It is this which sends her bustling along the Lane so often, for she has unerringly grasped the true significance of tea-drinking, which is—at any rate, in rural areas—that it provides an excuse to down tools and have a little gossip. So when the craving for tea overtakes her, it comes accompanied by a craving for conversation, and, adding a fur coat and a couple of extra scarves to her toilette (for the air in the Lane, it appears, is even more treacherous than that on the other side of the lantana), she trots off to visit someone. Similarly, should any of us drop in at the Griffiths' for a moment, she will cry gladly : " *Eh bien*, we shall have a nice cupper, isn't it ? "

This sometimes plays havoc with our quota of work, but always makes us feel that we are having a very jolly day.

When Ken Mulliner's sister comes to stay with him, Aunt Isabelle is in her element. She has a particular affection for Ken (the reason for which will become plain when we tell you about her arrival), so she dearly loves a long, cosy chat with Mrs. Jackson about his past matrimonial troubles, and the future matrimonial felicity which they are both determined he shall experience some day.

There is little else they can agree about, but this in no way diminishes the pleasure they take in each other's company, for they enjoy a squabble. Mrs. Jackson squabbles very politely, making much use of such phrases as : " Of course you *may* be right, but the way *I* look at it . . .", and : " Now *there*, Madam, I really can't agree with you." (She does not care for the casual familiarity with which we treat each other in the Lane, so she always addresses Aunt Isabelle thus, and the rest of us as Mr. This, and Mrs. That.) Aunt Isabelle squabbles in a more vehement, and less ladylike manner, but Mrs. Jackson puts this down to her being a foreigner, and makes allowances.

They are in accord, up to a point, about the state in which Ken keeps—or rather leaves—his house. This, consisting of a living-room, three bedrooms, a bathroom, a kitchen, and a long verandah is much too large for a solitary male—especially one who, like Ken, puts down the shallowest of roots. So he bunks out on the verandah, and eats in the kitchen, and the other rooms remain unused and untended except when his sister visits him. Then, however, the whole place undergoes such a sweeping and scrubbing of floors, such a shaking of mats, such a polishing of windows, such a washing of blankets and scouring of pots and pans, that Ken finds it uninhabitable, and gets more work done on the farm in a few days than during weeks when he is alone. Aunt Isabelle concedes the necessity for this periodical orgy of cleaning, but having done so, she considers the subject exhausted, and would prefer to pass on to something with more meat in it.

Mrs. Jackson's stroke-by-stroke description of how she swept out the living-room, fills her with indescribable *ennui*, and she hastens to turn the coversation towards Ken's habits and conduct, which she knows will afford them material for stimulating argument.

Mrs. Jackson considers her brother's philosophy of life to be deserving of the strongest censure, for it is strictly hedonistic, and she is all for Responsibility, Perseverance, Thrift, Self-denial and Christian Principles ; of these she speaks in a reverent tone, with capital letters. Aunt Isabelle views hedonism with an indulgent shrug, and remarks that while the pursuit of enjoyment may not appear a very lofty aim, it does not as readily lend itself to hypocrisy, censoriousness, long faces, and being the busy-body and how-do-you-say the wowser, as does the pursuit of things with capital letters. All the same, she is compelled to admit that there is no excuse for getting car grease all over a good pair of trousers, and burning holes in blankets with cigarettes.

Mrs. Jackson says, with a sigh, that trousers and blankets are mere material possessions, which are profoundly unimportant compared with spiritual grace ; it is this which she fears poor Ken so sadly lacks. Aunt Isabelle waves spiritual grace aside, and declares that Ken may be a nottee fellow, but he is a good boy.

Mrs. Jackson decides, after a moment's thought, that this curious remark can only be attributed to a faulty command of English. She insists that Ken is far too fond of gambling—for say what you like, the Casket is gambling, and the number of tickets he takes is just terrible. Moreover, who should know better than the wife of a policeman how much trouble he causes in the Rothwell bars ? Aunt Isabelle pishes, tushes, and protests that she does not concern herself with such piccadillies.

Mrs. Jackson then lowers her voice, and confides that although Ken tells her nothing of his manner of passing the time during his periodical absences in the city, things get around. She knows for a fact that he spends his money like water—receiving, she has been given to understand, enthusiastic co-operation from publicans, bookmakers and girls. Aunt Isabelle cackles, and cries : " Bravo ! "

This does not surprise Mrs. Jackson at all, for her articles of faith are far more numerous than the thirty-nine prescribed, and among them is a conviction that the morals of the French are not what they should be ; but she is annoyed. Therefore—well knowing just which criticism of Ken riles Aunt Isabelle most— she jerks her head towards the window facing the Lane, where there stands a contraption on wheels which is the apple of his eye, and goes by the name of Kelly.

This bomb is, like its owner, a bit of a larrikin, but by no means an anti-social one. It works hard while it is working and when it is not, loafs out on the side of the road, enjoying the heat on its paint, and peeling like a careless sun-bather. There is room for it under Ken's house, but he rarely bothers to put it there. It had a hood of sorts once, which vanished during a cyclone, so Ken took to throwing an old tarpaulin over it ; but there was another blow the following year, and the tarp was never seen again, so now Kelly just takes the weather as it comes. It only does about ten miles to the gallon, because its petrol tank leaks, and so far Ken has not got around to having it mended ; his bachelor existence allows him the little luxury of being feckless if he wants to. Its radiator leaks too, rather badly (you can always tell by a sinuous, wet streak in the dust when Kelly has been along the Lane ahead of you), but Ken carries a kerosene tin, and when he stops, he puts it under the leak, and when he is ready to start again he empties it back into the radiator, and this seems to work very well. It has no windshield, and no mud-guards. A few folded sacks on the seat serve as upholstery. The glass is broken out of one headlamp, and the other does not function. Ken, while admitting that its steering-gear is a bit crook, and its engine a bit noisy, points out that it has never failed to start up, and get him where he wants to go. As he frequently says, it's game—and thus it has come to be known as Kelly, in tribute to the immortal Ned.

Mrs. Jackson, then, gives this object a contemptuous glance, closes her eyes for a moment as though she found the spectacle unendurably revolting, and proceeds to bait Aunt Isabelle thus :

" As for that . . . that *Thing* of his out there, the money he's wasted on it would have bought him a brand-new utility twice over. It's not that I'm one for show, Madam. I don't approve of ostentation. If someone offered me a Rolls-Royce to-morrow, I'd say : ' No, thank you ; our own nice little Holden's quite good enough for me.' But there are limits. It's a matter of self-respect, that's the way I look at it. That Thing's a laughing-stock. It's . . . it's *sordid*, that's what it is ! "

Aunt Isabelle, whose bristles have been rising throughout this speech, says sharply : " Fiddlestooks ! Sordid, you say, is it ? Laughing-stock, you say ? I have myself studied the machinery of Kelly in motion when Ken has opened the lid, and it moves to admiration. Why ? I will tell you, for it is evident that you do not understand the qualities of this vehicle. It is not what-you-say mass-made on a row for the assemblage by a multitude of factory men who are thinking only that they must put the bits in fast, this bit, that bit, biff, baff, now the snatch, now the plug-sparkers, now the preferential, now the box of gears, now the pipes, clang, bang, it is all done and they may go home. In this way you may get your Holdens, but to get Kelly it has been the work of many years, it has been the labour of love to choose all these bits, one here, one there, and place them with care and judgment in positions the most advantageous. And for a result, this engine is of remarkable power, and will continue to propel the vehicle in such places where your Holdens would make what-you-say the sit-down-strike. And who then would be the laughing-stock—*hein* ? "

Mrs. Jackson looks pained, and says in a tone of patient for-bearance :

" I'm not saying the thing doesn't *go*—more's the pity. I'm only saying it's very wrong of Ken—very wrong and foolish—to squander so much money on it."

Aunt Isabelle enquires warmly :

" And if a man may not squander money upon the object of

his love—for he loves this Kelly dearly, and with reason—pray, upon what may he squander it ? "

" The way *I* look at it," retorts Mrs. Jackson, pursing her lips, " it's wrong to squander money at all. These days the young have no idea of Thrift. But now that you bring up the subject of . . . er . . . the affections, let me tell you his wife left him mainly because she couldn't stand the Thing, and the way he fussed over it. She said it made her look silly to the neighbours when he paid it far more notice than he ever paid her."

Aunt Isabelle eloquently lifts her shoulders, her hands and her eyebrows. *Sans doute*, she observes, this young woman had not yet learned that all husbands must be permitted their playthings. It is to be expected by any wife that the ardent attentions lavished upon her during the period of courtship, will quickly be transferred, after marriage, to some other object, person or pursuit. And is this a cause for a wife to shed tears ? *Pas du tout!* It is in the course of nature. For her part, she was well pleased to be spared the company and the conversation of the late M. Dufour, for these, particularly during his later years, were of a tediousness altogether insufferable, and must have driven his unhappy *belle amie* almost to distraction.

Mrs. Jackson finds her opinion of French morals confirmed by all this, and is glad that her own husband is not present to hear it. But since they have now arrived at the topic of Ken's love-life, there is tacit agreement between them that the time for squabbling is over ; they therefore fill their cups again, and settle down cosily to plot his recapture.

It must have been remarked by everyone that the sight of an unattached young man invariably gives rise to romantic speculation in the minds of the neighbours. Although Aunt Isabelle and Mrs. Jackson devote more time, thought and subtle machination to the problem of Ken's single state than do the rest of us, we all hope to find a nice girl for him some day. But it is a discouraging business, for when we do discover a promising specimen, we usually learn that he has already discovered her for himself, and passed on to someone else.

The experience of history should prepare us for the fact that schoolgirls become marriageable maidens—but the metamorphosis never fails to take us by surprise; so we were much astonished to wake up one morning and observe that EElaine Bell had— apparently overnight—been transformed from a somewhat lumpy adolescent into a young woman whose curves, though still on the generous side, were all in the right places. As soon as we had accustomed ourselves to this miracle, we naturally thought of Ken—but after thinking for only a moment, we looked dubious, and shook our heads.

Not that there was a thing to be said against EElaine; far from it. She is her mother's daughter—tall, buxom, comely, healthy, modest, virtuous, skilled in all the domestic arts, an expert case-maker, an accomplished packer, and wonderful with children. But we just felt, somehow, that she was not Ken's cup of tea. Of course Aunt Isabelle and Mrs. Jackson, who leave no stone unturned, examined her qualifications very narrowly; but in the end they shook their heads too. Mrs. Jackson said regretfully that she was a dear, good, home girl, and an example to all the other girls of the district with her interest in the Girl Guides and her Sunday School class; but she was not the sort Ken had ever taken to, though he might have done better if he had. Aunt Isabelle threw up her hands and invited all the world to look at the unfortunate child's clothes, for one must march with the times, isn't it, and such extreme decorum could not be expected to appeal to Ken, who was of the type lively and unconventional; nor could he possibly be allured by her manner or her conversation, for a man of this kind naturally prefers the company of a girl who comports herself a little *en coquette*—not shamelessly, you understand, but with the wit and merriment, the inviting glance, the pout, the downcast eyes, the playful *badinage*. Alas, it could not be denied that EElaine was quite without facility in such innocent arts.

We were just resigning ourselves to this disappointment when

Myra Dawson's niece came to stay with her, and we all sat up,
and said : " Ah-*ha* ! " This young lady has large, blue eyes, two
dimples, a silvery giggle and admirable contours. Her name is
Maud, and it is an appropriate one in so far as she possesses a
little head sunning over with curls, but her features are pert
rather than regular, and there is nothing icy about her. We
decided unanimously that this was just the kind of cuddlesome
armful a bloke like Ken would appreciate, and he was just the
kind of bloke into whose arms such an armful would be happy
to fall.

Sure enough, it was noticed that he had occasion to drop in at
the Dawsons' very frequently while she was there. Aunt Isabelle
reported that one morning when she chanced to be promenading
herself along the Lane, she observed him in Aub's packing-shed,
teaching Maud to pack pines. (". . . and for this occasion she
has made the *toilette*, you may believe me—the shorts very short,
the jumper fitting close, the white sandals, the varnish on her
toenails, the blue ribbon in her hair—oh, la-la, she knows her
potatoes, that one ! And across the Lane the poor EElaine is
packing with her brothers, in an old frock the most deplorable,
with a sack tied about her waist for an apron, I swear it, and on
her head that straw hat with holes, and on her feet the gumboots! . . .")

We had plenty of opportunities to observe Maud's toilettes,
and their effect upon Ken, for she paid several more visits to her
aunt, and he was always most attentive. Everyone expected an
interesting announcement any day, and prepared to receive it
with exclamations of delighted amazement. But no announcement was made. Mrs. Jackson dropped what she described as a
few tactful hints to Ken, and Aunt Isabelle, without bothering
about tact at all, sooled him on as hard as she could ; but he
only grinned, and replied with his favourite phrase : " What's
the hurry ? "

So while Aunt Isabelle and Mrs. Jackson sip their tea, they
discuss the news that Myra is expecting Maud again at Easter,

and they have much to say upon the probable outcome of this visit. They confess that their hopes are high. Though neither is entirely satisfied with Maud, they both allow that she will do. Mrs. Jackson thinks that she could with advantage wear more upon her shapely body, and Aunt Isabelle thinks that she could with advantage have more inside her curly head; but Aunt Isabelle meets Mrs. Jackson's objection by pointing out that she will soon cover her legs when she starts picking pineapples, and Mrs. Jackson dismisses Aunt Isabelle's with the remark that a lot of intellect is not needed in a farmer's wife. They finally agree that one must not expect perfection; that Maud is by far the most promising candidate who has yet appeared; and that matters will soon be brought to a happy conclusion. For when a young man has a young girl like that staying just across the road from him, there comes into operation a powerful force which Mrs. Jackson calls propinquity, and Aunt Isabelle calls sex.

Having settled all this, and drunk the teapot dry, they bring their conference to a close, and when Aunt Isabelle rises to take her leave, Mrs. Jackson escorts her to the gate. From here they can see a bit of the Bells' backyard, where EElaine is pegging out twenty-two shirts on the line, so they wave to her kindly, and she waves back.

" Such a dear, home girl ! " says Mrs. Jackson.

" Ah, that hat ! " sighs Aunt Isabelle. " What a disaster ! "

She shakes her head sadly as she bustles off down the Lane with Jake prancing at her heels. She hopes EElaine may find a husband some day—a worthy, sober man of mature years, a widower, perhaps, with several children—who will treat her kindly, and not care about the glamour.

Some Remarks upon
the Nature of Contrast

with Special Reference to the Habits and
Characteristics of *Ananas comosus* and *Lantana camara*
and an Examination
of their Economic and Psychological Effect
upon Homo Sapiens

In this district it may be said with little exaggeration that if you
are not looking at pineapples, you are looking at lantana ; nor
can it be denied that the general aspect of the landscape is
extremely pleasing to the eye. Ruskin has told us that contrast,
while increasing the splendour of beauty, disturbs its influence,
and if this be so, we may confidently state that the juxtaposition
of pineapples and lantana produces a type of beauty unequalled
both for splendour and disturbance.

Philosophers may ask whether the beauty which induces a mood
of serenity is preferable to the agitating kind ; it is a nice metaphysical point, but one which rarely engages the attention of
farmers, so we need not pursue it here. Of course they cannot
fail to observe the remarkable contrast between these two predominant forms of vegetation, and there is ample evidence that
the sight of either disturbs them, but the reason for this is
probably concerned less with æsthetics than with economics.

It was all very well for Mr. Crabb (who, we dare swear, never brushed a patch of lantana in his life, nor chipped a row of pineapples, but merely sat comfortably in his study playing with Synonyms), to point out that contrast, since it heightens the effect of opposite qualities which show, nevertheless, a likeness in degree, is of great utility among poets ; and no doubt poets have achieved some of their finest passages by skilfully setting against each other the fire and the frying-pan, the pot and the kettle, the devil and the deep blue sea. But the farmer, when he contrasts the control of lantana with the control of pineapples, is merely at a loss to know which imposes the greater burden upon his weary flesh, and his groaning spirit.

In our dealings with the vegetable kingdom we are apt to betray the same fallacious tendency which manifests itself in our attempts to divide our fellow men neatly into Goodies and Baddies. There are, we declare, Plants and Weeds—the quietest, most modest and inoffensive little number being a Weed if we have no use for it, and the thorniest, greediest and most troublesome rampager a Plant if it yields us something for our stomachs or our eyes.

Lantana is generally termed a Weed. We go further, hereabouts, and call it a Pest, to say nothing of less printable names. But in fact it is not altogether useless, and it is not so much wicked as crazy. It preserves, through all its misdemeanours, a kind of feckless innocence which, while often inducing extreme exasperation, still disarms hostility. We have become used to it—as those who work in lunatic asylums become used to mental aberration. Other weeds, such as Noogoora burr, Cobblers' Pegs, Crowsfoot, Groundsel and Stinking Roger, are systematic and purposeful enemies—Napoleons and Hitlers of the vegetable world, shameless aggressors bent upon territorial conquest ; but the lantana, poor fool, is not really greedy for *lebensraum*. Like an amiable, gangling half-wit who, without the slightest intention of incommoding anyone, gets under everyone's feet, it simply keeps alive, and grows.

And how it grows ! Nature—so neat and ingenious at devising

forms, patterns and routines—seems here to have become bored
with one of her creations ; to have informed it with life, and then
left it to its own devices. The result—as one might expect—is
frightful.

Other plants and weeds, endowed with a master plan providing
that the growth of one part shall contribute, in conjunction with
that of others, to a final harmony of shape and function, understand exactly what is expected of them, and address themselves
without pause or hesitation to the achievement of their task.
But a glance is enough to betray the sad fact that one stem of
the lantana knows not what the others are doing ; each sprouts
upwards, downward or sideways at will, guided only by an eager,
blundering vitality, a fervent, planless exuberance, a kind of
anarchic zeal.

We have used the word " stem "—but surely we mean
" branch " ? Or do we ? . . . Does this shrub (or should we say
creeper ? . . .) consist of a great many stems and no branches,
or a great many branches and no stem ? A stem—so we understand—is the ascending axis of a plant in contradistinction to its
descending axis, or root ; and a branch—if we have been properly
informed—is that part which grows out of the stem. This
definition may enable us to identify those stems which, having
emerged from the earth directly above their descending axis,
steadily and without further ado concentrate upon the business
of ascent, putting forth boughs and branches as they go ; but it
is no help at all with lantana. For although lantana certainly
ascends (and to prodigious heights), it can hardly be said to grow
upwards. It achieves, rather, what we might at first be tempted
to describe as an act of levitation, though closer research reveals
that the visible mass does rest upon an invisible foundation ; and
it is here, of course, that we must seek the answers to our
questions.

One's sensations, while crawling into the lantana's nether
layers must markedly resemble those of a psychiatrist groping
his way into the twilight of the unconscious, Great Heavens,
what a mess ! This demented confusion of naked growth cannot

but suggest the tortured complexities of obscure, Freudian urges. Here is activity without discipline or direction, an aimless rampancy of pullulation expressing itself in mad angles and frenzied excursions, senseless entwinings and interlacings, wild sallies and irrational recoils, brusque deviations, and long, random wanderings. The light is dim, and faintly green. The still air smells of secrecy, and through it the dead leaves softly fall and fall like yesterdays. Nowhere is any system discernible, nor any hint that the monstrous vigour of this afflicted weed is governed by a law.

Crawl and peer as we will, we can discover nothing which suggests an ascending axis. Here, indeed, is something which, from its superior girth, we might suppose to be a stem, but it is proceeding parallel to the ground, and—so far as our eye can follow it—betrays no inclination to ascend. From it there burst at intervals things which may possibly be branches, though some shoot skyward, some seem bent upon plunging into the earth, and others vanish horizontally in different directions ; and from all these there sprout, in turn, other growths whose behaviour is equally eccentric, and from these still others, and from these . . .

Now wait a minute. Let us keep calm, and classify these things. The biggest is the stem ; the things that shoot from it are the boughs ; the things that shoot from the boughs are the branches. . . . But no ; we recall the dictum that a branch is thinner than a bough, and thicker than a twig, shoot or spray, and the evidence of our eyes compels us to admit that these cannot be twigs after all, for they are in some cases thicker than the branches which, in any case, cannot be branches because they are in some cases thicker than the boughs. . . .

Enough. What's in a name ? We shall employ them all indiscriminately—stem, stalk, bough, branch, limb, twig and even peduncle. Only let us get out of this ; only let us rediscover sanity and sunlight ; only let us look again at a tree, a thistle, a clover-leaf, a cabbage—anything which comports itself with purpose and precision, anything which knows its own shape, and sticks to it. Shaken and defeated, we retire backwards on all-fours, emerging at last to stare up at the green crown of that hidden underworld. And from here we cannot fail to see that the unfortunate weed is really trying hard to be normal. It wears its veneer of leaves brightly, with an artless pride. As a simpleton apeing the labours of his rational associates may diligently perform absurdities, and invite applause the while, with beaming smiles—so this dim-witted clutter of vegetation zealously persists in the endless task of piling itself upon itself, and ingratiatingly adorns its gawky dishevelment with a peppering of silly little flowers.

But the penalties of stupidity are, alas, no lighter than those of wickedness. If lantana had the sense to stick to the boundaries, it might thrive for ever unmolested. But this it will not do, and when it encroaches too much, the tolerance of the farmers deserts them, and they take to it with brush-hooks.

Since anarchy begets anarchy, this operation proceeds without method or finesse. The blows by which an axeman performs execution on a tree fall with a grim and solemn rhythm ; those of a mattock uprooting lesser growths are dealt with economical exactitude ; the extermination of noxious weeds by poisonous sprays is governed by strict rules ; but the assault with a brush-hook upon lantana is mere slash and bash, from which the assailant himself does not emerge unscathed.

He steps in anywhere, and swings his weapon with a will ; but he cannot tell how much, or how little, resistance the stuff will offer, nor can he aim his blow at an angle which is correct for one branch without making it quite incorrect for half a dozen others. He strikes hard at the middle of the mass, and the brush-hook merely bounces. He summons all his strength and strikes again, whereupon everything gives way at once, and he over-balances on to his knees. He rises, breathing a little faster, grimly selects with his eye a promising, thick limb, and, with a fierce stroke, severs it ; promptly, from six feet above his head, another portion with which it appeared to have no possible connection, springs out and swipes him smartly across the face.

Now not only the stems of lantana, but all its et ceteras down to twigs, are furnished with a surface like coarse sandpaper, so this is extremely painful, and causes him to do his block. He swings again and again, more and more savagely. His shoulders ache. His arms smart from a hundred scarifying scrapes. Broken branches poke him in the ribs. Unbroken ones lie round his feet and trip him up. But he is making some impression. The wall is no longer solid, and he steps recklessly into the shallow breach. Now the damned stuff is all about him. Stalks spike his ankles with jagged ends. Boughs reach down and snatch his hat from his head. Stems leap backward from his blows. Twigs thrust forward at his eyes. The whole clownish tangle bounds and sways beneath the onslaught, frustrating his force with its infuriating elasticity. To pursue his advantage, he must now leave firm ground, and clamber over a network of interwoven undergrowth which heaves beneath his weight like a spring mattress. The damned and blasted stuff whips out at him from all directions as he lurches forward ; it catches in his hair, it tears large rents in his trousers, it sends a loop spinning out like a lassoo, and twitches the brush-hook from his hand. He strives, struggles and slashes while his muscles cry out in agony, the sweat stings viciously in his multitudinous abrasions, and from his lips there flows a steady stream of passionate profanity. . . .

Unfortunately (though perhaps understandably), he is in no condition to realise that the role of the lantana is that of a passive victim ; but so it is. The damned and blasted bloody stuff means no harm. It is just the way it grows.

But no crack regiment on parade was ever more orderly than a well-tended plantation of pines ; indeed, anybody who has ever driven past such a plantation will agree that his own movement creates so overpowering an illusion that its long rows are wheeling and turning in masterly execution of some complicated drill, that he almost finds himself taking the salute. Up and down the slopes they go—a strip of red earth, two green rows close together,

another strip of earth, two more rows—far away into the distance
in perfect formation, never breaking ranks, evenly deployed over
the surface of the ground, faithfully reproducing its contours,
each plant like every other plant, all the same height, all the
same colour, all the same shape, identity merged into slowly
turning spokes of *red*-green-green, *red*-green-green, *red*-green-
green, till the head swims, the eyes blur, and ghostly drums
beat out a marching rhythm. . . . Trrr*rum*-tum-tum, trrr*rum*-
tum-tum. . . .

Considering how often farmers are called upon to turn straight
from lantana to pineapples, or vice versa, it is a wonder that they
are not all schizophrenics, for the violent contrasts thus forced
upon their attention demand abrupt mental, manual, visual and
emotional adjustments which are enough to split any psyche
clean down the middle.

Both the Plant and the Weed are hardy and tenacious of
life ; but whereas lantana needs no help in overwhelming anything so ill-advised as to grow near it, and asks nothing of
man but to be left alone, pineapples imperiously demand that
human slaves reserve for them exclusive possession of their
earth.

Formerly the farmer achieved this by means of a primitive form
of labour. Those who have practised it, even briefly, marvel that
tyrants, while exploiting galleys, treadmills, and other torments
designed to break the spirits of their victims, seem never to have
heard of chipping. In chipping pines it is not—as in brushing
lantana—a case of plunging in anywhere, and laying about you
with heroic abandon ; it is a matter of beginning at one end of
the first row (taking care not to glance at all the other rows, far
less count them), dropping your chin on your breast, fixing your
eyes on the ground, and plugging away, row after row, till you
reach the last, by which time weeds are sprouting again in the
first. Your weapon is not a brush-hook to be fiercely whirled
about the head, but a push-hoe to be drearily shoved along the
ground. No mood of lively aggressiveness is required, but a
dogged patience. Here man is not a combatant, but a drudge.

Nothing bounces beneath his feet, nothing slaps him in the face, nothing resists him. He stands on solid earth, and progresses slowly, slowly, pushing his blade beneath shallow-rooted weeds which yield without a struggle. He cannot step to one side or the other, for he is held imprisoned between the rows; there is no escape until he reaches the end—and then another narrow passage opens to receive him. Nowhere on earth does he look so small, so lonely, so hopelessly engaged and so absurdly valiant as when he is standing waist-deep in the middle of a large block of pines, chipping.

But this is a labour-saving age, and chipping is now almost obsolete. The reason is, of course, that Science has come to the rescue with a spray. The immediate and visible effect of this upon the weeds is devastating, though what its ultimate, and less conspicuous effects upon all sort of other things may prove to be, we must leave to learned research workers of the future. For the moment we echo the prevailing cry that Science is wonderful. It has provided sprays for killing weeds, sprays for killing insects, sprays for speeding up growth, sprays for delaying it, sprays for making leaves fall off, sprays for making fruit stay on, selective sprays, pre-emergent sprays, and many others, all with very long names which we cannot spell, nor could you pronounce them if we did. Whether Dame Nature is properly grateful for so much expert assistance we do not know, but we rather doubt it, because she used to be considered wonderful herself, and no female likes to see the homage she once inspired transferred to a younger, upstart hussy.

Nowadays the axioms of our fathers are falling around us like ninepins, but that one still stands—and anything still standing in this iconoclastic age commands startled and respectful attention. Possibly we should do well not to rile this ancient lady. Possibly Hell hath no fury such as that which is even now consuming her, and if so, we had better beware, for she still has a few trumps in her hand. She can still insist, for example, that we must breathe, and though much of the spray which has freed us from chipping does undoubtedly descend on the weeds, and knock them cold, it may be that a residue rises to sport with the playful wind, which perhaps is already sporting with the residue of all the other sprays, and all the other by-products of our scientific genius, including atomic fall-out. Such an hypothesis tempts us to suspect that the old girl is sardonically waiting for us to discover that deep draughts of beautiful country air may no longer be confidently recommended, and that breathing is not what it was in the days when she had sole charge of it. True, we could (thanks again to Science) defy her even here with pig-like masks ; but though we might learn to eat and sleep in them, they would surely not be satisfactory for kissing—and there she has us again. There, in fact, is probably her ace of trumps. Deep as is our debt to Science, we should not thank it for building into our snouts a mechanical osculator, however ingenious.

And Science will, no doubt, add the last, the crowning contrast to those we have already noted between pineapples and lantana. Having received from it a spray for protecting the former, surely we shall soon be vouchsafed a spray for abolishing the latter ? Or perhaps an insect will be provided to prey upon it, and then a spray for abolishing the insect ? There is no knowing what measures Science may see fit to adopt, but we can be sure that it will presently elbow the fearful angels aside, and rush in brandishing a tube of something or other. We can also be sure that some churlish curses will be mingled with the blessings which farmers then call down upon its head, for not only they, but their wives, would confront certain problems if lantana vanished from the landscape.

It is not for nothing that a simpleton is often called a natural, for between him and nature there exists a strong bond of sympathy. And so long as the lantana still makes large areas inaccessible to the hustling, high-pressure system by which Science peps up the soil's productiveness, Nature may continue to build upon them, undisturbed and at leisure, a rich topsoil of rotted leaves, according to her own slow, old-fashioned methods. Moreover, she receives from her simpleton-child much sturdy co-operation in keeping the steeper hillsides from being washed down into the creeks, and thence out to sea—a thing which annoys her very much when it occurs, as it upsets both her marine and terrestrial arrangements. Formerly she kept the slopes at home by clothing them with dense scrub, but since the axes got busy she has had no hesitation in calling to her aid anything and everything that roots, including groundsel, blady-grass, couch, Stinking Roger, and, notably, lantana. But if lantana, too, be snatched from her, she will jump right in with something else— probably groundsel—and sit back in slyly malicious triumph to see how we like *that*. For she makes no distinction between Plants and Weeds. They are all Goodies to her, so long as they keep the soil where it belongs. It is a sobering thought that, in her eyes, we alone, out of all creation, may be Baddies.

It must be conceded, too, that the stiff, tough, soldierly pine-apples owe much to the feckless and slovenly lantana—for it is practically cow-proof. In gaining access to pines, a cow—despite its low I.Q.—is capable of great ingenuity and perseverance, and since one crunch, one slobber and one gulp suffice it for the devouring of each succulent fruit, the rape of a whole row may be accomplished with horrifying speed. Therefore the same superabundant vitality which makes lantana a pestiferous nuisance elsewhere, endows it with a certain value in those places where there lie, deeply buried beneath it, the rotting posts and the rusting wires of fences which would cost a pretty penny to repair. Small wonder, then, that the farmers are not unwilling to see it take over their road boundaries, and supply, at no cost to themselves, an impenetrable barrier to the poking and pushing of even the most pertinacious cow. And if you ask what cows are doing in the road, we can only reply that although no one, naturally, would dream of allowing his cattle to infest the Long Paddock, some are always there. As a result of this, the farmer who blesses the lantana from inside his property, curses it when he drives out into the Lane. We cannot fairly blame him for this apparent inconsistency, for the Lane, as we have already seen, is both narrow and curly ; so the sudden appearance of half a dozen cows—or even one cow—standing, with placid, incurious

eyes and steadily moving jaws, slap-bang in front of his bumper-bar, is enough to shake his nerves and try his temper. Thus the same high wall which earns his gratitude by keeping his own cows in, and stray cows out, becomes the target of his choicest maledictions when it confines to the dead centre of the public road those mysterious animals about whose ownership the less said the better.

Besides all this, we really do not care to imagine the plight of the farm wife bereft of the lantana, for it is without peer as a receptacle for otherwise non-disposable rubbish. When you are at your wits' end to get rid of something, it is the local custom, hallowed by long usage, to Throw it Down in the Lantanna; for the Lane is no suburban street, and Wednesday evening sees no housewives placing garbage-tins beside the back gate. Instead, the chook-bucket receives the scraps from meals, the burnable things are burnt, and for the rest . . .

Well, we put it to you squarely. What would *you* do with tins and dead marines? What would *you* do with the old iron bed-stead, the rust-consumed tank, the roll of useless wire netting, the ancient pram, the buckled bicycle wheel, the kettles, saucepans, egg-beaters and frying-pans which have earned an honourable discharge? What would *you* do with the broken vases, medicine bottles, crockery and looking-glasses; the half-used bag of cement, now set like a rock; the worn-out gumboots, and the mouldering remains of your late grandmother's buggy? True, an incredible amount of junk will go under the house, but there comes a time when space there is exhausted—and then how thankfully we turn to the lantana! With a soft crash, and a sound of splitting twigs, discarded objects of all kinds, shapes and sizes fall through the green leaves, and discreetly vanish into the twilit world below. If Science some day passes sentence of death upon our simpleton, many strange and embarrassing sights will lie revealed.

Perhaps at this very moment some deadly brew is being compounded in laboratories by people to whom a noxious weed is merely noxious; who have no cows, and drop their rubbish in garbage tins ; who have never lived with the fool of the family, cursing it to-day, and blessing it to-morrow ; who will some day hand it the poisoned cup, and, with scientific detachment, watch it die.

When that happens, you may go looking for Lantana Lane— but you will find only Black Creek Road.

Sweet and Low

TONY GRIFFITH is just eleven. He is one of those lean, light little boys whose movements are nostalgically observed by persons of middle age and increasing weight. Was there ever a time, they ask themselves wonderingly, when *I* had so small a burden of flesh to carry about with me, and carried it like that? . . .

For Tony hardly ever walks, and when he comes running, skipping or hopping down the Lane, or proceeds with a kind of dancing step—as if he were trying to keep his feet in order, and not succeeding very well—he has an air of being only temporarily and accidentally in contact with the earth, like a head of dandelion seed blowing along the ground.

It was probably the sight of some such little boy which first brought to a poet's mind the words : " *There was a time* . . ."; words to which, as we all know, he added many others about celestial light, bounding lambs, and trailing clouds of glory. He cannot have been ignorant of the fact that little boys are devils, and that lean, light little boys are the most diabolical of all, since a minimum of their horrifying energy is required for the business of moving them from spot to spot, and a maximum thus remains for the conception and execution of various devilishnesses. But he evidently decided (and we believe quite rightly) that their fiendish habits are abundantly redeemed by the intimations of immortality which they evoke in the minds of those about whom shades of the prison house have closed ; and no little boy ever more poignantly evoked them than Tony Griffith.

His face is as brown as a dead leaf, but as smooth and blooming as a peach. His nose is endearingly snubby and babyish, but the angle at which he holds it proclaims self-confidence, goodwill and indefatigable enquiry. His eyes—light-grey, and clear as water—stare at the world with an expression so genially and candidly searching that the world, if it had any shame left, might well blush and shuffle its feet. But the most noticeable thing about him is that he is never, never, never tired.

In any farming community the manifestations of fatigue are, of course, too obvious to be overlooked, and Tony is accustomed to the sight of his parents, his great-aunt Isabelle and his neighbours slumping into chairs at the end of the day, and exhibiting every symptom of exhaustion; but he is quite unable to comprehend what can be the matter with them. The opening of his eyes at five o'clock every morning brings into instant operation a powerful dynamo, incredibly concealed somewhere in his slip of a body, and this continues throughout the day to drive him at a furious and unfaltering pace. If he comes upon anything climbable, he immediately climbs it; if he chances upon anything that can be thrown, he immediately throws it; if a log, a wheelbarrow or a packing-case lies in his path, he not only jumps it, but returns several times to jump it again before proceeding on his way. He passes a great deal of time in hitting things—sometimes (as when he smites tennis or cricket balls with racquet or bat, or nails with a hammer, or tobacco-weed with a brush-hook) for some definite purpose; but sometimes (as when he puts in half an hour swiping at tufts of blady-grass with a stick, or belting stones along the Lane with a bit of board), merely because he feels like it. In either case, the vigour and impetuosity of his hitting are attributable to the fact that his dynamo produces so much surplus power that he must expend it rapidly, lest it burst his slender frame to smithereens.

This power is not only supplied to his muscles; it also floods his mind, sending forth, like a stream of crackling sparks, questions, comments, protests, petitions and conjectures. He says : " How ? ", " Why ? ", " What ? ", " When ? " and " Where ? "; he says : " Look ! " and " Watch ! "; he says : " Can I ? " (and, when corrected, " May I ? "); this last frequently leads him to " Why not ? ", and thence to a last ditch where he can always be depended upon to make a heroic stand, firing the word : " but," " *but*," " BUT," into the ranks of inimical adulthood until he goes down at last, with his colours still flying.

He does not lack companionship in the Lane. The Bell twins are his constant associates (though some might prefer the word accomplices), and there is also Daphne Arnold, who is twelve. She is unfortunate in that the Lane yields her no playmate of her own age and sex, so it is natural enough that she should turn to Tony ; but for a long time no one could understand why Tony welcomed her with such consistent cordiality, for not only did she always have her five-year-old sister, Joy, at her heels, but she is herself a very polite, ladylike and motherly little girl who is apt—like mothers—to be easily shocked. She almost invariably disapproves of everything Tony proposes to do, and reprimands him at length when he does it all the same. So it seemed rather a bewildering friendship, and even Sue Griffith took a long time to realise that it was not really Daphne whom Tony liked to have around, but Joy. This may appear stranger still until you know Joy ; but when you do know her, you cannot fail to see that she and Tony, out of all the children in the Lane, come nearest to being soul-mates.

Joy does not share Tony's physical characteristics, for she is a plump little person, and though she is untiringly active, she creates no illusion that her feet are winged ; on the contrary, one might imagine them to be equipped, like those of flies, with some kind of suction-grip, so firmly does she keep them on the ground. Her pastimes and Tony's are, of course, the poles apart, but the manner in which they pursue them is also subtly different. Tony is volatile ; Joy is constant. Tony is energetic ; Joy is busy. The activity of Tony's body frequently has nothing to do with the activity of his mind; but Joy's doing is always strictly directed and controlled by a fertile imagination, and her life is, consequently, one long, rich and coherent drama. Its theme (which is that of a lady burdened by many cares) never changes, though she improvises endless variations upon it. The more cares and responsibilities she can conceive for herself, the busier she can become, and her experience of life seems to have persuaded her that the most fruitful sources of care are maternity, illness and shops.

Tony is aware of himself only as we might suppose a plant or an animal to be, and if it is difficult for others to remain unaware of him, this is simply because any tremendous natural force is apt to be conspicuous. When he is present, the throb and pulse of his dynamo are almost audible, and the very ground seems to vibrate; but he does not court attention. Joy, on the other hand, is, in her own view, the absorbing and always vividly apprehended centre of the universe, and she finds it intolerable that the phenomenon of her existence should ever be, for one instant, disregarded by anyone.

From these traits arises, perhaps, the further difference that while she is extremely sensitive to criticism, Tony couldn't care less. If his mother, in a moment of desperation, tells him that he is, without exception, the most maddening and abominable child it has ever been her misfortune to meet, he merely gives her a blank stare from his limpid, grey eyes, and remains perfectly unruffled. But a hint of reproof, or even the shadow of a censorious expression, will cause Joy's rosebud mouth to droop, and her round eyes to fill with tears as she demands piteously: " Am I a *good* girl ? "

This is obviously a point of vital importance—for what would become of us all if the centre of the universe were less than perfect ? Cracks in its virtue are unthinkable, and therefore, upon learning that her perfection is, for the moment, slightly impaired, but that it may be speedily restored if she will do such and such, Joy hastens off to set things right, and returns for reassurance.

" Am I a good girl *now* ? "

" Oh yes, you're a good girl *now*."

" Am I a wery good girl ? "

" Very good."

" Am I a werry, *werry* good girl ? "

" Very, very."

" Am I a werry, werry *indeed* good girl ? "

" You're the best girl in the world."

The mouth no longer droops, and the tears have vanished. The peril has been averted. Joy is once more at her station, and all's right with the world. It may safely begin to revolve again, and she forthwith sets it in motion.

" Now," she says briskly, " we'll play shops, and you must be the lady, and I'll be the shop-lady, and these must be the money, and my Uncle Mont must be in hostable because he's werry sick, and you must ask me how he is."

All this being accomplished, Joy assumes an expression of quite heartrending anxiety, and distractedly waves her hands as she describes the predicament in which she finds herself. For it now appears, as the plot thickens, that not only Uncle Mont, but Auntie Flo and another character (of whom we learn nothing save that her name is Mary) are also in hostable, all suffering from fever, and all getting to be nearly quite dead. Thus Joy has the shop to mind, the housework to do, a large family of children to scold, and a heavy programme of sick-bed visiting as well. Here, becoming momentarily confused as to her identity, she thinks she will buy something to take to poor Uncle Mont ; but, observing her mistake, she deftly switches parts.

" *I* must be the lady, and *you* must be the shop-lady, but you mustn't have Uncle Mont and Auntie Flo, see, because I must have them." She pauses, considers, and adds magnanimously : " But you can have Mary."

With these alterations in the script duly understood, the drama is re-enacted, though by now Uncle Mont's condition has worsened, and the doctor has prescribed pills. In the confusion occasioned by hurriedly transforming the shop from a general store into a pharmacy, another switch of parts accidentally occurs ;

but the situation is so tense that this passes unnoticed. The pills having been wrapped up, and their cost fixed at one shilling and six pennies, this amount is handed over by the lady who receives, to her gratified astonishment, one shilling and eight pennies in change.

Now imbecilities of this kind are naturally beneath Tony's notice, and it must not be supposed that when Joy visited him he took any part in such nonsense. They were not playmates at all. What they recognised and valued in each other (until a regrettable occurrence which we shall presently recount put an end to their association) was the superb quality of their respective dynamos. They were like two great artists working in different media, who have no dealings with each other's arts, but still salute each other's genius. When the four older children played a game, Joy was neither invited nor forbidden to join in, but she was quite content to disport herself on its outskirts, turning it to her own purposes, and transforming it into something more her own. Nevertheless, she was, in a sense, more emphatically a participant than Daphne or the twins, for even her semi-detached gambollings at the periphery contributed to it a zest which was equalled only by Tony's. They were both very conscious of this. Like two royal personages in a crowd of commoners, or two millionaires in a suburban cottage, or two gangsters at a church social, they were always sharply aware of each other. But whereas Joy knew that Tony was aware of her, he did not know that she was aware of him ; whereas he merely felt her gusto, and enjoyed it, she not only felt his and enjoyed it, but enjoyed even more the knowledge that he was feeling hers. And this was why, on the fateful evening which we are about to describe, she ran away and hid in the dumpty.

The subject of sanitation is not one which is commonly introduced into simple, family tales, but since it is germane to this one, it must be briefly discussed. There are few houses in our neighbourhood which boast septic tanks, and in the Lane we are all resigned to, if not content with, a less elaborate arrangement.

This consists of a hole dug in the ground—a good, capacious hole, some four feet square and six deep—over which a suitable building is erected and furnished with the kind of seat appropriate to its function.

On the evening in question, Ding, Dong, Daphne and Joy were all at Tony's place, and Tony was practising on his fife. This had been given to him by Aunt Isabelle who—though not herself a performer on any instrument—comes of a musical family, and had often deplored the fact that Tony was prevented by his residence in this remote spot from developing the musical gifts which he must undoubtedly possess. She had accordingly presented him, on his birthday, with the fife, shrugging her shoulders the while, and protesting that—*faute de mieux*—it might serve to allay the hunger for melody from which the poor child was suffering.

Tony had no idea that he was suffering from anything, but he was delighted with the fife, and immediately began to experiment with it. After only a few hours he accidentally blew three notes in succession which formed part of a recognisable tune. After another hour he had thoroughly mastered these three notes, and could repeat them any time he liked ; but more than this, he had identified them as belonging to the well-known hymn *Once in Royal David's City*, and was tirelessly in search of the fourth note to put after them. This he discovered in due course, and followed it with the fifth, the sixth, and the seventh ; by this time he was so elated that only with the greatest difficulty could Sue persuade him to lay down his instrument for long enough to eat. She was clutching her head, and Henry was nearly frantic, but Aunt Isabelle was enraptured. Bless the little cabbage, she cried fondly, he executed the tune to a marvel, was it not ? Within a fortnight he could play the whole thing from beginning to end ; Aunt Isabelle, with proud tears in her eyes, said it was formidable, and Henry agreed that it damn well was.

Whatever his parents may have endured, the rest of the Lane (with one exception) quite enjoyed Tony's fife, and took a benevolent interest in his progress. Since distance lends enchantment to a view, it may, in like manner, soften the impact of sounds upon the ear ; at all events, the intimations of immortality which Tony had always exuded were, if anything, enhanced by the sweet and plaintive notes of his fife. Those who dimly recalled their poetry lessons at school found themselves thinking vaguely and sentimentally about Pan, and shepherd lads, and some boy or other who came piping down a valley wild.

Joy, however, did not like the fife. It provided her first experience of that terrible obsession known as Art, which causes otherwise normal people to become queer and distrait, and to go away into a world of their own, and cease to be conscious of anything outside it. All these symptoms Tony was now exhibiting. Daphne and the twins were rather taken aback when they found that he no longer wanted to play with them, but they just played together and—if the truth must be told—sometimes felt that things were simpler and cosier without him, if less exciting.

Joy, however, was in a terrible state. Tony was not aware of her any longer ; he was aware of nothing but his fife.

A woman scorned is popularly supposed to be fury personified, but she is a dove compared with a woman ignored, and on this memorable evening Joy had reached a stage where she would have stopped at nothing to detach Tony's attention from the fife, and transfer it to herself. There he was, sitting under the mulberry tree, tootling away at some notes which did not, as yet, seem to have any idea of co-operation, and looking rapt. She simply could not bear it. She tried singing a song at the top of her voice to drown his music, but he didn't seem to hear. She tried throwing pebbles at him, but he didn't seem to feel. Then she tried falling down and pretending she had hurt herself so werry, werry indeed badly that she couldn't get up again, but he didn't seem to see. This was so dreadful that she was just wondering if she could find his football and hammer a nail into it, when Ding happened to hit what would have been a sixer if Tony had not been in the way. The ball caught him on the wrist, knocking the fife out of his hand, and he sprang up wrathfully, yelling : " Hey ! Cut it out ! "

Joy went into action so fast that only a blur on the landscape betrayed her strategic move to a position behind him. While he was still stamping about, shouting revilements at Ding, and clutching his bruised wrist, she pounced, seized the fife, and ran.

She got away to a good start because for a few seconds Tony remained unaware of his loss. Then, with a vengeful cry, he gave chase. But she had disappeared round the back of the house, and when he turned the corner he could not see her anywhere. He looked behind the mango tree, he ran up and down the pineapple rows, he poked about in the lantana ; he summoned Daphne and the twins, and they all searched too. The sun went down. Daphne called, scolded and threatened. At last, addressing the empty air, she announced loudly :

" All right, I can't wait any longer—I'm going without you, and you'll have to come home by yourself in the dark."

Whereupon the door of the dumpty flew open and Joy shot out, bawling ; but, alas, without the fife.

The full truth of this deplorable affair is so securely hidden in the centre of the universe that we doubt if it will ever become known. To the question : " Did it fall, or was it dropped ? " we shall never really know the answer. But we have it on Heather Arnold's authority that Joy reached home still bawling, continued to bawl until bedtime, and refused to compose herself for sleep until she had been assured—not once, but twenty times—that she was a werry, werry indeed good girl. From this we may draw our own conclusions.

But there is no doubt at all that Tony's dynamo, stimulated by crisis, went into operation so powerfully that his parents, to this day, remember the occasion as one when they felt themselves driven and dominated by an irresistible force. They were reclining in their chairs, exhausted by a particularly tough day's work, when he presented himself before them wearing an expression compounded of outrage and invincible determination. He said bitterly :

" That beastly damn kid, Joy, dropped my fife down the dumpty."

" Tony," yawned Sue mechanically, " don't say . . ." She blinked, sat up, looked at him, and asked : " What ? "

" Joy," repeated Tony with terrible restraint. " My fife. Down the dumpty. And I want to practise, so come on." And then he burst out with sudden ferocity : " What's so funny ? "

For his parents—revealing a callous lack of sympathy which shocked him to his soul—had actually begun to laugh. Aunt Isabelle, however, had greeted his news with exclamations of dismay, and was now giving a rapid sketch of her views on the matter, which were that this instrument, though of an inferior kind not hitherto used, or even recognised, in her family, had nevertheless cost money, and was not to be flung away—and into such a place, *pfui!*—by a naughty and undisciplined child, for that little Joy there was, and had always been of the most mischievous, and could with advantage undergo chastisement which she herself would willingly administer, though it must be understood that she did not, as a question of principle, favour the punishment corporal, and had so repeatedly informed Henri when he had lifted his hand against *ce pauvre* Tony, who had now been so maliciously deprived of his instrument which, though of an inferior kind not hitherto used or even . . .

Tony, glad as he was to find himself with at least one ally, felt that this had gone on long enough, and could not be allowed to begin all over again, particularly as it seemed to be increasing his parents' scandalous mirth, rather than arousing them to a proper sense of the urgency of the situation. So he interrupted hotly :

" Mum, I never gave it to her ! It just fell out of my hand, and she sneaked up and grabbed it and ran away with it ! You're always telling me I mustn't meddle with other people's things, but when she does it, you only *laugh!* . . ."

Sue, smitten by the justice of this, remembered her maternal duty, wiped her eyes, and said soothingly :

"No, darling. I mean, yes, darling. I mean it was very naughty of her, and we're all very, very sorry."

Henry, belatedly contrite, reached behind his chair and patted Tony's leg.

"Yes—bad luck, old chap. But she's only a little girl, and I expect she didn't mean . . ."

"Didn't *mean* . . . !" snorted Tony fiercely. "She meant it all right! And I was just beginning to learn *Sweet and Low*!"

At this, Henry, for some inexplicable reason, suffered another paroxysm of misplaced hilarity, and Sue went off into a veritable fit of hysterics. Aunt Isabelle, eyeing them with astonished indignation, bade Tony rest tranquil, for although his parents appeared insensible of the anguish which such a loss must occasion to one of the artistic temperament, she was of a nature more *sympathique*, and would, at the first opportunity, buy him a new fife. . . .

"I don't WANT a new fife!" roared Tony. "There's nothing wrong with my old one, and I want to do some practice, so come *on*!"

Henry turned slowly in his chair, stared hard at his son, and enquired cautiously: "Come on . . . where?"

"To get it, of course," said Tony.

There was a long, hushed pause. Then Sue said briskly:
"Oh, come, darling, don't be silly!"

Henry was heard to chuckle indulgently; but from the way he settled himself on his shoulders and propped his slippered feet on another chair, it was plain that he had no intention of coming on anywhere. Tony stood looking at them in silence for a moment, drawing deep breaths and gathering his forces for battle. Within him the throb of his dynamo grew faster and stronger until the whole room seemed so charged with power that his parents exchanged glances of alarm, and shifted uneasily in their chairs. Sue—though she has described the later events of the evening with precision—has never been able to recall very clearly the exact details of the awe-inspiring struggle which now ensued.

She knows that Aunt Isabelle vaccillated, sometimes declaring that the child's resolution was *magnifique*, and repeating (with that air of triumphantly settling a matter which proverbs lend to those who quote them) "*Qui ne risque rien, n'a rien*"; but sometimes, when her imagination got the better of her, protesting, imploring, expressing profound repugnance, and recklessly promising not only a new fife, but also a bugle, a concertina, a ukelele and even a drum. She knows that Henry, eschewing argument altogether, performed a swift and masterly retirement to that impregnable position which parents always keep prepared, and thundered : "No! *No!* NO!" at frequent intervals. She is not sure what part she herself played in the scene, except that her lines all seemed to be short and unfinished. "Henry, dear, *please*! . . ." "Tony, you must *not*! . . ." "Isabelle, I wish you wouldn't encourage . . ."

But she is quite sure that throughout the engagement Tony was the attacker, and that they really knew they were beaten before they began. To every objection he unhesitatingly produced an answer beginning with "But . . ." To every bellowed "No!" he replied indomitably with "Why not?", and gained strength, as his adversaries weakened, from the obvious fact that they could put forward absolutely no valid reason why not. They could do nothing but shout, shudder, exclaim, wave their hands, make faces, and declare that he must be mad, it was out of the question, it was impossible, it was not to be thought of. And at last, when Henry, desperate and demoralised, unwisely exposed his flank by shifting ground and asking "How?", Tony knew that he had them where he wanted them. He told them how.

To his astonishment and disgust, he found that his admirably simple plan of action, far from being greeted with applause, provoked a fresh outbreak of protestations. Even Aunt Isabelle finally went over to the enemy, asserting that she was a realist, she, and had never demanded that life be presented to her *couleur de rose*, but there were undoubtedly certain aspects of it from which all civilised persons agreed to avert the eyes, and the proposal

of Tony, though made in all innocence, could not for one instant
be entertained. Tony was annoyed by all this time-wasting
chatter, but not seriously disturbed by the renewed opposition ;
he recognised it as being merely the sudden flare of a dying fire.
And, true enough, there were only a few more flickers—a few
weak, craven attempts at procrastination.

"But look, Tony," Sue urged despairingly, "not to-night.
Not to-night, darling, *please!* Dad's worn out, and so am I.
It'll be . . . easier by daylight, anyhow. Just wait till to-
morrow . . ."

Tony stood his ground, immovable.

"To-morrow you've got to start picking and packing early—
you'll say you haven't time. *I* know!"

"We-e-ll, yes, we *will* be busy in the morning—but in the
afternoon we could . . ."

"Have some sense, Mum, can't you ? " Tony cut in scornfully.
"It'll be worse then."

"Worse ? . . ." She stared at him. Henry gave a hollow laugh,
and said :

"Wake up, old girl ! Worse is right. It's now or never."

Light broke on Sue. "Oh, *dear!*" she cried. "Why do things
always happen to us ? Well, if we must. . . . I suppose we must.
After supper, then—yes, Tony, I promise. Oh, *dear!*"

Henry stood up suddenly, swept Tony out of the way, and
fetched from a cupboard the bottle of brandy they kept for
emergencies. True, they had never envisaged just such an
emergency as this, but the three adults immediately recognised it
as one calling for the Dutch courage which alcohol supplies. Sue
tossed off a stiff drink, and demanded another. Aunt Isabelle
(who is practically teetotal) downed hers with an air of martyr-
dom, as if it were hemlock. Henry, with his glass half-way to his
lips, paused and looked with disfavour at his son. "You," he
said coldly, "may have a glass of lemonade."

But what need should Tony have of artificial stimulants ? His
dynamo was pounding away as strongly and steadily as ever ; he
had expended fabulous amounts of energy, but he still had plenty

in reserve. Erect and inflexible, contemptuously observing their abject and lily-livered behaviour, he replied with dignity :

" I don't want lemonade. I only want my fife."

It was quite dark when the little procession emerged from the back door and passed in single file along the narrow, foot-worn path. No one except Tony had felt like eating much after all, and Sue, remembering what was in store for him, had queried the wisdom of his third helping of pudding ; but he had only stared, and said impatiently, " Why not ? I'm hungry." Now he strode ahead, marching fast and resolutely like a good officer who must instil confidence into his wavering ranks. Behind him—muttering that this was a nice, peaceful sort of evening for a man who had been working since dawn—came Henry with a torch. Sue followed, trying hard, now that the moment was at hand, to behave like a mother of Sparta, and not let poor darling Tony down. Aunt Isabelle (in whom the brandy seemed to have induced a mood of rather tearful sentimentality) brought up the rear, lamenting that Sue's late and so talented mother had not lived to see the incomparable resource and fortitude of this grandson, whose devotion to his art should be rewarded by the gift of a grand piano, and a musical education under the best masters of Europe.

When they reached the door, and Tony, without hesitation, entered, Sue's nerve wobbled, and she began to cry out : " Oh, no ! Oh, Henry ! Oh, Tony, darling ! Oh, no ! " Tony said sharply : " What's biting you ? Here, Dad, give us the torch a sec. I've just got to see exactly where . . ."

" Oh, no ! " babbled Sue. " Tony, you really can't . . . ! "

Aunt Isabelle now caught the infection of panic and, entirely deserted by her English, began a long and impassioned plea in French, the gist of which was that Tony must render himself more philosophical, and recognise that life was full of losses, ah, *Ciel*, did she not know of what she spoke, she who had lost her country, and her home, and her Sèvres dinner service the most elegant, and her silver spoons of the period *Louis Quinze ?* From such trials was character formed, and here was an opportunity—unlikely to be repeated in this land where all were apt to be *sans gêne*, and few encouraged the young to treat life *au sérieux*—for Tony to practise a mature self-discipline. He must therefore resign himself; he must renounce his life. She reached into the dim illumination of the torchlight, laid hold of his shorts, and urged desperately: "*Il faut t'en passer, mon pauvre, il faut. . . .*"

But Tony (who does not normally admit to knowing any French at all) jerked himself from her grasp and yelled in exasperation: "I will NOT! Why should I? I can see it as plain as anything!" At this Aunt Isabelle was seized with a fearful spasm of shuddering, Sue moaned faintly, and Henry burst out:

"All *right*, then, blast it! What the Hell are we waiting for? Here, Sue, you take the torch. Come on, Tony, lean over and I'll grab your ankles." Tony eagerly complied, and was presently suspended, head downward, over a black void.

"*Prenez garde!*" shrieked Aunt Isabelle in agony. "*Prenez garde de tomber!*"

"He can't," snarled Henry. "I'm holding him, aren't I?"

Sue remained dumb. She was watching, with fascinated horror, a fair head and a rosy, upside-down face disappearing slowly into unspeakable depths; but before it vanished, it opened its mouth to reproach her. "Stiffen the lizards, Mum, how d'you think I'm going to see? Give us some light down here, can't you?"

She gulped and obeyed, reaching round Henry and holding the torch at arm's length. Now she could see only that portion of her child which would usually be described as from the neck down, but which had become, in this nightmare, from the neck up. Slowly he sank from her view until nothing remained visible but his knobby knees, his lean, brown calves, his ankles—gripped in the vice of his father's hands—and his dear, darling, dirty feet. She turned her head away, and held her breath. Henry, his arms rigid and quivering, muttered that the damn kid was heavier than he thought.

Tony's voice, muffled, but gallantly cheerful, came up from the pit.

"A bit more, Dad . . . a bit more still. . . . Hɪ! That's *enough*! Oh, gee, Dad, pull me up a bit, quick!"

Aunt Isabelle whispered: "I can bear no more!" and melted into the darkness outside. Sue clenched her teeth, and thrust the torch lower. "Oh, darling, *do* hurry up!" she besought. "Henry, *do* hold him tight!"

But now, from the abyss, came a shout of triumph.

"Goт ɪт! Okay, Dad, you can haul me up now."

Aunt Isabelle met them at the kitchen door. She informed them that she was filling the copper with water, and lighting a fire beneath it. When the water was hot, Tony would kindly take a bath, to which she would add some disinfectant. Before entering the bath, however, he would be so good as to place the instrument (no, no, she did not want to see it, God forbid!) in the copper, where she would boil it for an hour. Better, for two hours. She rejoiced that he had once more his fife, and would thus be enabled to pursue his musical studies; but for herself, she was no longer young enough to support such incidents, and she would recommend that, in order to foil any further wickedness on the part of that Joy there, a strong catch be affixed high on the door of the *cabinet*. She then returned to the copper, and as Tony entered the house behind his parents, Henry barked at him:

"Don't you bring that revolting thing inside! Leave it on the step."

"Yes, Dad," said Tony, a model of docility.

In the living-room the brandy was still on the table. Without a word, Sue brought their glasses, and Henry poured it—straight. Tony was offered lemonade again, and this time affably accepted. He beamed at them over its rising bubbles.

"Gee, Dad, it worked well, didn't it?"

"It worked," said Henry.

"Thanks for helping me get it back, Dad. Thanks, Mum."

" Don't mention it, darling," said Sue, sprawled in her chair, and half raising her glass to him. " A ple-easure."

It was almost a hiccup, and she began to giggle weakly. Henry gave her a stern look, and said : " You're drunk, old girl."

Tony, advancing eagerly to stare, demanded with interest : " Is she, Dad ? Is she really dr . . . ? "

" *No!* " wailed Sue. " I'm only te-erribly tired ! . . ."

" Tony," commanded Henry, " go to your bath."

" Okay, Dad," said Tony, and went, with wondering backward glances.

So when faint, sweet sounds of distant piping are heard, we are all thankful to know that the music so nearly lost to us was saved, and that presently we shall see Tony coming buoyantly down the Lane, treading on air, his fife (two hours boiled) at his lips, and his clouds of glory trailing behind him. He has *Sweet and Low* to perfection now, and he is learning, at Henry's suggestion, *Safely, Safely Gathered In.*

The Deviation (2)

ONE DAY the word went round that surveyors were busy with their instruments on the main road half a mile short of Dillillibill. Aub Dawson saw them first, and reported that they looked decent enough blokes, but his grudging tone suggested that he was reserving his opinion, and could give no positive guarantee that they were not concealing horns, hoofs and forked tails.

Although these activities had no apparent connection with the Lane, we felt bothered. Perhaps this was because they had no apparent connection with anything else either. If we could have seen them as a first stage in straightening operations, later to be extended in our direction, and finally past our doors, they would have been, though upsetting, at least comprehensible. We should have known what we were worrying about. But just there the ridge is a veritable razor-back, and Nature has quite clearly ordained where the road is to go. Theoretically, it is two chains wide; but that, of course, is nonsense, and has always been treated as such by those whose properties debouch upon it. If it were indeed so constructed, its edges would pass on the one side through Bert Hall's front verandah, and on the other behind the Robertsons' packing-shed; and since it could hardly be supported, as these structures are, upon wooden stumps, it would necessarily float on air.

So, being unable to account for the presence of surveyors at this spot, we suffered from that vague uneasiness, that wobbling of common sense, which mystery occasions. We began to talk once more of The Deviation, sturdily agreeing that this strange visitation could not possibly have anything to do with us, but wondering, all the same, whether it might be a cunning ruse— a feint before springing on our Lane.

But to our amazement, it was observed that white pegs appeared, indicating that men with machines at their disposal are irresistibly stimulated by the thought of achieving the difficult, even if it be, also, the unnecessary. They were in no hurry, however. Having done their part, the surveyors disappeared, and three months passed peacefully without further official developments, though Kelly knocked out one of the pegs one night when Ken was coming home from a party, and a couple more vanished when the bank slipped during a heavy downpour, and a fourth was discovered in the Bells' backyard. Small boys are always bringing extraordinary things home, and as a matter of fact Gwinny found it quite useful as a wedge under her copper-stand.

Then, dramatically, men and machines appeared, and set to work with furious zeal. For a couple of hundred yards the road became a waste of deeply churned earth, guarded at either end by signs enjoining CAUTION and proclaiming MEN AT WORK. With vast labour, and the expenditure of a sum which, no doubt, would have exceeded the combined annual income of the Lane, the road actually was deflected four inches to the right in one place, and six inches to the left in another, thus eliminating a curve whose existence we had not noticed until then.

Bert Hall and Tom Robertson were a bit browned off about having to put in the best part of a day reorganising their car entrances—but they admitted it might have been a great deal worse. In fact Tom said he felt pretty safe now about having his packing shed on the road, because they weren't likely to start mucking around there again for a long time.

Sombrely we saw the men and the machines depart. The

incident was closed. Nothing had happened to us, and the inscrutable purposes of officialdom remained hidden in a Sphinx-like silence. Yet we were once more assailed and unnerved by thoughts of change. "Imagine that sort of thing in the Lane," said old Mrs. Hawkins, shaking her head. "It doesn't bear thinking of."

Nelson

AT PICANINNY daylight all the kookaburras laugh together, and all the farmers wake.

A little later, Nelson comes in from the west, flying low over the Hawkins' pines as he swoops up the hill. No one knows exactly where he lives, but he always appears from somewhere in the patch of scrub at the south end of the Sports Ground, and vanishes in the same direction when dusk is falling. The Lane is his daytime beat, and he commutes to and fro as regularly as a clerk travelling between city office and suburban home.

He flies swiftly eastward, and alights on the electric light pole outside the Bells' gate. This pole stands on the Lane's highest hillcrest, and its top is gilded as soon as the sun rises out of the ocean sixteen miles away, and far below. It is thus an excellent perch for a nippy winter morning, but it has, for Nelson, two other advantages: firstly, it is the best place from which to survey his territory; and secondly, it is right beside his breakfast.

Here, then, he sits for a while, fluffing out his feathers the better to enjoy the sunshine before embarking on the business of the day. Like all kookaburras at rest, he is a picture of placid inertia—motionless, ruffled and rather portly, with his great beak sunk pensively upon his breast. Not for him the restless hoppings, the alert head movements, the wild and wary sideways glances of other birds; he might almost be asleep. But his one round, brown eye is wide open, and observant; let a cricket stir a whisker in the grass, and—though he may, or may not be on to it with deadly speed and precision—he will know that it is there.

At this time of the morning he will usually ignore it, for he likes to begin the day with a good meal, and he knows that there is something more substantial than a cricket waiting for him nearby. So he saves the keen edge of his appetite for this, and addresses himself to his regular morning inspection of the Lane.

Very pleasant it looks, too. Most of the scene is still in shadow, but while he watches, the climbing sun touches the taller tree-tops, and then the ridge-poles of several houses built upon high ground. Presently, glinting along stretched wires, it makes its way from his own pole to the next, shedding a few beams in passing on long branches thrust up by the lantana to intercept it. Where the road dips, the wires elude it, but it leaps the gap, finds them again on the next hill, and runs along them, claiming more and more of the trees as it goes, and scattering light over the lantana walls, until, on the upward slope beyond Herbie Bassett's, it slides down another pole and comes to earth, painting a narrow strip of road with glowing red. Nelson watches this benevolent invasion from on high, and basks in its increasing warmth.

As yet there are no human sounds, but the Lane is far from silent. There is a good deal of complacent cackling going on in the fowlyards, Joe Hardy's Butch is barking, and the Achesons' Lassie is tirelessly mooing her detestation of the fences which separate her from the Hawkins' bull. Down in the scrub along the creeks the whip-birds are calling; a magpie is carolling away with full-throated abandon somewhere behind the Dawsons' house; and two butcher-birds in the Bells' hibiscus tree are spilling out notes like glittering drops of water. Nelson hears all this vocalism with composure, for he is not without his own talent, whose exercise has earned him greater fame than theirs.

He is, in any case, more concerned with his human neighbours. He likes to know in good time what they are all likely to be up to during the day, for many of their activities concern him closely. It is always worth while following anyone who has a spade in his hand; scythes and rakes, too, mean disturbance of the grass, and of the small, edible things that live in it. Most

rewarding of all are ploughs and rotary-hoes; he answers the
sound of these as though it were a dinner bell, and indeed, from
some convenient fence-post on the edge of the freshly-turned
earth, it is an acre of dinner-table that he surveys with his one
watchful eye, and a meal of many courses that he swoops down
to snatch.

So now he looks westward along the dipping, curving stretch
of road, and begins his observations at the Hawkins' place on the
corner. There he can see Bill crossing the paddock, bucket in
hand, to milk—and wading, it would appear, knee-deep in
diamonds, for the grass is drenched with dew, and the sun has
just reached it. But neither milk nor diamonds means a thing to
Nelson; nor is he interested in old Mrs. Hawkins, who is
emptying a teapot out the kitchen window. He has nothing to
hope from Uncle Cuth, either, whom he can see across the road,
pottering about in Joe's fowlyard. He notes with annoyance that
Tim Acheson is getting ready to spray his pines—for spraying is
something which Nelson simply loathes. Herbie Bassett is, as
usual, sitting on his verandah steps, staring, and Nelson hardly
gives him a glance—having come to regard him as being merely
a feature of the landscape. At the Kennedys' no one is visible
yet, but since Nelson will spend most of his time there later in the
day, his gaze does not linger now. Instead, it crosses the road
again to the Griffiths', where Sue is pegging some clothes out
on the line, and Henry is tinkering with his ute, and Aunt
Isabelle is standing beside him explaining what is wrong. Nelson
observes all this with indifference, but his eye pauses for a
moment, rather coldly, on Jake who is plunging around among
the spinach for a stick which Tony has thrown for him. Not that
Nelson is afraid of dogs—or of anything else except, possibly,
eagles—but he has reached a mature age, and he finds it tiresome
to be leapt at, and barked at, when he is busy with something on
the ground, so he visits the Griffiths rarely, briefly, and very
watchfully.

By now his researches have brought him almost level with his
own pole, and Aub Dawson, emerging from his packing shed,

sees him, and calls genially: " Kook ! Kook ! " Nelson cuts him dead. Aub has a habit of throwing him morsels of corned beef, sausage, cooked meat and even bread ; this is not the kind of human being one wastes time on. So he hops round on his perch to look for Ken Mulliner, who is erratic in his contributions but, when he throws anything, throws a generous and juicy lump of steak. Ken is just coming round the corner of his house, but it is immediately obviously that he is making for Kelly, where he will spend anything from an hour to a whole morning with his head inside the bonnet, so Nelson makes a little movement which is near enough to a shrug, and hops round again to see what the Arnolds are doing. And, to his intense satisfaction, Dick is carrying a can of petrol over to his rotary-hoe.

Nelson now has his day mapped out. As soon as he has break-fasted he will do some hunting in the wake of the rotary-hoe, and when he is tired of that he will look in on the Kennedys who are sure to have something tasty for him ; a dead mouse, perhaps, fresh from the trap. After that he will cruise around for a while to see what he can pick up. It is getting warm enough now for the snakes to come out, and he has a fancy not only for the gastronomic pleasure these afford, but for the excitement of closing his beak on their necks, fighting their wriggling resistance, exerting the full power of his wings to bear them aloft into a tree, and there methodically bashing them against a branch. Later he will return to the Kennedys' and pass the rest of the afternoon there, following them around ; for one does not live by meat alone, and they provide, as well, conversation and most agreeable homage.

Now he can turn his attention to breakfast. He hops round once more to face north, and directs his gaze downward at the Bells' house, almost beneath his beak. Alf, Tristy and Gally are visible picking pines in the middle distance, but Ding, Dong and Lynette are on the verandah, squabbling about something. It is time for Nelson to receive attention, so he announces his presence with a few casual clucks. They are too occupied with their own affairs to take any notice of him, but EElaine, coming out to make the beds, catches sight of him, pokes her head in at the door, and calls : "Mu-um! Nelson's here." Nelson settles down patiently to wait, but he has not waited long before Gwinny comes bustling out with her hands full of big, red lumps of meat which she lays side by side on the verandah rail. She is, as always, very busy, so she merely gives him a glance, and calls out hospitably : "Come on, Nelson! Here you are! Kook! Kook!" before bustling indoors again.

Nelson sails down and begins his breakfast. He picks up each piece neatly, bashes it on the rail, swallows it, and hops along sideways to the next. The lumps do not really need bashing ; he employs this technique partly from force of habit, and partly because the meat provided by humans differs from that which he catches for himself in that it sticks to the beak. Sometimes it sticks so obstinately that, before he can free it, he has to bash it many times, and shake his head with a violence which makes his beak rattle like castanets.

By now the children's squabble has ripened, and bedlam reigns on the verandah. Ding and Dong, locked in combat, are reeling from one bed to another, entangled in sheets and blankets, and Lynette is swiping at them both with pillows. EElaine, justly incensed at finding herself thus hampered in her morning task, is fiercely berating them, and slapping at any bare legs she can reach. But Nelson is well accustomed to this kind of thing, and takes no notice until a pillow grazes him, and almost knocks him off his perch as it flies past to fall on Gwinny's bed of lettuce seedlings. He regains his balance with a swift threshing of his wings, and EElaine cries accusingly : "There! Look what you've done! You've scared poor Nelson!" The children freeze, momentarily smitten by compunction ; but poor Nelson is already dealing with another bit of meat, and shows no sign of being disturbed by anything except its adhesive quality, so Ding declares robustly : "Aw, don't be so wet! Nelson doesn't care!"

But in this he is wrong. Nelson will put up with commotion if he must, but he prefers peace and quiet. So when he comes to the last mouthful he carries it back to his pole and, having bashed and swallowed it, sits there for a brief, post-prandial rest, sunning himself, and puffing his plumage out until he looks so round, soft and cuddlesome that he might have come out of a toy shop.

However, there is work to be done, and soon his feathers subside, his fluffiness gives way to a smoother, sleeker outline, his beak lifts and stretches forward, and his keen eye stares attentively over the Arnolds' roof; he no longer looks placid and amiable, but purposeful and predatory. Suddenly, with a thrust of his claws, a flap, a flutter and a flash of blue from his wings, he is off, arrow-straight, towards the sound of the rotary-hoe.

Nobody knows how long Nelson has lived in the Lane. One kookaburra is very like another, and he may have been around, unnoticed and anonymous, for years before the loss of his right eye transformed him into a recognisable individual. Gwinny says she can remember him when Ding and Dong were born, so he must be at least eleven. How much older than that a kookaburra can be, we have no idea, for we are not strong on ornithology; truth compels the admission that we are not even sure whether he is a he or a she. But what does that matter? The point is that no one could possibly refer to a creature so bursting with personality as It.

Since such quiz questions as the kookaburra's average expectation of life, and the manner of determining its sex, must be of interest to all intelligent persons, we are always saying to each other that we must look these things up, and it is quite possible that Bruce Kennedy may actually do so some day. But The Kookaburra is one thing, and Nelson is quite another. He is one of the neighbours, a fellow-resident of the district, and it seems natural to accept him as such, without impertinent probings into matters of this kind. Nevertheless, he does inspire other questions which really exercise our minds; but the trouble about these is—as Marge Kennedy complains—that it would be useless to seek the answers in books, because experts have a way of telling you everything about their subject except what you are fairly burning to know.

We wonder, for instance, what the other kookaburras think of Nelson. Do they approve of the extent to which he fraternises with us ? Of course they too, like all their kind, treat us with a good deal of familiarity, and Nelson is by no means the only fence-post sitter when the soil is being turned over. No member of this large and popular family will hesitate to approach a human who demonstrates goodwill by throwing a titbit ; nor upon rather closer acquaintance, decline to perch upon a knee, or accept a gift from friendly fingers. But Nelson goes so much further that he makes his relations appear, by comparison, quite stand-offish, and consequently we ask ourselves (having no one else to ask) whether they regard him, perhaps, as one who has carried traditional mateiness too far ? When they see him fly through the Kennedy's kitchen door, and emerge ten minutes later looking almost indecently replete, do they envy him the largesse he has received, or do they mutter among themselves of quislings and collaborationists ? Do they admire the confidence with which he alights on the toe of Bruce Kennedy's boot, and the nonchalant skill with which he remains there even when it begins to walk about—or do they look down their beaks and say to each other that there is such a thing as dignity, and you can be gracious without making a clown of yourself ?

And of course we should like to know how he lost his eye ; but we never shall. Perhaps it was in a fight ; or perhaps, like Joe Hardy, he got in the way of something during a cyclone. We do not like to admit even the possibility that some degraded human being took a shot at him, but if this was so, he has certainly exacted full compensation since.

Above all, we wonder why there should be between men and kookaburras the curious affinity which Nelson has so remarkably developed and extended in his association with ourselves. Did it always exist ? Were his ancestors as much at home beside the camp fires of our dark predecessors as he and his contemporaries are in our backyards ? Or did they, sitting on high boughs with their heads vigilantly cocked sideways, and observing that our cultivation of the soil turned up many worms and grubs, decide that it might be worth while to establish cordial relations ? Did they recognise our muskets as being more lethal than boomerangs, and reflect that the best defence against someone who possesses a horror-weapon is to make friends with him ? Kookaburras are extremely sagacious birds, and we think this very likely.

Whatever the reason, it must be a potent and subtle magic they have worked upon us since 1788 and all that. For have we not passed over the gorgeous parrot, the stately brolga, the sapphire-eyed bower-bird, the towering emu, the majestic eagle, and even that fabulous virtuoso of song and dance with the lyre-shaped tail, to find our *genius loci* in this plump, grey fowl which we at first called by the opprobious name of Jackass ? He must possess some necromantic art—and of course he does. He can laugh.

Secure in the knowledge that no one can contradict us, we relate that one morning when the mists were rising from the harbour where the First Fleet lay at anchor, a nameless marine espied a kookaburra on a branch, and raised his musket to his shoulder. His finger, crooked over the trigger, was just about to tighten when he observed a pulsing in its white throat, and heard a sound, half-chuckle and half-cluck, which grew louder and louder, faster and faster while the pulsation gathered strength and speed to match, and the powerful beak lifted and lifted till it pointed at the sky. The sound and spectacle of this preposterous bird as it sat there shaking from beak-tip to tail-tip with enjoyment of some private joke caused the stupefied marine to relax his trigger finger ; for although he was not, by the standards of 1788, a gentleman, and would have shot a sitting bird without compunction, he hesitated (not being particularly hungry at the moment) to shoot a laughing one.

Later, when he and his compatriots became very hungry indeed, anything went into the cooking pot, including the Jackass, who was contributing the only laughter heard just then. But because that laughter was the strangest sound in a strange place, it was

already identified more closely than any other with the land—
and this, no doubt, was the first stage of our bewitchment. From
that moment we were spellbound. For it was a sound growing
familiar as the place lost strangeness; a sound accepted as the
place became a home; and thus, at last, the very voice of a place
beloved.

Small wonder, then, that Nelson has us all by the short hairs—
especially the Kennedys.

When they first arrived he was sitting on the corner of their
verandah roof, so he had an excellent opportunity to study them
before they were even aware of his existence. It is probable that
he unerringly recognised them as the most promising pair of
suckers who had ever entered his territory, and certain that he
set out to woo them without delay.

It was a pushover. Now he has only to appear, and they drop
whatever they are doing, and hasten to the fridge where, in a
special receptacle, his food supply awaits his pleasure. He takes
up his position on the porch railing outside the kitchen door—
craning his head so that his good eye can see round the corner—
and watches the preparation of his meal with some slight impatience. Bruce often causes unconscionable delay by warming
the semi-frozen meat in hot water, and Marge makes altogether
too much fuss about cutting it up; does he not swallow a plump
mouse whole, and can he not get a smallish snake down in two
minutes flat? But at last, when they are finished with all this
nonsense, he flies in on to the table, and picks the morsels
delicately from their fingers. Should one stick to his beak, they
are quick to release it for him; should a shake of his head send
a broken-off fragment flying across the room to slap wetly on a
wall or a window-pane, they rush to retrieve it, and offer it again;
should he miss a scrap because it is lying on his blind side, they
assiduously push it into his line of vision. He knows as well as
anyone in the Lane when it is meat-day, for then Marge cuts his
portion from their own piece of steak, and Nelson lives in hope
that he may some day get off with the whole two pounds. He
makes a bold effort now and then; so far Marge has always

grabbed it back in time, although—with his claws braced against
the edge of the table, his strong wings flapping and his formidable
beak gripping like a vice—he makes her work for it. Bruce
(who never descended to baby-talk for his children) calls him by
absurd pet names, and offers him quite unnecessary encouragement by uttering peculiar, clucking noises. When he elects to
dine on Marge's knee, she babbles the most preposterous
endearments, and allows him to bash his meat on her skirt.

It is true that Bruce is often torn between his slavish devotion
to Nelson, and his strong regard for earthworms. From his
reading in the science of agronomics he has learned that a rich
acre may support a worm population of up to eight millions, and
he has also noted Darwin's estimate that these industrious
creatures will, in congenial conditions, deposit upon the surface
of the ground no less than ten tons of worm-casts per acre per
year. Being Bruce, he of course did the sum which these two
bits of data clearly inspire; but when he told Marge the result
of his calculations, she said she thought one-twentieth of an
ounce per worm, per acre, per year was nothing to write home
about. Bruce explained severely that this was a point of merely
academic interest; jeer as you might at the achievement of one
solitary worm, the fact remained that eight million worms constituted free earth-moving equipment by means of which nitrogen,
potash, phosphate, pre-digested humus and what have you were
placed where they would do most good. Consequently, when he
sees something pink wriggle in the earth turned up by his spade,
he glances furtively around at the adjacent trees and fence-posts,
and buries it again with all haste. But if Nelson finds his own
worm, Bruce philosophically adopts a neutral position, and
watches the contest with mixed feelings. For it must be understood that our worms are fine, muscular specimens up to two feet
long, and they do not yield without a struggle. Nelson, with one
end in his beak, digs his claws hard into the ground, leans backward, and pulls; the exposed portion of the worm stretches like
a string of pink rubber, but underground the rest of it keeps a
determined hold upon Mother Earth, and suddenly contracts with

a power that jerks Nelson forward on to his beak. He braces himself again, and the tug-of-war continues ; but the worm never wins. Sometimes it breaks in two, and the submerged half makes its escape while Nelson is busy with the rest ; this may fairly be called a draw. But more often Nelson is triumphant, and Bruce, seeing his humble, subterranean ally vanish inch by inch down the victor's throat, sadly accepts the fact that one-twentieth of an ounce of his topsoil will not be what it might have been.

Thanks to the Kennedys' hospitality, Nelson has learned much about the hazards to be encountered in houses. He has never forgotten how the back of a canvas chair swivelled under his weight, and shed him on the floor ; and he mistrusts newspapers, too, for a surface which looks quite solid may prove to be otherwise if it is projecting over the edge of a table. He is profoundly suspicious of basins, having perched on the edge of one which tipped up, and flooded him with milk, and upon another occasion, alighted in water hot enough to be uncomfortable. He also takes care that windows are really open before he flies through them, for he jarred his beak badly the day he cracked a pane of glass. There was one trying period when he almost decided to abandon the Kennedys altogether. This was when Marge was doing some painting, and it is debatable whether her nerves or Nelson's were the more sorely tried when he came in to land upon sticky window-sills. It was but natural that his own discomfort, as well as her agitated cries and gestures, should make him seek another perch as quickly as he could, but this often made her behave more strangely than ever ; to this day you can see, if you look closely, traces of his white footprints upon many of her possessions.

On the other hand, he has discovered that there is no more agreeable roost for a cold morning than a freshly-filled teapot with a cosy over it. Smoke-oh at the Kennedys' is apt to be complicated by this fact, for the cordial warmth seeping up through his down makes Nelson feel comatose, and he pays no attention when Marge asks him to move, so that she may pour a second cup for Bruce.

" Look, Nelson," she pleads, " get off, will you ? "

He blinks his one eye at her sleepily. She waves her hands in despair and cries.

" *Get off*, Nelson ! Shoo ! "

He settles himself more comfortably, and his beak nestles deeper into his fluffy breast. What a shame to disturb him ! She says grudgingly to Bruce :

" Well, if you really *do* want another cup, you'll have to lift him off, that's all."

And Bruce—poor doting ninny—replies quickly that he really doesn't.

About sundown Nelson calls it a day. But before he makes for home he usually joins a couple of his friends for a while on one of the electric light poles—and what passes between them we only wish we knew. There are confidential clucks, low gurgles of disbelief, more clucks, and a few throaty chuckles ; can he be telling anecdotes about us ? We have an uneasy suspicion that, if this is so, we appear in them less as lords of creation, awesome and powerful, than as comical creatures devoid of either wisdom or repose, but well-meaning enough, and eminently exploitable. At all events, he—or one of his companions—or some aunt or cousin elsewhere in the Lane—suddenly begins to laugh. Since nothing is more infectious than laughter, this naturally starts all the others laughing too. From everywhere within earshot they join in, lifting their beaks towards the golden sky, and releasing in chorus the wild, ripe, strident voices whose ribald joviality is a sly satire on the mellifluous notes of other birds. The air rings and shakes with hilarious sound until one subsides into ruminative chuckles, and then a second, and then a third ; and just as the last is recovering his gravity, the first is seized by another paroxysm which sets the whole chorus going at full strength again.

But the sun is setting ; it is almost down behind the Hawkins' house. Gradually they fall into silence, and one by one they fly away. The echoes of their laughter fade, leaving a hush soon to be broken by the sad cry of the mo-poke.

There goes Nelson, passing over Herbie Bassett's roof with a last ray of sunlight gilding his wings as he banks to turn towards the scrub. Now he is skimming low above the Hawkins' pines where the ground dips into shadow ; and now, grey in the grey twilight, he is gone.

But he will be back to-morrow to levy tribute on the Lane.

The Quick Return

THE POSITIVELY anti-social recklessness of those who deliberately go in for small farming has, we think, no parallel in human behaviour. It may be likened to the irresponsibility of artists, but it surpasses even this in impudence ; for whereas no artist expects more than a few ha'pence and some kicks, these would-be, must-be and will-be farmers actually believe that the world owes them a living, and expect to get it.

The thing is still more amazing when it manifests itself in the young, who are nowadays afforded every opportunity to learn that he who engages in small-scale and solitary effort, does so at his peril. We live, as our mentors so frequently remind us, in an era of expansion. Commerce and industry extend their operations, organisations multiply, and science reaches into outer space, thus setting the pattern which faithfully repeats itself in all our products and activities. Transport increases its capacity, and moves faster, buildings climb higher, newspapers grow fatter, roads grow wider, crowds grow bigger, problems grow tougher, cars grow longer, bangs grow louder and prices shoot ever higher, with wages in hot pursuit. In short, our age is content with nothing less than the super-colossal.

In such a society the properly instructed young person will do well to examine very narrowly the type of toil to which he commits himself. He will, if he is fully in tune with the times, eschew primary production altogether, for the greatest honours and rewards are undoubtedly reserved for the handlers ; but if he must engage in production of this kind, it is imperative that he should produce a lot. If he is prepared to weigh in with ten thousand bushels of wheat, or five hundred bales of wool, he will deserve—and receive—the support of a benevolent Government, and the plaudits of a grateful public ; but these are not to be expected by one who contributes a few crates of pineapples, or a few bags of beans. There is nothing super-colossal about that.

Similarly, if you let loose upon the world some fruit of your mind which proves tasty to vast numbers of other minds, you may win acclaim, and even some pecuniary advantage ; but the provision of nourishment for the few—however wholesome it may be, and however great their hunger—is a dilletante occupation which modern society regards with disfavour and suspicion.

For this there is good reason. The small-scale production of sustenance—whether mental, physical or spiritual—exposes the producer to certain subversive influences—namely, nature and solitude. These influences render him quite unfit for useful participation in the affairs of an advanced civilisation, for they make him think, and wait, and stare, and dream. The small farmer works alone, and thus communes a good deal with nature, in whose leisurely habits he necessarily acquiesces, since he cannot command the human and mechanical assistance by means of which the big farmer goads her into brisker activity. And the small artist—such as, for example, Shakespeare, Beethoven or Michelangelo—betakes himself to a solitary tower (which may, or may not be constructed of ivory, but in which, contrary to general opinion, he works like a beaver, and undergoes peculiar torments), and there coolly assumes that if he needs a year to achieve the right word, note or line, then a year he must have.

Can you imagine such presumption ? What makes small-scale activity so undesirable and dangerous is clearly the solitude it involves, and the temptation, inherent in solitude, to think. For thinking takes time, and in an expanding era the one thing which contracts is time. There is simply not enough of it for profitless nonsense of this kind. To do is recognised as the aim and duty of all good citizens ; to be is something that could exercise the mind of none but an irresolute mooncalf like Hamlet. To know how is the hallmark of merit ; to wonder what, why or whether is little short of sabotage. The proper study of mankind is not man, but matter, and its rich, abundant fruits may be seen all around us, from plastic dish-mops in the kitchen to Sputniks in the sky. And though we are already indebted for so much to those who pursue this study, our expanding society does not yet permit them to rest upon their laurels, but, like the Red Queen, tirelessly urges them forward, crying : " Faster ! Faster ! " But perhaps this is not a happy simile, for the Red Queen was getting nowhere at all, whereas know-how is well on the way to the planets, and may be expected to set its civilising mark quite soon upon those backward areas.

One might reasonably suppose that the splendour and spacious-ness of such an age could not fail to capture the allegiance of all young persons, and render the notions of growing spinach, or writing poems quite ludicrous to them. Heaven knows, we have spared no effort in demonstrating that only suckers make and grow, but clever people handle. It is disturbing, therefore, to find that some still entertain and even succumb to, such atavistic impulses ; and among the mature, as they faithfully pursue more useful avocations, one discovers an astonishing number of frustrated farmers and artists. This might be cause for serious alarm if one did not feel secure in the corrective power of modern environment.

There is, of course, one small problem whose solution as yet eludes us ; if there were no suckers to do the primary producing, there would be nothing for the clever people to handle. In a defeatist moment, one might envisage our society all organised some morning to proceed with its handling of the primary produce—and lo, there is none ! The shops are open, the assistants are present, the middlemen are at their posts, the trains, trucks, ships and factories, all suitably manned, are waiting, and the housewives are setting out with their baskets—but where are the fruit and vegetables ? . . . Where are the eggs and butter ? . . . The entrepreneurs are in their offices, the editors and publishers are at their desks, the paper-supply—all the way from standing forest to retail stationer—is being attended to, the paints, pianos and typewriters are provided, the concert-halls, theatres and galleries are prepared, the radio networks are ready to give out, the technicians are adjusting their mysteries, and the announcers are clearing their throats—but where are the stories and symphonies ? . . . Where are the songs and statues ? . . . Where are the plays and pictures ? . . . Is this a strike ?

Certainly not. Suckers have no idea of collective action. Their tendency to break ranks and march off by themselves quite precludes any such thing. They are notorious for their perverse and tiresome independence, and you simply cannot get them organised. No, no ; it is not a strike. It is the triumph of the *zeitgeist*. Like the dinosaurs and the pterodactyls, these dopes have failed to mesh with their environment—and they are gone. We are all handlers now, and while we look around for something to handle, we hear the ominous hiss of escaping air as our expanding age begins to collapse like a punctured balloon. . . .

But this is mere fantasy—a nightmare unworthy of the civilised mind. Science is at the controls, and will steer us safely to wherever we are going. As a temporary measure it will, no doubt, permit farming only upon a super-colossal scale, but we may rest assured that in due course it will devise means of producing all foodstuffs in its laboratories. And it will surely toss off (for even scientists have their playful moments) a machine to deliver works of art as needed—and not unsettling ones, either, like those we have been compelled to put up with in the past.

Thus reassured, and able to confront without too much apprehension the knowledge that suckers still infest the earth, we may turn once more to Lantana Lane, which harbours as many to the acre as any spot in the world ; and among them, we regret to say, Tim and Biddy Acheson, who are young enough to know better.

Some future author of a thesis upon the decline and fall of

suckerdom will eagerly seize upon Tim as one whose life provides an interesting case history in illustration of the transition stage. For Tim did not yield without a struggle to the fatal tendencies which at last landed him in the Lane. Having—in common with his contemporaries—clearly grasped the truth that whatever else one may be, one must not be a sucker, he valiantly suppressed the disreputable urges which he could feel clamouring within him, and became a bank clerk.

It must be evident to anyone that banking is the last word in handling. Other individuals or organisations may handle the primary produce at one, or two, or five, or ten removes, but banks handle what may be termed the produce of the handlers, and are thus the very apex of civilisation. Tim was, therefore, potentially one of the *élite*. He had a respectable position at a respectable salary in the most respectable of all human institutions, and he could look forward to a respectable future, with the probability of advancement to considerable heights of dignity and affluence. But he relapsed into suckerdom.

Perhaps if he had not been assigned to a branch in a rural district, this might not have happened ; but as it was, there were farms all about him, and even from his post at the teller's window he could see through the plate glass opposite a glimpse of pineapples growing on a distant hillside. . . .

But surely, you will say, shocked, he also saw something of farmers' current accounts ? True. He did, and what he saw kept him warily anchored to his counter for eight long years. But he went on looking at the pineapples, and his suckerdom—quelled, but not yet slain—went on whispering to him its age-old arguments. He needn't be rash ; he could save up, and *then* have a go. . . . He'd find a nice little place (a bit run down, for preference so that the price would not be too high), and he'd be able to put down the whole lot in cash (or very nearly all of it), so that he wouldn't start with a debt on his shoulders (or only a very small one), and he'd see that he had a few hundred in reserve to tide him over the first year or two, and he'd work like Hell, and it was a grand, healthy life, and you were your own boss, and with a cow, and hens, and home-grown fruit and vegetables you could live cheaply. . . .

In due course he found himself a girl called Biddy who had a dash of suckerdom in her too, and explained all this to her while she listened, starry-eyed. So they both saved up, and dreamed of the day when they would be married, and live on a little farm of their own.

Here they were, then, at last, in Lantana Lane. Their farm had three acres of citrus—two of which (one of oranges and one of grapefruit) had only recently come into bearing; there were three acres of pineapples (though one of these was overdue for replanting), and there was an eastern slope where bananas would do well some day. Except for the cow-paddock and the fowlyard, the rest was under lantana, but Tim planned to use it for avocadoes later on. He said he liked to have several different crops, because if you didn't catch a good market with one, you were sure to with another. There was a permanent creek, so they would be able to irrigate when they could afford to put in pipes and spray-lines and a pump. There was also a good Jersey cow, and she was in calf; Tim, as an ex-banker, named her Currency Lass, but they called her Lassie for short. Biddy fell in love with her, and so did Tim, though he preferred to stress the point that any heifer calves she produced would fetch a good price. The house . . . well, Biddy thought it could be made quite nice in time, with a new stove, and the white-anted floorboards replaced, and some new guttering, and plenty of paint.

The older citrus trees were fine big ones—and so they should have been, because they had begun bearing twenty years ago, and were now tired of it. Tim was disconcerted when he discovered this, but he consoled himself with the thought of the nest-egg tucked away in his bank account, and reckoned they could get along on what the pines and the new citrus brought in. Meanwhile, he set about the task of abolishing the worn-out trees, and decided to plant avocadoes in their place. He tried grubbing them out, but he soon realised that this was too slow a method to be economically sound, so he told Biddy they would have to plunge, and hire a bulldozer. It had half a dozen other jobs to do first, but it turned up one morning about a month later, and in no time had the whole patch as bare as your hand, and the slaughtered trees all pushed together in heaps for burning. But of course you cannot buy such miracles for nothing, and the bill was no joke. However, as Tim said by way of cheering Biddy— and himself—as he wrote out the cheque, time is money, and if you looked at it that way, they had saved more than they had spent. Biddy darted a sidelong look at her store bill, and wondered how she could pay it with time, but she said nothing.

Tim worked like a slave preparing the new ground, and a good deal more money went into it in the shape of fertiliser, and at last he was ready to replant. But somehow his savings were already dwindling faster than he had expected. As befitted one highly trained in the handling of money, he kept his books with meticulous care, and in the neat columns devoted to expenditure upon cartage, freight, case-timber, wood-wool, rates, telephone rental, sprays, petrol, oil, fence-posts and a new tank, he was able to see how the pounds were melting away. He was not one of those who, at a loss to account for mysteriously vanished pennies and shillings, reserve a kind of desperation-column called Sundry ; he knew exactly how much he had spent upon such trifles as nails, stencil-ink, timber-chalk, a roll of wire, a few screws, a few staples, an axe handle, a bag of lime, a sheet of corrugated iron, a new anchor bolt and a new hinge for the gate. The total looked disturbing when set against the total of his takings.

He therefore thought again about his newly prepared land, considered how much the avocado trees would cost, reflected that it would be a long time before they were producing anything, and decided to put in a small crop which would bring in a quick return. Beans, he told Biddy, were the thing ; you could get wonderful prices for beans in the winter, when it was too cold to grow them down south. And it need not hold up the avocado planting altogether, because they could put some in by degrees, between the bean rows, as they could afford the money and the time.

So he got pamphlets about beans, and studied them carefully, and bought the best certified seed, and laid out half of his acre with the aid of stakes and twine in admirably straight rows the approved distance apart; and that night—yawning mightily—he added bean seed, stakes and twine to his expenditure columns. Then he and Biddy spent two interminable days planting, and went to bed at night with such backaches as they had never known before; but for time spent he made no entry in his book.

While they were waiting for the beans to come up, Tim had plenty of maintenance and development work to do, and he did it with a will, feeling optimistic because the weather was behaving perfectly; it was surprisingly warm for April, and there were two nice little showers—about half an inch each time—which fell on the ground as lightly as a caress. Tim got half the old pines out, and a great pile of planting material ready, and what with this, and picking from the younger plants, and making cases, and packing, and doing a hundred other jobs as well, he and Biddy were hard at it from dawn till dark. But they stole a few minutes to visit the bean patch every day after the seed had been in for a week or so, and were quite excited when they saw the first little green loops pushing through. In another ten days that half-acre was a lovely sight with its fine, straight ribbons of lively green against the red earth. Practically a hundred per cent germination, Tim said jubilantly, which showed that it paid to buy good seed; if the warm weather kept up, and there were showers now and then, this crop would put them on their feet again.

The warm weather did keep up, and when the plants were a few inches high, a westerly wind began to blow from somewhere which was evidently warmer still, for in twenty-four hours the rows had began to look yellowish. It blew for three days, and then Joe Hardy said to Tim across the fence that he might as well give them beans away, because they wouldn't do no good now.

Tim still hoped a drop of rain might save them; in any case, it was time now to begin planting the second half-acre, so he decided to leave the first lot until that was done, and then see how they looked. This time he and Biddy were rather depressed at the end of the planting, and their backaches seemed to hurt more, but Biddy said you couldn't have that kind of bad luck twice, so they soon felt better. They had not been farming long enough to understand that there are enough different kinds of bad luck to last anyone's lifetime.

A week later there was an inch of rain, and this lifted their spirits considerably, for the wind-blighted beans seemed to respond quite gallantly, and Tim said he'd gamble on them, even if Joe Hardy did shake his head every time he looked across the fence. The second planting came up well, and there was no more wind; but there was no more rain, either, and by the middle of June Tim had to admit that the whole acre was looking pretty poor.

Biddy was expecting their first baby, and this is a thing which causes young husbands with dwindling bank balances to do a great deal of anxious thinking, so Tim went down to his creek one morning, stared at all the water running to waste, and thought hard. They had a little car, and when they decided to go on the land, they had bought an old and dilapidated ute for the farm work. The thing to do now was to sell the car, and put in some sort of irrigation. If he did it at once, Tim said to Biddy, they might save those beans yet. After all, they had meant to do it some day, and the sooner the better; it was crazy to think you could farm without irrigation. Then he remembered that he would have to get the ute registered for the road if they were to use it to get about in, and at least one of the tyres would have to be replaced; the thought shot through his mind that there was simply no way you could turn which did not lead straight to the expenditure column, but it was such a small and temporary difficulty to set against a great and permanent advantage, that he shrugged it away. Biddy declared herself enthusiastically in favour of the idea, but she, also was visited by a shooting thought; there would come a moment when Tim would have to take her to the hospital, and the ute—having no hood, and practically no springs—was not the ideal form of transport for such an occasion. But this, also, was a trifle to be shrugged away. She just hoped it would be a fine night.

When they sold the car it did not bring quite such a good price as they had hoped, but, on the other hand, the pump cost less than they had feared, because Tim happened to hear of a man who had a good second-hand one for sale. More disturbing was the fact that these transactions took so long to complete; Tim was by now sharply conscious of the perpetual presence at his elbow of that old, bald sexton, Time. But at last everything was assembled, and he began to set up his irrigation system, slaving at the job like one possessed. It was a great moment when all was ready, and it was only necessary to start the pump; but the pump would not start.

Tim is a fair mechanic by now, having learned the hard way, but in those days he knew little about engines, so he asked Jack's advice, and Jack said the best thing he could do was to get Ken Mulliner to have a look at it. Ken spent the best part of the day tinkering with it, while behind the lantana all along the Lane, the neighbours listened anxiously. When they heard a few half-hearted sputters, they said: "He's got it going." When the sputters ceased, they shook their heads, and said nothing. But there is really not much that the owner of Kelly cannot do in the way of coaxing temperamental engines, and towards evening when the sputtering began with a strong, determined note, and kept on, everyone rejoiced in the knowledge that water was at last falling blessedly on Tim's thirsting beans.

Just after dark, it began to rain.

Tim—half a stone lighter, and looking ten years older than he had a few weeks ago—stood on his verandah with Biddy next morning, watching it come down, and said: "Wouldn't it?" But after all, water is water, whether it comes from an irrigation system or from the sky, and he was glad enough to see it—at first. The difference is, of course, that you can control what comes from pipes, but you just have to take what the sky sends, and the sky, at present, was in a munificent mood. It poured down eight inches in the first twenty-four hours, and six in the second, and six in the third, and then it settled down to rain quietly for another two days. Tim and Biddy put on their gumboots, waded down through the mud to look at their beans, and presently waded back again, not saying much. The second lot had been practically washed out of the ground, but—as Biddy remarked brightly while she made a cup of tea—most of the first lot was still *there*, and might produce a few bushels. . . .

After a while Tim said suddenly :

" There's still time to replant."

" Y-e-es," said Biddy.

" Of course the seed's pretty expensive. . . ."

" And it'd be getting late when they came in. . . ."

" And the market's not so good then. . . ."

" And Amy Hawkins was saying you have trouble with bean-fly when it's warmer. . . ."

But Tim was worried, for there was nothing coming in except from the pines (and that wasn't much), though there seemed to be always plenty going out. Besides, his young orange trees were Sevilles, and everyone said there was not much demand for those ; grapefruit, too, caused more head-shaking than he liked to see. He felt that something had to be done quickly, so he decided to replant the second half-acre of beans. He reminded Biddy that Lassie was due to calve next month, and if the calf were a heifer they could sell it for enough to pay for the extra seed and fertiliser. Biddy said yes, of course, and she didn't remind him that Gwinny had told them all Lassie's calves except one had been bulls.

So Tim replanted. Biddy was not able to work such long hours now, but she did what she could to help, and in due course the beans came up, and promised to flourish quite as wonderfully as their predecessors. By now Tim was looking quite haggard, and would have liked to relax a little, but after the rain the weeds were fairly leaping up from the ground, so he had to start cleaning his pines. He perceived that he must wait till next year to get the avocadoes in; but he could not have paid for them just now, anyhow.

One morning Biddy got up soon after six (she was sleeping in a bit at present), and found Tim getting the mattock and spade from the packing shed. " Lassie's calved," he said, barely looking at her. " It's a bull."

She sat down on a crate and watched him walk away with the tools over his shoulder. Well, she thought, there was no harm in hoping. Then a rather frightening flash of perception told her that the harm—oh, the peril, the disaster, the failure and defeat ! —would be in not hoping. For what else can keep a farmer going ? Maybe the market will improve ; maybe the drought will break ; maybe the rain will hold off for a week or two ; maybe the next lot of case-timber won't be warped, the price of fertiliser will fall, the hares won't get the peas, and the next calf will be a heifer. Maybe.

It was one of those clear, cool, still, dewy, cobwebby mornings that make you think of innocence. Everything about it seemed new, young and tentative ; the sunlight was delicately golden, the shadows long and light, the blue of the sky pale and pure. A butcher-bird in the custard-apple tree was singing a few phrases over and over in an absent-minded undertone, as if it were only half awake. Biddy felt very strange because she was naturally preoccupied just now with her baby, and she found that she could not disentangle her constant awareness of it from all the things she thought, and did, and saw. Consequently, the loveliness of the morning, the malevolence of fate, the thought of Lassie's calf, and the recollection of Tim walking away with the spade and the mattock, were all blended with the consciousness of her own coming maternity in a confusing and oddly heart-piercing manner.

She stood up, and went to the corner of the shed. From here she could see Lassie grazing near the fence of the paddock, with the calf beside her ; she could catch glimpses, too, of Tim's head and shoulders behind a clump of lantana near the adjoining fowl-yard, as he bent and straightened in his digging. She wanted to run away from all this, but she began, instead, to walk slowly down the hill towards it, not even trying to understand her strange feeling of compulsion and despair. When she came to the cow-paddock gate, she saw Tim's .22 rifle leaning against it, and a pair of Willy-wagtails flirting about on the top bar. She turned aside, and walked down along the fence, and Lassie, looking up briefly, acknowledged her presence with a mellow, contralto moo.

The calf, propped unsteadily on its widely-straddled legs, was sucking vigorously, and butting its head against the swollen udder. The wagtails flew down from the gate and perched on Lassie's back, tipping and fidgeting, and peeping down over her flanks at the calf, which presently stopped sucking, and backed away a few steps. It seemed to become aware, for the first time, that there were other things in the world besides the warm body of its mother, and stood gazing earnestly at a rusty tin lying among the grass. It took a few experimental steps towards this curious object, but paused then, and looked back uncertainly, as if mistrustful of its own success. Lassie was oblivious of its mute appeal for reassurance, however, so it accomplished an awkward turn, found its way back to her, and once more thrust its head importunately against her udder. But it was no longer hungry ; having satisfied itself that the one comprehensible fact of its universe was still there, still warm and soft, still provided with available nourishment, it began to circle the cow, keeping very close to her side. Lassie nuzzled it as it rubbed against her nose ; for a moment the two heads were close together, and very alike with their mild faces, and their large, dark, long-lashed eyes.

But the calf was now interested in its legs, their odd behaviour, and the remarkable sensations of locomotion. Suddenly it broke into a clumsy gambol which carried it a full ten yards away, and brought it up in confusion, with its front hoofs inexplicably crossed. It stood rocking, looked down at them with an air of perplexity, and then turned its head enquiringly towards the indifferent cow. Once more ignored, it cautiously lowered its black, twitching nose to the problem, and then jerked it up again sharply as a broken stalk of lantana pricked it. The problem, forgotten, resolved itself, and was replaced by the problem of this hard, injurious substance. The calf stared at it, jumped nervously, backed away, and slowly returned. Its front legs spread themselves widely as its nose went down again, warily explored, lingered for a moment among the blades of dewy grass, and lifted, sniffing, along the broken stem. This brought Biddy into its line of vision ; it stared at her for a long time, and she stared back at it. The pale, biscuit colour of its rough coat shone faintly in the sunlight ; over its knobby forehead the hair lay in moist, irregular waves ; its delicately flaring nostrils, its sensitively twitching ears, its dark, wondering eyes, and the very breath that moved its flanks in a barely perceptible rhythm, seemed to be savouring the promise of life, the miracle of its first—and last— morning.

Biddy turned away, and began to hurry up towards the house as if she were frightened—as indeed she was. She knew all the answers to the wild protest in her heart. You can't keep a bull calf to eat pasture that is only just enough for your milking cow. You can't even leave it with its mother till it is old enough to make veal for the butcher, or for your own table, because what you gained in money or in food would not make up for the milk you lost. You can't spare the time to poddy it when the days are already too short for more productive work. She knew it all, and didn't believe a word of it. Waste, she was saying fiercely to herself as she stumbled up the steps on to the verandah—just wicked waste ! But she was not thinking of veal, or of money ; she was not really thinking at all. She did not even know that she was frightened, and if anyone had been there to ask her what was the matter, she would have replied, very sensibly, that she was just feeling a little upset, and she supposed it was all part of The Business. And so it was. Maternity recognises itself across all divisions. It is a touchy thing, jealous of its inviolability, quick to take fright when it sees life being squandered, passionate in resentment against callous disregard of its long, and solitary ordeal. So Biddy was angry and afraid, though she tried to regain her composure by telling herself that one must not be sentimental about these things. Lassie wouldn't care. Within a few hours she would have quite forgotten the calf. Dairy cows were like that. Everyone said so. (But how did they *know* ? . . .)

Unfortunately all this common sense failed to obliterate from Biddy's mind the picture of a small creature newly ready for life, and trusting in it ; she flung herself face downward on the unmade bed, and when she heard the shot she began to cry as if her heart would break.

But a farmer's wife may not for long indulge in moods and vapours. There is too much to be done. By now they were harvesting the Sevilles and the grapefruit, and while Tim picked, Biddy made cases. She never managed to drive a nail with one tap and one bang, but she could nearly always do it with one tap and two bangs. She also became very expert at packing, and liked to show Tim how, when she ran her hand over the top layer of exactly graded golden globes, not one of them budged.

But perhaps the less said about the citrus the better. Not many people want Seville oranges, but very many are so addicted to juicy, bitter-sweet grapefruit that they will pay quite astonishing sums for them in the shops, and we are therefore unable to explain why Tim, instead of receiving a cheque for this fruit, should have received a bill for the expenses incurred in dumping it. He was naturally disappointed, but he was far too busy to brood over mysteries.

He had been grabbing an hour or two here and there to get ready for his new pines, and the patch was rotary-hoed, and ploughed, and fertilised, and prepared for contour planting. Though Biddy grew tired rather quickly now, she insisted on laying out some of the butts for him when he began to put them in. They were in good spirits, for the weather was really co-operating ; it was warm and sunny, rain had been coming along at nicely spaced intervals, and the beans were leaping ahead.

When the planting was finished, and they stood on their verandah looking out over the farm, they felt quite proud of it.

The bearing pines were as clean as a whistle, and the elegantly sinuous curves of the newly-planted ones were a joy to behold. The magnificent appearance of the new beans almost compensated for the fact that Joe Hardy had been right, and the old ones must be written off as a dead loss. Tim had found time one Sunday to mow down the long grass round the house, and straighten some of the fence-posts, so altogether the place was losing its dilapidated air, and beginning to look like a well-tended, self-respecting little farm.

They were not surprised, or unduly alarmed, when the bean-fly got to work. They were prepared for it, and Tim got to work too, and kept them down with spraying. Of course the spray cost money, and the job took time, and meanwhile the weeds were again beginning to make a green film over the earth between the pinapple rows. At last the flies were routed, the bean plants grew ever sturdier and bushier, and their rich green, much darker now, was liberally besprinkled with white flowers. Soon the flowers were replaced by clusters of tiny beans, and still the weather was perfect, so they grew apace, and Tim's hopes kept up with them. But he was cautious, too ; he halved his order for bean bags—because, after all, he could always get more if he found he needed them. Biddy sat in the shed doing the branding with Tim's stencil, and when that was finished they were all ready for the crop.

Then one day the crop was all ready for them, and they began picking.

" There's no need for you to help," Tim protested. " It'll make your back tired."

" Look," said Biddy mutinously, " I held strings to get those rows straight, and I helped to hoe them, and I went along them putting the fertiliser in, and I went along them again dibbling the holes, and again planting the seed, and again covering it over, and again hilling up the plants, and again keeping the weeds down —and now I'm damn well going along them to pick some beans if it kills me."

So there they both were at daybreak one momentous morning,

stooping over the rows, and moving slowly from plant to plant with their kerosene tins. You never saw such beans. They were fat, and crisp, and long and perfectly straight. Biddy found one which she could lay across the top of her tin, and walked half-way down a row to show it to Tim, and there were many only a little shorter. But no one who has picked beans will be surprised to learn that by half-past eight she said apologetically that she thought she would have to stop for a while. Tim replied that it was time they got some breakfast, anyhow, so they straightened their backs with difficulty, and went up to the house. After break-fast Tim returned to the beans, and Biddy joined him again in the afternoon. They stopped at sundown, and when they had finished their evening meal, and washed up, they took the lantern down to the shed, bagged the beans, and got to bed by ten o'clock. Tim said he thought they should be able to afford to get the electric light connected to the shed in . . . But he was asleep before he could complete the sentence, and Biddy had only time to wonder drowsily whether he meant in a few months, or a few years before she was asleep too. In the morning they put the flag out for Doug Egan to stop, and saw their bags safely loaded on to his truck, and began to talk about how much they would fetch.

But it had been warm down south too, and the bean market was considerably depressed ; so were Tim and Biddy, when their cheque came back. Still, it was something—if not very much when you thought of the time, labour and money which had gone to produce it. The second picking was a little bigger than the first, and the cheque for it was about the same. Then Biddy was not very well for a week or so, and Tim said she was to take it easy, and not do any more picking. But he had to have some help if all the beans were to be got off before they became post-mature, so he hired a youth from Tooloola to give him a hand. When the cheque for this picking came back, and he deducted the youth's wages, and the other costs, he perceived that his profit was very small indeed. The crop was now past its peak, so he picked the next lot alone, and this time, when he came to do his reckoning, it was clear that he was not even squaring expenses. Others in the neighbourhood who had been making similar calculations arrived at a similar conclusion. Both Joe and Alf assured Tim that if he and Biddy liked beans, the best thing they could do now was to eat them, because it wouldn't pay them to send any more to market.

So Tim and Biddy ate beans. Jack Hawkins had tried half an acre, too, so he and his family also ate beans. But even with the best appetite in the world the Hawkins and the Achesons could not eat all the beans those lusty plants were still producing, so everyone in the Lane ate beans, and still there were more going hard and knobby on the stalks. Biddy said rather rebelliously that women in her condition were entitled to food-fads, and what she really wanted was pickled onions ; but she took some more beans, and conceded that they were probably better for It. The last figures in Tim's banks statement were now ominously printed in red, but strangely enough he was more cheerful than he had been for months. It oftens happens this way with suckers. The more you bash them down, the more they bounce, and Tim was already explaining to Biddy why it was quite inevitable that they should have better luck next year.

Biddy need not have worried, of course, about going to the hospital in the ute, because when the time came she could have had her pick of any vehicle in the Lane. It was a very wet night, as it happened, but she went in the Arnold's car quite comfortably, and despite all her anxieties, exertions and afflictions, little Jeremy was as fine an infant as you could see anywhere. For farming is a healthy life ; she had spent much time out of doors, drunk gallons of Lassie's creamy milk, and eaten pounds and pounds of beans.

The Nuts that were Ullaged

DICTIONARIES inform us that ullage is that amount by which a receptacle is short of being full. Some of them stand pat on casks and bottles; they quite ignore such things as crates, cases and bags—thus implying, if we understand them rightly, that it is, though non-existent, always liquid. Others apply the word, rather confusingly, to what is left in the bottoms of wine glasses; but since this would appear to be piling ullage upon ullage, we, for our part, shall stick to dregs.

The lexicographers also allow us a verb *to ullage*—a very versatile verb, for it may mean to calculate the amount of nothing in a vessel, or to replace the nothing with something, or to draw a little of the something off; but by this time its versatility has greatly impaired its usefulness, and we are left with no clear picture of an ullager in action. The verb we use in the Lane is entirely different, and much better. Everyone who sends any sort of produce to market knows that somewhere between its harvesting and its destination it may be, and occasionally is, ullaged. Consequently our verb has just one grimly simple meaning— namely, to pillage what used to be where there is now nothing but ullage. And an ullager is a ... well, we have a number of words to describe ullagers, but not one of them is printable.

The tale we have to tell concerns the ullaging of some Bopple-nuts. It must be understood that although other kinds of nuts have long been seriously grown, seriously investigated by scientific persons, and so seriously regarded by importers, exporters, wholesalers and retailers that the public needs to think very seriously indeed before buying two ounces in a cellophane bag, it has been quite otherwise with these things, which just grow wild. They have always lived in the scrub hereabouts, and of course it is known all over the world that what nature grows at your own back door is hardly worth a glance. Therefore, although Bopplenuts have been eagerly conveyed to other lands, and there grown, harvested, processed, packaged, sold and generally treated with the respect they deserve, they have had but little honour in their own country. This may seem strange until you remember that, owing to the Curse, small farmers have become so accustomed to crops which drive them grey with worry, that they feel a strong mistrust of something which, in its native habitat, just keeps on growing and producing for a lifetime without causing any trouble at all.

Everyone in the Lane has at least a couple of Bopplenut trees—usually in some spot too steep, or too dry, or too wet, or too low, or too high, or too exposed for anything else—but all bear nuts, and if their owners are not too busy with their real crops, they gather these up from the ground and send them to market ; for, as they say indulgently, Bopples are not a bad little sideline.

Bruce Kennedy quite likes his because they supply him with endless statistical material. He can tell you in a moment the relative weights of a gallon in the husk, a gallon in the shell, and a gallon of kernels ; he knows how many nuts go to a pound, how many pounds to a kerosene tin, how many kerosene tins to a bag, and how many bags to a ton. Once, when a cyclone almost stripped his trees of their immature crop, he went down on his knees, counted the little round, green corpses in a square yard, and came up with the intelligence that the total casualties numbered thirty-eight thousand five hundred and forty-six. Marge said coldly that she would have preferred not to know.

Like everyone else, Bruce has a packing-shed which gapes on to the Lane, and in this he has built a rack for his nuts, pending their despatch to market ; it will hold (the figures, of course, are his) three hundredweight, two quarters and nineteen pounds.

One day he looked sharply at this rack, and realised that his nuts were being ullaged.

It was a staggering discovery. Strangers, as we have pointed out, do not come into the Lane, and Lane dwellers do not ullage. Nevertheless, someone had been ullaging, and in order to explain this mystery we must turn, with regret, to the n̖ost juvenile inhabitants.

Tommy Hawkins is a month or two older than Jeremy Acheson, and a couple of months younger than Joy Arnold, and long before they were born their mothers used to say fondly that they would be such nice little playmates for each other. During the time when they were no more than bundles they were, indeed, thrown much together, but the moment they could toddle it became noticeable that they showed a marked tendency to toddle away from each other as fast as they could. Joy preferred the company of older children ; Tommy had his own brothers and —better still—Herbie ; and Jeremy was a child who favoured the contemplative life.

Children frequently mislead their parents, and arouse all kinds of hopes or fears by manifesting, at a tender age, a fierce absorption in some particular pursuit. One will indefatigably collect pebbles, so that his mother feels sure he will become a world-famous geologist ; but no—he turns out to be a restaurant proprietor. Another will display so ardent an interest in bones that it seems certain he will eventually put up a brass plate ; but in the end he takes to dry-cleaning. So we dare not prophesy too confidently that Joy will some day preside over what is known as a mixed business ; we merely state the fact that by the time she was rising four, she had begun to develop a passion for selling things over a counter.

For this it is of course necessary to have customers. The older children were rarely willing to co-operate, so Joy—whose passion was riding her relentlessly at the time we have to deal with— found herself forced back upon her contemporaries, and actually managed to infect them, for a while, with her own enthusiasm.

She perceived that Jeremy was ill-equipped by nature for a role which calls for loquacity and a great deal of spirited haggling, so Tommy was cast as the customer; Jeremy, as his little boy, had nothing to do but stand by and recite at intervals : " Daddy, c'n I have'n ice-cream ? " His little sister, Jennifer, and Keithie Hawkins, were both, at three, too small to be entrusted with any lines, but they made the shop look busier.

Now Joy's father has half a dozen nut trees, and one day when Joy had borrowed the kitchen scales for her shop, and lost the weights, he provided her with a gallon tin, promising her three-pence every time she filled it with nuts ; this, he told Heather optimistically, would keep her out of mischief. Joy was at first unimpressed by the offer, for she was unable to see that real money was much use to her without real shops, and although she did visit the store about once a fortnight, she could not con-template such infrequent spending sprees with much excitement. On the other hand, pretend money was perfectly adequate for pretend shops, and of this she need never be short while there were leaves on the trees or pebbles out in the Lane. But it suddenly occurred to her that she might have her cake and eat it —a prospect which even adults find irresistible—if she collected nuts as pretend money for pretend shops, and later, when a visit to a real shop was imminent, exchanged them for real money.

So she announced to her customer and his hangers-on that henceforward the only currency acceptable to her would be nuts. They protested that leaves were easier, so she was compelled to take them into her confidence, and promise them a rake-off from the vast sums she would receive from her father when they had collected thousands and millions of nuts, and spent them freely on her merchandise. Being simple souls, they agreed to this, diligently searched the ground under their own home trees, and presented themselves at her counter with brimming jam tins and bulging paper bags. Soon—as always happens when money is plentiful—inflation set in, and they found that instead of charging five pennies for a stone representing an iced cake, the rapacious Joy was demanding twenty-six.

But suddenly the nut supply failed. The reason for this was that Amy and Biddy were saving up to buy a Mixmaster between them, and Biddy had suggested that they might as well collect their nuts, and pool the proceeds for this purpose. When they went out with their tins, they were surprised not to find more, until Dave and Daphne explained that the kids had been taking them to play shops with. The mothers only shrugged; for in the Lane pines, oranges and avocadoes are sacred, but no one grudges the children a few nuts as playthings.

Thus Joy found the economic situation dramatically changed. The inflation was over, and a sharp depression had set in. Prices tumbled. You could now buy an iced cake for one penny. When things became so desperate that Tommy began trying to pay in leaves again, she faced disaster, and almost decided to close her shop. At this critical time a new source of supply was discovered by—of all people—Jeremy Acheson.

Wandering down the Lane one day, with Jennifer at his heels, he had spied beneath the Kennedys' packing-shed an empty breakfast-food carton. As all the world knows, these cartons supply the young not only with breakfast, but also with jet aircraft, space-ships, sabre-toothed tigers, fiendish masks, cards with pictures on them, and other things which make them highly prized; so Jeremy naturally lost no time in crawling under the shed to secure this treasure-trove. And what should he find beside it but a nice little heap of nuts. Even as he stared, another nut fell from above. He looked up, and observed a crack between the floorboards which, at one spot, widened to a hole. He poked an enquiring finger into this, and immediately a little stream of nuts descended. He tried again, with a similar result. He takes things as they come, so he did not wonder why nuts should be falling through the floor, but the fact was that he had happened on a rat-hoard.

Rats have such a taste for Bopplenuts that they will employ much time and ingenuity in providing themselves with a cache where they may lay up a supply for future use, and in Bruce's shed they had found arrangements readily adaptable to their purpose. There was a rack nearly full of nuts ; there was a nice, dark corner of it strategically hidden behind a pile of packing-cases ; and directly below this there was a crack in the floor. A creature which can gnaw through the armour-plated shell of a Bopplenut, thinks nothing of gnawing through hardwood, so the crack was easily widened at the appropriate spot ; and with a little more gnawing at the corner of the rack, and a little pushing aside of its wire-netting base, the sagacious rodents were able to exploit the law of gravity in such a manner that their larder was practically self-replenishing. For although a pile of Bopplenuts will come to rest above a small hole, the merest touch from below is enough to release a temporary trickle, and thus the hole in the rack deposited a pile on the floor, from which the hole in the floor shed a pile upon the ground.

But this interesting lesson in natural history was quite lost on Jeremy. He merely filled the carton with nuts, and crawled out with it to rejoin Jennifer, who accepted the miracle with a composure equal to his own.

The moment Joy saw that one of her customers was in the money again, she put her prices up and began to rake in more pennies from Dick. Of course she asked Jeremy where his riches came from, but he replied only with a sweet smile, nor would Jennifer say more than that he had got them from a Nole—which, indeed, was all she knew. But every financier understands that money has no smell, and Joy took the business-like view that so long as she got cash for her goods, it was unnecessary to enquire too closely where it came from. She merely kept a shrewd eye on Jeremy, limiting her demands only by his capacity to pay. When he abandoned jam tins and paper bags, and began to bring his money along in his billy-cart, her prices became astronomical.

Alas, the sudden and ostentatious flaunting of wealth has been the downfall of many crooks. Even the most absent-minded and overworked parents wake up some time, and when Dick discovered one day that both he and Heather had been cleaned right out of small change, it suddenly dawned upon him that there was something odd about this endless stream of nuts. They could not possible have all come from his own trees. And almost simultaneously it dawned upon Bruce that although he threw a kerosene tin full into his rack now and then, it did not seem to be getting any fuller.

Then the fat was in the fire. Joy, hard pressed by Dick and Heather about her source of supply, protested that it had all been acquired by perfectly legitimate trading, and tearfully sought assurances that she was a werry, werry, indeed good girl. Dick said he gravely doubted it, and put the screws on harder. Joy then said that Jeremy had millions and millions of nuts which Jennifer said he got out of a hole, and this, though certainly not a solution, was at least a clue. Jeremy, under interrogation from Tim, was all co-operation, and volunteered, sweetly smiling, to show Daddy where he had found the nuts. By now, naturally, the whole affair was a *cause célèbre* among the children of the Lane, and they were there in force when Joy and Jeremy, in the custody of their respective fathers, halted before Bruce's packing-shed, and Jeremy invited Tim to crawl beneath it. This Tim declined to do, saying that he had his good trousers on, but he summoned Bruce, while all the children waited, round-eyed and whispering.

Now Bruce had already noted the depression in one corner of his rack, traced the leakage through both holes to the ground, and recognised the work of rats; but there was ample evidence to indicate that their depredations had been extended by some human agency, and the effort of disbelieving the clearly demonstrable was causing him much mental anguish. Therefore, when all was revealed to him, his relief was so great that only urgent protests from Dick and Tim prevented him from treating the culprits with most unwise and jovial indulgence. He yielded, however, to their muttered exhortations, and stood beside them wearing an expression of awful severity while Dick made a solemn and very moral little speech, in which he explained to his awestruck audience the extreme impropriety of ullaging, and sternly commanded Joy to make full restitution.

Painful as this prospect was to Joy, she perceived that it was necessary for the restoration of her virtue. But she was still a business woman, and she wanted a clear understanding on the matter.

" Will I be a good girl then ? " she enquired searchingly.

Dick, Tim and Bruce all answered emphatically in the affirmative ; and that ended what we are proud to say is the only case of ullaging in the Lane's history.

The Dog of my Aunt

THIS TALE will require careful handling. A single yeasty character leavens the lump of normal, human dough from which all tales are basically compounded; two make it froth a bit; three create an almost unmanageable ferment; but when you find yourself committed to a narrative containing no less than four, it is impossible not to feel that the whole thing may blow up in your face, obliterating your literary style, and playing havoc with your efforts to create a serious and shapely work of art.

However, the inescapable fact is that we have four barmy characters to deal with—namely, Aunt Isabelle, Ken Mulliner, Jake and Kelly. We do not hesitate to include Jake and Kelly, for barminess is by no means restricted to humans. Animals can be quite screwy. So can plants—lantana being, perhaps, the outstanding example. So can inanimate objects, many of which are undoubtedly animated by something which makes people stare, blink, and suffer sharp misgivings as to their own sanity.

In this last category cars now take first place, having supplanted houses owing to their additional advantage of mobility. For a house is, by definition, a stay-at-home affair, and may absorb only those experiences which come to it; but a car gets around. In both, personality reaches its full flowering with old age, but whereas a house is commonly mellowed by the years, a car becomes, quite invariably, a tough rapscallion, a buccaneer, a cynical adventurer who has been everywhere, seen everything, and knows all there is to be known about mankind. This is, of course, the reason why those whose own personalities have never ripened, buy new ones so frequently ; no one likes being made to feel adolescent by a bit of machinery.

Ken is still quite a young fellow, but his personality is ripe beyond his years, and there can be no doubt that this is largely attributable to his association with Kelly—though he would be quite effervescent enough even without the influence of his barmy vehicle. This Thing (for, like Mrs. Jackson, we can find no other word for it), already had a long, long history when Ken first acquired it for thirty quid just after the war. It must once have been of some identifiable make, but he was still in short pants when it shed the last emblem, legend or bauble which proclaimed it a This, That or The Other, and since then its internal arrangements have been so swopped, modified, removed, replaced, repaired, rebored, recharged and generally readjusted that possibly even he does not now remember what make it was. To this day he is always buying parts out of other jalopies and incorporating them into Kelly as its own parts give up, or fall out, but these operations seem to enhance, rather than diminish its rich and aggressive personality.

These two in combination afflict the beholder with an uneasy sensation of impending crisis. They cannot even go in to the store together without turning the trip into a hair-raising adventure, and on their meat-day the Lane finds itself listening tensely for the racket which announces that they have successfully accomplished their errand. We swear each time that we shall not view this everyday expedition as if it were a commando raid ; nevertheless, the air is electric with excitement, to which Ken adds by his dramatic manner of delivering our meat. " We made it ! " he yells jubilantly, thrusting Biddy's roast and chops into her hands. " We made it ! " he shouts, dumping steak and dog's meat into the Griffiths' box. And all the way down the Lane we may follow his victorious progress by the appalling noise of Kelly's brakes and gears, and the sound of his voice exultantly proclaiming : " We made it ! We made it ! "

It has been said that modern life consists of tedium enlivened by disaster, but Ken does not subscribe to this view. He argues that tedium cannot sneak up on you ; there is plenty of time to see it coming, and take suitable action. When he perceives that a job is about to become boring, he stops doing it, and when he becomes tired of a place, he leaves it ; but as a rule he finds any job interesting simply because he is doing it, and any place seething with drama simply because he is there. As for disaster, he recognises it only in one form. It is a disaster to be dead. But even this, as he points out, cannot be regarded as unmixed disaster, for it lends a peculiarly zestful enjoyment to all the time when you are not dead.

Such, then, are two of our characters. We have already glanced in passing at Jake, and mentioned that among the adult members of the Griffith family there is a tendency to disown him. Any time you visit there, you are likely to find Henry swearing, or Sue tearing her hair over the latest iniquity committed by that awful dog of Aunt Isabelle's, and Aunt Isabelle fiercely asseverating that her responsibility for the animal came to an end when she delivered him into Tony's arms. But you will also find that he has his loyal champion, for it is precisely in such moments of tension that Tony makes no bones about admitting that Jake is exclusively his, and will be defended by him against all slanders and revilements, because the poor old boy didn't understand, and never meant to do it.

This is perfectly true. Jake possesses some admirable qualities, but not even Tony has ever claimed that intellectual prowess is one of them. When he first appeared among us he was only a puppy, and it was charitably hoped that he would get more sense as he grew older. He is now nearly as big as a calf, but this hope has not been realised. Life has always puzzled him, but he never despairs of finding out what it is all about, and when he stands gazing at anything, with his head on one side and his forehead seamed by a thousand wrinkles of perplexity, it is a safe bet that he will presently launch himself at the mystifying object in order to subject it to a close, and usually destructive examination. His coat is smooth, and golden-brown, but it is a little too large for him, so when he shakes himself (which he does very frequently, as if he could thereby free himself from the manifold problems which bedevil his existence), its loose folds flap like sheets in the wind, and such mud, water, manure or nameless offal as happens to be adhering to them, is scattered far and wide. He is an indefatigable rummager in the lantana, where he collects old boots, rotting fragments of rag, decaying corpses of birds or bandicoots, snake skins, tattered remnants of sacks smelling to high heaven of blood-and-bone, and many other loathsome matters ; these he brings home, and lays upon Tony's bed. His pendulous cheeks, his bulldog nose and his bloodshot eyes combine with his bulk to lend him an intimidating appearance, but his disposition is so friendly that unless you see him coming, and brace yourself for the shock, his ecstatic leaps of greeting are apt to land you flat on your back. As he grows bigger and bigger, his inspired clumsiness naturally has more and more dog-power behind it, and this excessive bonhomie has become one of the major hazards of life in the Lane. In the circumstances, it surely speaks volumes for his beautiful nature that we all love him dearly.

With Aunt Isabelle we are already pretty well acquainted. Her abrupt and totally unheralded appearance in our midst would have dumbfounded Sue and Henry even if she had made her entrance alone, and in a more orthodox manner ; for it was barely a month since they had received one of her very long letters, posted in Paris, and containing no suggestion that she ever proposed to leave that city, where she lived a busy life doing nothing in particular, but doing it with so much verve that it seemed to herself, and everyone else, tremendously exciting. As it was, there were aspects of her arrival which might have made them doubt the evidence of their eyes, had there not been other witnesses. These were Dick Arnold (who was helping Henry put a new stump under the tank-stand), Marge Kennedy (who was returning a mincer she had borrowed from Sue), and Dave Hawkins (who was playing with Tony). Ken was less a witness than a *deus ex machina*, for the vehicle from which Aunt Isabelle alighted, clad in a boiler-suit, a fur coat and hob-nailed boots, and clasping the squirming Jake in her arms, was Kelly. It will readily be seen that a combination of these four is strong medicine, and one wonders that Providence should ever have allowed them to come together, especially on a Sunday.

But there they were, and for some moments—what with Aunt Isabelle's cries of greeting, Jake's yelps, Tony's enraptured exclamations and the clamorous questionings of Sue and Henry —the situation was extremely confused, and . . .

But things are getting out of hand already, and we are telling the end first. We feel rather despairingly that even if we attempt, by scrupulously observing a chronological sequence, to lend this account the majestic, step-by-step inevitability of Greek drama, the chances are that it will come out in a form (or perhaps we should say a formlessness), more reminiscent of the brothers Marx. Nevertheless, we must explain how Aunt Isabelle came to possess Jake, how they made the acquaintance of Ken Mulliner, and how Kelly brought them all to Lantana Lane. We shall do this methodically if it kills us.

It must first of all be understood that although Aunt Isabelle frequently declares herself to be a realist, she is a romantic as well. Contrary to general belief, this is quite possible. A little mental agility is required, but she has plenty of that, and finds no more difficulty in switching briskly from romance to realism, and back again, than she would find in removing one dress in order to put on another.

For the romantic adventure of emigrating, she cast herself as a pioneer—having eagerly read two books, written in 1849 and 1857, upon life in the Antipodes. But her realism compelled her to recognise that facilities for making perilous, six-months' voyages in sailing ships, and subsisting upon weevily biscuits and a daily pannikin of water, no longer exist, so she philosophically allowed herself to be whisked through the air in perfect comfort, cheering herself with the thought that every hour was bringing her closer to The Bushes, where interesting privations surely awaited her. And although she descended from the 'plane clad in everything that was suitable and *soignée* for an elderly Parisienne upon her travels, she had her boots and her boiler-suit readily accessible against the moment when pioneering should begin.

She was somewhat dashed to learn that it was now quite a long time since the coaches of *Cobb et Cie* had ceased their picturesque operations, and that she must perform the next stage of her journey by train. But once more, as a good realist, she accepted the inevitable with composure, and engaged a taxi to convey her straight from the airport to the railway station ; for she was resolved not to lose a moment in coming to grips with her new life. However, as she explained to the taxi-driver, she wished to purchase a little gift for the son of her niece, and would therefore be obliged if he would take her, *en route*, to some appropriate shop. To this he replied that it was Saturday after-noon, and all the shops were shut; but he must have been a quick thinker, for he immediately added that he had kids himself, and if she asked him, he'd say there was nothing a little boy liked better than a dog. Now it so happened (he continued) that he had an exceptionally fine Boxer pup which was worth fifteen quid any day, but which—since he didn't like to see a lady disappointed —he would let her have for five. Aunt Isabelle was delighted, and requested him to take her at once to inspect this animal, which he willingly did.

Just as they were walking up the side path towards the back-yard, and the taxi-driver was explaining that it was necessary to keep a valuable, pedigreed dog shut up because it might get pinched, his third youngest child at last succeeded, after many attempts, in opening the door of the shed where Jake was incarcerated, and Jake, thus released, bounded out and knocked down a clothes-prop which supported a line of washing. The taxi-driver, shouting vituperations, gave chase, but was impeded by the fact that he did not like to trample all over the washing, and Jake (who had no such inhibition), always managed to be on the side where he was not. The third youngest child at first tried to help, but his father—rightly regarding him as the author of this contretemps—fetched him a clip on the ear in passing, which enraged him so much that he retired to the coal-heap, threw coals at everyone, and screamed. The fourth youngest child now appeared from somewhere, carrying the youngest child whom she set down on her father's best nylon shirt so that she might take part in the pursuit; but at this moment, most unfortunately, the second youngest child emerged from the house with a kitten in her arms, and joined the youngest child on the nylon shirt, where it was very contentedly pushing coal into the pocket. In order to assist with this, the second youngest child put the kitten down, and the kitten wisely decided to withdraw from a scene of so much uproar; but alas, Jake had seen it, and as it whizzed through the kitchen door he was practically on its tail, and the taxi-driver, the children and Aunt Isabelle were practically on his.

Inside the kitchen, Jake lost no time in overturning a small table upon which was set a tray of cups and saucers, and the taxi-driver, in a lunge to avert this catastrophe, upset a bucket of water. The kitten leapt on to the window-sill, and Jake tried to follow it, but his legs became entangled with each other, and he fell heavily, bearing down with him the second youngest child, who was trying to rescue the kitten, and now raised her voice in such piercing sounds of distress that the third eldest child, who had been peacefully reading on the front verandah, dropped his comic, and hastened in to see what was happening. The kitten had by now taken refuge on the sink where the washing-up was piled, and as there was a chair adjacent, Jake managed to get up there too; but of course the kitten was immediately on the floor again, and Jake, in a rash attempt to emulate its graceful, feline leap, skidded on the draining-board, and fell into a greasy frying-pan.

The taxi-driver—as Aunt Isabelle freely conceded, when she was relating all this—did his best, but his difficulty was that wherever he set his foot, there was a child, a dog or a kitten beneath it. The third eldest child was more agile, and, seizing a broom, gained the sink, and proceeded to swipe at Jake with such effect that most of the crockery was dislodged, and fell to the floor with a crash which penetrated the virginal daydreams of the second eldest child who, however, was varnishing her nails, and did not wish to be disturbed. She therefore thrust her head through the bedroom window, which commanded a view of the next-door verandah, and yelled to the eldest child, who was there exchanging badinage with her boy-friend, that she better come and do something about the damn kids and the bloody dog before they wrecked the place. This summons was heard by the taxi-driver, and so enraged him that he took time off to burst in upon his daughter and demand why the hell she didn't come and do something herself. The kitten, perceiving another open door, dashed through it, leapt upon the dressing-table, and upset the bottle of nail varnish so that Jake—who was the usual three jumps behind—received its contents on his back. The taxi-driver and his second eldest child dived to capture him, but he, feeling a sticky trickle between his shoulder-blades, braced his paws firmly, and shook himself with such vigour that they found themselves liberally bespattered with the varnish, which was of a deep magenta shade named Seduction.

Meanwhile, Aunt Isabelle had been borne into the passage upon a surge of children, and as the kitten emerged from the bedroom—closely followed by the incarnadined Jake—she, with great presence of mind, opened the front door, taking cover behind it as the hunt streamed through. When she stepped out on to the verandah, she found that the third eldest child (still armed with his broom) was dodging to and fro at the foot of the steps while Jake dodged to and fro at the top ; the taxi-driver, emerging just behind her, saw the quarry thus momentarily and comparatively immobilised, made a grab at him, trod on some marbles belonging to the third youngest child, stumbled, and hit his nose against the verandah post, causing it to bleed profusely.

Aunt Isabelle says that from this moment his active participation in the affair ceased. He sat down on the top step to nurse his nose in his handkerchief, and for some little time her attention was necessarily concentrated upon him—for, as she explains, she is anxious to perfect her knowledge of the local idiom, and she was busy committing to memory certain words and phrases which she was later able to repeat to Henry, who advised her to forget them again. Presently, however, an increasing clamour caused her to look up, when she observed that the kitten had escaped over the fence into the street, and all the children of the taxi-driver, reinforced by half a dozen belonging to the neighbours, and also by the boy-friend of the eldest child, were now involved in the chase, so that no less than twenty-eight hands were trying to seize Jake (". . . an attempt the most difficult, owing to the grease.").

Proceedings were at this stage when the taxi-driver's wife erupted through the front door, demanding shrilly of her husband whether she might not slip up the back lane to place a bet without all hell breaking loose, that damn dog, not a cup left, the floor swimming, talk about H-bombs, and what did he care if she had to do all the washing again ? . . .

It was at this moment that Aunt Isabelle realised she held trumps. The fourth youngest child, and the third eldest had at last secured Jake by falling on him ; they were all three lying in a heap, panting, and Jake's expression conveyed very clearly that he had had a whale of a time, and would willingly have continued the entertainment had he not been too exhausted. Her heart went out to him. Here, without doubt, was the perfect companion for a spirited little boy. (". . . for say what you will of Jacques, he possesses the *élan*, the *joie de vivre*, to a degree unparalleled.")

She therefore tapped the taxi-driver on the shoulder, and got down to business.

" You wish to dispose of this animal—yes ? "

She relates with the warmest admiration that he lifted his nose from his handkerchief, and said : " Five pounds." She begs her hearers to consider this reply, for does it not, she asks, reflect that spirit which, in two world wars, earned for his countrymen the reputation of not knowing when they were sunk ? It was *magnifique*. She saluted him. But she could not perceive the necessity for parting with five pounds, or even fivepence, so she addressed herself to the realistic sex, enquiring whether she was right in supposing that Madame would be prepared to part with this dog which, though handsome, and perhaps even valuable, seemed to require more room than he was here able to command ? . . . Madame replied with intense feeling that she wanted neither hide nor hair of the great, clumsy galoot, and the sooner someone would take it out of her life, the better she would be pleased. Aunt Isabelle courteously expressed her satisfaction at finding herself in a position to gratify this wish ; she would make no charge for removing the animal, but would be enchanted to do so as a favour to Monsieur and Madame. Monsieur would, of course, convey her—with her dog—to the railway station in his taxi, and if, in the circumstances, he insisted upon waiving the question of his fare, she would gracefully accept his generous gesture.

The taxi-driver looked up at her over his bloodied handkerchief, and said :

" Lady, you win."

Aunt Isabelle arrived at the station in the best of spirits, for although the taxi-driver and his family were not engaged in taming the wilderness, they had provided her first encounter with the indigenous population in its native habitat, and she had found her brief encounter with them stimulating. Moreover, she was quite enraptured by Jake, and discerned in him qualities which clearly equipped him to play a major role in her pioneering drama. It was not only as a playmate for *le petit Tony* that he would prove invaluable. He would help Henri bring in the cows ; he would defend the lonely farmhouse against bushrangers and maddened buffaloes—both of which had figured largely in the books she had consulted ; and if Tony should become lost (a misfortune which these same authorities presented as practically routine for all small boys), he would guide searchers to the rescue. In short, one could not look at him, immature though he still was, and fail to recognise a dog destined for heroic adventures.

Her parting with the taxi-driver was amicable, for he had

thought things over, and come to the conclusion that it was, after all, worth a good deal to have a few hundred miles between himself and Jake. So (not entirely without ulterior motive) he produced from his pocket a length of cord which he reckoned she might find handy for a lead, and then, having accepted the small *pourboire* which she thought proper to offer him, wished her luck, and drove away so fast that his tyres screamed.

Aunt Isabelle, retaining only her fur coat and a small suitcase, delivered the rest of her luggage into the hands of a porter, tied a handkerchief round Jake's neck, fastened the cord to it, and made her way to the ticket window. Here a sharp-faced official sharply informed her that the last passenger train to Rothwell had departed ten minutes ago, and there would not be another till to-morrow at nine fifty-three ; but in about an hour there would be a slow goods with one passenger coach attached, and she could go by that if she liked. Aunt Isabelle was delighted by the prospect of travelling in a goods train, and made haste to protest that if Monsieur contemplated providing a passenger coach solely for her convenience, it was most courteous of him, but quite un-necessary, for she would think nothing of making the journey in an open truck, particularly since she was accompanied by her dog which, though young, was of immense courage and devotion, and would with ferocity defend her against any outlaws who might hold up the train.

This was, of course, a bad blunder. The official, leaning forward to stare down at Jake with cold disapproval, replied that he didn't know anything about anybody holding up trains, but passengers were pribbetted from travelling in trucks, and animals were pribbetted from travelling in passenger coaches, so if she didn't want to pay no fines she better put the dog in the guard's van, and if it bit the guard there'd be compensation.

This rocked Aunt Isabelle. She felt that such pernicketty niceness was misplaced in a rugged, pioneering land. But she immediately resolved that Jake should on no account be parted from her, so she cunningly beamed acquiescence, and declared that she would first take him for a little walk—accompanying these words with a glance so archly meaningful that the official was quite covered in confusion.

She then retired with Jake to the Ladies' Room, and considered their perilous position. A moment's reflection persuaded her that it would be advisable to assume a disguise, so she changed into her boots and boiler-suit; but as there seemed to be no way of disguising Jake, she realised that he must be concealed. Fortunately not many ladies had occasion to enter their sanctuary during the next hour, for he disliked being suddenly extinguished under the fur coat; however, in the intervals between these crises Aunt Isabelle began teaching him to beg, and as their acquaintance improved they found each other increasingly congenial, so the time passed pleasantly enough.

When the train at last came in, she took her suitcase in one hand, bundled Jake—swathed in the fur coat—under her other arm, and, after some wary reconnoitring, stepped out on to the platform, only to find herself confronting an ominous looking person in a peaked cap, who had suddenly emerged from another doorway. She did not falter (". . . for, as we say in France, *toujours l'audace!* . . .") but undoubtedly she owed much to her disguise; for the sharp-faced official had circulated among his colleagues a warning that an old girl would probably attempt, in contravention of By-Law No. 6889112, to sneak a dog into the passenger coach, and as a result of this, the peaked cap was keenly looking out for her. But the description with which he had been provided did not at all tally with her present appearance; nor was any dog visible. So his gaze passed over her without suspicion, if not without some small surprise occasioned by her curious gait. The fact was that Jake, struggling against suffocation with the strength of a mastiff, was slipping down from beneath her arm, thus compelling her to assume the role (". . . for the theatricals I possess a natural gift . . .") of one afflicted by lameness, convulsive spasms, and advanced curvature of the spine.

Thus she was able without molestation to find the passenger coach, and take possession of an unoccupied compartment. She observed the little door in one of its corners, and noted it as providing a last, desperate line of retreat, but judged it wiser for the moment to seat herself innocently by the window, with Jake —still firmly parcelled—on her lap. She opened the folds of the coat now and then, in case he should want to breathe, but dared not allow him to emerge, for the peaked cap was still vigilantly patrolling the platform.

It was not until the train was about to start that this person suddenly smelt a rat. No elderly lady of the kind described to him had appeared . . . but had there not been something fishy about that old bag with the boots . . . and the suitcase . . . and the lump of coat bundled beneath her arm ? . . . Might not a suitcase contain a change of attire ? . . . Might not a coat conceal a dog ? . . . He began to stride purposefully towards the passenger coach, and Aunt Isabelle, who had been keeping a close eye on him, immediately recognised disaster.

There was nothing for it but the last ditch. Clutching Jake in her arms, she leapt for the little door, entered, slammed it, and shot the bolt home. But the situation was still extremely tricky, for Jake struggled free as she did so, and the notion of holding parley through the closed door, and indignantly denying all knowledge of a dog, could not, she feared, be seriously entertained in view of the fact that he was putting on a barking turn which suggested not one dog, but half a dozen. In that bitter moment, with defeat staring her in the face, her eyes lit on the basin, and the button above it which said : PUSH.

(". . . I do not hesitate. I push. The basin descends itself. I seize Jacques. He is downside up, but what would you . . . ? There is no time to make the adjustments. In my haste to close the basin, I nip his tail. This I regret, but freedom is all. It is done—he is safe. He is also silent ; I think he is perhaps a little confused. With my heart between my teeth, I open carefully the door a small crack—and what meets my eyes ? . . . Thrust through the window, I behold the head of the Persecutor ! ")

Good, strong, dramatic stuff, no doubt—yet we feel that this title leans towards overstatement. True, the peaked cap promptly demanded what the lady had done with that there dog, but the question, aggressive as it was, emerged in a curiously apologetic tone. Aunt Isabelle was quick to detect this, and no less quick to understand the cause. (". . . the prudishness of the Anglo-Saxon temperament is well known. . . .") She therefore moved swiftly to attack, and was enquiring in an outraged voice whether, in this country, passengers of the female sex might not retire themselves without being subjected to vulgar intrusion, when a large, red-faced man appeared at the elbow of the now quite sheepish Persecutor, and signified his desire to enter the compartment.

Aunt Isabelle at once modified her role to meet this new situation. She now became a poor little old lady who, though courageously determined to resist oppression, was only with difficulty mastering her terror and restraining her tears. She bravely expressed astonishment that one whose duty it was to promote the comfort of travellers should, instead of opening the door for Monsieur, continue to incommode him by standing in the way and talking nonsense about dogs, when it must be evident to anyone in possession of his eyesight that the compartment was entirely innocent of dogs, unless, indeed, it was supposed that she had a dog packed in her suitcase, or concealed in her handbag, and as for the *cabinet*, she felt a certain natural delicacy, but if she were to be spared no humiliation let all the world observe for itself that no dogs whatever. . . . (". . . and here I fling wide the door, but hearing that Jacques is now making some small squeaks, I begin to weep loudly, thus rendering them inaudible to our enemy. . . .")

The effect of all this was excellent. The red-faced man, much moved by her distress, menacingly intervened, urging the peaked cap to stop worrying the lady, and shut his ruddy mouth, and take his big feet out of the way or he'd get them trod on by accident. The peaked cap—baffled, if unconvinced, and not really caring a hoot anyhow—withdrew, and Aunt Isabelle, tremulously smiling upon her champion, helped him to open the door and scramble in just as the train began to move.

So far, so good. But she was now in something of a predicament. (". . . for I fear that *le pauvre Jacques* may be a little discomfortable. . . .") However, remembering that *l'audace* had already served her well, she re-entered the *cabinet* extracted Jake from the basin, boldly conveyed him into the compartment, and set him down on the floor ; meeting the astonished gaze of the red-faced man, she said genially : "Now we may all be happy together, isn't it ? "

No doubt her heart was once more between her teeth as she awaited his reaction, but it might as well have stayed in its appointed place. Mr. Benson (for by this name he presently introduced himself), let loose a tremendous bellow of laughter which quite reassured her—though Jake was so startled by the sudden eruption of sound that he yelped, and fell over backwards. But his courage, and his determination to examine even the more alarming phenomena of existence, overcame his apprehension ; he righted himself, and staggered forward to investigate the fingers which Mr. Benson was invitingly snapping before his nose, and which immediately began to pat his head, tweak his ears, roll him over on his back, tickle his stomach, and pay him other attentions of an agreeable and stimulating nature. Aunt Isabelle, watching with the keenest pleasure, digested a new and valuable item of knowledge concerning local customs—namely, that anyone will, at any time, and with the warmest enthusiasm, assist anyone else to evade a regulation.

Very soon they were all friends. Aunt Isabelle diplomatically assured Mr. Benson that his presence was a great consolation to her, for she—being an old woman, and a stranger in a strange land—naturally welcomed the protection of a gentleman ; particularly, she added, with an admiring glance at his burly shoulders, one who so clearly combined prodigious strength with a tender heart, and instincts the most chivalrous. Mr. Benson made modest noises, but was much gratified, and at once set about demonstrating the two latter qualities by lifting Jake on to the seat beside him, arranging Aunt Isabelle's coat over her knees, and enquiring after her comfort with anxious solicitude.

Little is needed at any time to ensure Aunt Isabelle's comfort save an opportunity to talk, so she truthfully declared that she had never felt cosier, and they became so engrossed in conversation that they ceased to pay any attention to Jake who, having found a small tear in the leather upholstery of the seat, occupied himself in making it larger, and pawing the stuffing out. Aunt Isabelle explained that she was going to join her niece and her nephew-by-marriage on their pineapple farm, and Mr. Benson revealed that he was a pineapple farmer himself. She begged him not to be misled by her fur coat and her diamond rings into imagining her to be an idle and pleasure-loving member of the *haut monde*, for these she had only brought with her so that they might be pawned, or sold, should a financial crisis arise in the affairs of her niece's husband; and Mr. Benson replied judicially that, since such crises were regrettably common among pineapple farmers, he reckoned her niece's husband would be real thankful to know there was something around he could pop.

As darkness fell, he produced from his pocket a large packet of ham sandwiches and a small flask, expressing the hope that she would share a bite and a little nip with him. She explained that her medical advisers ordained, much to her regret, that she must remain a teetotum, but she accepted a sandwich, and drank his health from the railway tumbler, filled from the railway carafe, afterwards inserting Jake's nose into it so that he had a nice drink too. Mr. Benson voiced his concern at finding her unsupplied with food for so long a journey, and insisted upon presenting her with the sandwiches left over from their repast.

At length they all composed themselves for sleep, and in the small hours of the morning the train stopped at a little station where Mr. Benson prepared to alight, and Aunt Isabelle and Jake roused themselves to take leave of him. He declared that it had been a pleasure to make their acquaintance, and hoped that her nephew would get by without popping her rings, which he might if prices didn't go any lower, and expenses didn't go any higher, and he tarred his drains.

By now dawn was slowly merging into daylight, and Aunt

Isabelle remained glued to her window, nibbling her sandwiches and eagerly observing the landscape, while Jake once more applied himself to worrying at the tear in the seat, and eating the stuffing he extracted from it. She was deeply interested in what she saw, for this was the kind of setting in which she was to enact her role of pioneer. She decided that the bananas were pineapples, and the sugar-cane was bananas, and the pineapples were prickly-pear, and deduced, after some cogitation, that the tall posts upon which the little houses stood were designed to protect the inhabitants from crocodiles. Throughout the rest of the journey the only people to invade her compartment were two schoolboys who avidly devoured science fiction, and had long ago ceased to find ordinary human beings and animals worthy of a second glance.

Thus, at about eleven o'clock on that Sunday morning of bright sun and gusty wind, the train at last drew into Rothwell.

Ken had driven into town an hour earlier to see a poultry farmer from whom he had arranged to take delivery of six bags of fowl manure for himself, and a dozen pullets for the Dawsons ; when this business was concluded, he had parked Kelly near the railway yard while he dropped in on a mate of his who lived nearby, and who could always be depended upon to have a few bottles of beer on hand.

It will be recalled that Ken's sister is married to a Rothwell policeman named Bert Jackson. It so happened that Bert, serenely pacing the streets in the course of duty, saw Ken take his leave of this friend after a pleasant and convivial interlude, and immediately fell a prey to the uneasiness with which the sight of his brother-in-law always afflicted him. He would have been the first, mind you, to admit that Ken carried his liquor well. Too well, in fact ; for when a man is muzzy in his speech, wobbly on his legs, and behaving in an unbecoming manner, he is, for all the world to see, fair game for a copper. But Ken could sink incredible quantities without harm to his speech or his gait, and its effect upon his manner (which was to make him as solemn as an owl, and extremely dignified), merely gave him the appearance of being the only sober person in a bar full of boisterous yahoos. And yet—as his sister often bitterly remarked—you could be sure of trouble when Ken started behaving like a bishop.

So Bert, full of gloomy misgivings, crossed the road to investigate, and was inexpressibly relieved to find himself greeted with a genial : " Hi, there, Podge ! " instead of the ceremonious : " Good morning, Jackson " which he had fearfully anticipated. Ken, he decided, was perhaps a trifle lit up, but by no means stinko. His satisfaction increased when he learned that his relative had no further business in Rothwell, and was about to set out for Dillillibill with his bags of manure and his crate of fowls.

" You want to watch out what you load on to that old tin can of yours," he observed, " or it'll fold up under you one day. Where've you left it ? " He looked around rather nervously, for Ken is notoriously unable to read parking notices. The goods train had just pulled in, and a small crowd seemed to be gathering about someone or something on the station, but there was nothing to indicate a breach of the peace, so his gaze passed over it perfunctorily. He had seen a crowd gather round a dead goanna. Ken, with a negligent wave of his hand, explained that he had left his vehicle parked down there by the goods yard, and Bert, looking in that direction, blenched, and caught his breath sharply. Kelly was . . .

Well, you might say that Kelly was just standing there. You might add that an inanimate object constructed of rusting metal, dubious rubber and odd bits of timber secured by odd bits of wire could—God help it—do no other. Yet Bert—guardian as he was of law and order in Rothwell, and custodian of its fair reputation—felt his blood run cold. There wasn't any regulation, he reflected uneasily, about having a crate of fowls in the back of your ute, and it'd be stretching things a bit, even on a Sunday, to say they were committing a nuisance by poking their heads through the slats and squawking ; it was legitimate to carry bags of manure, though somehow they looked more noisome on Kelly than elsewhere; the owner of a parked vehicle couldn't be blamed if the wind blew a ragged bit of hessian from the seat, and wrapped it round the steering-wheel so that it fluttered with a kind of shameless bravado, like a disreputable banner; and if he wanted to stuff an old pair of khaki shorts half under the bonnet to stop some of the rattles—well, he was within his rights. As for the kerosene tin standing under the radiator with water dribbling into it, you might think it was hardly decent, but you'd have your work cut out to prove it before a magistrate. Such things, Bert felt, would temporarily impair the dignity of even the most self-respecting ute, but Kelly had no dignity to start with, and these items added an almost unendurable touch of impudent squalor to an aspect already sufficiently outrageous. The object seemed to be leaning against a telegraph post—but that was probably because its offside wheels were in rather a deep gutter. It seemed to be squinting wickedly straight at him—but no doubt this was due to its one blind headlamp. It was obviously in the last stages of decrepitude, and yet—like many deadbeats and hoboes whom Constable Jackson had known, and now vividly recalled—the impression it conveyed of sly, rakish and rascally vitality was so powerful as to be frightening. He said in an awed voice:

" Blow me down, Ken, if that thing was human, I'd run it in ! Parked, eh ? To me it looks like it was loitering with intent. For Chrissake, feller, take it back to the farm, and keep it there ! " He sketched a farewell gesture with a hint of panic in it, and his departure was a flight. Ken grinned at his retreating back, and went cheerfully on his way.

But by the time he had reached Kelly, he too had noticed the little crowd on the station, and since he had found that exciting events were frequently generated in crowds, he crossed the yard and the railway tracks, vaulted up on to the platform, and found himself looking over the heads of the bystanders at Aunt Isabelle and Jake.

Aunt Isabelle was in a spot of trouble. As she alighted from the train, Jake (being in considerable distress, and this time not only from lack of oxygen), had suddenly wriggled with such desperate violence that he fell out of the fur coat just as the stationmaster walked majestically by.

Now Mr. Brownlee cultivates a majestic tread because his position as the big shot at an important railway station like Rothwell clearly demands it, but he is, in fact, an easy-going bloke who always prefers to turn a blind eye upon minor infringements of the by-laws, since so many of them are always being infringed by everyone, and no harm seems to come of it. So he would have failed to notice Jake if it had been possible for him to do so. But of course Jake, being Jake, could not stand still and be sick where he fell ; he had to stagger forward and be sick over Mr. Brownlee's boot. Mr. Brownlee was therefore compelled to pause, and point out sternly that dogs were not allowed to travel with passengers.

Aunt Isabelle, who sometimes finds it helpful to be helplessly uncomprehending, chose to interpret his remarks as being admiring rather than admonitory, and affably agreed that this was, indeed, a remarkable dog, well born, what-you-say an aristocrat, and with a temperament the most docile, who had passed the entire journey sleeping quietly at her feet, and had no fleas at all. Mr. Brownlee replied coldly that, fleas or no fleas, he had no business travelling on the railway except in the manner permitted by the authorities, and Aunt Isabelle decided to fall back upon the pathetic-old-lady role which had already proved so successful. She therefore requested, with a quaver in her voice, that before she was haled to prison, she might first arrange for her niece to take charge of the faithful creature whose only crime had been to mount guard over her throughout the night, and discourage bandits from entering her compartment, and murdering her in her sleep.

Mr. Brownlee pondered this for a moment. He did not fail to note a contradictory element in her two statements, and he was by no means certain that Jake's innocence was as spotless as she would have him believe ; for, glancing down with distaste at his boot, he felt a strong suspicion that what he was seeing was damaged Government property. But a certain delicacy prevented him from pursing this aspect of the matter, and he wisely decided to refrain from entering into an argument about whether Jake had passed the night slumbering or keeping vigil. The point was that he shouldn't have been there at all. In the end, however, he resolved not to harp on this either, for he was very conscious of the interested audience gathered about them, and well aware that his countrymen were, as a matter of principle, always against officialdom in any dispute. In fact, he had just heard Ken Mulliner remark to nobody in particular that you'd think an old lady could have a nice little pup like that to keep her company on an all-night journey without getting bullied, and threatened, and frightened out of her wits ; and he had observed that Aunt Isabelle at once began to look very frightened indeed, and to dab her eyes with a handkerchief—a bit of business which was bringing indignant murmurs of sympathy from the onlookers. So he declared magnanimously that there was no question of immediate arrest, but she'd better not do it again.

Aunt Isabelle thanked him with great cordiality, and put her handkerchief away. She suggested that *Monsieur le Chef de Gare* might add to his kindness by telling her where she could find a conveyance to take her to the farm of her nephew-by-marriage, whose name was Henri Greefeeth, and who lived at a place called (and here she knit her brows in concentration as she enunciated each syllable with careful distinctness), Dee-lee-lee-beel. Ken pricked up his ears at this, and she—proud of having got her tongue round so strange a name—beamed at the assembled company, and caught his eye, which promptly winked at her. She was just about to wink back when Mr. Brownlee said that the Dillillibill bus didn't meet the goods, so she'd better take a taxi.

This really wounded her. Already she had put up with a train only because it appeared that neither stage-coach nor covered waggon was available. Now she was far from the city—she was in The Bushes—she was Out the Back—she had changed into

her boiler-suit—she was ready and agog to embrace hardships—
and this species of a donkey talked about taxis !

Enough realism is enough. Aunt Isabelle was now dressed for
romance, and romance she was going to have. Entirely ignoring
Mr. Brownlee's preposterous suggestion, she announced that the
discomfort, the slow progress, the peril—all these were of no
significance ; she snapped her fingers of them. In some parts of
this country, so she had been reliably informed, camels were
employed as a means of transport, and she was quite prepared
to travel by camel. If not by camel, then on horseback. She had
been, in her time, a notable horsewoman. It was true, however,
that her valuable dog, and her no less valuable luggage must be
considered, so it might be more advisable to hire the services of
a peasant with a cart ; a mule-cart, perhaps . . . ?

Mr. Brownlee, taken aback, protested that there were neither
camels, mules nor peasants in Rothwell, and if there were any
horses, which he doubted, not having set eyes on one since he
didn't know when, they were probably pulling pineapple slides,
though most of the farmers used tractors nowadays ; so the lady
had better just go across to the taxi-rank and . . .

From the outer rim of the crowd, a voice said helpfully :

" There's the bullock team."

A dozen pairs of incredulous eyes swivelled towards Ken
Mulliner, and then exchanged among themselves glances which
said you could always trust Ken to come up with some remark
that was just plain nuts, but which seemed to borrow from its
context a kind of maddeningly elusive logic. For although it was
true that there were no camels, no mules and very few horses in
Rothwell, there *was* a bullock team. The owners of the eyes
considered that this was one too many, for they were not
romantic, and had no patience with relics of the past; they were
also well aware that, in spite of the fact that it did haul logs to
the mill now and then, its main functions were to impede motor
traffic, and to be photographed by tourists. Never before, in the
whole history of the town, had anyone so much as hinted that
it might be employed as a vehicle for the conveyance of passengers.

Yet Mr. Brownlee had left hanging in the air a suggestion that camels, mules and horses must be ruled out simply because there didn't happen to be any around, and this seemed to leave Ken with quite a strong case for the bullock team. The thought flickered across several minds that it was no wonder he started arguments and won bets in bars, for a clear head was needed to keep up with him.

Aunt Isabelle, however, was entranced. She turned her back on Mr. Brownlee, waved the intervening citizenry aside, and advanced upon Ken, who stood with his thumbs in his belt, and beamed down at her from under what remained of his army hat.

The manner in which soul-mates recognise each other is a mystery. Probably it is a question of wave-lengths. At all events, as these two stood face to face, a powerful current of something or other leapt between them, shedding a rain of sparks in passing upon Jake, who at once began to plunge about between their feet as though electrically charged, and to exhibit every symptom of having discovered the very source of rapture.

Aunt Isabelle, with great animation, expressed her gratitude for so excellent a suggestion, and begged that Monsieur would be kind enough to direct her—or, better still, escort her—to the beefs. And Ken—with the current shooting red-hot streaks of remorse into his heart—explained in great haste that now he came to think of it, the bullock team was out, because the bloke that owned it had got bitten by a taipan only that morning ; and besides this, the bullocks had stampeded last night, and broken out of their yard on account of hearing the booming cry of a bunyip from the scrub—this being a thing which no bullock can endure. But it happened that he himself lived at Dillillibill, and if the lady liked, he'd be glad to give her a lift. . . .

A murmur of horror and protest arose from the bystanders, but Aunt Isabelle, firmly in the grip of the current, abandoned the bullock team without a pang, and enquired eagerly :

" You have a cart—yes ? "

" I got Kelly," replied Ken with simple pride.

Aunt Isabelle's reference books had neglected to inform her of

Kellys, but her faith in Ken was already absolute. She had no difficulty at all in placing him. He was not a peasant, this one ; no, he was unmistakably a soldier. In her youth, during the First World War, had she not seen hundreds like him—and even, as she tenderly recalled, enjoyed a flirtation the most amusing and delightful with one of them ? It was, she said (with a glance which owed something to this charming memory), most amiable and obliging of Monsieur to extend so kind an invitation ; she would be happy to accept it. She drew his attention to Jake. " My dog may be accommodated in the Kelly, isn't it ? And my portmanteaux ? And my hatbox ? "

" Bring 'em all on," Ken told her encouragingly. " I got some hens and fowl manure aboard, but Kelly can shift a ton load, easy." His eyes wandered over the crowd, from which certain jeering sounds, and offensive guffaws had come, and he asked hopefully : " Anyone want to argue ? . . ." No one did, so he turned with a brief sigh to a junior member of the railway staff, and instructed him to fetch the lady's luggage, and bring it across to Kelly, and handle it careful if he didn't want to get tonked.

The audience was then privileged to behold a little scene of the kind which barmy people can put on at a moment's notice. Aunt Isabelle advanced one step, contriving, despite her boots and her boiler-suit, to look like a lady about to tread a measure with her cavalier ; Ken made a half-turn, removed his revolting hat, bent slightly at the waist, and offered her the curve of his elbow, into which she delicately placed her bejewelled fingers. As they moved with grace and ceremony towards the edge of the platform, Mr. Brownlee bethought himself of urgent business in his office, whither he quickly retired, and through its window watched Ken illegally making his way across the railway lines with Aunt Isabelle on one arm, and Jake beneath the other. A row of trucks, one of which was full of young pigs, had just been shunted into a siding, and exactly what happened when they passed out of sight behind these, no one really knows. But there was a clang of metal, followed by porcine squeals and canine yelps, after which they reappeared, moving with quiet dignity towards the gates, and the goods yard was suddenly alive with dementedly charging piglets. Ken—grave and aloof as a whole bench full of judges—ignored the resulting commotion and, having introduced Kelly to Aunt Isabelle (who clasped her hands and exclaimed how it was beautiful), gave his whole attention to the task of replenishing the radiator.

Constable Jackson was by now a quarter of a mile away. The first he knew of the affair was when, as he turned a corner, a pigling charged between his legs, and he observed three others scampering across the road. His wife has told us (in strict confidence, for everyone has agreed that there must have been something wrong with the fastenings of the truck, and accidents will happen), that he immediately said to himself : " Ken—or I'm a Dutchman ! " No sooner had he formulated this thought than Kelly came into view, doing a brisk forty, and pursuing an erratic course among the piglets, whose numbers multiplied with every second. To the metallic rattles of its superstructure, the paroxysmal coughings of its engine, and the continuous blaring of its singularly discordant horn were added the congratulatory cries of Aunt Isabelle as each pig was successfully avoided, and the frenzied barking of Jake, who was straining on his leash in an attempt to hurl himself out and pursue them.

It was Aunt Isabelle who first spied Constable Jackson standing transfixed on the edge of the footpath, and she at once drew Ken's attention to the presence of a *gendarme*, suggesting that it might be prudent to take a side turning before they reached him ; but Ken, far from acting upon this advice, steered Kelly to the kerb, pulled up beside his relative, and expressed in strong terms his disapprobation of a police force which permitted pigs to infest the streets, endangering the traffic, and violating the Sabbath peace. He then said : " Giddap ! " to Kelly, who roared, bucked, leapt convulsively into motion once more, and tore off along the road to Dillillibill, leaving behind a trail of water, a trail of petrol and a fuming policeman.

Very soon Ken was being regaled by his passenger with an

account of her adventures. This made him laugh so heartily that he was unable to give adequate attention to Kelly's rather eccentric steering-gear, and the amusing things which consequently happened on curves and corners interrupted Aunt Isabelle's narrative, and made her laugh so much that Ken laughed harder than ever. Although the streets of the town had been almost bare of traffic, the road was quite busy with carloads of picnickers, surfers, fishermen, bowlers and tennis players hastening to their sundry appointments. Kelly's approach caused eyes to bulge, mouths to fall open, and heads to crack round on craning necks as it shot past ; this was not merely because of its normal peculiarities, but because certain physical phenomena are produced by a very high concentration of barminess, and it was travelling in a shimmer of blue light which emitted, from time to time, small puffs of mushroom-shaped cloud.

It was by now obvious to Ken that his new friend, like himself, did not see eye to eye with those who prefer their journeys to be characterised by safety, comfort and uneventfulness, and—being one who truly understood the art of hospitality—he resolved that while she was in his charge, these trials should not be inflicted on her if he could help it. So he took advantage of the next brief silence when she was drawing breath, to warn her that Constable Jackson was a malignant and revengeful nark who could not take a joke, and who would certainly send a posse out after them.

Greatly stimulated by this intelligence, Aunt Isabelle professed herself ready for any measures which he might think proper, and warmly applauded his suggestion that they should throw their pursuers off the trail by leaving the main road, and proceeding to Dillillibill by a dangerous and unfrequented route. So presently Ken turned off the bitumen on to a steep horror-stretch which is locally known as The Goat Track, and, bidding her hold on tight to whatever she could find, put Kelly into bottom gear, and began to negotiate chasms and boulders with reckless, but skilful abandon.

Now the only person who uses The Goat Track nowadays is Jeff Jenkins, who has the misfortune to own a farm to which it

is the sole access, and who, consequently, has come to regard it
as being, though a poor thing, exclusively his own. It so happened
that he had chosen to employ that morning in making it a little
more trafficable, and to this end he had fixed a plug of gelignite
into one of the solid rock bars which traverse it at intervals, and
had just lit the fuse when he heard Kelly approaching. In great
alarm, he ran down to the corner, and stood there yelling and
waving his arms in a manner which looked so threatening that
Aunt Isabelle at once assumed they were being held up by a
bushranger. Unluckily, Ken and Jeff had not been on the best
of terms since Ken cut in on Jeff and his girl-friend at the last
Masonic Ball, and took her for a drive in Kelly which lasted
until three in the morning. So the genial greeting which would
have quickly disabused Aunt Isabelle of her notion was lacking ;
indeed, she can hardly be blamed for finding herself confirmed
in her belief by the determined way in which Jeff commanded
them to halt, and the truculence with which Ken—continuing to
urge Kelly forward—invited Jeff to stop them if he could.

Filled with admiration for her companion's intrepid behaviour,
and eager to make it clear that she entirely supported him in his
defiance, she began to offer verbal encouragement, but was forced
to scream it because Ken and Jeff were both bawling, Jake was
barking, the hens were squawking, and Kelly in bottom gear
must be heard to be believed. Consequently, no one understood a
word of what anyone else was saying, except that Aunt Isabelle
did hear Ken demand with passion whether the ruddy drongo
thought he owned the flaming road. He then sounded three
tremendous blasts on the horn, and trod hard on the accelerator.
Kelly, gladly responding, plunged forward and upward over the
rocks and gutters with so much goodwill that Jake was hurled
bodily into the air, and came down on top of the rocking crate
with a broken lead dangling from his neck.

In the circumstances one could hardly have censured Jeff if he
had shrugged, and left them to their fate. But he jumped on the
running-board as it went bucking past him, and attempted direct
action where persuasion had failed. Not unnaturally, Ken resented

this move, but there was little he could do about it except yell threats, and poke Jeff fiercely in the ribs with his elbow, because he needed both hands to keep Kelly away from the twenty-foot drop at the side of the road.

Aunt Isabelle, however, was free to act. She saw Jeff's desperate manœuvre as blatant and unprovoked aggression which she, as a good democrat, was bound to resist with every means at her disposal. Apart from her fluent tongue—which she continued to employ without pause—the only means at her disposal seemed to be a large pineapple which was lying on the seat for no particular reason except that in this district there usually is a pineapple lying around somewhere. It was a good, solid Fifteen, and, grasped by its green top knot, made a very passable black-jack, as Jeff discovered when it descended with considerable force on his head. He abruptly disappeared. Kelly continued to plunge forward. Ken, delighted with the manner in which his companion had acquitted herself, shouted : " Attagirl ! " Aunt Isabelle, much elated, gazed back, waving her pineapple over her head in triumph, and crying : " *A bas, le Drongo!* " As they turned the next corner she had a last glimpse of Jeff sitting in the middle of the road, and staring after them. His hands were clasped tightly over his ears, and his face was strangely screwed up. It crossed her mind fleetingly that he looked like someone waiting for something to explode.

Facing the front again, and observing that Kelly was about to tackle a kind of rocky staircase, she had barely time to exclaim : " *Allons, mon ami, courage! En avant!* " before the road blew up.

We are happy to say that it blew up behind them. Kelly has passed unscathed over many nasty bits of highway by adhering to the simple rule that the best way to be sure of getting anywhere is to keep going as fast as possible ; and on this occasion it had kept going just long, and just fast enough. Even now it would have kept on going if Ken had not been so startled that he stalled the engine just as it was successfully climbing up a step some fifteen inches high. Disgusted, it uttered a raucous snarl, and stopped short with a jolt that lifted its passengers high into the air. Ken and Aunt Isabelle, having come down again, sat still on a seat now leaning backward like a dentist's chair; Jake lay still on a manure bag, more than ever at a loss to understand the whimsicalities of existence; Kelly stood still, emitting deep breaths of steam from its boiling radiator. For one long, long second, before a rain of small stones, earth and assorted debris descended on them, there was an oddly peaceful silence.

Then, sharply ejaculating: "Suffering snakes!" Ken leapt out and tore back down the hill towards the corner. Obviously, thought Aunt Isabelle, he was going to chastise the bushranger, who, having failed to halt them by intimidation, had hurled a grenade at them, and richly deserved his punishment. Anxious not to miss this interesting spectacle, she clambered hastily out of her seat, and was preparing to follow when she perceived developments on the spot which needed her attention.

At some stage of the journey, the rusty wire securing the hinged flap at the rear end of the tray had burst asunder; the crate of fowls had slid bumpily backward during Kelly's essay at mountaineering; the jar of their halt had precipitated it on to the road; and the impact of its fall had broken two slats. Through the escape route thus provided, the hens were emerging in great disorder, and Jake was in the act of leaping joyously into their midst. It will be recalled that Aunt Isabelle was prepared to lean heavily upon inherited instinct for guidance in her rural life—and rightly so, for she now heard its voice urgently proclaiming that fowls were property, and property must at all times be sedulously guarded. So she seized one of the hens, thrust it back into the crate, and turned to seize another. Alas, they came out faster than she could put them in; to this day she repudiates Ken's assertion that there were only a dozen, and stoutly maintains that she counted twenty-two before they foiled her by adopting a a policy of dispersal. At last she saw with consternation that they were making for the scrub on the lower side of the road. (". . . where, being now a little fatigued by my efforts, I feared I could not pursue them with any hope of success.")

Jake, of course, was not at all fatigued, and entertained no doubt of his ability to capture the absconders, so she was relieved to see Ken reappear, carrying a bucket of water. This he hurriedly placed on the ground as she shrieked an appeal to him, and was just in time to grab Jake by the tail as he prepared to leap from the bank into a thicket of impenetrable lantana. As he dumped his captive back into the ute, and re-knotted the broken lead, Aunt Isabelle perceived that there was blood upon his hand. She enquired with interest :

" You have killed the Drongo ? "

Ken blinked. His interview with Jeff had passed from exclamations, questions, reassurances and handsome apologies to cordial handshakes, back-slappings, expressions of mutual esteem, and fervent agreement that the sheila didn't live that two good blokes like themselves wouldn't be mugs to fight over. But he now reflected that since Fate had not only so admirably seconded his efforts to provide entertainment for his passenger, but had also prevented her from witnessing this scene of rapprochement, it would be a bit tough to spoil her fun with an anti-climax by revealing that the blood came from his own wrist, which had got in the way of an unguided missile, and that Jeff was enjoying (apart from a slight headache) his usual robust health.

So he replied that although bare-handed slaughter had indeed been his intention, he had spared the life of the poor coot on discovering him to be dingbats. Aunt Isabelle demanded : " *Qu'est ce que c'est*—dingbats ? " Ken explained that he meant off his kadoover. She enquired : " *Qu'est ce que c'est*—kadoover ? " He tried again with loopy as a snake, and she asked : " *Qu'est ce que c'est*—loopy ? " So he gave up, and tapped his forehead with his finger, at which she, a trifle offended, declared that if he meant nuts, he should say nuts, for of the idiomatic English she possessed a command the most extensive.

She then went on to explain the disappearance of the fowls, and assured Ken that he need not fear for the safety of Kelly while he went in search of them, for if the Drongo should attempt another assault, she and Jake would resolutely defend it. But Ken was beginning to be hungry, and he did not want to be bothered chasing fowls which would, no doubt, find their way down to Jeff's place, where he could later collect them at leisure. So he pointed out that the scrub around here was that thick a dog couldn't bark in it, and he might hunt the perishing things for a week without getting a sight of them, so he reckoned the best move would be to kiss them good-bye, and make tracks for home. Aunt Isabelle was very scandalised by this, and began to deliver a homily on thriftlessness which Ken feared might go on indefinitely ; so he said he hadn't wanted to alarm her, but the fact was that every one of those fowls would be by now quite beyond recovery, for the scrub teemed with pythons which enjoyed nothing better than a nice, fat pullet. This certainly stopped the homily, but inspired, instead, pleas that he would at once conduct her to see a python, and he was only able to check these by reminding her that the lunatic might return during their absence, and commit an act of sabotage upon Kelly.

So she regretfully took her seat again, and Ken—having filled the radiator, and left the bucket by the side of the road for Jeff to pick up—took his. Kelly coughed, shuddered, heaved and got under way again. Aunt Isabelle asked hopefully whether they were likely to encounter any more adventures, and Ken said he thought not, unless the posse should be lying in ambush for them at the top of The Goat Track ; but when they reached this spot, and came again on to the highway, there was no one to be seen except a small group of Dillillibill citizens making their way home from Church. Kelly put on a nice turn of speed, but it was long after midday when they turned into Lantana Lane, and drew up at last outside the Griffiths' gate. Aunt Isabelle, with glad cries of : " *Suzanne! Henri! Mes enfants!* " soon made her presence known, and, as we have already related, became the centre of a scene so tumultuous and confusing that Dick and Marge could only look on in amazement, until stray words emerging from the hubbub revealed that this was a family reunion of some kind. They then made tactful movements of withdrawal which were quickly circumvented by Aunt Isabelle, who declared, embracing them both, that the friends of her niece were also her friends, and it was charming of them to be here to welcome her, and of course they would stay to luncheon which she herself would help Sue to prepare, for it must not be thought that she expected to lead a life of luxury and idleness in her new home, *au contraire*, she had come prepared to play her part as they could see from her boiler suit which, though perhaps lacking in *chic*, was most suitable for labour in the fields, and in her luggage she had also a peasant scarf which had descended to her from her great-great-great-grandmother whose husband had been a *vigneron*, but it would serve equally well, no doubt, among the pineapples.

At this moment her thunderstruck audience became aware of the ear-splitting racket which, as the Lane well knows, means that Kelly is starting up. Ken was giving them all a wave of his hand as he prepared to drive off, but Aunt Isabelle, with a scream, rushed at him, plucked him from his seat, and introduced him to his neighbours as her very dear friend, Moolliner, who had conveyed her safely to her destination through many perils, having not only intervened to save her from imprisonment, and outwitted the *gendarmes* sent in pursuit of them, but also courageously defended her during an encounter with a dingbats Drongo. She added, cackling wickedly, that had she been younger, he would himself have constituted a perilous adventure on a road so unfrequented, and it now gave her great pleasure to present him to her niece, who would naturally insist that he join them at luncheon. Poor Sue was by this time so dazed that when the graceless Ken solemnly offered her his hand, she actually said: " How do you do ? " but came to her senses in time to slap it away instead of shaking it, and bid him scram before she hit him on the head with the mincer.

Aunt Isabelle now turned her attention to Tony and Jake, who were rolling about on the grass together, enjoying a mock battle, and proudly invited everyone to admire the valuable, frolicsome and intelligent dog which she had brought as a gift for her little cabbage. Everyone complied, and Marge—having rubbed her eyes and looked more closely, said in a weak voice that she loved Boxers, but she hadn't ever seen one with spots before . . . and weren't they an unusual colour ? . . . Aunt Isabelle was just beginning to explain about the nail varnish when Jake got through Tony's guard, and seized a tempting bit of shirt-tail which had escaped from its retirement during the scuffle. There was one of those horrible, rending sounds which women hate to hear. Sue uttered a cry of dismay. Tony sat up, inspected the tatters which now most inadequately draped his person, and said consolingly, like the kind little boy that he is : " Pipe down, Mum ; it's only an old one."

But Jake, rudely recalled from the simple world of dogs and children to one which the bewildering commands and tabus of the larger humans always made so difficult, was alarmed to find himself surrounded by a ring of these creatures—all staring at him in an unsympathetic way which was dreadfully familiar. With his head on one side, his forehead painfully wrinkled, and a ragged fragment of khaki cloth depending from his jaws, he stood and returned their gaze, his expression eloquent of sad, anxious and puzzled enquiry. Tony—who had frequently been the target of similiar stares—understood at once just how he felt, and hastened to the defence, protesting : " Gee whiz, he's only a puppy, Mum ! " And he added that phrase which was, alas, to be so often on his tongue thereafter : " He didn't understand . . . he never meant to do it ! "

All the creatures immediately perceived how true this was. Sue's heart melted in her breast. She fell on her knees, gathered the culprit into her arms, and cried :

" Isn't he *sweet* ? "

Little she knew.

Serpents

IT WOULD be pleasant to believe that Science, when it grouped snakes under the name of Squamata, was indulging in a spot of imaginative whimsy, for the most conspicuous thing about these creatures is their manner of locomotion, and for this no more aptly descriptive term than squamatous could possibly be invented. But imaginative whimsy would, of course, be a very improper thing for Science to indulge in, so we must regretfully accept the fact that the word refers to their scales, and not to their movements.

All the same, it is the erroneous interpretation which will probably linger in our minds, for the attitude of most people to snakes is less scientific than emotional—an attitude which, we suggest, dates from the very earliest recorded association of man and reptile. We do not wish to harp unduly upon the Garden of Eden, but it naturally keeps on popping up, for the events which took place there set the pattern for much that goes on in the Lane, including the uneasy relationship between ourselves and representatives of the order Squamata.

It will be remembered that when sentence was passed upon Adam and Eve, the Serpent also did not escape uncursed. Indeed, grim as were the words which condemned our first parents to swink for ever among thorns and thistles, they seem almost mild when compared with those which so terrifyingly pronounced doom upon the Serpent. UPON THY BELLY SHALT THOU GO, AND DUST SHALT THOU EAT. Appalling! The mere sound of it is enough to chill the blood—and that, apparently, is exactly what it did. When there is added the further decree of perpetual enmity between men and snakes—the former neglecting no opportunity of bruising the latter's head, and the latter making a dead set at the former's heel—no mystery remains in the fact that the generally prevailing good-neighbour policy in the Lane here comes up against a formidable psychological obstacle.

It is true that the sons of Adam are inclined to be tolerant of carpet snakes, and when they see one basking in the sun, spread out along the tops of the pineapple plants, they will usually allow it to slide away with its head unbruised. But the daughters of Eve, on their own ground, are less forbearing. " I know it's harmless," they will say, gazing with distaste at eight feet of richly patterned reptile squaming indolently across the verandah, " but I just don't *like* snakes, and I *will not* have them in the house, so you just get a stick while I watch it."

What makes the gentle sex so savage is precisely this habit snakes have of entering houses. The women allow them to be a fair enough hazard out of doors, but resent finding them in the bath, or lying along the kitchen mantelpiece behind the tea and sugar. And who can blame them ? It was surely not unreasonable of Myra to be riled when a copper snake fell out of Aub's shirt as she picked it up ? And when Marge, having found a four-foot Black crawling into the top drawer of her dressing-table, seized a broom and violently pushed the drawer shut upon it, can we fairly censure her for gazing in sombre triumph at the corpse which Bruce presently extracted, and flung out the window ? As she said indignantly : " I was just going to get a pair of socks, and I might have put my *hand* on it ! "

Note the form of this protest. She does not complain that it might have bitten her ; she merely has the horrors because she might have touched it. Had it been a carpet snake, Bruce would undoubtedly have made the asinine, and typically masculine reply that it wouldn't have hurt her if she had; but this point of view is totally irrelevant, for what women feel towards snakes is far less fear than aversion.

Consider, too, the illuminating lament of Heather Arnold when she perceived a sinuous shape stealing across her bedroom window-sill, which is at least ten feet from the ground. " I can never," she cried passionately, " get used to the way they *climb* ! " This is the very voice of evicted Eve. In the time of innocence before the Fall, she must often have watched, with admiration and pleasure, the Serpent elegantly weaving its way through the top-most branches of the Tree of Knowledge—but now her deepest instincts are outraged by the sight of a snake climbing anything. They clamour that the wretched thing should stay down on its belly in the dust, for thanks to its machinations she was landed with domesticity, and if she must work out her sentence, should it not do likewise ? Insult, she feels, is added to injury when it assumes the perpendicular for the purpose of invading her own exclusive domain.

So snakes of any kind are for it once they cross the threshold or the window-sill, and the poisoners are for it anywhere, unless they can make a fast getaway. Not that they don't have a good run for their money indoors, where there are so many things for them to retreat behind, or beneath, and one cannot swipe at them so freely. The one that got under Amy's wardrobe stood seige for nearly an hour, defying the united efforts of the family to eject it. But Biddy effected what is unanimously allowed to be the neatest capture in the history of our community, and she did it all by herself, too, for Tim had gone to Rothwell, and she was alone in the house, except for the children. Admittedly, the snake played right into her hands by entering the fridge when she had it open for defrosting ; but she slammed it shut like lightning, and turned on the current, so presently hibernation set in, and when Tim came home the creature was too drowsy to know what hit it. This execution—so clean and simple—was in marked contrast to the bloody massacre which took place under the Dawsons' bed. That invader was a really big Black, and when Aub and Myra came in and switched on the light, it decided to make itself inconspicuous by stretching out under the bed, close up against the skirting-board. This was not a bad idea at all, and

would have been successful if it had not passed between the
wall and one leg of the bed, leaving its tail protruding. The tail
was not noticed however, though Myra must have almost trodden
on it when she arranged her pillow ; the discovery was made only
because Aub stood on one foot while he removed his shoe from
the other (a thing which Myra is always telling him he is no longer
young enough, or slim enough to do), lost his balance, and
bumped the foot of the bed, thus pushing its head hard against
the wall. In such circumstances even the most stoical snake must
have betrayed its presence by a convulsive movement.

For once there was no question of you-watch-it-while-I-get-a-
stick. The thing was caught, and the only problem was how to
hit it. If you have ever tried to hit a snake which is pressing
itself closely into the angle of floor and wall underneath a low
double bed, you will understand why Aub's efforts merely made
him very hot, breathless and profane. At one stage he even
advocated pulling the bed away, and letting the ruddy so-and-so
escape, because at this rate it would be time to rise before they
got to sleep. But Myra vehemently opposed this suggestion, and
in the end they both crawled under the bed, and Myra pinned
its head against the wall while Aub cut its throat with the bread-
knife.

The harmless snakes are pretty safe out of doors, though. (Of
course the word " harmless " is rather ambiguous, and the affair
in the Griffiths' fowlyard shows that there are limits to the
indulgence of the menfolk.) Packing-sheds are, by tradition,
sanctuary for carpet snakes, and Biddy just has to put up with the
one that lives in theirs. She tries to find consolation in Tim's
assurance that it saves him pounds a year by eating the rats which
would otherwise eat his wheat and laying-mash ; but all the same,
when she is packing pines she keeps a wary and hostile eye on the
squamiferous coils looped round the rafter above her head.

Sue Griffith used to be the weak spot in the women's united
front, for she is by temperament disposed to love all creatures—
even snakes. This may have been all right, perhaps, for St.
Francis of Assisi, but it is an extremely difficult stance for farmers

to maintain. We are surrounded by so many creatures, nearly all of which seem to exist for the purpose of impeding or frustrating our efforts to make a living. We may manage, with a good deal of determination, to subdue our feeling of malevolence towards Brother Leech, for he merely sucks our blood, and we can spare a little of that without actual damage to our bank accounts. We can forgive the Brother Tick who confines his attentions to ourselves, but we are implacably hostile to the one who attacks our cattle. And it calls for a greater degree of Christian forbearance than even Sue can command, to love Brother Borer, Brother Fruit-fly, and a host of other brethren whose activities contribute so largely to our financially depressed condition. It is also discouraging to observe that while we strive conscientiously to love as many creatures as possible, they make no attempt to love each other. Sue frequently finds herself troubled and embarrassed by Brother Snake's penchant for devouring Brother Frog, and by the rapacious appetite of Brother Hawk for little Sister Chicken.

Nevertheless, she used to insist—before the episode in the fowlyard—that she quite liked snakes. There is reason to suspect that she has deliberately taken her eyes off some which Henry has bidden her watch while he fetched a weapon, thus conniving at their escape ; and she always used to speak heatedly about the wickedness of slaying poor, inoffensive carpet snakes. She declared indignantly that no snake had any real wish to intrude, and, when it accidentally did so, was only too anxious to withdraw without causing any trouble. No one argued about this, but the other women said it was not the point ; when she ganged up with the men about carpet snakes, and even sabotaged operations against more dangerous Squamata, they took the view that she was letting the side down.

But all that is changed now, and we shall tell you why.

One evening, when Tony and Aunt Isabelle, escorted by Jake, had gone to a birthday party at the Bells', Sue and Henry settled down for a nice, peaceful evening. Henry went to sleep in his chair with an open book on his knee, and Sue went to sleep in hers with some knitting on her lap, and the nine o'clock voice of the A.B.C. composedly reporting the sensations and disasters of the past twelve hours, fell upon two pairs of happily deaf ears. But although tidings of floods, tornadoes, revolutions, murders, juvenile delinquencies and exploding H-bombs failed to disturb their little nap, an ominous outburst of noise from their own backyard brought them both to their feet in a split second.

Seizing a torch, Henry dived out the kitchen door, with Sue close upon his heels. It happened to be one of those quite abnormal occasions when neither moon nor stars glorified our sky, and the night was inky black. From the henhouse came the kind of hysterical clamour which only panic-stricken poultry can emit. The ray of the torch, sweeping to and fro, came dramatically to rest upon a long, dark, shining, gliding shape. "Holy smoke!" exclaimed Henry. "What a whopper!"

At the same moment, the whopper (which was next morning found to be, by Bruce Kennedy's precise measurement, twelve feet two and a half inches long), realised that escape rather than banqueting must now be its aim, and, doubling swiftly back upon itself, sought egress from the fowlyard by the same hole in the wire netting which had allowed its entry. Perhaps it takes some time for the rear end of so long a snake to grasp what its front end is up to; at all events, there was a brief, but fatal hitch in its execution of this manœuvre, owing to the fact that it found the hole still plugged by about three feet of its own tail. This seemed to confuse it a little, and Henry, summing up the situation in a trice, called out to Sue: "Grab it while I get a stick!"

Much may happen in the human mind during a second or two of crisis; indeed, almost the only thing which does not seem to have occurred to Sue was the advisability of retorting: "*You* grab it while *I* get a stick." Instead, she apparently condensed into one tick of the clock enough anguished spiritual indecision to have kept Hamlet going for a year. To grab, or not to grab? That was the question. On the one hand were her Franciscan principles—for not only was this a poor, inoffensive carpet snake, but it was doing everything in its power to demonstrate the truth

of her contention that Squamata in general only want to get away.
To grab, therefore, would be shocking. On the other hand, she
was, as custodian of the chooks, aware that her egg-money would
be gravely jeopardised if poor, inoffensive carpet snakes were to
consume her hens whenever they felt so disposed. Not to grab,
therefore, would be silly.

And yet—quite apart from Franciscan benevolence—she
hesitated. For although she is always handling such things as
frogs, mice, spiders, crickets, worms and lizards, the only snakes
she had so far handled had been dead ones, and she was now
astonished to discover in herself a strong, emotional disinclination
to obey Henry's command.

Meanwhile, Brother Snake had got his problem worked out,
and his head was posted beside his tail, superintending its withdrawal from the hole; a bare two feet now remained outside the
wire. Henry, rummaging about on the wood-heap for a suitable
weapon, was holding the torch in such a manner that its light
played only dimly and fitfully over these proceedings, and the
smoothly flowing movement, half-seen, of dark and shining coils
filled Sue with a sudden abhorrence which brought her vaccilla-
tions to an end. She perceived that if she did not stop the tail
from going in, the head would speedily come out, and for more
reasons than one, this was clearly undesirable. So she took a deep
breath, jumped forward, and grabbed. It was comforting to
know that Henry was just behind her, and, presumably, now
armed.

" Oh, blast," said his voice in a tone of mild annoyance, " this
stick's rotten. I'd better go and get the brush-hook."

And with these words he departed, taking the torch with him.

Darkness closed about Sue and the Thing which she was
grasping. Perhaps, since it wrapped itself so fiercely about her
wrists, we might say with equal exactitude, that it was grasping
her. At all events, they were joined together in a struggle as
fearful and implacable as man's struggle with sin. There was a
terrible sound of thudding and threshing; the earth vibrated,

the fence-posts creaked ; something splintered. The wire netting strained outward under the writhing weight hurled desperately upon it ; then it strained inward as Sue, dragged forward, lost her footing and fell against it on her knees. Awful thoughts jostled each other in her mind. It was very old netting. It probably had other holes in it. There might be one quite near. It could give way anywhere. She might suddenly feel great, cold, powerful coils encircling her. She scrambled to her feet, dug her heels into the ground, and pulled with the strength of terror. The Thing in her hands—the hard, chilly, muscular, squamiferous Thing—leapt and wrenched and dragged against her. She could hear its other extremity banging against the bit of corrugated iron on the gate. Perhaps it could get under the gate ? . . .

She screamed.

" What's wrong ? " called Henry from the packing-shed.

" What's *wrong* ? " shrieked Sue between gasps of panic and exertion. " Have I got to stand here all night hanging on to a bloody snake's tail ? "

" Calm down, old girl," said Henry rebukingly. " It's only a carpet—it's harmless. Tony must have left the brush-hook out somewhere, damn it. Don't let go, will you ? "

" I *can't* let go ! " yelled Sue furiously. " I *daren't* let go ! It might be coming out under the gate ! How do I know where its other end is ? Oh ! Oh, Heavens ! *Hurry up. . . .!* "

The last words were a squeal of despair, for the Poor In-offensive had changed its tactics. It had now anchored itself firmly to a post of the fowlhouse, and was settling down to a really serious tug-of-war. Sue lifted her voice in frantic appeal.

" Quick ! Oh, Henry—*quick* ! It's pulling ! "

" Good grief," cried Henry disgustedly, " what do you expect ? I'll be there as soon as I find this ruddy brush-hook. All you've got to do is hold it."

Sue's plight was now dire indeed. She gave ground inch by inch. Her hands, dragged down and down, touched the earth, scraped along it, and came up against the wire. In darkness atavistic memories stir, and ancient evils breed. Never, since the first day of the Creation had there been a darker darkness than this. She was no longer grappling with a mere marauding reptile, but with a monstrous and malevolent force out of the time when time itself was young, and innocence was first imperilled. . . .

Well, it is remarkable what powers of exorcism may reside in a four-and-ninepenny Woolworth torch. "Hullo," said Henry, approaching behind a blessed beam of golden light, "got you down, has it? Never mind, just hang on a few minutes more—I've got the brush-hook."

When the execution had been accomplished, and the still writhing remains flung upon the wood-heap, Sue stumbled up to the house on legs which wobbled slightly.

"What's the matter?" enquired Henry when he saw her in a good light. "I thought you liked snakes?"

Sue has not told us what she replied to this, nor have we asked. There are moments in every marriage when husbands must expect to hear, in precise and forceful terms, just what their wives think of them.

Sue is still kind to spiders, and goofy about frogs. She still pleads for mice, and declines to tread on scorpions. But she no longer rushes to intervene when there is a scurry out of doors, and someone calls for a stick. To her, nowadays, as to all true daughters of Eve, every snake is The Serpent.

Bulldozed

KEN MULLINER'S property stretches down the steep, eastern slope at the end of the Lane, and some distance out on to the flat below, but when he bought the place there was no access to this level area save by a narrow foot-track winding round the contours of the hill, and hemmed in by Stinking Roger eight feet high. Enriched by the slow wash of topsoil from above, watered by a spring, and sheltered by protruding ridges on either side, it was too good a bit of land to lie idle, and Ken's neighbours were always urging him to do something about it. Once he did begin to put in an hour here and there making a road with pick and shovel, but he happened to mention it to Bruce before he had done more than about five yards ; Bruce, having enquired how long this had taken him, went into a mathematical trance from which he presently emerged to inform Ken that, if he kept on working at the same rate, he might expect to get it finished in about thirteen years. Ken stared, and said : " Strewth, I don't want a road *that* bad ! "

The next summer, in one of his sporadic fits of industry, he cleared half an acre at the bottom, and planted tomatoes. There had never been tomatoes grown in the neighbourhood to equal them, but by the time Ken had trudged up that slope half a dozen times, lugging his harvest in kerosene tins, he lost interest— particularly since, having thus got it to the top of the hill, he sold it at the bottom of the market.

" What you want's a flying-fox," Aub told him.

" Got to have two to work those," Ken objected. Aub shrugged.

" Okay, what you want's first a wife, and then a flying-fox."

" Look, mate," said Ken, " if having a flying-fox means having a wife, I'll leave the flaming land under lantana till kingdom come."

And there the matter rested for a long time.

Then, a year or so ago, he won fifty pounds in the Casket. He gave the Lane a fine beer-party, but—to everyone's amazement—did not afterwards disappear for a spree in the city ; instead, he announced his intention of hiring a bulldozer to make a road down his hill. Everyone deduced from this that he must be seriously contemplating matrimony at last ; there seemed to be no other way of accounting for such a sober and responsible decision. Yet it was a long time, now, since Maud had visited the Lane, and a long time since Ken had left it ; nor had she been writing to him. (Of course we are not vulgarly inquisitive about each other's correspondence, but when you collect the mail you cannot help seeing the handwriting and postmarks on envelopes.) Moreover, we had only recently learned from Myra that Maud was all but engaged to a sports commentator. Aunt Isabelle immediately wrote to Mrs. Jackson to find out what girl Ken had been going around with in Rothwell lately, but Mrs. Jackson replied that, so far as she knew, there were just the usual half-dozen, so we all subsided into baffled curiosity.

Bill Brown at Rothwell has two bulldozers, and the one he sends up to do jobs in this neighbourhood is usually driven by a youth named Barry James. Bill came up and looked over the terrain critically when Ken summoned him to give a quote ; he chewed a blade of grass, pondered a while, and said :

" Looks okay, Ken, but you never know when you might strike a band of rock."

" Suppose you don't ? "

" Easy as falling off a log. Meat pie and a cuppa tea. But you might, see, so I couldn't guarantee to do the job under a hundred quid."

" That's fifty more than I got."

" H'm. How about I give you fifty quid's worth, and we call it a deal ? "

" Suits me."

" Mind you, it might take her down to the bottom, or it mightn't. Depends."

" Well, give it a go, sport. I got nothing to lose."

So Barry set to work one morning at eight o'clock.

Once youths took pride in being good horsemen, but nowadays they prefer something with an engine, and Barry loves his bull-dozer as devotedly as that character in the poem loved his Arab steed. He has wonderful hands, too, and a wonderful seat, even when the thing is lurching down a steep hill on a sideways cant of forty degrees, and shoving the landscape in front of it. He likes to have a job in which he can demonstrate its speed and efficiency, so he fairly licked his lips when he saw Ken's hill. He likes an audience, too, so he was pleased to see that Mrs. Jackson and her two boys, Len and Derek, were present. He was even more pleased when these lads told him they had spent two solid days pestering their mother to bring them, but he was not surprised because (having been thirteen himself only six years ago), he understood that the sight of something huge and powerful making so much mess in so short a time has an irresistible appeal for boys.

Presently Dick strolled across the road to watch for a while. He was closely followed by Aub (who lost no time in persuading him to take two to one against the job being finished that day), and hard upon their heels came Bruce Kennedy, accompanied by Marge. Bruce's interest was, as ever, academic and statistical ; having estimated the time required to complete the road by manual labour, he now wished to observe the bulldozer in operation, and make further calculations for comparison. As for Marge, she was there in the spirit of one who visits a gaol or a slum ; such things are deplorable aspects of the civilised world, but the responsible citizen must look them in the face. For Marge—as she sadly acknowledges—was born a century too late. She feels that since human beings have never been really sure what they ought to do, and have usually guessed wrong, it was better in the days when they had to do it slowly and laboriously, because that did impose some slight check upon their enthusiastic blundering. She is therefore profoundly out of sympathy with machines—particularly ones which can devastate the face of nature with a speed formerly reserved to earthquakes.

Barry, as may be imagined, was gratified to find his gallery thus increased, and sprang lightly to his lofty perch; even the man from Snowy River can never have sprung to his saddle with so gallant and insouciant an air. His actions then became reminiscent of a pianist who, with eyes fixed upon the ceiling, runs his hands over the keys to establish a rapport with his instrument. Gazing at the sky, he pulled, pushed, pressed and turned various knobs, gears, switches and what have you, with the result that the monster lifted its snout from the ground, and began to growl fee-fi-fo-fum in a menacing undertone. This indication that the show was about to begin made Len and Derek caper with excitement, and utter loud cries of encouragement, but Barry paid no attention to them. His face was solemn, his eyes intent, his whole bearing that of one dedicated to the performance of a momentous enterprise.

In the kitchen, Mrs. Jackson had just finished beating up a cake for the morning smoke-oh, but when these sounds reached her ears, she tidied her hair, put on a clean apron, and hastened out to join the audience. Making her way to Marge's side, she assumed her most social manner, and addressed the assembled company as follows :

" Good morning, Mrs. Kennedy, it's real nice of you and Mr. Kennedy to come along and watch . . . and Mr. Dawson, too . . . and Mr. Arnold . . ." She bowed graciously in the direction of the men who—a trifle startled to find themselves thus transformed from mere spectators into guests—mumbled confused acknowledgments, and felt that they should have put on ties. " I always think," pursued Mrs. Jackson, " that it's nice to show an interest in what your neighbours are doing. It's neighbourly, I always say,

though of course it can be carried too far. I'm pleased you could
all find time to come, because Ken's always saying how farmers
never have a minute to call their own."

Marge and the men, now haunted by the suspicion that they
were gate-crashers irresponsibly neglecting their duties in order
to indulge a vulgar curiosity, maintained an uneasy silence, but at
this moment the monster's growl became a roar, and Mrs.
Jackson turned to regard it with a proprietorial eye.

"Wonderful, isn't it?" she remarked complacently. "Progress,
I mean. The things We invent, and the things We can do with
them! All the same, Mrs. Kennedy, the sermon last Sunday was
on not being vainglorious about the works of men, and that same
evening it came back to me when I was looking at the sunset,
because when all's said and done, there's nothing like nature, is
there? Bert and the boys couldn't think what had come over me,
the way I stopped what I was doing all of a sudden, but it seemed
to take hold of me, if you know what I mean, and do you know
what I said? . . . I just turned round to Bert, and I said : ' Well,
really ! . . .' And then it sort of came into my mind that all our
inventions are done under Providence too, and I was telling the
boys only this morning that we shouldn't give way to pride about
bulldozers, and television, and electricity, and fission and things
like that, because when you come to study it out, it's all God."

" Oh, yes," said Marge—but rather unhappily. For though she
had no quarrel with this statement, she could not but suspect that
before the grass and weeds grew once more over the torn hillside, the rains would have washed many tons of earth from it
into Black Creek, and thence into the Annabella River, which in
turn would deposit it in the ocean, where it would nourish
neither pineapples, nor tomatoes, nor even uneconomic weeds.
This she could not feel to have been God's intention, and she
wished that we might employ the marvels we invent with a
little more wisdom and restraint.

She was rescued from her morbid thoughts by jubilant yells
from the boys, and some eager muttering from the menfolk. She
turned her head in time to see the monster move forward towards

a slope which, to her horrified eyes, seemed almost vertical, and since no barrier interposed itself save a clump of lantana, she clutched Bruce's arm in panic, and cried : " What's he doing ? . . . He can't possibly go down *there*! . . ."

Bruce was far too absorbed to take any notice of her, so she continued to stare, at once appalled and fascinated. In some dark and nasty corner of her mind she would have quite liked to see the law of gravity take charge of this snorting object, and send it crashing down the hill to destruction ; but her vindictiveness did not extend to Barry—a nice lad, who had probably never read Samuel Butler, and could not be expected to recognise himself as one of the race of machine-tickling aphids foreseen by that perspicacious Victorian.

And, she conceded, you had to hand it to the boy that he knew his stuff. For the monster, when it appeared to be teetering on the very brink of disaster, suddenly veered away, lowered its head with a snarl, sank its teeth deep into the turf, tore up a large section, swung it sideways, and contemptuously spat it out down the hill. It then backed, and prepared for another onslaught. Marge said nervously :

" I still don't see how he can help turning over on that slope."

" You needn't worry," said Dick reassuringly ; reassuring ladies is frequently necessary in beauty salons, and he has quite a technique. " It's perfectly safe. It makes its own road as it goes."

And so it did. After only a few more charges had been made, and a few more tons of earth tossed aside, the plan began to take shape. Where there had been a steep slope of green grass, there was now a perpendicular red gash some five feet high on the upper side, a long, red bank on the lower, and between them a sweetly sloping red strip, already recognisable as the beginning of a road.

Now the monster had tasted earth, and was working with rapid and methodical ferocity. It charged again and again, with lowered snout ; its blade ripped great slices of the ground away, rose, swung outward dripping soil, stones and sods of mangled grass, and hurled them down. Shrubs which a man might have spent an hour grubbing out, it scooped up and tossed over the bank in seconds, and rocks which he could not have moved with a lever, it flung about like pebbles.

Ken came to stand beside Marge, and she noticed that he was wearing an expression which, from time immemorial, has caused dismay and foreboding in the minds of the anxious sex—that which a mother descries on the angelic countenance of her infant son, when he first discovers the enchanting fact that many objects will break if he flings them on the floor. It is an expression with which the passing years will make her exceedingly familiar. She observes it again when, seated on the floor beside his tower of blocks, he demolishes the edifice with one ecstatic sweep of his arm; and many times throughout his boyhood when, with infinite relish, he throws stones at bottles, prowls about with a tomahawk, hacking at everything he can find, pushes rocks over cliffs, registers delight when a tree falls, and counts himself favoured by Heaven if he may witness the collision of two cars, or the derailment of a train. For bangs, crashes, the sounds of splintering and the roar of explosions are as music to his ears.

In due course he arrives at physical maturity. Whether man ever attains maturity of any other kind is a question which woman answers crisply in the negative; but he does, in time, become an adult member of the sex which built the Pyramids and the Rockefeller Centre—to say nothing of castles, cathedrals, bridges, banks, mansions, milk-bars and suburban bungalows without number— and he therefore regards himself as one dedicated to constructive activity. His helpmeet, however, is not deceived. Since her weakness is confined to muscular development, and does not at all affect her eyesight, she has not failed to note that the types of construction which most excite his enthusiasm are those which demand, as a preliminary, excavation or demolition on a massive scale. She will most willingly concede that his structures, when completed, deserve her commendation. They are grand; he has made them very nicely; she will pat him on the head, and tell him so. But she well knows that it was the preparatory mess which he really enjoyed; and what is more, she knows that even now, in some unacknowledged corner of his being, he would just love to put a few sticks of gelignite under them. She therefore reads without surprise of the belligerent past, and quails at the thought of a belligerent future ; she perceives that ever since he became the only tool-using animal, he has been building things, and knocking them down again, and she is piercingly aware, if he is not, which process it is that makes him look as Ken was looking now.

" Pretty good, eh ? " he said exultantly. The other three men assented—but in tones which betrayed varying degrees of fervour. Bruce was impressed, and had already collected data for his calculations by consulting his watch at intervals, and pacing out distances. Dick sounded a note of jubilation, for at this rate he could hardly fail to collect from Aub at the end of the day. And Aub, with this selfsame thought in mind, expressed his concurrence rather moodily, though hope was beginning to revive in his heart. For Barry had reached a point where the grass gave way to a dense growth of every known weed, among which there grew some smallish trees, including a few self-sown exotics gone native—a couple of lemons, a little grove of paw-paws, a clump of bananas—and here, where Ken's foot-track plunged into the Stinking Roger, he was having his first spot of bother. It was not, of course, the vegetation which incommoded him, nor was there any band of rock ; but there were rocks—and large ones, too, whose dislodgement and removal called for more circum-spection, and took more time than did the disposal of mere earth. Moreover, the grade had become steeper ; the wall of earth on the upper side was now ten feet high, and on top of it the monster's excavations had left a particularly vast boulder so unsteadily balanced that any more undermining would obviously bring it crashing down. Down it must come—but not in its own time and manner, for though the metal giant had already taken the buffetings of many falling rocks with perfect indifference, this one was big enough to give it a very nasty buffet indeed. Barry was attending expertly to the problem, but it was delaying the dramatic speed of his advance.

The monster backed, paused, lifted its snout high into the air, made a quick sally and a lightning jab, and retreated again, leaving the boulder quivering for a few seconds before it settled on its base once more. The beastly contraption, admitted Marge to herself, was revealing unexpected qualities. It was not all savagery and brute force ; it was capable, under Barry's expert hands, of subtlety, finesse and delicate manœuvring. It moved as lightly as a dancer ; it positively pirouetted. Again and again it thrust at the rock, and swung nimbly back out of danger; again and again the rock trembled and subsided, while cascades of earth and stones fell away from around it. Aub's gloomy face grew brighter and brighter. " No hurry, son," he called solicitously, " take your time."

Barry may or may not have heard this gratuitous advice, but he gave no sign. He had backed away, swinging his massive vehicle dexterously on its tracks until it lurked close beneath the bank, like a huge beast of prey in ambush, and from here he was studying the rock with an expression which boded it no good. Softly and warily he sneaked up on it again, fiercely and accurately he jabbed, and swiftly he retreated as it slid forward, and remained hanging so precariously on the crumbling brink that Marge decided not to look any more. Nor did she—until a dull crash, almost drowned by congratulatory cries from the audience, proclaimed the climax ; then she turned to see the boulder leaping down the hill, gouging a deep scar through the undergrowth, smashing a shapely sapling, and fetching up with a sickening thump against a large log at the bottom. Aunt Isabelle, suddenly appearing at her side, remarked appreciatively that this was an operation the most interesting and educational, to which Marge replied sadly that maybe it was, but the hillside used to look so pretty.

Aunt Isabelle treated this with robust contempt. How, she demanded, would the agriculture flourish if good land were to remain uncultivated because its natural state was pleasing to the eye ? This was the view of an unpractical aesthete, and however appropriate in artistic circles, entirely out of place here. For herself, she had resolved to recreate herself in the likeness of her peasant ancestors, who, in their time, must have despoiled many and many a flowering hillside. . . .

" Not with bulldozers," objected Marge.

Aunt Isabelle very properly made short work of this feeble reply. Let Marrrrge not mistake herself, they would have been enchanted to use bulldozers had it not been their misfortune to live before the age of these mechanical marvels. It was unbecoming, she added sternly, to speak with the disapproval of this wonderful invention, for such machines were undoubtedly among the greatest benefits which Providence had conferred upon mankind.

Marge gave up. This continual passing of the buck to Providence depressed her, and she began to think rather crazily about a new version of Genesis in which an eighth day was devoted to the creation of bulldozers. And while she was thus absurdly and unprofitably engaged, Barry—stimulated by success and applause—was working with concentrated fury. He was getting through the troublesome bit, and making up for lost time. Lesser rocks tumbled about him as he sliced into the wall ; a landslide bore down two young paw-paw trees and a dead stump ; a large groundsel bush, crowned with a froth of white blossom, descended gracefully, still upright, and a burnt log rolled down on top of it ; the front edge of the banana grove toppled, and vast leaves sank slowly, like green sails. The monster, advancing and backing, swinging and turning, scooping, pushing and rending, implacably flattened them into a mangled mass, shoved them over the lower bank, and continued to tear its path out of the hillside, leaving behind it a trail of devastation.

But it left behind it, also, a road, and so exhilarated was Barry by this miracle fast growing beneath his hands, that an invitation to share the smoke-oh which Marge and Mrs. Jackson carried down from the house, was austerely declined. " Suits me best to keep goin' mate," he declared when Ken went down to fetch him. " Once you start on tea, it's just natter, natter, natter for

an hour, I seen it too often. Anyway, me breakfast's still ridin'
nice and high."

This Spartan attitude abashed the spectators slightly, but not
enough to blunt their appetites, or still their tongues, and they sat
on the grass, natter, natter, nattering while they watched the road
extend and descend like a bleeding wound across the slope below.
Dick was jubilant, but Aub, though shaken, refused to admit
defeat. The kid might strike trouble yet, he insisted hopefully ;
but Ken slapped him on the back and told him he might as well
part up at once, because there wasn't any more rock down there,
and by the way things were going the job would be done by
lunch-time. He looked so elated that Aunt Isabelle patted his
hand fondly, declaring that this step he had taken to enlarge his
farm was both bold and prudent, as the actions of a young man
about to assume grave responsibilities should always be, and she
begged—speaking with emotion—that he would lose no time in
bringing his sweetheart to the Lane, that all might take her to
their bosoms. It was well and movingly done, but Ken did not
rise. " Break it down, Auntie," he protested, clipping her round
the waist and planting a kiss deftly on her cheek, " what would
I want with any other sweetheart when I've got you ? "

Towards midday the amazing truth could no longer be denied,
even by Aub ; the road would be finished inside another hour.
The audience had grown by now, though its composition had
altered as one or another of its members reluctantly mooched off
to do some work, and someone else arrived to watch. Dick and
Bruce had gone, but Aub (perhaps still hoping against hope for
a band of rock) had stuck it out. Doug Egan had parked his
truck outside the Arnolds', and come in to take a gander ; Wally
Dunk had left his alongside Kelly, and just nipped down on the
thin excuse of telling Mrs. Jackson they were temporarily out of
cinnamon at the store. This news he had not imparted, however,
for Mrs. Jackson had earlier withdrawn to the house, after
explaining that although it was real nice sitting out in the sun,
she somehow couldn't enjoy it while there was work waiting to

be done, some could, of course, and she wished she could too, but she was funny that way. Henry Griffith had turned up because, he said, it was plain that one would be socially a dead loss in the Lane for ever if one had seen nothing of this remarkable event; and Sue had promptly followed him because she darned well wasn't going to be the only mug left slaving at home. Alf, EElaine, Tristy and Gally had been and gone, but Amy and Gwinny had turned up together, and brought their knitting. Ken had spent much time prowling about on the road as if proving its existence to himself by walking on it, but he had now rejoined the group and was arguing with Aub about whether Kelly would be able to get up it after rain. At this stage Jack and Joe arrived, and it was Jack who presently remarked that it looked as if Barry might finish with a bit of time to spare before he ran out the fifty quid.

" That's right," agreed Ken, consulting his watch. " A good quarter of an hour, I reckon. Might be twenty minutes, even."

" Them things can do a lot in twenty minutes," observed Joe.

" I'll say ! " said Doug with enthusiasm, staring at the road.

They looked at the bulldozer far, far away at the foot of the hill; it was still backing, thrusting and manœuvring, but on comparatively level land now, and the job was all but done.

" Might as well get him to shove out a bit of that lantana on the flat while he's here," said Ken. " I'll need to fix up a few fences down there before I put anything in. If the kid could just clear me a line along where the old south fence used to be, I'd get it done in half the time—eh, Jack ? I reckon there might be some of it still left under the lantana."

" How's he going to know where the line is, in all that muck ? " Aub objected.

" I can show him, can't I ? See that bit of a track through the thickest part ? That's where I brushed a path last year when the kids wanted to get down to the creek for a swim. It goes right through the fence line, and comes out on that little clear, grassy patch—see ? Well, that's about fifty yards the other side of the fence. All Barry's got to do is follow me along that till

I tell him to stop, and then clear a line at right angles. Easy as winking. I'll just nip down and word him about it."

Everyone got quite a kick out of seeing him tear off down the road which had not existed a few hours ago, and Gwinny caused much astonishment by announcing that although Alf hadn't ever held with the Casket, he said it did make a difference what you did with the money, and he reckoned it was real sensible of Ken to have the road made.

Presently a strange silence fell as the bulldozer came to a standstill, and ceased its sputtering roar. Ken and Barry were seen in consultation, pointing and gesticulating. The road, it seemed, still required a few finishing touches, but at last Ken marched off towards the lantana, and the monster lumbered powerfully after him. He entered the thin thread of track, his blue shirt making a bright spot of colour against the green, and the onlookers above could see him pushing his way along it ; Jack remarked that it must have grown over a lot by now, and he'd have done better to take a brush-hook with him. The bulldozer came up against the green wall where the track entered it, and began to shove.

" Cripes, she shifts it, all right ! " exclaimed Joe admiringly.

Indeed she did. She shifted it so effectively that it piled higher and higher before her ravening snout ; the ground was firm and level, so she moved at a good pace, too. It was suddenly observed that the blue dot began to exhibit signs of haste and agitation, moving ever faster along the track, and turning frequently to hold up its hands in a gesture which those above had no difficulty in interpreting as an attempt to halt the traffic. " By golly," breathed Aub ecstatically, " the flaming thing's got him on the run ! "

Through the ocean of lantana the bulldozer moved remorselessly forward like Leviathan, pushing a high wave of greenery before it, and along the track ahead scuttled the blue dot, leaping, ducking and wildly gesturing. Aunt Isabelle clasped her hands to her breast and shrieked : " *Halte!* He is trapped ! *Halte!* " " Save your breath, old lady," said Henry soothingly. " He can't hear you. He can't even hear Ken."

It was too obviously true. Barry could neither hear nor see the unhappy fugitive he was driving before him. The hungry roar of his monster drowned all other sounds ; the mountain of lantana piled before it shut off his view of the ground immediately ahead. In the overgrown track, pushing, stumbling and tripping, Ken could not move fast enough to increase the distance between himself and his pursuer ; nor had he time to effect an escape by struggling into the lunatic undergrowth before he should be overtaken. He could only flee—and he fled. Up above, his unfeeling neighbours were by now convulsed with laughter—all but Aunt Isabelle who, wringing her hands, exhorted them to hasten to his aid. Finding this plea quite disregarded, she warmly declared them a set of miserable poltroons, announced that she herself would shame them by proceeding to the rescue, and was half-way down the bank before Sue seized her and dragged her back.

" Keep calm, Isabelle," she besought. " For goodness' sake, keep calm. It'll be all over long before anyone could get there."

Admittedly these words were not well chosen, but Sue was excitedly intent upon the spectacle, and she spoke in haste. Aunt Isabelle uttered a scream of horror.

" All over ! He is to be murdered, and you tell me to keep calm ? See how it pursues him ! He is mad, that boy who drives ! He should not proceed when he can no longer see before him ! *Halte! Imbécile!* Henri, you must act ! . . ."

" What for ? " asked Henry callously. " Ken's showing all the action that's needed. Just look at him—what more do you want ? "

" Reckon he must be getting pretty close to where the fence used to be," said Joe, staring raptly.

" Somewhere near," Jack assented. " Wonder if there *is* any of it left ? . . ."

" By jings, he'll need to be nippy if there is ! " Doug exclaimed. " I wouldn't want to get through a fence with that thing right on my tail ! "

" Me, neither ! " agreed Wally fervently.

" Bad enough getting through a good fence," said Aub, " but an old one—all loose barbed wire tangled up in lantanna ! . . ."

" He could get hung up in that good and proper," said Doug.

" Too right, he could ! " said Wally.

" Monsters ! " screeched Aunt Isabelle.

" Now if it were a bull chasing him instead of a bulldozer," observed Henry with detachment, " a fence would be a help. But Barry'd drive that little runabout of his clean over any fence without even knowing it was there."

" *Fi, donc!* " raged Aunt Isabelle, stamping her foot at him. " For shame ! Shut up ! Oh-h-h-h—it moves faster ! . . . See it breaking down all before it ! Henri, you must prevent this disaster ! I command it ! Ah, my poor Ken, my poor boy ! . . . He stumbles ! . . . It overtakes him ! . . . Release me, Suzanne, or he is lost ! " But Gwinny and Sue had her by the arms like wardresses, and she struggled in vain.

" Lost ? Not he ! " scoffed Aub. " He's holding his own, I reckon, don't you, Wally ? "

" He's doin' all right if he don't trip too often. Put on a bit of pace, there . . . musta struck a clear bit. . . ."

" Cripes, he's down ! " cried Aub. " Okay, he's up again, and moving pretty good, too. Watch your feet, son ! It gained on him then—eh, Doug ? "

" Run, my poor Ken ! " screamed Aunt Isabelle. " Faster, for the love of God—faster ! Ah, that terrible machine—*quelle abomination!* "

" Come on, boy ! " yelled Doug. " Put on a bit more speed ! "

" He's drawing away ! " cried Aub. " Fence must be gone, Jack—he never stopped. Fifty yards more and he's out in the clear ! Jeeze, he nearly took another header then ! . . ."

" He did ! " Joe cried excitedly. " He must've done—I've lost him. . . . Or d'you reckon he's found a place he can crawl off at the side ? . . ."

" No fear," said Jack, " he's still going. Bit of a bend in the track, that's all. See, there he is again. . . ."

" That'll lose him a few yards," remarked Henry. " Tough luck."

" That's right," agreed Jack, " the 'dozer travels straight."

Aub was bouncing at the knees, and his hands were sawing on invisible reins. Clearly he was back on the racecourse, and he had his shirt on Ken. Voices rose exultantly in chorus :

" Come on, Ken ! "

" Boy is he moving ! . . ."

" Keep it up, sport, you're doing fine ! "

" Stick to it, Ken ! "

" He's coming up the straight ! . . ."

" *Courage, mon cher*—you arrive ! . . ."

" Finishing in style, too, I'll say that for him ! "

" He's home and dry ! *Hooray!* "

Ken shot out into the clearing, veered sharply sideways, and staggered to a halt, flailing his arms in groggy gestures which, at last, Barry could see. Leviathan wallowed out of the lantana, stranded on the sward, and stuttered into silence. Aub cupped his hands round his mouth, and shouted : " Nice work, feller ! Nice work ! "

Ken was seen to turn and stare upward. He waved, and shook his clasped hands over his head. He hadn't much breath left, but he used what he had, and his meat-day pæan came faintly up the hill. " I made it ! " he proclaimed triumphantly. " I made it ! " And everybody cheered.

Everybody, that is, except Aunt Isabelle. She was very cross.

" Make no mistake," she scolded, " I write to the Government about this outrage ! I write to the newspapers ! I write to the Bishop and the Agriculture ! I ask is it permitted that these wicked machines crush into the earth like an ant so good a boy as Ken ? Tch ! tch ! He is not crushed—I see it—am I blind ? This is only because he is of a type the most athletic, and has great resourcefulness. Not all possess these qualities. Are these others to be squashed while *tout le monde* stands by making the buffoonery ? It is a scandal ! I write to the Prime Minister ! I demand the investigation ! I write to the criminals who make this bull-roarer. As for that Barry there, I tell him off—I give him the works on the carpet! Figure to yourself—a youth, a *blanc-bec*, a veritable child like this to be entrusted with such an engine of assassination!"

Marge murmured sympathetically. She perceived that in future there would be one other person in the Lane who did not regard a bulldozer as a Christmas box from Providence.

Time Off

It is a fact worth pondering that the trials heaped upon human beings by nature rile them far less than do those which they devise for each other; which makes it all the more peculiar that they should so assiduously seek to abolish or mitigate the former, while applying themselves with ever greater zeal to an endless multiplication of the latter.

Little as we Dillillibillians like the cyclones which periodically come ashore on our part of the coast, and play merry hell with our affairs, we prefer them to certain recurring, man-made afflictions which we have to endure—as, for instance, income-tax returns. This is quite reasonable. A cyclone gives you a sporting chance, which the Taxation Department never does; for though potentially disastrous, it is, like Macbeth, infirm of purpose, which the Taxation Department certainly is not. Even after our wirelesses have warned us in calm and cultured accents that a severe cyclonic disturbance is reported off the coast, we know that it may dither about for days before deciding exactly where to go. At noon, the news that it is moving south-west may make us look to our roofs and window fastenings; by evening we hear that it is veering northward, and begin to hope that someone else may cop it after all; next morning we learn that it is heading out to sea again—but our sighs of relief are premature, for in the evening we are informed that it has mended its pace, increased the velocity of its winds, and is charging straight at us. Even then there is still the possibility that it may miss us.

But once we hear the annual intimation that Forms A, B and C are now available at all post offices, we realise there is no escape. The Commissioner has our address, and we can do nothing to save ourselves, for it is not a bit of use shutting doors and windows. Moreover, waywardly flibbertigibbet behaviour is far less trying than drearily efficient implacability ; a certain stimulation may be derived from the unpredictable vagaries of a cyclone, but filling in a dreadful form is just dull agony. So if our bank balances are to suffer another assault, let it, we say, be by Act of God rather than by Act of Parliament.

The proof of all this—if proof were needed—is that no one has ever invented a pet name for the Commissioner of Taxation ; but cyclones always have pet names. These—bestowed in the first instance, one supposes, by some waggish gentleman of the Press —are invariably feminine, and usually of the down-to-earth variety. It may not be too fanciful to suggest that they exercise a subtle influence upon our attitude ; names such as Annie, Maudie, Bessie and Clara, when combined with the natural characteristics we have mentioned, do seem to transform cyclones from menacing and impersonal meteorological phenomena into romping girls— rough, noisy and given to practical joking, but without malice.

So we accept an occasional visit from one of these hoydens philosophically enough. Recently, however, the Coral Sea spawned no fewer than three of them in three weeks, which was quite abnormal, and due, as everyone agreed, to The Bomb. What made it more abnormal still, and more unbearable, was that (although cyclones usually blow in during the summer, and are the wettest feature of the Wet), these three turned up in July and August, when the sight of those forms lying around the house made us feel that we already had quite enough to cope with.

Worse still, the last was called Celestine. This is a pretty up-stage sort of name, and when the newspapers jocosely drew attention to its meaning we all thought they were carrying waggishness far beyond the permissible limit. Such a pleasantry might go over well enough in the city, where walls are thick, roofs are strong, the earth is firmly held down by pavements, and practically the only form of cultivation is indoors, where the more palatial banks and insurance offices go in extensively, nowadays, for potted cacti. But it was coldly received in Dillillibill, and no wonder, because we had already, in the space of three weeks, suffered visitations from the other two girls, whose names were Ada and Bella; we were therefore fed up with cyclones, and in no mood for whimsy. We might possibly have accepted a Maggie or a Daisy with better grace, but we fairly snorted when this third wench was introduced to us, with a broad wink, as, forsooth, Little Heavenly One.

Ada made a lot of noise, blew the roof off the school (of course all the children were safely at home, eating hot buttered toast), demolished a car shed out on The Other Road, and brought down most of the citrus crop; but she never really came ashore, and the full force of her playful energy was expended on the ocean. Bella was rather a weak sister, as cyclones go. Apart from causing a landslip on the Tooloola road, tearing off a great many branches, snatching an old tank from its decent retirement in the lantana, and dumping it on Biddy's vegetable garden, washing out a row of pines here and there, and wrapping a canvas blind from the Arnold's verandah round the top of an adjacent telegraph pole, she did not incommode us very much.

But hard upon her heels came Celestine—and she was a humdinger.

She fell upon us tooth and claw, screaming, raving and carrying on like Alecto, Megaera and Tisiphone rolled into one; indeed, those artists who have depicted the Furies as winged virgins with serpents threshing about in their hair as they fly upon their vengeful errands through a sky full of torn cloud and howling wind, might well have drawn their inspiration from the Lane at that time. In a frenzy of destructiveness, the Little Heavenly One uprooted trees, flattened fences, blacked out electricity, silenced telephones, unroofed two houses and five sheds, whisked a chair from the Bells' verandah, and flung it on the Dawsons' roof, snatched up Amy's clothes-prop and hurled it like a javelin into

the ground fifty yards away, and tossed a packing case through
Herbie's window. She sent torrents tearing down the pineapple
drains, turned the paddocks into lakes, and the roads into angry
rivers. We could hear Black Creek on the one hand, and Late
Tucker Creek on the other, roaring down their gullies to the
Annabella River which, rising to unprecedented heights, submerged the railway bridge, and flooded the farms of our lowland
neighbours. The Achesons' cow vanished. She was discovered a
few days later at Tooloola, but we will not go so far as to say
that she was blown there.

During all this commotion we Lane dwellers lay low in our
houses, and those whose roofs held were snug enough, except for
some leaks in the ceilings. It was very dark, even in the daytime,
and very cold. Habit betrayed us into pressing switches for light
and warmth no longer available, but when we had found lamps
or candles, and set our chairs round the roaring kitchen range,
our spirits rallied, and only those irrational folk who expect their
fellow-men to be rational at all times, will be surprised to learn
that a certain holiday atmosphere began to pervade our be-
leagured homes. True, our crops were being ruined. True, it
would take us weeks to clean up the mess. True, our careful
budgeting would now be nonsense. But there was not a thing
we could do about all this at the moment, so we might as well
sample the sweet uses of adversity, brew cups of tea, browse
through magazines, play a hand or two of cards, make toffee, and
discover, in unaccustomed idleness, a curious peace amid the
uproar.

For we were now able to enjoy the advantages of escapism
without incurring its odium. Nothing could get at us except
Celestine herself—and so far we were withstanding her siege. No
doubt the Great Powers were still snarling insults and accusations
at each other in their efforts to reach a peaceful settlement ; but
we had no means of hearing about it. No doubt depressing
reports of prices at the Fruit and Vegetable Markets were being
broadcast on the tortured air ; but they were not reaching us.

No doubt a lot of people had sent us bills; but it was unlikely that the Postmaster General had been able to get them any nearer to us than Rothwell. On the other hand, we were for the present powerless to replenish our larders, but we could open tins: Bruce Kennedy even declared, not without complacency, that if Celestine had to bring all normal activity to a standstill, she could not have chosen a better time to begin than his meat-day.

And when we compared notes later, it was found that although this interlude would have afforded us a perfect opportunity for tackling Form B, not a soul had used it for that purpose.

It seemed very quiet when Celestine had gone. The prophet Isaiah relates that both Ar and Kir of Moab were in the night laid waste and brought to silence, and very much the same thing appeared to have happened to the Lane when we woke early one morning to a strange hush, an almost awesome stillness. In a sky of washed-out blue the sun shone palely upon a world from which the busy stir of multitudinous small sounds and movements had quite departed. On the battered trees the leaves hung motionless; on the sodden ground the grass lay water-logged; no whip-birds called from the scrub, the magpies were mute, there was no aubade from the kookaburras; the dumb inertia of exhaustion lay upon the earth. Goodness knows how long this uneasy spell might have lasted if fowls were not the prosaic creatures that they are; but an egg is an egg even after a cyclone—and perhaps at such a time more than ever worthy of celebration—so when the cackling began, we pulled ourselves together, and prepared to deal with life once more.

There was plenty to do, and perhaps—having heard much of our powers of resilience, and our hard-working habits—you may expect to learn that we addressed ourselves to it without delay. The men did, in fact, put on their gumboots and squelch about their farms looking at the damage, and the women did begin doing their chores in a desultory way; but our routine had been brutally interrupted, and we felt a reluctance to establish it again.

Marge, whose bathroom is under the house, stood in its doorway for quite a long time, contemplating the concrete floor upon which there lay not only an inch of mud, a mass of slimy leaves and the shattered door, but also six worms, a cake of soap, five oranges, two towels, several scorpions, eight aspirin tablets, a broken looking-glass and a dead frog covered with talcum powder. It was while she was trying to overcome a strong disinclination to do anything about all this, and vaguely wondering whether to fetch a rake or a shovel, that Tony appeared at her elbow, bursting with news.

" Hey, Mrs. Kennedy, you know that big tree outside Herbie's place ? The old, nearly dead one ? Well, it's blown down ! "

" So what ? " replied Marge, turning lack-lustre eyes upon him. " The wonder is that there are any trees left standing."

"But listen . . ." urged Tony excitedly, ". . . it's fallen right across the road ! Me and Dave Hawkins found it first. Well . . . of course Herbie knew, and I s'pose the Achesons must have, too . . . but we're going round telling everyone else, because you see it's no good anyone trying to drive in to the store, even with chains. Not the slightest bit of good. It's right, bang, *plonk* across the road ! We're marooned ! " His eyes, bright with pleasure, looked past her appreciatively at the bathroom floor. " Cripes ! " he said genially. " You've got a mess there all right, haven't you ? "

" Yes," said Marge.

" I'll go now," continued Tony politely, " because you want to get on with cleaning it up, don't you ? "

" No," said Marge.

"Well, you better, anyway," admonished Tony and, like Hermes, lightly departed with his tidings, on winged feet.

There must have been many other trees blocking roads in various parts of the area just devastated by Celestine. Trees are always doing this, even without the aid of cyclones, and it is rarely a matter for concern, or even comment. You can either go by some alternative route, or, more simply still, just drive off the road and find a way round one end or the other ; and once such a detour has been pioneered, everyone else has only to follow it until the obstacle has been removed by those whose business it is to do so.

But in a dead-end road like the Lane, offering no alternative route to the outside world, such an event is of the first importance, and if Marge had not been feeling rather punch-drunk, she would have received Tony's news less lethargically. But she soon woke up, and discerned, hidden among its obvious and tiresome implications, others of a quite cheering kind. And, as the word went round, so did everyone else. This fallen tree was a serious matter. It would be sheer irresponsibility not to go and take a gander at it. With a view, of course, to its removal.

One of the rarest and happiest experiences of life is to find duty marching with inclination, and this happiness was now vouchsafed to us. We had been cooped up inside for days, with no opportunity for neighbourly gossip, or even those waves and shouted greetings which keep us pleasantly aware of each other's proximity. Things had happened to our crops, our trees, our fences, our roofs, our cows, our fowls, and we were dying to talk about it all. So we were delighted to recognise a heaven-sent, made-to-order, incontestably legitimate excuse for abandoning the dreary task of rehabilitation, and getting together. We embraced it eagerly. Of course nothing was pre-arranged. No rendezvous was made. But within an hour all the farms were totally deserted, and everyone was assembled at the Tree.

When Jack Hawkins and Joe Hardy strolled down, with Butch at heel, they found Nelson and Herbie Bassett already there, but taking no notice of each other. Nelson was sitting on a telegraph pole, and looking rather disreputable, as he always does after wet weather. His plumage was askew, his white breast stained and ruffled; he had been on short rations during the cyclone and, unwilling to wait for breakfast at Gwinny's, had begun digging worms at daybreak, so his beak and claws were heavily encrusted with red mud. He was also put out, for the meal Gwinny had at

last provided was disgracefully meagre, and she had even tried
to palm off a bit of cooked sausage on him. Offended by this,
he had flown straight off to the Kennedys', but they—though
lavish with endearments and apologies—had found nothing better
to offer him than the dead worms from the bathroom floor. Then,
cruising disconsolately along the Lane, he had found one of his
favourite perches no longer perpendicular. To a bird of pretty
fixed habits, all this was gravely disturbing.

Herbie had been up since daybreak too, but so far he had done
nothing except place outside his gate a packing-case upon which
he was still seated, staring with great contentment at the brand-
new spectacle so conveniently provided right opposite his house.

It was worth staring at, too. Lying as it did at the foot of the
Lane's first hill, the tree had formed an effective dam, and there now
stretched out on its western side quite an extensive lake of muddy
water. This so altered the aspect of a familiar spot that not only
a confirmed starer like Herbie, but any resident of the Lane, could
be excused for finding it worthy of prolonged study. Its vast roots,
towering nakedly above the lantana, were festooned with ancient
barbed wire, for it had elected to grow exactly on Herbie's
boundary, and its downfall had torn out what was left of that
part of the fence. Its head—which consisted of several bare
branches, and one which still boasted a few tufts of leaves—had
come down well inside the Achesons' property, and across two
rows of their pines. One glance was sufficient to assure Jack that
no vehicle now east of it—not Aub's jeep, nor Bruce's Land
Rover, nor even Kelly—was going to get out of the Lane till it
was removed. This was a matter of some moment to himself, for no doubt the meat and the mail would get through
to the store to-day, and since Herbie had no car, and Joe's
ute was not registered for the road, and all the others were on
the wrong side of the tree, it would clearly be up to him. He
sighed.

" No hope of sneaking round this one," he observed.

" Not Buckley's chance," agreed Joe. " Take a bit out of her
—that's the only way."

They waded through the lake, clambered over the trunk, and stood back on the other side to consider the problem.

" Made a mess, hasn't she ? " Jack remarked with that note of appreciation which anything superlative inspires, even a superlative nuisance.

" Always reckoned she'd go some day," said Joe. " Never thought she'd last as long as she has. Pretty near dead these last ten years, she's been."

Jack nodded.

" She has, too. Done in your fence, Herbie."

" No matter," replied Herbie placidly. " The cows ain't going to get past the roots."

Jack inspected the roots, and grunted acquiescence. He crossed the road and studied the other end. " Won't worry Tim much, either—the lantanna's close around it." He peered into the mashed up vegetation. " Hey, Joe," he called, " see that bit of rusty iron sticking up there ? . . . Bet you don't know what that is ! "

" Looks like a plough," said Joe.

" It is, too." Jack stared at it with a kind of awe. " Old plough my dad dumped there. Must have been pretty near twenty years ago ! Dumped an old stove at the same time—that might be it a bit farther in . . . see ? "

" Go on ! " said Joe, impressed. " And that there," he added, pointing, " that'd be the mudguard off Harry Maxwell's Ford— remember ? It conked out a few years before he sold to Tim. He must've chucked his old wire-netting there too, when he put up the new fowlyard. What's that pink thing ? . . ." He climbed on to the trunk for a better view. " Cripes, it's a real big mirror with roses painted on it—not broken, or nothin' ! Who d'you reckon would throw out a good thing like that ? . . ."

" Me," said Herbie. Joe turned to stare at him.

" What for ? "

" It got in me way."

" Break it down ! " protested Joe. " How'd a mirror get in your way—just hangin' on the wall ? Real artistic, it is. I reckon it's a shame, throwin' out a nice article like that." He was shaking his head as he climbed down from the trunk and rejoined Jack, who was now prodding into the lantana with his brush-hook. " What's that you found ? "

" Only old fencing wire. All tangled up with the lantanna. There won't be any cows poking far into that, so Tim's pines ought to be safe enough. But the tree's flattened some of them already."

" Pretty near due to come out anyhow—that lot," said Joe. They returned to the middle of the road, and stared hard at the trunk again.

" Have to get her shifted," said Jack.

" Too right," responded Joe. " We'll get cracking as soon as a few others turn up. Here's Tim comin' down now."

Tim and Biddy were both coming—but slowly, for they were followed by Jeremy and Jennifer, who were finding it heavy going in the slippery mud, and required constant encouragement. They all gained the road at last, however, and after greetings had been exchanged, Tim related his adventures while crawling about inside the roof looking for a leak, and Biddy chipped in at intervals, describing her agitation as she imagined the roof going, and Tim, presumably, going with it. This recital was interrupted by the arrival of Tony, who spattered everyone with water as he jumped from the tree trunk into the lake, where he was joined almost at once by Dave and Tommy Hawkins. Biddy, after some fruit-less attempts to persuade her offspring that they didn't really want to play in the nasty, muddy water, said resignedly that, after all, everything was too wet for them to keep dry anyhow, and gave them permission to go in. " They're in already," Tony pointed out, and was deservedly ignored.

Conversation then began again, and Joe stated that he never took much notice of cyclones now, because he reckoned there wasn't much more they could do to bother him—but Uncle Cuth, he had the wind up properly. Jack described the row made by a four-gallon oil drum as it rolled down the iron roof, and told what had happened to Amy's clothes-prop. Herbie, when asked

for an account of his experiences, merely smiled, and replied that
he had spent most of the crisis in bed and asleep ; he could not
be bothered explaining that a cyclone is not a rewarding thing to
watch, on account of its restlessness.

While they were chatting thus, Aub and Alf came along, and
as soon as they were within earshot, Aub shouted his intention of going straight back into the newsagency business just
as soon as he could find some ruddy lunatic to buy his farm.
Nelson burst into loud, derisive laughter, and Alf made
rumbling noises which his neighbours understood to mean that
cyclones were fair cows, but it didn't do to let them get you
down.

The Lane at this moment provided a spectacle probably unprecedented in the whole of its history. It is not possible to take
it in from ground level however ; what is needed is a bird's-eye
view, so we cannot do better than to borrow Nelson's. His most
noticeable characteristic, as we have already indicated, is im-
perturbability, but any member of the group below who had
happened to glance up at him now would have remarked an
uneasiness amounting almost to agitation in his demeanour. For
the whole road, both to the east and the west, was dotted with
the figures of those who, by immemorial custom, should at this
hour have been variously employed behind their own lantana,
but who were, instead, converging singly, in pairs or in groups
upon this spot. Rather in the manner of a spectator at a tennis
match, Nelson was turning his head rapidly from side to side in
an attempt to keep them all under observation.

Heading the procession from the east came Bruce Kennedy,
but he was presently overtaken and left behind by the Bell twins
and Lynette, whose excitement on gaining the top of the hill, and
observing the aquatic gambols in progress near the Tree, lent
wings to their bare feet.

" Yippee-ee-ee-ee ! " yelled Ding and Dong, charging down the
slope.

" Come on ! " shouted Tony unnecessarily.

" Yee-ee-ee-ee ! " shrieked Lynette with such breath as she

could spare from the task of keeping up with her brothers. They arrived in a body, scrambled on to the fallen trunk, and leapt gladly into the water ; but the adults had moved back in time.

Bruce had stopped to wait for Dick and Henry, and these three were the next to arrive, closely followed by Daphne who, with motherly solicitude, was holding Joy by the hand to keep her from slipping—an attention which Joy was fiercely resisting. Behind them came a hilarious group consisting of Sue, Marge and Aunt Isabelle, escorted by Ken, and surrounded, as it were, by Jake. Turning once more to the west, Nelson perceived another hand-in-hand pair approaching, namely old Mrs. Hawkins and her youngest grandson, Keithie, but—whether owing to the age of the one, or the youth of the other—their progress was very slow, so he clicked his head eastward again to watch the rest of the Bell family swinging along at a good pace, as the Bells always do, heads up and shoulders back, and Gwinny marching every bit as smartly as EElaine and the boys.

By the time all these had added themselves to the group at the Tree, there were twenty-nine persons present (not counting Nelson, Jake and Butch), which is only five short of the Lane's full muster. The meeting had noticeably assumed the character of a social occasion, so it seems advisable to repeat that the adults, at least, were still informed by a commendable spirit of duty and communal self-help—proof of which was to be seen in the axes, brush-hooks and crowbars with which all the men had equipped themselves ; and though the ill-natured might say they seemed in no hurry to use them, the fair-minded might justly retort that there had so far been no chance to do so. For each new arrival had to report the character and extent of the damage his property had suffered, and the others were naturally required to repeat for his benefit an account of their own ordeals. Aunt Isabelle's discourse, in particular, took a very long time, for besides describing events, and giving a detailed analysis of her emotions, she touched upon such matters as the effect of noise upon the nervous systems of Sue and Henry (". . . me, I am unaffected . . ."), the efficacy of will-power as an aid to sleep, and the purpose of Divine Providence in allowing cyclones at all.

Yet even with all this to engage their attention, the men did not completely forget the real purpose of the gathering. Now and then one of them would make a remark about the Tree, and there would be a pause in the chatter while everyone stood and looked at it, pondering. Joe, for instance, expressed the opinion that the white ants had been at her, so Jack prodded the trunk with a crowbar, and Bruce knocked out a few chips with his axe, and Aub gave it a kick, and Ken took a swipe at it with his brush-hook, and they all gravely agreed that the white ants had, indeed, been at her. Then, a little later on, Jack remarked, eyeing it critically, that he reckoned they could do the job with two cuts ; and Aub objected that she was all of four feet in diameter, and if you put one cut *here*, and the other *here*, you'd have a twelve-foot length to get rid of ; and Henry said hopefully that maybe the jeep and the Rover between them could move it. Bruce then did a few measurements with a stick, squatted on his heels making cabbalistic marks in the mud, and presently announced that the cut out length would have a content of about a hundred and fifty cubic feet ; did anyone know, he enquired, what a cubic foot of hardwood weighed ? While all the women were respectfully waiting for the men to answer this, and all the men were knitting their brows, and trying to look as if they really did know, but had forgotten for the moment, Biddy suddenly said in a bewildered voice that the trunk was round, and she thought cubes were square ? . . . Bruce replied quite civilly that cubes were cubic, and Biddy retorted that anyway, they weren't *round*, and she couldn't see what square cubes had to do with a round trunk. Bruce, in a tone of slightly strained patience, pointed out that the trunk was not round, but cylindrical, and Biddy—her Irish blood well up—said that even if it was, all the cylinders she had ever seen were round, so what were they arguing about ? This led to a general and extremely animated discussion (accompanied by much drawing of diagrams on the ground, and much quoting of such examples as pennies, wedding-rings, tennis balls and water pipes), about the nature of discs, globes, spheres, circles and cylinders, from which it seemed to transpire, rather to everyone's astonishment, that simply nothing at all was round.

It is pretty universally accepted that in any undertaking theory should be mastered before practice is attempted, so it cannot be said that this excursion into the theoretical, mathematical, etymological and (one might almost say) metaphysical aspects of chopping through a tree trunk was a waste of time. But it certainly made everyone feel thirsty, and the loudly cheered appearance of the five missing Lane dwellers could not have been more opportune. Here we may note, too, another demonstration of how unnecessary organisation is when the common need is understood by all; for there, coming down the western hill, were Amy Hawkins and Bill, with baskets containing mugs and scones in their hands, and a kerosene tin full of tea slung on the copper stick between them; and there, coming over the eastern hill at precisely the same moment, were Myra and Heather, bearing more baskets containing more scones, more mugs, and more tea in thermos flasks.

That, you will say, makes four—not five. But we have yet to explain that the fifth was Uncle Cuth who, having seen the tea set out, had hurriedly scuttled forth in pursuit, and was now, despite his years, gaining upon it so fast that everyone was much impressed, and gave him a cheer all to himself.

For an hour or so after this no one pretended that it was anything but a picnic. The only dryish places to sit were Herbie's packing-case—to which he gallantly conducted old Mrs. Hawkins —and the Tree itself, so they all strung themselves out along its trunk like sparrows on a wire, eating scones, drinking tea, swopping anecdotes about cyclones, and talking shop. The sun —earlier so cowed and pallid—took heart as it climbed the sky, pouring down abundant warmth, and sucking up moisture from the earth in a fine, silver steam. Colours glowed and ripened under its caress; leaves whispered and shone; grass sat up and sparkled; coats and cardigans came off; optimism revived, and self-respect returned; no doubt—no doubt at all, we have a perfect winter climate.

But alas, the devastation wrought by Celestine could not be very long forgotten. Work was waiting—not only here, but behind the lantana all along the Lane—and at last, by unspoken but unanimous consent, the Tree ceased to be a seat, and was once more acknowledged as an obstacle.

Ken declared that what this job needed was a cross-cut saw, not a lot of ruddy axes, and Joe said too right it was, and he reckoned Bill Weedon would be glad to lend them his. Jack observed gently that Bill would let them have it like a shot, but the trouble was to get hold of it; so far as he knew nobody had ever got up or down that last hill on The Other Road just after a cyclone. Aub said truculently, without thinking, that he'd give anyone any odds they liked that his jeep would do it with chains, and Henry replied, tapping the tree trunk with his brush-hook: " Chains and wings, old boy—chains and wings." When the laugh against Aub subsided, Dick said there must surely be another cross-cut saw somewhere in Dillillibill, and Ken assured him that there was—down at Jeff Jenkins' place on The Goat Track. After this there was a brief, baffled silence until Tristy Bell said simply that maybe a saw would be better if they had one, but seeing they didn't have a saw, what was there against doing the job with axes seeing they did have axes? No one offered any objection to this line of reasoning, though a few looked dubious, and they all began to study the Tree again.

Bruce said wistfully that if only someone could tell him the weight of a cubic foot of it, he could work out whether his Land Rover and Aub's jeep could shift the log when they got it out. Aub snorted, and asked why worry about working it out, because the Rover and the Jeep between them could shift anything. Jack then mildly intervened, explaining that the log wouldn't be *that* heavy, because he hadn't meant to cut it *here* and *here*, but *there* and *there*. Gwinny promptly objected that if they did this, there would be only room for one car at a time to get through and Ken exclaimed : " Well, blow me down, what more do you want ? "

It needed hardly a moment's reflection for everyone to realise that nothing more could possibly be wanted ; it wasn't, Aub said, as if a bloke were ever in so much of a hurry that he couldn't pull up and wait for another bloke to get through. So the men took up their axes, and ran their thumbs along the edges, while the women bustled about clearing the trunk of mugs and coats and packets of tobacco, and threatening to send the children straight home if they got in the way. Then Aub announced loudly that he had an idea, and this idea turned out to be that they should make a contest of the chopping—north side of the Lane versus south side—how about it ? This suggestion was at once vociferously acclaimed by the children ; the women eagerly approved it ; the men grinned, protested, looked at each other, grinned some more, and finally said they didn't see why not.

With Joe and Uncle Cuth excluded on the grounds of disability and age, it worked out very neatly into two teams of six, and after some consultation it was agreed that each team should put its men in, two at a time, one on each side of the trunk, to chop in shifts. Jack said they had better knock a bit of the mud and rubbish out from under the tree to let the water get away, and this was rapidly done by Tristy and Gally, despite some cries of bitter protest from the children.

Then Aunt Isabelle vehemently objected that the proposed arrangement would not be sporting, for the north side—with Tim, Ken, Henry, Tristy, Gally and the less youthful, but equally redoubtable King Kong to make up the half-dozen—would enjoy an unfair advantage over the south side, whose champions, with the exception of Bill Hawkins, were all of mature age. This provoked an indignant chorus of denial from all men, women and children of the south side, and an inevitable offer from Aub to give anyone odds of ten to one on Souths. For a moment it seemed that the takers would be both numerous and clamorous, but it was remembered in time by a few—who conveyed it by means of winks, frowns and nudges to the others—that Alf was unshakably of the opinion that betting wasn't right ; so there was a little delay while those who felt that it would be a crying shame not to have a bob on, this way or that, went aside and negotiated in pairs so discreetly that Alf was able to appear quite unaware of what was going on.

Then Gwinny—unanimously recognised as the only person capable of keeping her eyes on a watch without having to take them from the axemen—was declared time-caller ; Jack and Ken were appointed captains of their respective sides, and drew for positions on the trunk ; the spectators disposed themselves in rows on either side of the road, and the teams stood ready to begin. It cannot be denied that Norths had the stronger team, but fortunately the draw had given Souths the position nearer to the head of the Tree, where its girth was slightly less, so everyone anticipated a close and exciting contest.

We only wish you could have seen and heard it. The barrackers never stopped yelling for a moment from start to finish. It is true that the women were sometimes yelling less to encourage their menfolk than to call their children down off the ends of the trunk, or out of the way of flying chips, but this made no difference, because on such occasions words do not matter, but only noise. And so far as noise went, the honours were dead even. No one watched more closely, or screamed more effectively than Gwinny, who had a husband and two sons to cheer, yet her call of " TIME ! " rose punctually above the uproar to release two pairs of panting heroes, and summon two more to the battle. Old Mrs. Hawkins was at first diffident about her vocal capacity, but when she heard Uncle Cuth's performance, she determined not to be outdone, and was not, though she wore red flannel round her throat for days afterwards. Norths had the advantage of six children to South's five, but Jeremy habitually relies upon his smile to express pleasure, adding in moments of extreme excitement only a kind of subdued twittering, and Jennifer found some scones left over in a basket ; whereas all five of South's juvenile supporters have voices like steam engines, and gave undivided attention to using them. Norths claimed both dogs, but Jake (though normally far more vociferous than Butch), was not much

help, for he leapt, reared and plunged about so madly that he had
breath only now and then for a few gasping yelps; Butch, however,
being older and wiser, sat like a rock at Joe's feet, and barked
steadily in a fierce baritone. Only Nelson, up aloft, was silent—
and very fidgety. In his experience it was kookaburras, not
humans, who made a row in chorus, and this pandemonium
therefore appeared to him as a monstrous reversal of natural law.

As for the contestants, we do not suppose that more in-
domitable spirit, or more heroic effort has ever marked a wood-
chopping event in any part of the continent. The finer points of
technique might, perhaps, be more in evidence at the Royal
Agricultural Show ; connoisseurs might have detected in our
teams some deficiency in style and polish ; Herbie's physique
might have been judged too slight, and Aub's too rotund, to
permit of really classic execution ; a ruthless critic might have
said that Dick's condition was not what it might have been, that
Bruce's blows did not always fall with perfect accuracy, owing to
the way his glasses kept misting over, and that Henry wasted
wind he could ill afford by laughing ; purists might even have
objected that the bulging muscles of Alf and his sons did not
quite make up for a certain savage and overhurried violence, and
that Tim, on the other hand, exhibited more elegance than speed.
But we defy anyone to fault the performance of Jack and Ken
who, valiantly supported by Bill and Gally, leapt in last, to
provide the thrilling climax.

The great trunk, now almost severed in two places, shuddered
beneath their blows. They had discarded their shirts, and sweat
streamed down their backs. The children, dancing in an agony
of excitement, splashed mud over everyone. Jake dived hysteri-
cally between Tony's legs, and upset him in a puddle. Uncle
Cuth screeched angrily that he had never seen such a lotta lousy
chopping in his life, and Joe bellowed at him to shut his trap.
Nelson succumbed at last to panic, took off from his perch, and
headed for the scrub as though jet-propelled.

Now it could only be a matter of seconds. The axemen put
forth their reserves of strength, and chopped as if the price

of pines depended on their efforts. The barrackers, filling their bursting lungs, produced a volume of sound which was heard across the gully in Dillillibill. At this moment, Aunt Isabelle, shrieking encouragement to her beloved Moolliner, clutched at the nearest arm, and realised that its owner seemed to be making no noise at all. Shocked, she turned to stare, and astonishment paralysed her vocal chords in mid-scream—for she flattered herself that she could recognise *l'amour* when she saw it gazing starrily from a maiden's eyes. " *Holà!* " said Aunt Isabelle to herself. " What is this that we have here ? No, no ! *Pas possible!* " Yet the signs were unmistakable. The face of the lily maid as she gazed at Lancelot can never have betrayed her heart more surely than did that of her namesake now, as she gazed at Ken. And at this moment, as the trunk fell apart under his final blow, and he stood back triumphant, his eyes immediately sought EElaine, found her, and, for an electric second, communed intimately with hers. Aunt Isabelle lifted her shoulders to her ears in eloquent acknowledgment of the unbelievable. Ah, the cunning ones ! That they should have arrived at the stage of exchanging such glances without the Lane perceiving what was afoot ! That the Lane should have seen Ken's bulldozed road, and yet failed to appreciate the advantages of a trysting place so secluded, where none passed by ! But surely the good Gwinny, whom nothing escaped, had known all, for was she not now glancing from Ken to EElaine with an expression the most maternally indulgent ? . . . Aunt Isabelle whisked a happy tear from her eye, and resolved to compose that very night a long letter to Mrs. Jackson, acquainting her that the problem of Ken's love-life had found its own solution here in Lantana Lane.

Norths had won—but only by a whisker. The middle section of the trunk lay free, and the twelve champions stood back to contemplate their handiwork, and receive the congratulations of their supporters. But Ken (perhaps a little above himself as a result of that stimulating glance which Aunt Isabelle had intercepted), suddenly jumped forward again, seized a crowbar, and called out : " Well, come on, fellers, what are we waiting for ? "

They were waiting for the Land Rover and the jeep, and the older men, at least, would willingly have gone on waiting. But in Tristy, Gally and Bill that chemistry of youth which immediately replaces expended energy was powerfully at work ; they had ergs and ergs available already, and they hastened to range themselves beside Ken. After that, of course, no one could hang back. Levering with crowbars and shoving with shoulders, they all attacked the log. " One—two—three—*heave* ! " chanted Bill, and it moved. " One—two—three—*heave* ! " chanted everyone together, and it moved some more. The kids crowded into small spaces, and heaved too. Jake—having for some reason taken a dislike to the log—pranced at their heels, seizing every opportunity to rush in and bite it. Uncle Cuth stood well out in the road making gestures like a traffic cop, and crying : " Bring 'er round a bit, can'tcher ? Whatcher lettin' 'er slip back for ? Spare me days, I never seen such a lotta goofy muddlers ! " But the north end swung slowly towards the west, and the heavers, encouraged, toiled with a will. "One—two—three—*heave* ! " sang the womenfolk. " One—two—three—*heave* ! " yelled the children. Aub called out gaspingly to Bruce that in case he still wanted to know, a cubic foot of the blanky thing weighed a bleeding ton ; and Henry was heard to mutter that they might as well be Neanderthal men for all the good it did them living in the machine age. But despite such small symptoms of disaffection, everyone kept on heaving, with the happy result that the log was at last manœuvred into a position where it was hardly in the way at all. And the road was open.

It was a proud moment. Aunt Isabelle felt that the last few days had richly fulfilled her expectations of the pioneering life. They had been in peril, they had suffered, they had found themselves cut off from the world—but by their own united and courageous efforts, they had triumphed. She looked in some astonishment at the other women, who were busily packing baskets, and assembling children, for she thought it fitting that someone should now deliver a brief oration. But the only valedictory remark came from Jack, who called over his shoulder as he walked off up the hill :

" Okay, Bruce, now you can nick in and get our meat."

That evening, just after dark, Joe came limping down from his shack, and scrabbled about in the lantana near the Tree. Herbie saw him climb the hill again with something under his arm ; he was a little surprised, for he had never suspected Joe of aspiring to Gracious Living.

The Deviation (3)

RECENTLY another pair of decent young blokes from the Department of Main Roads turned up, and this time they came right into the Lane. But they drove no pegs ; they were equipped only with armfuls of maps and papers which—to judge from their hot and harassed faces—were driving them nuts. They called at several of the houses, bade us good morning, and explained rather cryptically that they were just checking.

We courteously accepted this mysterious statement, offered them tea, of course, and tried not to betray the curiosity which was consuming us. But when they began, very civilly, to ask us questions, we immediately understood the reason for the corrugation of their youthful brows. They were enquiring, if you please, about boundaries.

Now the thing which infallibly distinguishes newcomers from old inhabitants of these parts is an absurd preoccupation with boundaries. They soon get over it, but just at first they exhibit a quite morbid anxiety to discover exactly where their properties end, and those of their next-door neighbours begin ; and this is a matter which—though simple enough in the suburbs—is pretty complicated in Dillillibill.

Along the Lane we know our boundaries all right ; that is to say, we know they are somewhere in the lantana. There are long stretches, too, between our properties, where a fence marks the division perfectly clearly ; and it goes without saying that when a boundary fence is also the fence of a cow-paddock, we attend most scrupulously to its maintenance, so how the cows keep on getting out all the same is a problem upon which it is quite fruitless to ponder.

But all our farms slope down more or less precipitously towards the creeks, and since most of us have under cultivation as much land as we can manage, if not as much as we need, we leave the steepest acres to the native scrub. Down there, in those dim, damp, tangled, primeval fastnesses, we have, of course, other boundaries—but just exactly where, we wouldn't know.

And why should we? When Dick Arnold first came, he felt the usual urge to determine how much of what he surveyed he was monarch of, and he thought he would begin by following down the fence between his place and Dawsons'. Luckily he encountered Aub before he had gone very far. Aub was picking pines, but he dumped his basket, and came pushing along between the rows with all the alacrity of a man not only willing to help, but glad to be interrupted.

" Boundary ? . . ." he repeated, when Dick had explained the purpose of his expedition. " Well, there you've got me, mate. Went looking for it myself once, but I gave it away when I got down near the creek. Got hung up in a lawyer-vine for long enough to think it out, see? Said to myself: ' Aub, that boundary's *there*. You've seen it on a map. It's not going to run away. It'll pay you better to leave it alone, and get on with your chipping.' "

" You can't just follow this fence down ? . . ." asked Dick wistfully.

" You can follow it down as far as it *goes*, and that's into that big patch of lantana down there."

" It doesn't go into the scrub at all, then ? "

" What'd be the use ? Only reason for a fence is to keep something in or out. Right ? "

" Well, mainly, but it marks the line, too."

" Point is, does the line need to be marked ? If you're a grazier —well, then you have to have a fence, and it matters if it's a coupla feet out, this way or that. Lot of grass in a two-foot strip a mile long. But we're not graziers—more's the pity. We're not trying to keep anything in. Or out. Cows don't go in the scrub ; nothing for them to eat. It's no skin off our nose if the line's a yard or ten yards out, so long as we aren't *using* the land. What do we care if there isn't a line at all ? And if you did find it, and bust your bank balance putting a fence along it, what'd happen to the flaming thing ? It'd rot away, that's what. Just give it a few wets, and it'd rot clean away. Look, sport, you come on up to the house, and meet the wife, and have a cupper tea, and forget about boundaries. All you'll do down there is tear your pants."

Thus was Dick's error in thinking swiftly and painlessly corrected, and in some such manner have most of us, at one time or another, adjusted our attitude to boundaries. Our scrub is God's Little Acre, and so far as we are concerned, God is welcome to it. Ken Mulliner did clear a bit of his once for bananas, and it was not until he had finished planting that he began to wonder if about a quarter of it mightn't be in the Bells' place ; so just as a matter of form, he summoned Alf to have a look, and Alf said he thought it probably was, but no matter, and how were Ken's new pines coming along ? Little accidents of this kind are bound to happen now and then. The classic example occurred out on The Other Road after the Jones and the Warburtons both sold their farms at about the same time, and the new owners, running true to form, and messing about with plans, and tapes and compasses, discovered that a good half-acre of Warburton's pines had been planted on Jones' land. But when further investigation revealed that over on the other side of the ridge about an equal number of Jones' pines were doing nicely on Warburton's land, they very sensibly decided to let well alone.

So we were not always able to answer very explicitly the questions asked by the two young men, whose names were Don and Denis. But it was only at the Arnolds' and the Dawson's that they made searching enquiries about the scrub boundaries —and this we regarded as grimly significant. Aub naturally

offered at once to get a brush-hook and take them down to
have a look round for themselves, but they thanked him,
and said it would not be necessary at present; they were just
checking.

It is inevitable that there should be a difference in approach
between those trained to see a boundary as a line clearly drawn
upon a sheet of paper, and those taught by custom and experience
to regard it as being, like the bunyip, a myth somewhere down in
the scrub. Consequently, although the Arnolds and the Dawsons
did their best to be helpful, and although the boys seemed
appreciative of their efforts, the interviews were not very
illuminating to anyone. All, of course, were intellectually aware
that a relationship exists between place and map. But Dick and
Aub, in whose view the map possessed less substance and reality
than the place, would keep on pointing out the window; while
Don and Denis, to whom the place seemed less important, and
much less reliable than the map, were extremely reluctant to lift
their eyes from it.

When they did, it was not to see what was being pointed at,
but to regard the pointers with a forlorn and baffled expression.
Did Mr. Dawson, they asked, not know where his Pegs were?
" Too right, I do," declared Aub roundly, and went on to explain
that they were buried somewhere down there under the accumulated forest debris of the years—if, indeed, anything remained of
them at all, which he considered most unlikely.

The boys looked shocked. After all, said their reproachful eyes,
other decent blokes of their craft had once, long, long ago,
struggled about in that gully, braving the lawyer-vines and leeches
in order to fix and mark those boundaries—and for what? . . .
So that Aub, scratching his head, should give their successors no
greater comfort than to say that, so far as he knew, the line
between his place and Dick's went just above that Strangler Fig
—or maybe just below it; so that Dick, shrugging his shoulders,
should confess that he wasn't sure, but he thought his south-east
corner peg must have been a bit across Late Tucker Creek, where
there was a big rock beside a Gympie tree.

The boys stared, sighed, and turned once more to their maps, which treated these matters with rigid exactitude, and had no use for rocks, Figs or Gympie trees. But their very silence was an accusation of fecklessness—if not something worse ; for it was plain that in their fraternity Pegs were sacred objects, to be guarded no less reverently than Israel guarded the Ark of the Covenant.

This being so, it was no wonder that they looked wan. Denis confided to Dick that not only boundaries in the scrub were causing trouble. There, though they might be elusive, they did, presumably, stay still ; but over on the steep pastures of the opposite ridge near Tooloola, they slipped. And what was the good, asked Denis sadly, of finding a Peg when it might be thirty yards downhill from where it was last week ?

We all grieved them, even when their researches were concerned only with frontages and corner posts along the Lane. We thought we knew all about those, and spoke of them with blithe assurance, but it turned out that even here things were not quite as they should have been. A corner of Jack's front garden, opposite the green ute, had somehow strayed out into the road, and a strip of the road had somehow found its way into the Kennedys' fowl-yard. Doug Egan's truck had skidded one wet day, and knocked out the rickety corner post between Bells' and Griffiths', and it now appeared that when Alf and Henry put it back, they had just shifted it a foot or two eastward to give Henry a bit more room for his gate. And Herbie's whole frontage was completely crazy because—as old Mrs. Hawkins recalled—Mrs. Herbie had liked two trees which once grew on the roadside, so Herbie had run his fence outside them to keep them safe.

But our reasonable explanations only made Don and Denis look more baffled than ever, and we began to feel that they had been given insufficient briefing in the facts of life. Leaves fall, damp wood rots, and steep hillsides slip ; these are but natural hazards which any Peg must be prepared to face. We suspected that these lads had not been warned of the extreme disillusionment which awaits those who confuse theory with fact, or taught that although a boundary on paper is, *per se*, an admirable thing, a boundary on the ground is transient and unreliable, being subject not only to the assaults of time, but also to the incorrigible disorderliness of human beings. In short, we could discern in them no symptom of awareness that the art of living is the art of continual little adjustments ; that while perfect theory is quite proper, it must submit to being fiddled with in practice, lest society become a strait-jacket.

But they were certainly triers. Kneeling side by side on the floor, heads down, sterns up, they pored in an agony of concentration over their vast, crackling and intractable map. They traced laborious paths with pencil tips along mazy lines peppered with microscopic figures. Muttering together in desperate undertones, they compared this map with a second, and both with a third, and shook their heads unhappily. Time after time Don pounced upon some promising hieroglyph and—while Denis hurriedly consulted a sheet of paper—held it imprisoned beneath his hot forefinger, only to release it at last, with a heavy sigh, and pursue another down the labyrinthine ways.

We could not but feel sorry for them—and yet, as Aub pointed out later, it was their own fault if they had to sprain their brains because, when you came to think of it, why call a farm Sub 1 Res 1 Sub 2 & of Res C & of Res 2 Sub 2 Res B Sub 1 Por 11v, when you can just call it Dawsons' ? In any case, there was little we could do to help except stand on the end of the map to stop it rolling up—but this we did, with a patience which was surely commendable, and even, in the circumstances, magnanimous. For we all knew that this was the beginning of the end. At the Kennedys' Marge offered them beer instead of tea, because she thought they might see their problems in better perspective with the aid of a little alcohol ; Herbie actually abandoned a spider he was watching to try and comfort them about his frontage ; and Henry was moved by their distress to suggest kindly that it might be less trouble not to make The Deviation at all.

But at this the boys, exchanging startled and embarrassed

glances, hastily protested utter ignorance of any deviation, and repeated, with great earnestness, that they were just checking.

We do not know to this day what they checked, or what, if anything, was the result. It was not for them to make premature announcements concerning major public works, and despite our subtle probings, they gave nothing away. Upon this matter, so nearly touching our lives, we expect no further enlightenment until some day one of us goes in for the mail, and returns to distribute notices of resumption all along the Lane.

We shall survive it. When we discuss the matter among ourselves, it is still mostly the compensation that we talk about, and to hear the note of relish in our voices, you might think we anticipate this great event with the unmixed approbation which all good citizens accord to manifestations of progress.

But never forget that we are Anachronisms. We are not entirely convinced that speed and convenience add up to civilisation. Should we be required to state just what does add up to civilisation, our tongues would halt, for we have never given the matter much serious thought. But not all the triumphs of science and technology, nor all the persuasiveness of mass communications, have quite succeeded in banishing from our minds a vague notion that in order to become civilised, one must, first of all, remain human. And being human, we feel, has at least something to do with treading on earth, getting sweaty, seeing the sun rise, making things grow, having animals around, using one's muscles, taking one's time, getting on with one's neighbours and feeling no need of tranquillising pills. Nor have we failed to note that the faster we move, and the more conveniences we acquire, the less of our brief, precious and irreplaceable time we have to call our own.

Therefore (but strictly in communion with our own hearts), we admit uneasiness. Perhaps a few gossamer-threads of primitive belief in man's identity with his place still drift about the world —tenuous, but oddly strong; too frail to be grasped, but obstinately clinging. At all events, we pick at teasing doubts in our minds, as we might pick at cobwebs blown across our faces.

Oh, we shall gain much from The Deviation; no argument about it. And if you ask us what we shall lose, how are we to answer? Are we to say that we fear Nelson will not like it? Are we to voice an apprehension that it will spell doom to Kelly —that tough old battler who surely can survive only if the odds are all against him? What will he have to be game about when the bitumen passes his door? Are we to protest on behalf of Aunt Isabelle? Was it for this that she crossed the world in search of the pioneering life? Are we to babble of a little boy with dancing step, whose faint, Arcadian piping once told so clearly all those things about the Lane which we, with clumsy words, have so miserably failed to tell? . . .

Heaven forbid! We confess to some slight taint of ana-chronism, but such absurd and mystical flapdoodle we utterly reject. We may think—and even say—that the Lane will seem quite different. We may admit that imagination baulks at the picture of it nakedly exposed on its high ridge, bereft of its lantana, bounded by stiff posts, and straining wires; not only recognisable at a glance as a trafficable road, but marked on all maps, and known to all Tourist Bureaux as a through highway; perpetually infested by passing strangers whose cars confound our ears with unfamiliar horns; so wide, so smoothly surfaced, that in our own comings and goings we shall be travelling too fast to call a greeting, or even wave a hand. We may mention to each other with a half-apologetic shrug that it will be queer when the green ute no longer stands embowered at the corner; when no kids trundle their billy-carts at leisure past our gates, and no cows surprise us in the Long Paddock; when the Bump is gone, and the Dip drained, and no vestige of the Tree remains at the foot of Hawkins' hill to remind us of the morning when we celebrated our deliverance from Celestine. But we shall not ask each other what compensation we may claim for all this—for who could pay it, and in what coin?

The shade of St. Chrysostom perhaps observes us sympatheti-cally—for did he not recommend withdrawal from the highway, pointing out that it is hard for a tree growing by the wayside to keep its fruit till it be ripe. We have lived round the corner from the world, with not even a signpost to betray our whereabouts ; we have ripened a few fruits besides our oranges and pineapples ; and if the treasure we have accumulated makes no show upon our bank statements, neither is it subject to income tax. Thus, with our wealth safely invested, we need not repine too much when the highway catches up with us. The world and his wife will come whizzing past our doors, but we shall know, if they do not, that this mile-long strip of glassy bitumen was once Lantana Lane.

THE END